Rosalie Ham is the author of five previous novels, including her sensational number-one bestseller *The Dressmaker*, now an award-winning film starring Kate Winslet, Liam Hemsworth, Judy Davis and Hugo Weaving. Rosalie was born and raised in Jerilderie, New South Wales, and now lives in Melbourne, Australia. She holds a Master of Arts in creative writing.

MOLLY

Rosalie Ham

PICADOR

Pan Macmillan Australia

Pan Macmillan acknowledges the Traditional Custodians of Country throughout Australia and their connections to lands, waters and communities. We pay our respect to Elders past and present and extend that respect to all Aboriginal and Torres Strait Islander peoples today. We honour more than sixty thousand years of storytelling, art and culture.

First published 2024 in Picador by Pan Macmillan Australia Pty Ltd
1 Market Street, Sydney, New South Wales, Australia, 2000

A catalogue record for this book is available from the National Library of Australia

Typeset in 11.6/15 pt Adobe Garamond Pro by Post Pre-press Group, Brisbane

Printed by IVE

The author and the publisher have made every effort to contact copyright holders for material used in this book. Any person or organisation that may have been overlooked should contact the publisher.

The paper in this book is FSC® certified. FSC® promotes environmentally responsible, socially beneficial and economically viable management of the world's forests.

I am a part of all that I have met;
Yet all experience is an arch wherethro'
Gleams that untravell'd world whose margin fades
For ever and forever when I move.

From 'Ulysses', Alfred Lord Tennyson

Chapter 1

MOLLY DUNNAGE STARTED 1914 with a stint in the city watchhouse.

The day had begun well enough. The Dunnages rose early to prepare for the campaign and, over a substantial breakfast of August's homegrown eggs and homemade bread, they clarified the precise position of the Women's Political Association. The WPA were against Prime Minister Joseph Cook's new conservative government, who had no sympathy for the women of suffrage or for women in general. Mr Fisher's Labor Party, on the opposing side, had pledged to increase the old age pension and establish a five-pound maternity payment. August pointed out that they also wanted to adopt a uniform railway gauge and promised to provide funds for pressing health concerns, like cancer and heart disease.

'And consumption,' said Aunt April.

And Molly said, 'We must remind Gladys of the issues.' She stopped spreading jam on her toast. 'Orphans! Mr Fisher will provide for the care of orphans.'

August Dunnage added, 'Hear, hear.'

'Indeed,' said her aunt, and wondered aloud if Gladys would be allowed to join them today for the campaign. Gladys's foster mother, Mrs Sidebottom, was a supporter of Prime Minister Joseph Cook, so disapproved of the Dunnage family, maintaining that they were a corrupting influence on her ward.

The Dunnages remembered well the day Gladys arrived next door from the Mallee, a distant desolate place that bred bushrangers. Little Gladys was a hesitant girl with unbrushed hair and Mrs Sidebottom immediately put her to work doing laundry and housework. She was eight.

When she showed up in the classroom the teacher pointed at Molly Dunnage. 'Sit next to her.' The new girl walked through the sniggering class towards Molly, who made room on her bench.

Unity Palmer and her gang stared at them. Finally, Unity said, 'Molly Dunnage stinks.'

Gladys sniffed. 'I can't smell anything.' It wasn't a comment in defence of Molly, just a fact, but Molly put her arm around her new best friend anyway.

When their school lives ended, Molly and her best – and only – friend got jobs; Mrs Sidebottom found Gladys work in an odious horsehair mattress factory and Molly got a job making corsets. Less than one week enduring terrible working conditions and the girls joined Aunt April and her friend Miss Berrycloth at their suffrage campaigns.

But five years later, their terrible working conditions remained, and so Gladys and Molly took up campaigning for the WPA and the Labor Party as well. Due to Aunt April's ageing feet and painful hips, her pet issue shifted to insufficient public toilets for women in the city. Urinals for men were on almost every corner; they could use one while, behind them, their horse drank at a trough. Toilets for women, however, were underground, few and far between, and cost a penny to use. Miss Berrycloth and Aunt April petitioned ardently for more public toilets, to no avail.

'It is cruel,' said Aunt April. 'They want us all to stay at home.'

'Which is why men design corsets and dresses to hobble us,' said Molly.

August knew better than to say anything. He'd heard the arguments, over and over: that men liked to see women faint, gasping for breath and weak from lack of blood; in this way, men could be strong and protect the weaker sex . . . keep them confined, under control, all the while gazing at their slim waists and upheld breasts.

Today's campaign, titled 'Equality', was more general than working conditions and ablutions, and was designed to amplify Vida Goldstein's Women's Political Association, an organisation the Dunnages were passionate about. Posters rammed into their front garden declared:

TRUE EQUALITY FOR WOMEN IS BEING ABLE
TO MAKE LAWS AND ELECT LAWMAKERS.

EVERY WOMAN HAS THE RIGHT TO
SELF-DETERMINATION AND TO BECOME HERSELF.

As his daughter and sister prepared to depart, shoving the banner into a rucksack and binding the posters, August tried to rouse their morale. 'With only a one-seat majority, the Liberals are a shambles. They're useless.'

'It'll end badly,' said Aunt April, 'as surely as blowflies are green. But it means that Vida has a chance at the next election.'

Thunder rumbled across the sky.

At the door, Molly handed her father a ten-shilling note. 'If we are not home for tea . . .'

'I'll find you.' His daughter was drawn to conversation and so when seeking her he usually looked for a melee, or at least a group in discussion. Molly was often misjudged. She didn't present as decorous, as most young women did, and was actually twenty-four, but people were taken by this pretty slip of a girl with inquiring sea-blue eyes, her curiosity and willingness to listen . . . until they found she was happy to share her own opinions about their opinions.

After Aunt April visited the toilet one last time, Molly gathered their posters and helped Aunt April thread her arms through the rucksack straps, buckle up and apply her flag sash. She positioned the cup to hold the pole so that her flag would fly high over her left shoulder and applied the other flag sash and cup to hold one end of the banner – Miss Berrycloth always held the other end – and the leather sashes crisscrossed to cleave her bosom in opposite directions. She clutched pamphlets – pleas for fairness in divorce, the benefits to society of emancipation and equal pay, education and employment, pensions for deserted wives, custody of children in marriage breakdown and the right for women to own property and control their own earnings – and then it started to rain.

'Every time!' cried Molly. 'Every time we join a rally it rains.'

'The weather is organised by men, no doubt.'

The women ignored August's comment.

'It's only rain,' said Molly, and Aunt April said, 'You'll bake some bread and turn those leftover vegetables into a pie, won't you, Augie?'

He'd make a salad as well, use the tomatoes before they spoiled and the lettuce before the leaves were nibbled to lace.

Aunt April saluted her brother. 'Once more unto the breach.'

And her brother replied, 'Dishonour not our mother.'

Mrs Sidebottom usually left early for the counter-campaign, to avoid having to travel on the same tram as her neighbours, but today, her poster was still standing tall in her garden:

For God and Home and Native Land.

Agitate – Educate – Legislate. Temperance In Everything Is Requisite For Happiness.

Between her veranda posts, a banner declared:

Safeguard the Interests of the Home, Women and Children

Molly rang the cow bell at the Sidebottoms' gate and Gladys appeared, dressed to seduce in a pretty new outfit – Gladys spent quite a portion of her wages on pretty new dresses.

'What on earth are you wearing?'

'What?'

It was Gladys's habit to stuff cotton balls into her ears so that she couldn't hear Mrs Sidebottom. Molly pulled the cotton balls from her ears. 'You're not wearing that, are you?'

'I am.' Gladys swayed, showing the blue satin moiré. The dress had a modern high waist and lace trim. The neckline was square – a little low for day wear – the sleeves long and tapered to a cuff, and the skirt narrow.

'And I suppose you're wearing a corset? How will you run?'

'I don't run, you know that. It's not ladylike.'

It was almost impossible to run in a long dress and corset, which was why suffragists didn't wear them to campaigns, but Gladys's goal in life was to find a wealthy husband, so she made the most of what she had and tried to look pretty. And if there was a fracas during campaigns she simply lowered her poster and stood still, which seemed to mollify the enemy – enough that they didn't assault her. Aunt April thought it best Gladys stayed hobbled in her corset and skirt rather than being in public, pink cheeked, dishevelled and panting.

'When I perfect my new corset design,' said Molly, 'we will be able to play tennis and run away and be as unladylike as we want.'

Gladys buttoned her coat and opened her umbrella. 'Anyway, I thought we were campaigning so we didn't ever have to run.'

'At this stage we still have to run. I'll mend it for you when it gets shredded.'

'It won't.'

Mrs Sidebottom appeared carrying a poster.

INSURANCE: BE RESPONSIBLE FOR YOURSELF.

'Good morning, Mrs Sidebottom,' Molly said.

'I suppose August Dunnage is unwell again today?' Mrs Sidebottom, as an ardent admirer of Mr Joseph Cook, thought his latest promise for a 'great national and social insurance' scheme a triumph. She waved her poster.

'He's quite well, thank you.'

'August should join Mr Cook's program. It is a gift to the nation: all he has to do is make a contribution that will cover sickness and you can also pay for maternity, accident and unemployment. We will all be responsible for ourselves.'

'We already are,' Molly said. 'That's why we're campaigning. The greatly disadvantaged people who cannot pay for insurance need support too.'

Mrs Sidebottom turned to Gladys. 'You stay out of trouble or you'll be sleeping in the park tonight.' She headed off to the tram, head thrust forward and her unnecessary bustle bouncing.

'She won't pay for insurance for Freddy,' said Gladys, and they looked to the rotunda in Curtain Square where Freddy Sidebottom sat, his thin legs crossed. Mrs Sidebottom would not tolerate her husband's drinking, which he'd taken up with a vengeance when he'd returned from the Boer War. Gladys's memory of the eight years before she came to Curtain Square was vague: a farm, chooks and sheep, cold feet in winter and bindies in summer. If she tried, she could bring to mind the floral fabric of her mother's dress, but that memory brought the shouting man who hit them. She was hiding in the cooper's barrel when the hands reached for her: 'It's alright now,' and it was alright. She went to a big house with a grown person who gave her food to eat, and there were lots of children who showed her what to do and slept beside her through the fearful nights. And then she was at Mrs Sidebottom's. The Sidebottom boys weren't very friendly but the Dunnages next door were, and they behaved like a family. Somewhere deeper in her mind an impression existed of a man hiding under a bed, bellowing, and somehow she knew it was the fault of 'the war', and that neither Freddy nor the man could be held responsible for it . . . whatever *it* was.

Across the road, Mrs Raven stood at Mrs Cross's front gate. They watched Mrs Sidebottom turn abruptly and march towards the Rathdowne Street tram, while the WPA supporters turned east towards the Nicholson Street tram. It was doubtful Mrs Cross and Mrs Raven supported anything, except Church. Their children attended Catholic schools and came home at the end of their day to conventional mothers wedded to their 1900 bustles and trains, blousy bodices and high collars. Both women still wore hats with upswept brims, clotted with lace, bows and flowers. Together, their husbands went off to work each morning in their sober suits and bowler hats. Both families kept to themselves and it was well known that a gate in their backyard fence joined their properties.

Left to a quiet house, August shut his sister's door against the odour of her experiments – ripening mould and festering infections in the summer heat – and headed for the pea patch. He stopped in the kitchen to drink a cup of beef stock, which his sister had made earlier and left to cool. He was even taller under the low ceiling of the cottage, and while he sipped he admired the pictures that crowded the walls, framed images from magazines and newspapers, the odd paintings of fruit in bowls (April's), and his own: lots of birds, from emus and kookaburras to bald eagles and Andean condors. All sorts of farm animals: sheep, cattle, dairy cows, a couple of dogs and horses. Dreams and memories.

In the pea patch he was soon defeated by rain so he went to his studio and the dodo he was painting onto a jug, the bird book open in front of him. His table was piled with paint pots and hundreds of fine brushes standing upright in tins. There were also hake brushes and fat brushes, and others thin or flat, round or shaped like seeds, some long as clothes pegs. The stacked paint palettes leaned together into an apex and rags curled like sleeping mammals. Waiting for adornment were towers of bisque crockery, white and earth coloured, plump bowls, slender plates, mugs and cups, saucers and butter plates and tea sets of all styles. Crowding the benches along the walls were books on great art and artists, birds, animals, portraiture, vegetables, fruit and traditional English landscapes, seascapes, mountains and the harsh vegetation around sluggish Australian rivers. Lined up like surgical instruments were pottery tools, rasps and sanding papers, knives for carving, scraping and trimming and sculpting. There was also an assortment of cutlery Molly regularly returned to the kitchen.

He dipped his brush into the paint, made the end fine with his lips, staining them yellow, and applied it to the bird's feet. In the ceramics world, August Dunnage was famous for his fine brush-strokes and less-than-usual depictions. Molly often said he would make more money if he painted English gardens rather than emus and sparrows, but everyone did English gardens.

August proceeded to paint, entirely content with his home and the rich life he enjoyed. He was soon overcome with a familiar creeping weariness. It was the humidity. He put down his brush to listen to the gentle patter of rain, grateful that the yard was softened by a shower and his vegetables watered and dusted. The garden had helped many over the years – Mr Luby, the Sidebottoms, the Crosses, Ravens and even the hotel – especially during the 1890s Depression. It needed attention, weeding, harvesting, the ground composted and turned over, but these days those things fell to Molly, when she had time. He again picked up a paintbrush and worked on the dodo until he accumulated the strength to prepare dinner, and as he did, he steeled himself for a probable trip to the watchhouse.

Miss Berrycloth waited near the Victorian Women's Suffrage Society assemblage, on the Princes Bridge side of the new Flinders

Street Railway Station. Such a modern, impressive building, four storeys of red brick with bluestone, and shops along Flinders Street.

As they approached, Miss Berrycloth started hopping, gesturing towards the WPA banners flying high above the crowd, 'They're here! Over here!'

Neither Aunt April, Miss Berrycloth, Molly nor Gladys would ever become Women's Political Association 'insiders'; they would remain mere fringe supporters. Aunt April had ruined her chances years ago, when she attended the regular discussion of the Book Lovers' Library. It was run by Vida Goldstein's sister, Elsie, and Aunt April raised her hand at question time and asked about the lack of toilets; she then explained how not providing places for relief for women contributed to disease of the elimination system. Her lecture then segued to excretion in the world of pathogens and swamp ecology, whereupon Aunt April was politely interrupted and the subject changed.

But the night was still generous. Miss Berrycloth, a scrap of a woman who wore a close-fitting cotton cap over her balding head, stood and walked across the room, interrupting the view of the low stage and its important occupants to sit next to Aunt April. Miss Berrycloth said – loudly – that her brother, a farmer, would not countenance her own strong opinions but her upbringing had exposed her to the equality and efficiency in the natural world, and she found April's speech to be 'a very important topic'.

Aunt April was further restored and affirmed when, over tea and biscuits, Miss Berrycloth boasted that she had shaken the hand of suffrage pioneer Miss Henrietta Augusta Dugdale then, unabashedly lifted her short overskirt revealing the skirt beneath – it was divided, the very practical Henrietta Dugdale split skirt.

Miss Berrycloth joined Molly, Gladys and Aunt April beside the Women's Political Association and League of Women Voters and their posters:

Support Vida Goldstein and support fairness,
independence and opportunities for women.

Men see only men's need, but a woman
will understand a woman's.

Molly's poster begged, *Move Factories to Toorak; Pollute Waterways in Rich Suburbs Instead.* Gladys's placard said, *Safer Working Conditions For Everyone.*

Bravely, Aunt April and Miss Berrycloth each balanced an end of April's banner in their leather flag holders: *One toilet in the city for 300,000 women is an act of oppression.*

They were an unlikely pair, tiny Miss Berrycloth and Aunt April, a stout woman with a substantial jaw from which her fleshy throat hung. Her top lip was short under a plump nose and her remaining teeth small. She wore round glasses for long sight, which she nested in her frizzy hair and swapped for her large magnifying glasses when she was near her microscope. The two women gave each other a crisp, encouraging nod and gripped their banner.

Molly lifted her overskirt and buttoned it to the waistband of her culottes, freeing her legs to run (and kick, if necessary). She stayed beside her aunt. Gladys looked to the clouds and then to her new outfit.

The mob began to move, slow and orderly, their boots working hard beneath their hems, their grey overcoats darkened in the rain. Aunt April, made twice as big by her rucksack and rain dripping from the buckled brim of her old boater, stepped out first, her small group with her. Gladys kept an arm at Miss Berrycloth's elbow. Miss Berrycloth was not particular about her grooming and Gladys vowed she would keep money aside for eyeglasses so that she could see herself in a mirror when she was older.

'You will hold me if you stumble, Miss Berrycloth.'

It was perhaps to keep herself upright in her heels; in any case, it was less trouble to help Miss Berrycloth to her feet than Aunt April.

'I can see Muriel Heagney,' whispered Aunt April, and they looked with admiration at Muriel standing with her father, Patrick, of the Political Labor Council. Muriel was bespectacled, straight backed and serious, and an impressive crusader for equal pay for women. It was said that she had the makings of a great reformer but, as she was a woman, few men would consider her seriously.

Most of the unions were represented and, naturally, the trade unionists and their giant banner for *A Fair Go For Workers* were close by. The campaign was advertised as a general campaign for women's rights, but the crowd was swelled by all types and Molly decided that they, like her, thought the Commonwealth Liberal Party needed to do better for their causes. The Saviours of Animals and Children, the flat earthers, the Nihilists and Anarchist Group each had their own issues and therefore their own chants and pamphlets. Not far behind them was a huge turnout for the Temperance Society and, behind them, the National Anti-Sweating League. The Bulgarians were there too, protesting an attack from Greece and its allies, and began to chant, 'We denounce the Treaty of Bucharest.'

'Surely there won't be another war,' said Molly.

'Surely not,' Gladys replied, thinking of all the potential husbands lost.

There were so many campaigners that passage through the Central Business District of Melbourne was sluggish, obstructed by women made bulky by voluminous skirts and large hats, who sharpened the crowd with their placards, poles, spikes and banners. The horses, carts, carriages, traps and automobiles had to stay at the kerb and a tram was forced to stop while the campaigners passed, like a mob of sheep around a tree.

'See if you can spot Adela Pankhurst,' said Miss Berrycloth, half expecting to see the recent immigrant front and centre of an army of savage English suffragettes.

Molly frowned and said, 'I hope she's been told we don't use violence here, we're simply campaigning for equality in everything.'

But she understood why Adela was here, that she'd fled persecution in the United Kingdom, that the Pankhursts and their suffragette comrades were done standing on street corners, ringing bells and subjecting themselves to abuse, mockery and missiles – rotten eggs and excrement, sputum and bricks. After decades, the Women's Social and Political Union no longer asked for permission to participate in policy that affected them. Asking got them nowhere, so they employed tactics of disruption and civil disobedience. And when this had no effect, plight became fight: 'Deeds not words.'

Molly wasn't so dedicated as to throw herself under a politician's car or run in front of the King's racehorse, nor would she ever bomb a politician's house or a church – it only brought more persecution and imprisonment. She didn't want a criminal record; she was an outcast as it was. A lifetime of abuse and being shunned was enough. In the end, she had been awarded the gift of life and she would have it, no matter what it was. There was pleasure in the trees in her backyard and the music at the rotunda, and in the love and loyalty of family.

'The suffragettes are up the front with Vida,' whispered Aunt April disapprovingly. They didn't want the visiting British suffragettes handing out diagrams explaining the protest tactic of starvation and how to cope with the prison's policy of force-feeding. The newspapers had been reporting their actions more scathingly than usual and the entire suffrage movement had been maligned.

The crowd moved onwards, the police shepherding them, the cage doors on their trucks open and ready to hold as many women as they could bag.

Some general suffragettes and reformers at the back of the march began to push, forcing the centre to press against the head of the crowd. Meanwhile, the orbiting pamphleteers scattered their propaganda. Black and white pamphlets were glued by rain to fences, lampposts and footpaths, and stuck underfoot, causing people to slip and fall.

In the pushing and chanting, Molly and Aunt April, and Miss Berrycloth and Gladys at the other end of the banner, became wary. Behind them Mrs Sidebottom and the Australian Women's National League punched the air with their posters:

SAFEGUARD THE HOME TO SAFEGUARD THE FUTURE.

WOMEN'S POTENTIAL IS IN THE HOME.

It was the rogue faction of fierce British suffragettes at the back who began to really push, dislodging a small crowd of humanists and advocates for euthanasia. This caused other campaigners to stumble against office workers, shoppers, ladies at luncheon, businessmen, traders and hawkers going about their daily business. It was wet and steamy, and people were trying to get to and from Flinders Street Station, jostling in doorways, crammed at tram stops. The march began to heave and sway, broiling women churning under their umbrellas.

The police moved in, breaking the march in half to let pedestrians through. They called the stalled campaigners faddists and pests, dragging them away, and, as they did, other women were shoved, stumbled or fell. A sergeant shouted, 'You're not making it easier for anyone,' to which Molly replied, 'On the contrary, women make things easier for everyone.'

'And we're exhausted,' said Gladys, feigning a yawn.

Mrs Sidebottom and her AWNL chums began to merge with Molly's Women's Political Association group. An older woman shaped like a rainwater tank snarled, 'We oppose socialists!

Our responsibility is to safeguard the home, children and each other.'

'Good,' said Molly. 'You stay in the home and obey your husband, but don't stop me from realising my own potential.'

Suddenly, things ignited; the fracas became a brawl and a horse was frightened, rearing. The driver, frustrated with the women, slashed the top of a lady's hat with his long whip. A man of the cloth, religion unidentified, tore a suffragist's poster from her and snapped the pole over his knee, then limped in circles, rubbing his bruised thigh. Aunt April, anchored by her end of the banner, cried, 'Men have plenty of public toilets, women do not, yet God gave us the same elimination system.' The man of God put his fingers in his ears.

Another placard was snatched away by a gust of wind – *Women understand women's needs, men see it only from their needs* – and lifted away, scything through the air, sending passers-by running and ducking. The placard narrowly missed Eva Hughes, head of the AWNL, and hit Mrs Sidebottom, who was just behind her. Mrs Sidebottom held her bleeding head, and Miss Berrycloth ran to her with a handkerchief. She slapped Miss Berrycloth. 'Traitor!'

The sympathetic crowd, seeing only Mrs Sidebottom's bloodied nose, began shoving the WPA members into the gutter and tearing the cardboard pleas from their arms. Those who could, retreated.

Miss Berrycloth, being the size of an ant, was among the first to scuttle away from the melee. She looked back from the steps of Flinders Street Station and saw police and other men shoving the women, one after the other, so that they swayed and lost purchase, a great dark wave of them falling on top of each other.

That's when the suffragettes came running.

'Here come the British,' someone called, and Aunt April, dishevelled and askew, forgot her vow of non-violence and yelled, 'Kill the enemy!'

The ladies from the motherland, accustomed to brutality, fought hard, slashing any man in reach with their umbrellas and poster stakes. There was an eerie absence of screaming for such a struggle, just men grunting, the thud of flesh on flesh, fist against teeth, the occasional yelp and the sound of more police, dozens of them, all running, their voices – *'Police, stop!'* – pointless. Someone dragged Mrs Sidebottom to a wrought-iron picket fence, which she clung to, and Molly was unable to get her aunt up on her feet. She sat on the gravel road, her boater at the side of her head and her bosom dislodged from the cross-chest straps.

'Run, Molly,' Aunt April commanded, but a policeman grabbed Molly, his fingers digging into her forearm, while another pulled on her aunt's rucksack.

'Come on, fatso.'

Molly called out, 'Gladys! Run!' But Gladys remained perfectly still in her pretty dress, her placard high, protected from the light rain by an umbrella she'd picked up. All around her comrades fell down fighting.

A policeman held Molly by her coat-tails, his shins out of range of her boots. 'You are cowards and thugs!' she snarled. 'Let my aunt stand up, she's old.'

He laughed, but Aunt April scrambled to her feet, reached into her bosom and brought out a vial. She pulled the cork with her teeth and splashed the contents all over both constables' coats. They coughed and retched.

She smiled. 'Bacteria.'

Molly's captor cried, 'You women stink!'

Molly was able to say, 'It's you,' and pointed to the wet stain on his lapel.

Aunt April was shoved to the ground again and dragged away by her rucksack, a turtle on its back, smiling and tossing pamphlets in her wake. Molly felt the constable's smelly arm around her neck like a steel bar, pressing her throat, as she was frogmarched all the way to the watchhouse in Russell Street with dozens of other bloodied and bruised women.

Gladys lifted her skirt and tiptoed through the puddles and the wounded, their own skirts limp with rain and muddy horse manure, and their coat buttons popped. It was a battlefield scene, and Gladys moved from one brave friend to another, helping them regain and secure their footing. Then she brushed herself off, picked up the discarded placards and leaned them along the wrought-iron fence. She made her way to the tram, scattering her remaining pamphlets under the slippery shoes of the crowds hurrying to their warm, dry homes.

The door opened immediately. August had his hat on and one arm in his coat sleeve, his binoculars hanging around his neck in case he saw a bird.

'City Watchhouse,' Gladys said, and went to face Mrs Sidebottom.

Chapter 2

WHILE SHE WAITED for August to bail her out, Molly thought about Paris, her failed path to a career as a seamstress and her fall to factory work – and now jail. She seemed always to be *prevented*. How was she to grow if she had no new world to see?

First, there was Miss Archambeau's small, exclusive dress-maker's atelier. One week after she left school Molly arrived exactly fifteen minutes early to start work as a shop assistant. An apprenticeship wouldn't pay her enough to contribute to the family, but it was agreed she'd learn how to make dresses while she was helping to run the shop. The perfect start.

Alive with hope and shaky with happiness she ignored the *Closed* sign on Miss Archambeau's door and knocked. No one came. She knocked again, watching the clocks in the window of the neighbouring jewellers crawl towards 8 am, when she knocked again, but still no one came. She paced along Little Bourke Street and checked again that she was at the right shopfront, knowing full well that she was. The sign still read *Miss Archambeau, Couturière*, and the front window featured a faded picture of the famous soprano Dame Lily Pert, wearing a Miss Archambeau gown. Through the lace curtains she could just make out a dressmaker's dummy resting on the counter.

Her usual inclination would have been to stomp off but this was her dream, her future, her life, so she banged and rattled the door and was about to kick it when the woman from the Ham and Beef shop next door came out waving a meat cleaver. 'No amount of banging's going to wake her up.' The woman looked at the indignant, red-faced girl. 'She's dead.'

'Dead?'

'As a post.'

'You're kidding.'

'Why would I kid about that? Miss Archambeau dropped dead yesterday afternoon in the middle of Daisy's send-off.'

'I'm replacing Daisy.'

'Not anymore.'

Molly could not speak. She just looked at the door, hating it, willing it to open and end the catastrophe that was the first day of her new life, the new life that was to rescue her from her world of plain people wearing drab dresses, her life of scrimping and saving and begging. In her cold dark home in lower-working-class Carlton, Molly Dunnage had always looked to the light. And it had just been snuffed out.

'You a relative?' The woman pointed her cleaver at Molly.

For a moment she thought of lying, somehow claiming the salon and its customers.

'Because if you are, you need to take her, they haven't come to collect her.'

'That's because they live in Paris, France.'

'Ha! A tall story that one, she's from Morwell, born and bred.'

'She had a French accent.'

'Anyone can get one of them. Any rate, no one to pay the undertaker, and I can't have my customers getting wind of it, if you get my drift.'

Molly peeked through the lace curtains and recognised that the dummy waiting on the counter was in fact the slender form of dear Miss Archambeau, liar, not at all a genuine French seamstress, trained in the couture houses of Paris, and now draped in some sort of netting, its feather trim as still as death.

'A mere setback,' said August, when Molly railed against the unfairness of the death of her career.

'Come and work with me,' cried Gladys, but a horsehair-mattress factory job would be the very last resort. 'Or you could be a nurse.'

Molly said she'd rather die than be a nurse and her aunt said she probably would: 'Of diphtheria, typhoid fever, yellow fever, TB, cholera, pneumonia, dysentery or malaria.'

'Or gunshot,' said Gladys, and they all thought of the nurses who had gone to the Boer War.

Molly found no *Positions Vacant* or *Hiring Now* signs at any atelier or dress shop anywhere, and so she headed to Slutzkin's warehouse in Flinders Lane. Slutzkin's made and sold ladies' white underwear, superior corsets and undergarments, the first of their kind manufactured in Melbourne. For a girl with firm ideas on underwear it seemed like a good alternative.

The people of Flinders Lane appeared to all know each other, and everyone was cheerful. The footpath was narrow and there were many warehouses, some small, some big, all with grand doorways and wide windows showing the industry within, and the crude displays of passementerie and costume jewellery, artificial flowers, beads, feathers, leather trims, buckles, belts, sequins, fans, lace and weaving materials. The whole of Europe and half of Asia made up the throng, and the food shops and food hawkers added voice, spice, herbs and a general pizazz to the air.

'Well, off you go,' said Gladys, nudging her to open Slutzkin's door. 'A step towards your fashion empire, Molly.'

Her heart pounding, she inhaled, but it was a hot day and she couldn't quite get enough air into her lungs.

At the sound of the bell tinkling, a man arrived and introduced himself as Mr Slutzkin. Molly introduced herself and asked if there were any vacant positions for seamstresses or machine girls.

Mr Slutzkin smiled, shook her hand, saying, 'Many girls have come through this door since school ended.'

'I have brought samples.'

Mr Slutzkin's features were big, his smile kind and his accent European, and he was sprinkled in a fine cotton thread. Beyond the reception area wall, sewing machines thrummed. Mr Slutzkin studied her samples. 'They are lovely. Why would you like to work for Slutzkin's?'

'Because you make good corsets. And functional underwear, or the lack of it, interests me.'

'In this day and age do you think women will continue to wear corsets?' he asked.

'I think they'll serve a purpose for the right reasons. I'd make them so that they allow more flexibility. I have ideas that I think are better than the corsets we are currently enduring.'

He raised his eyebrows.

Molly pressed on. 'I don't mean to be disrespectful, but the narrow-hipped, narrow-skirted silhouette means corsets are lengthened over the thighs and that changes the position of the hips. Women want to move more and be active. We play more sports these days and there are new dances from Europe.'

'But these corsets you disapprove of allow for a higher, wider waist, and they allow for movement.'

'It's an illusion: they're still restrictive.'

Again, his eyebrows rose. 'You made the dress you have on?'

'Yes.'

'Lace with tartan, I never thought . . . Also an unusual cut . . . And the embroidery is lovely.'

Molly nodded, beaming. Mr Slutzkin offered her his hand again.

Outside, a great draught horse, dragging a four-wheeled dray piled with fabric bolts, pulled up and Mr Slutzkin's eyes flicked to it then back to Molly.

'Thank you for thinking of us, I wish you all the very best.' He dismissed her with a polite nod.

She turned to the door, dizzy, her legs suddenly insubstantial. Her last chance was gone.

'I will offer you some advice.'

Molly looked into his sincere brown eyes, and in a very gentle tone, he said, 'When I shook hands with you just now, without gloves, it was as I suspected. You have sweaty hands . . . you cannot work with fabric with sweaty hands.'

'But I am nervous.'

'Quite. You will become relaxed, no doubt, but it remains that you can also become nervous again, and then your hands will sweat.'

She stepped onto the street and was conscious of the great animal beside her, smelling very much like a horse, and her rage at the man who had kindly decapitated her future.

Sweaty hands.

She focused on Gladys, red-faced and pacing in the heat, smiling at passing men, appraising them.

'Molly, you look like you have seen an elephant fly past.'

Mr Slutzkin watched from his door, saw the overdressed lass with the dated bonnet embrace the applicant, and the applicant's shoulders shake as she wept, her beautiful face contorted, inconsolable. Later, when he settled into his bed in his room above the factory and thanked God for the chance he'd been given in this new country, he remembered the girl, so passionate, and wished he had asked her name and address.

Molly and Gladys got off the tram at Curtain Square and sat for a moment on the rotunda steps. They looked across to their homes on the other side of the gravel road, lined with a fetid depression, a gutter of sorts, for manure and any rubbish that had somehow evaded the family incinerator.

Aunt April's poster said:

THE WOMEN'S POLITICAL ASSOCIATION SUPPORTS
EQUALITY FOR WOMEN – AND A VOTE FOR
THE WOMEN OF THE MOTHERLAND.

And Mrs Sidebottom's defied it. Between her veranda posts, a banner declared:

AUSTRALIAN WOMEN'S NATIONAL LEAGUE DOES
NOT SEEK PLACE OR POWER; WE DO NOT
WISH TO SEND WOMEN TO PARLIAMENT.

Because the girls had assumed their lives would be better than those of the generation before, they usually let Mrs Sidebottom and Aunt April do all the squabbling. But in the short time since they'd left school, life had shown no promise of being better at all.

Molly made her announcement – dramatically – from the head of the table in the crammed kitchen. 'Today is the end. First it was the death of Miss Archambeau that stalled my ambitions, and now they have ended completely. I have sweaty hands.'

Her father lowered his newspaper and her aunt looked up from her book, *Achievements in Public Health, 1850–1900: Control of Infectious Diseases.*

Molly held her palms out to her audience. 'It's the truth. I will never be employed and so I will stay at home and calmly sew dresses for a living.' They gave her their full attention. 'I'll ask Mr Luby if I can use his shopfront when I have saved enough. It's a good position on the corner.'

Aunt April and August exchanged glances. It was her father who cleared his throat and spoke first. 'People are as suspicious of Mr Luby as they are of us. You won't draw any customers.' Mr Luby was a pale, black-eyed man, a timid hoarder whose crowded dwelling bred rats. But he was harmless and handy if you needed a chair leg or a newspaper from 1904.

Aunt April added, 'Molly, dear, you are a good seamstress, but it won't make you a fortune.'

Molly

In the Dunnage household there was a chronic shortage of funds. August was unwell, and his big sister beyond employment, and they survived largely on August's small government pension, his income from his work as a ceramic artist, and the stipend from a very small investment their parents had left for Aunt April.

'We'd all benefit greatly,' Molly's aunt said, 'if you could contribute a little to running our home.'

That afternoon, August returned home and put one hand gently on his anxious daughter's shoulder. 'I have found you a job. The factory of Emrys Pocknall will be taking girls on the first of January. They make corsets.'

Molly was momentarily speechless. The corsets Pocknall's made defied her principles on freedom and style. Eventually, she said, 'Pocknall's is a sweatshop.' She pointed at the *Better Working Conditions* badge on her aunt's breast. 'I'll die in a fire, my life will end like those poor wretches in New York.' Their minds went back to the picture in the newspaper of the shirtwaist factory girls, big falling embers, flaming as they plummeted from the windows of the third storey.

'The machines at Pocknall's are all on the ground floor,' August reasoned.

Aunt April said gently, 'If the WPA succeed, you could be promoted to designer. Opportunity is what you make it, daughter. And Fitzroy is close, you could walk there.'

'Fitzroy's a slum.'

Her father and aunt glanced around their shabby, porous house. 'Molly, everyone starts at the bottom. If you learn the basics of how to make a decent corset, then you can make it so that it'll fit anything.' Her aunt was right. Undergarments supported everything; a good corset dictated what you could wear and what you could do.

'Alright,' she said. 'I'll start at Pocknall's – at the bottom – but I'll get promoted every year. I'll make wonderful underwear. I will make garments that people *should* have, not what they want. I'll make corsets so that women can feel free to wear anything they want. I will invent corsets that people need, not what they *think* they need. Our neighbours will look at us differently when I am in Paris.'

'When are you off to Paris?'

'Give me three years.'

'Make it five.'

The sergeant at the desk pointed to the cells with his fountain pen. 'Take your pick, many as you like.'

There were at least twenty women squashed into the minuscule space, squatting side by side, leaning on each other, some lucky enough to be sitting on the bunk. August's daughter, a girl with her mother's delicate face and her aunt's stoic demeanour, was perched on April's knee, looking like thunder.

Then Molly saw him and her expression changed – she was surprised by his appearance. He was unwell. She had seen it happening but close proximity meant she hadn't noticed. It was only here, a place other than their kitchen or the studio, that she saw him as others did: as a pale, depleted man, though his expression was cheery.

Molly clambered over the squatting ladies, her aunt trailing, dishevelled but triumphant.

The sergeant thumbed in the direction of the doorway and said to August, 'Get 'em out of here.'

They stepped into the fresh Melbourne air.

Molly stopped and looked earnestly at the footpath for a few moments, working something through in her mind, and then an undisputable truth dawned on her, an impenetrable, flawless truth. She declared, 'Nothing is fair.'

'Good things come from disappointment,' said her aunt but Molly continued.

'But it isn't fair, it's just not. My life . . . I am like a beetle trying to climb out of an empty teacup.'

August had never heard such defeat come from his indefatigable, doughty offspring. Her resolve had frayed. The life force of Molly Dunnage, oppressed in a factory for five years, had weakened.

She'd failed to find better employment close to home so had ploughed on, earning extra money by seamstressing for local ladies on weekends. For nourishment, when Gladys had polished, dusted and tidied Mrs Sidebottom's house, she and Molly took trips to the bay or went to the rotunda band of a Saturday afternoon – they always got a good spot with an uninterrupted view because no one dared sit next to a Dunnage. Gladys's search for a husband continued at life drawing classes, which they attended together, though Molly's motivation was to know more about the human form. She felt it helped her with dressmaking and corsetry and, most importantly, drawing her designs for pattern making. It was hard to imagine what was hidden under corsets, voluminous bloomers and skirts.

It was all very well and it seemed their lives were full, but Molly wanted something for their 'emotional health', their sense of worth. She and Gladys were 'underutilised'– Gladys had not found a husband, Molly was prevented from making modern corsets, neither of them had been promoted, there were not enough Sundays to sew good dresses for decent profit and, standing outside the city watchhouse with her frail father and unflagging aunt, she felt she was trudging through life knowing the frayed drawstring in her bloomers could snap at any moment.

August put his hat on. 'Now, my brave battle angels, a chariot approaches to take us home.'

A tram rattled around the corner, slowed and, seeing them outside the watchhouse, hurried on.

Chapter 3

MOLLY'S ILL TEMPER accompanied her to work Monday morning, the bruise of her stint at the watchhouse adding to the general discomfort of the machinery din and the sharp odour of decaying teeth and sweat – new and old. She understood all too well that these indignities were exacerbated by low pay, but still they added their flavours to the heat radiating from the factory's corrugated roof and walls. And Snakelegs was stalking. From time to time, Molly reminded the manager of Pocknall's that the factory was an oven, and a draughty ice box in winter. She could not stop herself and added to her complaint that sweatshop conditions were a reportable offence.

Mr Addlar was called Snakelegs because he was low to the ground, didn't blink, and walked with a smooth gait, propelling off the ball of his foot into the next step rather than pulling forward with his front foot. Delighted with Molly's insubordination, he turned and pointed to the lines of first machinists. Molly dutifully abandoned her place at the cutting table, where it was removed from the general clamour, to replace Lizzy at the noisy machines. Working the machines was all about rapid sewing, and it was difficult to sew straight lines on a curved corset panel. It stole Molly's fury because it required total focus. A lone crooked line meant a shilling less in your pay packet for the ruined corset, and there were hundreds of boning channels – up and back, up and back – before all the panels had to be joined.

The girl detailing corsets kept the pile next to Molly's machine tall and whipped the finished corsets away without a word.

No one left space for her on the bench along the wall at lunch, but it was not fury; their co-worker's hurt was summoned by her stalled, frustrating life. Nothing was as she'd dreamed, and nothing was fair.

Now, sent back to the machines, she told herself that it couldn't last. Alathea Pocknall would notice, hopefully sooner rather than later.

Molly had only been at the factory a few weeks when she complained to Snakelegs for the first time. She asked for toilet breaks when required, rather than just at morning tea and lunch. Often the queue was so long some girls were late back to their machines, and they were then hounded by Snakelegs, who slid around the tin and canvas walls and up and down the banks of workers, hissing at them.

Her request for toilet breaks relegated Molly to bodice stockmen, commonly known as torsos – 'ideal midriffs of the ideally shaped woman' – for the next two years. As torso girl she was required to check the busks and panels, the metal eyelets, the hooks and eyes, and put aside any corset with faults. Next, she had to latch the top and bottom hooks and eyes, thread the back closure with a cotton lace two yards long, and pull, though not too tight, before inserting the baleen into the boning. She grew expert at all of these procedures, but no one, least of all Molly, found any part of it pleasurable. Most girls coveted the embroidery table: seated, stitching pretty pictures, attaching silk or cotton lace, beads or ribbons, and, for exercise, embroidery girls were also required to fold and pack.

For four years Molly longed for a treasured position at the table with the white cotton garments, and when she finally got there, she excelled. Then Alathea Pocknall noticed her superior embroidery.

The boss's daughter often came to the factory, though she usually remained in her father's office, and every so often Miss Pocknall had someone bring samples to her so that she could choose new undergarments for herself and her friends. Mr Addlar was unfailingly courteous to her, but spoke as if she were both slightly deaf and six years old. She couldn't look into his pale eyes when it was necessary to speak to him – it required her to look down on him – and this, Alathea Pocknall suspected, was the seat of his attitude. She spoke to his eyebrows: 'Who sews the fine embroidery on the corselets, drawers and undershirt samples?'

Mr Addlar replied, 'Dunnage. A difficult girl with a poor attitude, defiant and opinionated.'

'Her humour might improve with affirmation of her skills.' Alathea looked down at his legs, which were unusually short, as if they were someone else's. She then turned and walked away.

That very afternoon, Snakelegs moved Molly from embroidery back to torsos, but, over dinner, Alathea Pocknall proposed a line of special-occasion undergarments to her father. 'Molly Dunnage has good workmanship; her talents are useful for advertising.'

'I've taught you well,' said her father, reaching for his wine glass.

To Molly's delight, she was sent back to the corner table to embroider opposite Colma. Colma, the self-appointed mother of the factory, and holder of a certificate in Anatomy and Hygiene of Corsetry and Surgical Fitting, was toothless, long-nosed, sharp-chinned and threatened by Molly's fine needlework. Mr Addlar said nothing, just opened the windows above the table. The light was appreciated, but at the time it was late July, and in that dank, gloomy corner of the factory, the cold caused pain. After only an hour, Molly's neck and shoulders were like marble and her stiff fingers hard to manoeuvre. Soon her fingertips were punctured, but she endured with the help of a scarf and fingerless gloves. She felt Colma's hatred across the way, but, at the embroidery table, Molly Dunnage no longer complained, until today.

Marching home that night, hot and sticky with cotton dust, her ears ringing from the thrum of machines, her mind boiled with the unfairness of the world.

Chapter 4

JUST OUTSIDE THE house, Molly came across Gladys's so-called brothers. The Sidebottom boys were throwing stones at a dead bat caught on telegraph wires and their faces lit up when they saw the neighbourhood witch. Manfred said, 'Want it for your cauldron?'

'Otherwise we'll squash it under our boots,' Aubrey added.

As usual, Molly ignored the remarks. 'My aunt will want that bat.'

'How much is she offering?'

'Depends how squashed it is.'

The boys returned to their retrieval; Molly continued on her way. It was choir night, and Gladys could not go if Molly wasn't there to walk her home. Rounding the corner, she looked back to see Manfred had climbed onto Aubrey's shoulders to poke at the creature with a long stick.

Two years prior, Gladys and Molly were lying, toe to toe, on their favourite grave – Cornelius O'Mahony, 1840–1879, Gaelic scholar and supporter of Irish independence – when Molly said, 'I can sing, you know.'

'That's something I've never forgotten, Molly.'

At school, Molly had been asked to sing 'My Shepherd Will Supply My Need' at the end of year assembly. The applause lasted minutes, and the schoolyard persecution much longer.

'I think we should join a choir for our emotional health.' And then, to really persuade Gladys, she offered, 'Men sing in choirs.'

The conductor, the pianist and the committee heard their audition. Gladys sang a few lines and was thanked, but Molly managed a complete verse before she was told by Mrs Blinkhorn that they already had adequate sopranos.

'We know,' Molly replied. 'But what you need is *good* sopranos.'

To defuse the appalled silence, the conductor suggested they could sound the note for each song at Tuesday rehearsal when the pianist wasn't available.

'And you can prepare the supper,' said Mrs Blinkhorn, a thin, pearl-draped woman who wore far too much face powder and hid her chin behind a high clerical collar. 'Tell me, Molly Dunnage, how did you come by that blouse you are wearing?'

'I stole it off a clothesline.'

Gladys replied eagerly on her behalf, 'She made it herself. That's what she does.'

'Well, then,' said Mrs Blinkhorn, sitting up straight. 'You can also have responsibility for the wardrobe. You will attend to any mending or adjustment to the robes and see to it that they are ready for the choir at each performance.'

'Can we sing?'

'If you must, just not anywhere within earshot.'

Gladys said thank you and the two girls rose as one and headed outside.

And so, years later, the girls were still manning the refreshment counter and sorting the robes and failing every audition.

Aunt April looked up from her microscope and moved her magnifying glasses to the tip of her nose. 'Did you ask me if I wanted a dead bat?'

Molly removed her hat; it was straw with a narrow brim and a deep, wide crown. She'd trimmed the band with roses made from dry leaves and orange and red fabric scraps. 'The boys are retrieving it for you now.'

Aunt April pushed her glasses up to the top of her head and hurried to the front gate. Molly continued through the house, her spirits a little sunnier. She turned on the kitchen light, one of only two electric lights in the house, to illuminate her cubby through the window. It was a warm summer night, mosquitos buzzing. Factory offcuts, mostly muslin and satin, provided privacy from the laundry and washhouse at the other end of the veranda but no protection from insects. A hen leapt from her bed and ambled out, and Molly sat to change her boots.

Gladys hurried down the hall, the ribbons from her bonnet floating behind and two eager teenage boys following. Aubrey carried a long stick and Manfred a sack, and they looked like they'd just slain a monster.

August heard the commotion from his studio. He was painting a dinner plate, a private commission from the local doctor's wife, who wanted her children's portraits on plates for the dresser, and looked up to see the two Sidebottom boys, strapping now and both in long pants. One – he wasn't sure which – pulled a bat by the tip of a fine, spiked wing from the bag. He went back to the plate, consulting the photograph of the doctor's youngest son. The jug-eared boy would do well on a teapot. But curiosity got the better of him and August went to find out why next door's enemy foot soldiers had gathered in his kitchen. He arrived just as Molly called, 'Wash your hands. Bats carry death-making diseases.'

'You'd know all about that,' said Aubrey.

'My aunt's the one to avoid if you want to live. I'm just a harmless sorceress.'

Manfred stepped away from April.

August found the girls readying to go out and remembered it was choir night. They were going to audition, as they did every year, for the annual performance. This year, it was arias from *Madame Butterfly*.

'Do you think you'll get a part?'

'We might,' said Gladys, and Molly said there was always a chance, especially now there was a new choir secretary.

'He's also the conductor's understudy,' said Gladys, as if it was very important.

'He'll notice you can't sing if you audition,' Manfred sneered.

April handed the boys a penny for the dead bat and pointed to the door. 'You may go now.'

'If we don't get a part this time I've got a good mind to quit,' said Molly.

Gladys cried, 'No! I want an invitation to hear the new choir secretary's gramophone.' Gladys was wearing a scarf no one had seen before. Gladys often wasted her savings on new accessories. 'I'm not invited to anything, ever.'

Molly secured her boater. 'If you do go to hear the gramophone, remind Mrs Blinkhorn that she owes me two pounds.'

Mrs Blinkhorn had turned up the day after Molly and Gladys failed their first choir audition. 'I'm here for a dress,' she said.

August replied, kindly, 'This isn't a dress shop. But I'm assuming you're here to see Molly?'

'I am.'

Molly appeared. 'Good afternoon, Mrs Blinkhorn, you will need to make an appointment –'

'I just want to ask a few details.'

'You need to make an appointment. Saturday is bath day, and you are lucky we didn't answer the door wrapped only in a towel.'

Mrs Blinkhorn took a step back. 'How much do you charge?'

'It depends on what you want. You would need to purchase the fabric, of course, and depending on the pattern and the fabric, then I would purchase the linings. And, as you know, the more highly decorated the buttons and trimmings, the more expensive they are. Basically, you are looking at about six pounds or more for a basic dress. Appointments are Saturday from four until five and Sunday from eleven until noon. Sharp.'

'You are very expensive – six pounds is almost the basic wage.'

'You can pay at least double for the same dress at Myer. And sewing is cumbersome and time-consuming, it can take weeks.'

'You keep a record of your hours?'

'I do, and I also record the time it takes me to detail that time and I can also explain how I have spent the hours labouring, which will of course cost extra time.'

Mrs Blinkhorn removed her gloves. 'Very well, I'll try you out and if I don't like what you do –'

'Then you will forfeit your deposit.'

'Deposit?'

'The amount depends on the garment. Come back next Saturday at four if you like.'

'Today is Saturday.'

'Yes,' said August, 'and it's only two.' August put his hand to his nightshirt buttons and said, 'I'm off to my bath.'

Mrs Blinkhorn fled, her Victorian propriety still intact.

As they hurried towards the front door, August reminded them that if they failed to get a part and quit, all they had to do was open the front door every Saturday to hear music from the rotunda.

'The rotunda band hasn't played anything new in twenty years,' said Gladys.

Molly and Gladys ran, the gate slamming behind them.

Aunt April spread the bat with a pair of tweezers and lowered her magnifying glasses, reaching for her scalpel.

A mosquito came buzzing and August slapped at it, then splashed a little turpentine into the old saucepan filled with dry manure and threw a match onto it. The smouldering mass filled the air with rancid smoke, but the mosquito buzz eased.

Next door, Mrs Sidebottom sniffed the air and, looking at her drying sheets, shook her head.

Despite their musical failings, they still enjoyed choir. Gladys loved the 'social aspect' of serving supper, while Molly occupied herself with the music and the play of relationships and the quiet skirmishes in the hierarchy. When they arrived at the hall, the new choir secretary was sounding the note for running through scales.

Gladys apologised for being late, a little too earnestly, Molly thought. There was something about the choir secretary. He was reasonably tall and well built with good teeth, but his lips were the type that would flatten to a thin crease with age and his fair hair was almost yellow, not a shade she'd ever seen. Despite all this, Gladys had taken a shine to him, or perhaps to his gramophone.

As the choir warmed up, Molly and Gladys assembled the cups and saucers, poured milk into jugs, put biscuits on the tray, teaspoons beside the sugar bowl and the kettle on the gas ring. And then the auditions began.

When they were called, Molly and Gladys did their absolute best. The committee listened politely, sitting at their table with notepads, pencils and sheet music. But it was only the new secretary who clapped enthusiastically while the committee murmured among themselves.

Mrs Blinkhorn thanked the young women. 'You've prepared supper?'

Molly and Gladys took their places behind the canteen counter. The choristers came and took their tea and biscuits, ignoring the girls. The new secretary approached them and told Molly their audition was outstanding.

'I thought so too,' said Molly, and the new secretary stepped in to the counter and leaned close to Molly.

'You have a remarkable presence.'

'People find it grating after a short time.'

Gladys gushed. 'Thank you for listening to us, we are very grateful, sir.'

The new secretary turned to Gladys. 'Call me Evan.' He put down his empty cup and saucer and returned to the songsters.

Molly watched Gladys watching the new secretary. 'He is too old, Gladdy, at least thirty, and I thought you wanted someone rich.'

'I heard his mother is wealthy.'

'He has no lips.'

'He has a gramophone.'

Molly decided she would put aside her reservations. He was not worth an argument with Gladys.

They tidied their kitchen, noiselessly, as they had learned to do, feeling the piano through the thin leather of their shoes. It tickled and filled her with happiness. Gladys swayed and turned long slow circles across the kitchen floor. Then Cio-Cio-San's voice pierced the air, the conductor winced, the chorus failed to unite and Gladys stopped dancing. She took her cotton balls from her sleeve and put them in her ears. After three more attempts, rehearsal arrived at an impasse. The conductor, alarmed, called for an end to the evening and the committee gathered in the corner, then dribbled out, muttering.

Molly and Gladys tidied the hall, hung the gowns and went to check the stage door was locked, all the while discussing Fanny's inferior voice.

'Poor girl sounds like a train whistle,' Molly said, and Gladys said even she could do better.

Then a voice came from the back of the dark hall. 'Would you like to audition again?'

They froze.

In unison, Molly said, 'No,' and Gladys said, 'Yes.'

'Sing something for me now.'

Evan Pettyman emerged from the gloom. 'Go on, stand there, exactly where you are, and sing me a song together.'

They remained there in the middle of the stage, torn: to sing for the choir secretary or not?

Evan vanished into the dark end of the hall and called, 'SING!'

Gladys stood tall and started to sing 'By the Light of the Silvery Moon', but Molly wasn't going to sing 'We'll be cuddling soon, by the silv'ry moon' for anyone.

Suddenly the floor vanished from under them and they plunged into complete darkness, landing on a dusty mattress, all around them cobwebs. They heard his laughter and then, in the square of light above them, he appeared. 'Got you!'

Gladys laughed but Molly was furious. 'How dare you! You're a fool! We could have sprained an ankle, broken something, and there are spiders down here.'

'They wouldn't dare take you on.'

Molly told Gladys to search for a door, but Gladys refused. 'Spiders,' she whispered. It was Molly who groped around in the dark, recoiling when she put her hand on a sharp brittle thing covered in fur. 'HELP!' she bellowed.

'No one can hear you,' sang Evan.

'This isn't fair, you tricked us!'

'Give us a kiss and I'll get the ladder.'

'I'd rather stay here,' said Molly.

Gladys said, 'Spiders.'

Evan got to his feet and walked away, calling, 'Suit yourselves.'

'I'll kiss him, Molly, I don't mind,' Gladys said.

'No, you won't! Give me a leg up.' Molly lifted her ankle and clutched the rim of the hole. They heard the front door close.

'Gladys, get hold of yourself; better still, get hold of my ankle and give me a leg out.'

After two attempts and then a mighty heave by Gladys, Molly was able to claw her way out of the hole, her long skirt dragging. She unlatched the access doors at the front of the stage and Gladys crawled free, dust smudged and anguished.

Outside, Evan appeared, cajoling. 'It was just a bit of a laugh, a bit of fun! You look like fun girls.' He put his derby over his heart. 'Will you forgive me?'

'No,' said Molly, for she'd decided that there was a certain beady-eyed quality about him and something about the way he licked his thin lips that she didn't trust. She took Gladys by the hand and dragged her away.

'He said he was sorry,' Gladys said, as Molly led her through the cemetery.

'He *said* he was sorry, but he enjoyed every second he had us trapped. And he's older – why is he still alone?'

'I don't want my future to be just horsehair and housework.'

They arrived at the corner of Curtain Square. The cow bell sounded.

'How does she know, Gladys? It's as if she can smell you at fifty yards.'

Down at her gate, Mrs Sidebottom called, 'It is not healthy to loiter in the park, and you're late.'

They weren't late, they were always home by nine, but there was no point arguing.

'She hates it when I enjoy myself.'

They brushed off the last of the dust and cobwebs.

'It seems all of society's against us, Gladdy.'

Gladys shrugged. 'See you tomorrow night for drawing class.'

Through the window Molly could see Aunt April at her desk, an angel with a halo of frizzy hair, one pair of glasses on her head ablaze with lamplight, the other pair where they should be on her nose. The house smelled of earthy woodsmoke and manure from the compost at the back. Over at the square the young trees moved in the breeze and there was starlight above the rotunda, vacant save for Freddy Sidebottom stretched out along the bottom step, his hat over his face. She thought of her father's birds in the trees, asleep with their beaks pressed under their wings, and the wildlife that provided her aunt with subjects to study. What Molly was passionate about wasn't so attainable.

Her aunt was bent over the fruit bat, dissected and pegged out on her desk, her nose perilously close to the mammal's innards. Aunt April was sketching its calm, big-eyed face into a notebook using a blood-smeared pencil.

'Don't they carry disease?' Molly asked.

'No more so than any other animal.' While Molly removed her coat and hat, Aunt April expanded on viral pathogens. 'It's a matter of being cautious and washing hands. Pathogens are dedicated. Unlike normal flora, they cross cellular and biochemical barriers, eliciting specific responses from the host that enable them to thrive and multiply, so they colonise the host, circumvent the immune responses, settle in, build lives, then move on to a new host via a bat and establish another family. Very skilful and practical.'

'That's my ambition,' Molly said.

'To colonise a host?'

'More or less. One day I'll be autonomous, society will be my host. I'll circumvent the social norms so that I can thrive and multiply my underwear design.'

Her father called from the kitchen, 'People will always need crockery and underwear.'

Aunt April pointed her sticky red pencil to a stack of her pamphlets. 'You will succeed when we women of the world get our way. Have you quit?'

'No, but we didn't get a part.'

Her aunt scoffed. '*Madame Butterfly* is just popular song. It has an unlikely synopsis that romanticises an innocent, possibly stupid girl who has endured fallen circumstances because her father is weak and obedient to a cruel tyrant, and thus she must prostitute herself and is taken advantage of and cruelly cast aside. Then she kills herself.'

'They're just singing the tunes.'

'Dying's a serious thing.'

'They were going to take Cio-Cio's child from her,' Molly said.

'She could have got on with things, the child might have come back. Anyway, the point I am making is that popular song is akin to whistling, which is useful to summon dogs and direct crane drivers.'

'You sound like someone from the Temperance Society,' Molly said and joined her father in the kitchen, smoke from the burning manure drawing up through the hot plates. He was reading Aunt April's copy of *Woman Voter*.

'You must be the only man in Melbourne who reads that newspaper.'

'Some men read it.'

'Before they tear it into wipe-sized squares and nail it to the toilet wall.'

His daughter was in an indignant mood. 'Molly, my dear girl, such language.'

'Accurate, though.'

Molly went to her cubby, lifted the chook from her bedhead and retrieved her money box from its hiding place. She totalled her savings in her little book, as she did every week, sometimes twice a week, then hid the money box again.

Over the past five years, though her plans to conquer Paris had faded as her frustrations dominated, her imagination and determination remained. As long as life continued as it was, if her father's health was maintained, if her aunt held steady, if nothing went awry, she would eventually have enough money to open a shop, perhaps in three years, perhaps even two . . . or one day Mr Luby would die, and she would clean out his house and use his shopfront. She might yet get to Paris.

Chapter 5

THE NEXT EVENING, after the tedium of Pocknall's, Molly looked forward to home, but when she turned the corner into Newry Street she saw Mrs Sidebottom standing on the very edge of the veranda, as far away from the contaminated air floating out from the Dunnage home as was possible. She cradled a dozen eggs in newspaper and turned from August to Molly. 'Gladys is late, where is she?' Her injuries from the campaign were now just a vague yellow and purple tinge.

Molly shrugged. 'Poor exhausted Gladys has probably fallen asleep from the hard work at her factory job and her nights stirring a boiling copper.'

'Gladys has never worked hard in her life.'

'As I say, she's exhausted.'

'Hard work brings profit, mere talk leads to poverty.'

'That's why you're poor, Mrs Sidebottom.'

'I'm not poor.'

'Then perhaps you could pay your docket,' said August, 'to which I'll add these eggs.' Then he closed the door before Mrs Sidebottom could continue.

As Molly put the kettle on, her aunt came in, washed, and scooped a thumb of butter from the pat to rub into her old coarse hands. 'How are things at the factory?'

'Frosty.' Molly poured them all tea, the sewing machines still thrumming in her ears and her mind filled with visions of the cotton-reel boy run off his feet, boxes piled up at the stacking post and piles of corsets toppling at the machines.

'I wonder where Gladys is,' said August.

Molly said, 'It's drawing class tonight, she'll be home soon.'

Drawing classes were held in the craft room at their old school, and as Molly and Gladys trekked through the cemetery, they called hello to Molly's mother's grave, as they often did.

'Why were you late, Gladys?'

'Oh, I just got chatting to someone and missed my tram.'

They arrived in the classroom to find the desks already pushed to the wall under the window, which glowed red with the setting sun. Two lines of timid people, mostly women, were sheltered behind easels, with a tall stool within reach and their sketching pencils sharpened. One or two held notebooks.

Mr King – quiet, immaculate and passionate – wore a long royal blue vicuna coat and a colourful African kufi hat made from handwoven cotton. He stood in front of two satin-draped easels and faced the class. Mr King explained that he would reveal two paintings from which the students would choose one to replicate. He placed his hand on his chest as he spoke. 'Infuse your heart with the emotional content of the picture and it will travel through your imagination and onto the canvas.' He turned to the easels and ripped the sheets away, revealing two images: Francesco Hayez's deep, emotional painting *The Kiss*, and Gustav Klimt's passionate gold and silver depiction with the same title.

'Behold *The Kiss*!' Mr King wrapped his arms around himself, embracing his own small shoulders. 'These show an expression of love' – he turned to them – 'a symbol, or an approach, to the *ultimate* expression of wondrous love, the moment of connection that leads to coupling.'

Gladys was all ears and eyes, Molly a little self-conscious.

Mr King closed his eyes and shook his head, as if to break a trance. 'A kiss is a truly beautiful *precursor*, a singular, *natural* impulse that sees two people entwined to the exclusion of *everything else. Every.* Thing.' He stepped towards the class, his tone serious, 'This is not about titillation, the nudeness of a body, breasts, the genitals of *The Victorious Athlete,* the depiction of the statue we explored last week. No! What is it about?'

No one said anything.

Mr King sighed in frustration. 'It is about love, obviously. Now, Molly Dunnage, what is it you can see, about either painting, that expresses specifically the bond between these lovers?'

'Oh,' said Molly, startled, feeling even hotter under the electric light and the gaze of the classroom. Molly had not been kissed and had not really seen such a thing in real life. But she understood the closeness of the act, had imagined the melding of lips, teeth, even the proximity of the tongue. Seeing, but not really recognising, the erotic domination in the Klimt and the impulsive action in the Hayez, she decided it must be, as described in novels, total enrapture. Both pictures conveyed willingness and seemed somehow urgent. Molly decided the kiss was about the rapture and goodness of love, and the pleasure of coupling, but she also feared it a little. It looked dangerous. She would not kiss anyone until she was in love, until there was a miracle and she found that man.

'Well, as I see it, in Hayez the way his hand holds her face, her jaw – it is protecting, cupping, a loving gesture. And then there is her hand sitting so comfortably on his shoulder, drawing him to her, and her rich and pretty dress makes the image . . . pleasing? And he also shields her with his hat. It's about oneness.'

'Thank you.' Mr King clasped his hands at his heart again, his eyes closed, nodding. 'Anyone else want to add anything to this portrayal of love that they can see? What have Molly and I missed?'

Hands shot up all over the class: 'The splash of red, for passion.' 'The setting, it is an unexpected encounter.' 'No, he has just come home, he's been away, you can tell by the way they hold each other.'

Gladys added, 'The shadow they cast is intriguing, it suggests something dramatic.'

And then Mrs Wrench, an older lady who favoured lacy Edwardian bonnets and Queen Victoria collars, said, 'I see both are about the love of God.'

A quiet young man at the back of the class, who no one had ever heard speak, said, 'Well, you would.'

In the silence, all eyes turned, students leaning out from behind their easels, to inspect Master Farrat, a pale young man whose physique Aunt April would have said was one that would 'gain a pound a year'. He was the youngest in the class by far, his moustache more duck down than hair, and while most people wore an apron, Mr Farrat wore a smock, an 1880s buttoned shirt that gathered and fell from the bodice. Its full sleeves buttoned at the wrist, and its green buttons matched his cheerful green paisley tie.

Mr King begged, '*Please*, feel free to speak *more*, young man.'

The young man's name was Horatio – Molly knew that much – and he was a fine drawer. His depictions of fabric were lush, as if the cloth could be touched – his mother was Mrs Farrat of Mrs Farrat's Hat Shop, Darling Street, East Melbourne, and she'd trained him well. He once drew a woman wearing a very fine hat which Molly re-created when she got home, though she stuck pine-tree sprigs into her hat because she had no ostrich feathers.

'Mrs Wrench sees the world through the eyes of God but I see that the artist is depicting passion, *human* love. This art has more to do with human nature than religion. There are no icons, no halos, candles or arched windows, and I doubt there's a virgin in either depiction.'

Mouths fell open. Horatio had uttered the word *virgin*.

Mrs Wrench merely said, 'The love of God showed us all how to love *truly*.'

'But these images speak strongly about yearning and the pleasures of the flesh.'

There were audible gasps in the class. Gladys giggled. Mrs Wrench blushed crimson.

Horatio looked to the class. 'Surely everyone can see that?'

'I can see the physical nature of their love,' said Molly.

And Gladys said, 'Me too.'

In the silence, people retreated behind their easels again, and so Mr King clapped twice. 'Very well, thank you for your thoughts. Art is, after all, about interpretation. Thus, I want to see on your page the emotional content of what you see in this painting. I want your pencil lines to *move* me.'

At the end of each class, Mr King walked between the easels making comments, and suggested they work on their drawings at home. On this night he studied Molly's drawing. 'Think about the style of Paul Rubens. This is schematic rather than École des Beaux-Arts. Do you want to be an artist?'

'No.'

'That is fortunate.'

As they packed up, Gladys went to Horatio. 'I am Gladys, and you are?'

'Horatio Farrat, how do you do?'

'I am well. Tell me, Mr Farrat —'

'Horatio, please.'

'What do you do, Mr Farrat?'

He straightened a little. 'I am a police officer, a constable.'

'That's a good steady job. You look far too young to be a policeman.'

'I have only just joined.'

'You must be brave.'

'I don't get much conflict in the Lost, Found and Stolen Department.'

'Your depictions of fabrics are wonderful,' Molly said.

'I like fabrics — in fact, I like clothing in general. I like to guess what people are like by what they wear.' And before Gladys could say anything further, he said, 'Now I really must catch my tram. Goodnight.' Horatio Farrat strode from the room with his smock under his arm and his pencils neat in a small pink leather case.

*

The two young women wandered home through the cemetery gates, down Centre Avenue and then the Ninth, the headstones standing sentry as they passed, their sketch books under their arms.

Molly sighed. 'I always find art class so inspiring.'

'Mrs Sidebottom thinks we draw fruit.'

'We started with fruit.'

'And now we have moved on to naked athletes and kissing.' Gladys sounded triumphant. 'And it has sent Mrs Wrench running out the door, even though she is married. I can't wait to be married, everything will be settled.'

Gladys had always been curious about men, but she had never discussed what she wanted in a husband except that he love her and be wealthy enough that she didn't have to wash clothes or dust and polish drawing-room appurtenances.

'I'd be careful of marriage if I was you, Gladys.'

'Careful?'

'Don't rush. Wait until you meet the right man, someone who is honest and will let you express yourself as you really are.'

'Molly, my friend, Mr Right probably went elsewhere while I was stuffing horsehair into a steaming machine.'

'You don't want to get stuck with someone then find you don't really like him.'

'That's my life now! I'd rather live with anybody other than Mrs Sidebottom and her smelly boys.'

'Gladys, I don't blame you for settling for security, but don't you want to be independent, aim higher?'

'I am an orphan and I wash other people's soiled linen. Wherever I aim it's higher.'

'Point taken.'

They said goodnight at Gladys's front gate, Mrs Sidebottom at the curtain with a candle.

Chapter 6

MOLLY'S JOURNEY AROUND the factory floor had taught her about almost every aspect of production. She knew the suppliers and the quality of what Pocknall's provided, could identify inferior material and what it meant to meet output demands. Snakelegs taught her much about how to treat workers: Molly would not use threats or force; her workers would like and respect her in her exclusive corsetière's establishment, and she would appreciate their insight. Her business also would be efficient; she'd have a time and motion specialist come in to increase production. Gladys had shown her that selling more popular styles to suit the 'feminine and fashionable' trends would fund her more adventurous designs. When her time came, she would work with dress designers, make corsets to match coming trends, and then fashion outlets would recommend her underwear.

'You have a lot of dreams,' her father said, but it was her dreams that kept her going to Pocknall's every day, and the fact that her father was ill and needed medications, good food and a life without worry.

Occasionally, when Mr Addlar was otherwise occupied, Molly made use of the cutting table and the electric lighting during the lunchbreak. She was embroidering flowers onto the yoke of a pale blue cotton blouse with a high band collar for Gladys, when suddenly the factory lights went out. She looked across the two rows of machines, with their high-wire arms like frozen ballet dancers and their cotton threads like cobwebs, and there, behind the bodice stockmen and walls of fabrics, stood Mr Addlar, his hand on the light switch.

From across the room Molly felt his repugnance and knew her hopes to get back to embroidery were dashed. When she joined the girls along the wall in the sunshine they said nothing, though they would have seen Mr Addlar turn out the lights. But no one could ever be a friend to Molly Dunnage; you'd be punished by implication.

Mr Addlar announced that he would stagger breaks from now on, to increase production and stop the workers 'stealing'. There would be first and second breaks. It was his custom to draw crosses on their aprons then give commands according to those with crosses and those without. Torturing Molly was a great joy to him, and on this day, Molly looked down at her cross and felt the hatred from some of her starving co-workers. She focused on the boning channels, running straight lines up and down panel after panel, passing them on for the busks and shell to be attached.

And then Emrys Pocknall and his daughter Alathea arrived.

Miss Pocknall, a tall woman with an important bearing, was friendly despite her privilege. She was sometimes written about in the social pages. Only last week Molly had read that she had become engaged, and with her new fiancé was seen at the Town Hall Ball in the company of Dame Lily Pert, renowned prima donna.

Snakelegs saw the Pocknalls enter and moved quickly between the machines to them. Emrys Pocknall, a neat man stiff with age, made straight for his office, taking the steps one at a time, hauling himself up with the handrail. Alathea stopped Mr Addlar with a raised arm, pointed, and spoke to the top of Snakelegs's head. The girls waited to see who would be made responsible for choosing a selection of undergarments to place in her pale, perfectly mani-cured hands.

Alathea watched the rows of mousey sweatshop girls lean away as Mr Addlar passed. Molly just kept on running the panels under the foot of her machine, up and down, up and down, stewing over the ill treatment and her miserable job – such a waste of her talent, so crushing to her spirit. And then she felt a breath like a blade of grass across her neck. Knowing it was Mr Addlar, she did not turn around.

'Take a selection of undergarments to Miss Pocknall, Dunnage. She'll wait in the office. And Mr Pocknall will be there, so mind your mouth and manners.'

She had selected items for Alathea before, but it was always Mr Addlar who delivered the garments to the boss's daughter, carrying them as if they were made of snow.

'Do it now, girl.'

Miss Alathea Pocknall represented opportunity. With consideration, Molly chose a selection of corsets, a corselet, nightdresses, bloomers and petticoats and, her arms laden with white lacy underclothing, she ascended the steep timber stairs to the glass walled office. She knocked and waited, nervous but elated.

Emrys Pocknall opened the door, smiling, though it was more of a squint. He tilted his head to his daughter. 'She's the boss today.'

Alathea had removed her hat and was unbuttoning her jacket. She looked at Molly as she would a favourite ferret and pointed to her father's desk, where a large flower basket waited. Molly took a moment to understand it was Alathea's hat.

'The hat . . .'

'Yes, quite a statement, isn't it? The marvellous Mrs Farrat made it for me. Just lay the garments there on the desk next to it.'

Emrys Pocknall carried his air of entitlement sheepishly. Molly decided he was a man who had happened upon good fortune rather than striving for it. But he wore his immaculate suit well. The fabric was fine wool, granite coloured, and beautiful. The jacket was close over his shoulders and smooth over his gently humped back; the lapels did not gape or flap but curved snugly at his waist. His trousers fitted perfectly, no bulge at the knees or pockets, though she knew they held a handkerchief and flints, cigars and spectacles, a wallet and tobacco, pencil and watch. The tailoring was so sharp that Molly could scarcely tear her eyes from it.

'You're the one with nimble fingers and a good eye?'

'I'm Molly Dunnage.' She'd been caught staring.

'You make her sound like a pickpocket, Dad.'

He laughed, sat at his desk and sifted through some papers.

Molly displayed the undergarments around the hat on the mighty oak desk, Alathea wordlessly picking pieces up, inspecting them, and replacing them carefully, which Molly appreciated. She didn't like the way Mr Addlar treated their delicate embroidery. She had seen him blow his nose on one of Edith's pieces.

Mr Addlar appeared on the landing outside.

'Close the louvres, will you, Molly?' Mr Pocknall said.

Molly closed the Florentine louvres and all that was left of Mr Addlar was a dark form, like a shark beneath an evening sea.

Alathea put her hands on her hips, quite nicely rounded for someone so slender – no need for her to tightlace her corset. Her hair was dark and her blue eyes made vivid by drop earrings that Molly assumed were sapphire and diamond. She inspected the trims on a selection of bloomers and petticoats, selected two undershirts, a corselet, a nightie. When she was done, Molly collected the remaining undergarments, said thank you and headed towards the door.

'Stay for a minute.'

Molly stayed.

Mr Pocknall wandered to the door. 'I'll have a word . . .' he said vaguely and joined Mr Addlar on the landing to look down at the factory floor. He was loyal to Mr Addlar, who he knew started as a street urchin at a cotton mill before being thrown out when he turned twelve and was entitled to more pay. Replaced by an infant, young Addlar found himself homeless, but was given a chance by Mr Pocknall. The factory was his life so when

Alathea started to assist with wages and accounts, he grew livid with resentment.

Alathea shut the door behind her father and shoved the extraordinarily long hatpin through her hat and carefully piled New Woman hair. In a tone you'd use to mention you were off to the letterbox, she said, 'I'm getting married.'

Molly told her it was lovely news and congratulated her.

Alathea shrugged. 'It's not lovely at all and you know it, but it's not terrible either.'

'No.' Molly was shocked that Alathea had confided in her.

'I have seen you at those protests with your mother.'

Once Alathea had passed in a grand barouche.

'You saw me at a campaign with my aunt. My mother died.'

'So did mine.' She explained that she supported women's causes and donated to suffrage groups. 'I've even been known to show up at campaigns, ironically to progress conditions for those less fortunate. Not all of us bother, that is, women like me. Most are not inclined to defy our men, but up until now I have not had a man to placate.'

Molly nodded.

Miss Alathea Pocknall had not been raised to simply marry, procreate and be happy. Her father expected more of her – she would take over the factory – and so had been raised knowing the truth of the culture she lived in. Her father made sure she knew how to work in it, how to succeed. She knew that men would not expect her to have ideas, and would afford her no credit. But this could be useful; she could use this attitude to her advantage.

'You and your warring associates and your earnest, ethically correct humanist campaigners need to use subterfuge. You need to outmanoeuvre your opponents,' Alathea said.

'There are more of them than us,' Molly replied simply.

'I know it sounds ludicrous coming from me with all my privilege. I could give it up and join you, but that would be even more ludicrous.'

'Yes.'

'You wonder why I don't make a stand here, at this factory, don't you?'

Molly shrugged, sensing the less she said the more she'd hear.

'I will change things when I inherit this place. I will run it – you will see me here every day. But I can't cause a fuss now. I don't want to give anyone cause to challenge my father's wishes. I want him to leave the factory to me, not be persuaded to leave it to my husband.'

'I see.'

Alathea stepped closer to Molly. 'I don't need to tell you these things.'

'No.'

'And you don't need to tell anyone.' Her eyes moved to the louvres.

'I won't, but I'm sure everyone will be pleased when you take over.'

Alathea smiled. 'Right. Now here's what I want. I want a corselet but I want to be comfortable so I can ride my bicycle – fast.'

'Well, Colma –'

'Colma would build me a cloth-covered bird cage complete with padlock and spikes.'

'I can build you something painless and fetching.'

Alathea nodded. 'I want shape, too.'

'Of course.'

'I want something defining and supportive, but not restrictive.'

'It's about design,' said Molly. 'The style and art of line and form, the space and light, the colour, texture and pattern of fabric on a body. The foundation garment has to marry the body to the garment, so to speak . . . It's not about fashion or disguise.'

'Is that so?' Alathea grinned, and Molly cautioned herself not to be too bold. Over the years she'd perfected a way of agreeing to her weekend clients' demands, then making what was required. So far, no one had complained they had not got what they'd paid for.

'Tell me your thoughts on fashion and disguise, then, Molly Dunnage.'

'Fashion makes people look the same, not like themselves. Fashion's like theatre, a costume that's a fiction. Style tells the truth about someone.'

Alathea pointed towards the louvres. 'That man has the girls on the factory floor making patriarchal instruments of torture to appease the male gaze.'

'I couldn't agree more.'

'You're not a fanatic of the Rational Dress Society, are you?'

'No,' said Molly, 'but I do believe in dress reform. Corsetières still appreciate the idea of the silhouette. A corset shapes by compression: it's smaller than you so it restricts and therefore strengthens, but it could simply enhance, it doesn't need to be restrictive. It's about pressure points and the pressure exerted by the body inside, and the underpinning needs to be even and constant to the right body points.'

'Quite, and if that's all correct then a corset will support and allow movement without pinching. And those things you're holding, I want you to make some especially for me – make them *bridal.*'

Molly looked at the cloud of soft cloth in her arms and thought about the paintings, *The Kiss.* 'Discreet or bold?'

Alathea grinned. 'I need to at least attempt to provide an heir.'

'I understand.'

'But respectful. I will be respected in my marriage; that is what I have agreed to. And I'd quite like an heir, hopefully a girl so that she can progress my work and I might have an ally.'

'Could you please ask Mr Addlar if I can take the garments home?'

'I most certainly will not. I will *tell* Old Snakelegs that you are to alter these garments for me during your work hours and that he is to supply the fabric and thread and anything else you ask for. And if he doesn't, Molly, send a note and I will have him dragged behind a cart at peak hour Friday evening, before the street sweeper gets to the horse droppings.'

They laughed, and outside Mr Addlar turned his ear to the giggling women.

When Alathea had driven her father away in her sporty buggy, Snakelegs slid to her through the undergrowth of machinery and hissed, 'Don't think making underwear for the boss's daughter allows you any privilege.'

'It's not privilege,' she retorted, 'it's recognition of my talent and potential.' She immediately cursed herself for speaking. Mr Addlar would see to it that she was stepped on, like a snail on a path. Still, she did enjoy it when Mr Addlar was left speechless.

Molly found herself skipping home. She stopped, but then began skipping again. It was the start of her future, at last. She was on her way to Paris, or at least to her own shop. From now on, Molly would try harder not to antagonise Mr Addlar, she would sew for Alathea in her lunchtime, discreetly.

Chapter 7

MOLLY RANG THE Sidebottoms' cow bell and Gladys appeared, overdressed and carrying her folio and far too many pencils. And she dawdled, stopping to button her gloves, unpin her hat and smooth her hair, lingering at the kerb to let trams pass when there was ample time to cross. Gladys relished a late entrance, especially if she'd bought a new dress.

No one noticed their tardiness, their eyes only for Mr King and the satin-covered object on the desk behind him. Gladys took an easel close to the front, knowing everyone would see her before they saw Mr King's display. Molly happily set up next to Horatio. He was far too young to have thoughts of marriage – especially with someone over the hill, like Molly – therefore they could be friends.

Mr King whipped away the red satin cloth from the easel to reveal a print. 'This,' said Mr King, 'is the foot of the Egyptian Goddess, Isis. And, as you can see, Isis's foot is naked, except for the light sandal, or, as the Romans would say, a *crepida*. This foot is located in the Via del Piè di Marmo in Rome. The other picture is of Emperor Constantine's *piede*, which is also held in Rome at the Musei Capitolini.'

He spoke with an effective accent, though it was unclear if it was Italian. 'We can only imagine the majesty of the sculptures of Isis and Constantino in their full height, but looking at Constantino's piece, his foot, one can make assumptions about him, about what he was like. Tell me, students, what was he like?'

'We can tell he was poor because he rarely wore shoes,' said Mr Kalkman, knowledgeably. 'His toes are quite splayed.'

'Warm weather, so little need for lace-ups,' said Molly, though no one, apart from Horatio, recognised the irony.

Horatio called, 'I think he was a noble, because his foot is pedicured, and I, for one, can sense his upright and noble deportment.'

Mr King clapped his hands once. 'Quite! Now I urge you to communicate an emotion through your particular depiction of an ankle. Please focus on what is present and real, but what does the foot *say*? The foot and ankle before you are quite naked . . .' He stopped, and looked around the class, as did everyone else, but Mrs Wrench's easel was vacant.

Horatio whispered, 'Mrs Wrench would have draped its toes in thorns and driven a holy nail through them.'

Soon there were many awkward pencil drawings of feet kicking footballs, children's stubbed toes, broken ankles, ankles peeping from hems, even a bandaged ankle. Gladys drew an *en pointe* foot in a ballet slipper, the emotion being 'grace', though she had forgotten to give the foot a heel. A few of the students coloured-in their foot – pink with yellow toenails. Most had clothed their foot in a shoe or a sock, conscious of the pious element that Mrs Wrench had brought to the class, or perhaps drawing toes was beyond the students' talent? Horatio drew an ankle and foot, the toes reaching upwards and back from the ground. He declared it, 'Yawning.'

'It's very creative,' said Molly.

At the end of class it was Horatio's drawing that Mr King complimented, guessing it expressed 'surprise'. As they folded away their easels, Horatio asked Molly if she sewed.

'I work as a seamstress on weekends.'

'You made your dress, I bet. I sew, too, because of Mother, I suppose. I've designed new uniforms for the police force,' he said proudly.

'You've been commissioned?'

'No, I just like to contribute. Police should look impressive, authoritative, but I feel like a damp sofa in my uniform. And it's too hot in summer and too cumbersome to run in, not that I ever feel compelled to run. A costume, or uniform, can transform. We could be admired and respected rather than assaulted.'

She couldn't imagine the police force looking smart, nor anyone taking any notice of a constable.

'I see you're doubtful, Molly. If Paul Poiret hadn't made that costume for the actress Gabrielle Réjane, he wouldn't be where he is today, with all his fortune and fame. I'll make up a prototype and show them.'

'I'd like to see it.'

'I'll show you first. What do you think of crepe?'

'It's popular but I prefer the Japanese cotton crepe, or the moven from Britain.'

'Gosh, that's sixpence per yard.'

'Some only costs about two and threepence, depending on the quality, and shops only seem to stock white, but it is a beautiful fabric.'

They talked of the firm cotton fabrics known as cloth maids or matron's, and Quaker cloth, which were mostly made in a new hue called butcher's blue; they were recommended for indoor morning wear but, both felt, could be worn anywhere. But they came back to 'old friends' poplin, standard favourites like delaine and chally, before considering cashmere versus light tweeds, silks and silk wool or silk cotton blends, and another new fabric called Drap de Paris, a silk and wool blend with a cashmere finish, though it cost about six-shilling sixpence a yard.

'It wears splendidly,' said Horatio, 'and looks well on elderly and middle-aged women, as do woollen crepes or crepoline.'

'Expensive, though.' Too expensive for her clients, Molly regretted.

They parted, Molly walking with Gladys towards home and

Horatio to his tram, and each felt they'd made a new friend. Molly and Gladys's discussion turned to the extra rehearsals for *Madame Butterfly* on Saturday afternoon. Mrs Sidebottom had objected to this additional activity, and they'd watched the woman turn red and fling her arms about. Gladys had her cotton wool earplugs in place so had not heard a word of it, but there would be no further extra rehearsals.

The following Saturday started as every day did. Molly woke to the smell of the fire under Mrs Sidebottom's copper and the back-yard full of woodsmoke. On this day, given the wind was right, the air in her room was tinted grey, and she got up and out of bed coughing.

At the factory, she worked on Alathea's corset, which she adored. It was all but finished: a black sateen, wasp-waisted corselet, edged at top and bottom with black and pale-blue broderie anglaise which she had purchased herself. She matched this with pale-blue decorative flossing. Molly had machine-corded the side-front and side-back panels using string, not whalebone or metal, and made the boning channels at the back slim, inserting two very fine baleens to support the metal eyelets. The side panels had no binding, no steel, no bone. It would be firm for Alathea, but malleable – shape without restriction. And it was *bridal*, sumptuous; the bust gussets featured horizontal cording so fine that they could be pushed down easily. Molly had also cut it high over the hips to allow the legs greater movement. And she made the suspenders detachable. Alathea Pocknall would adore it, and she would make Molly a designer.

At home, she was pinning the corselet to the dummy when Aunt April appeared in her room, her palm to her cheek. 'What a fine construction, Molly.'

'You have another toothache, Aunt?'

She nodded and winced.

'You poor thing.'

Her aunt studied the corselet. 'It's for Alathea Pocknall?' She winced again.

'You should see the dentist.'

'He's a greedy, callous man.'

'What about the bacteria in your mouth?'

'*Streptococcus mutans.*'

'Have you had a tot of whisky?'

'And I have chewed cloves. I'll get Augie to it with the pliers later. I'll still have enough teeth left to chew on the other side.'

'Do it when I am out.'

Gladys was late for their departure for choir, and then she did not arrive at all, which meant Molly had to face Mrs Sidebottom. At the sound of the cow bell, Sidebottom faces appeared in the windows and Mrs Sidebottom came to the door. 'She went about half an hour ago.'

'Went where?'

'She's gone to choir, of course.' Mrs Sidebottom was pleased that she had wounded Molly Dunnage, just a little.

The rehearsal of *Madame Butterfly* arias meant extra work, and it was out of character for Gladys to go anywhere with alacrity if it meant extra work. Molly stuffed Mrs Sidebottom's letterbox with WPA pamphlets – *Support fairness and independence! W.P.A. for equal rights and equal pay* – and walked quickly away.

She found Gladys at the piano, wearing her best velvet skirt and a new blouse Molly had embroidered for her.

'I went to collect you, as usual.' When Gladys turned away, Molly grabbed her arm. 'Have you got cotton in your ears?'

'Mrs Sidebottom was complaining, so I just left.' She removed and folded the piano cover.

'Well, you could have collected me on your way past.'

'You'd better fill the kettle and start the cups.'

Molly was left to ponder her friend's mood as she set about arranging the food. Perhaps she'd place the tinned tuna sandwiches on the same plate as Mrs Blinkhorn's butterfly cakes, just to be annoying. The pianist started, Pinkerton and Butterfly began to warble, and Gladys joined Molly to serve refreshments.

Evan Pettyman was especially charming, complimenting Gladys on the tea. 'Nice and hot, and a good colour.'

Gladys offered, 'The trick is to pour the water into the pot while it's on the boil.'

'Aha! Good to know.' He winked and walked away.

Molly rolled her eyes. 'He's insincere.'

'You are suspicious and cynical, he's simply charming.'

They watched him move through the crowd, greeting and smiling.

'And he's older, why is he not married?'

'You are ungenerous, and you might be happy to be a spinster, Molly Dunnage, but I'm not.'

The singing started, and Gladys marched to the other side of the hall again, and at the end of the evening, she was nowhere in sight. Molly washed the dishes and cleared and wiped down the bench. The tenors stacked the chairs and the sopranos delivered any abandoned teacups and saucers. Then, as she swept the floor, August appeared at the hall.

'Why are you here?'

'Mrs *Bustle*bottom sent me to chaperone. She said Gladys was *up to something*. And your aunt still has a toothache.' He picked up a tea towel and started drying the teaspoons and milk jugs.

'She should see the dentist.'

'You've never had to see a dentist, so you don't understand.'

It occurred to Molly just then that she hadn't ever been an orphan either, working two jobs with only one obvious path out. And yet Gladys was generous. She collected the teaspoons her father had dried and put them away. The choir secretary wasn't a big enough reason for a rift with her oldest friend.

She waited under the peppercorn tree in the yard with her father and, eventually, Gladys came around the corner of the hall with the new secretary and his followers: the 'Music Group'. Molly went to her.

Gladys put her hand up, *stop*, and turned to August. 'Don't wait to walk with me, Mr Dunnage, I will walk home with the music girls.'

'The *music girls?*' Molly was incredulous and, again, hurt.

August said, 'It's my responsibility to get you safely home to Mrs Sidebottom, though she'd be better than me at fighting off ill-intentioned men.'

Gladys glanced at the crowd moving towards the tram stop. 'I'm going to the secretary's place to drink coffee and hear the gramophone.'

Molly reached for her. 'I'm not invited?'

Gladys shrugged her off. 'I know, a bit rude, but you don't like people and you probably have underwear to make.'

Gladys had never spoken to her so dismissively before. Molly would always be her one true friend, but there was a chance here, a group of friendly people who might lead her to something better, somewhere she could forget about horsehair and laundry.

'Someone will walk me home, Mr Dunnage. Please go without me.'

'No,' said August, gently. 'I made a promise to Mrs Sidebottom.'

But when it came to it, Molly was anxious to heal what looked like a rift. 'It's a perfectly normal activity for adults to listen to music with other people, Dad.'

'Eating your young is a perfectly normal activity too, for crocodiles. Come, Gladys, you can go next week when Mrs Sidebottom has agreed.' He offered her his arm.

'I'm nearly twenty-five,' Gladys huffed, 'and I'm never going to get out of North Carlton.'

It was after they had left a sullen Gladys at her front gate and paused at their own letterbox – Mrs Sidebottom had shoved all of Molly's pamphlets inside it – that August spotted the choir secretary pretending to be interested in the elm saplings in Curtain Square, in the dark. And it was for this reason that August chose to raise the prickly subject of his daughter's future. He sat at the stove, his sister beside him.

Over bedtime supper, August said, 'We are concerned about your future happiness.'

'I'm not,' Molly said. 'Alathea Pocknall will tell all her friends about my underwear. And she will make me an underwear and lingerie designer as soon as her father falls off his perch.'

'Daughter! Such language.'

Aunt April stirred the fire. 'You'd already be a designer if Vida Goldstein had been voted into the House of Representatives.'

August and Molly looked at the flames licking up through the hot plate.

'There'll be an election soon,' August continued. 'You can't open a newspaper without seeing reports of the senate obstructions and general ructions. So on that subject, what about marriage?'

'Of course. I'll just pick one of the blokes that line up at my door every Sunday to take me walking.'

'Well, if you *tried* to find someone,' said her father, and Aunt April suggested she might want children one day.

'Did *you*?' Molly asked.

Aunt April nodded. 'But my beau, Hurtle Rosenkranz, was felled by TB.'

Mycobacterium tuberculosis was an ordinary bacterium but it wrecked people's lives, and almost completely ruined April May Dunnage's life. Molly's amiable aunt seemed to be living freely and independently these days, but her true trajectory had been foiled in 1881. April was twenty-seven when the University of Melbourne announced it would accept women into its courses. Her passion for study was strong, but she and her brother faced facts and decided she should not spend her meagre inheritance on the large university fees given her chances of a career in micro-biology were weak. This didn't mean she would have to give up her passion for pathogens though. Access to the library was free for everyone. And it happened that she was searching the lower shelves in the microbiology section of the University of Melbourne library when she bounced off someone. She turned to apologise and fell in love with Hurtle Rosenkranz.

'Did you find it?' he asked, pointing at the books.

'Yes, you're holding it.' April felt she was looking at a familiar entity, someone who had been with her always.

He moved the book from one hand to the other but had not taken his eyes from hers. 'What's your favourite? Viruses, bacteria, algae, fungi, slime moulds or protozoa?'

'I like all pathogens.'

'Well, in that case, I like you. You can have this book tomorrow. Come to my rooms.' He wrote the address on a slip of paper. 'I'll meet you at reception, what time?'

'Four?'

'I look forward to it. We shall drink some wine.'

Right there between the stacks April Dunnage felt her life change. It was different from what it was mere seconds before and she was not surprised to find herself still talking to Hurtle at nine o'clock the next evening. They'd eaten in the hotel dining room and were on their third glass of wine. He was a big man, older – possibly forty-five or more – and economical in his movements. He was unfashionably clean-shaven and wore his receding hair swept back from his high forehead. She loved his mouth, loved every word that came from it, as well as his teeth, crooked as they were, and yearned to press her lips against his. April had never met a malacologist, specialising in bivalvia (specifically clams and molluscs), let alone a man who really listened to her. They swapped stories of archaea versus bacteria, viruses and proteins, and they reached conclusions . . . together. It was glorious fun.

Hurtle, too, was taken by April Dunnage; she was intelligent and smart, an armful of womanliness; she had no artifice and was not the least bit flighty. He knew he would not return to his wife as a true husband and found himself asking April if she would be his inamorata. 'On a permanent part-time basis, because I cannot marry you, but I love you dearly.'

She nodded. 'I doubt I could endure life without you now.'

He took her hand. 'Shall we unite?'

'I feel it is the natural response.' When he closed the door to his rooms, they removed their spectacles and reached for the buttons on their cuffs. Then Hurtle swept April into his arms and they fell back onto the bed.

Later that night, he lit the bedside lamp and looked down at April, with her hair like unravelled string about her head, and said, 'I see now that I have been waiting for you my entire life.'

A few short weeks later, after an energetic and lusty afternoon, Hurtle coughed and wiped his mouth with the white bedsheet, staining it red.

She ceased loving all pathogens.

All these years later, whenever Aunt April thought of Hurtle, she felt the same sensation that she'd felt when he said those words to her; 'I see now that I have been waiting for you my entire life.'

She was flooded again, the love still palpable in her. She had been *seen*. Hurtle Rosenkranz loved *her*; he had loved her then and she still felt his love. But, more importantly, she had been able to know what it was like to love, to live in love and to return love, and for that she was grateful.

But Hurtle was lost to her and it was a scar that pained her, and sitting across from her, Molly saw the pain on her dear aunt's face. She had asked her aunt a tender question and regretted it. It was a foolish and cruel question, but still, Molly couldn't contain her exasperation. 'Well, just because I'm not invited to music club . . . I understand that you're concerned that I will be left on the shelf . . . you'll never get your dining room back.'

'It might be a bitter pill to be stuck in unfriendly Curtain Square with two old sorcerers as we crumble and age,' said August.

'*Someone* has to look after you.'

'Your aunt and I have looked after each other since we were born.'

'We intend to continue doing so,' said April. 'We don't want you to miss out.'

'I am perfectly content.' Molly would not be bitter, though she knew she appeared to be at that moment. She would create a life as her father and aunt had, if she had to. She would make the life she ended up with rewarding and fulfilling, one way or another.

Later, she took a pound note from her savings and gave it to her father. 'Take Aunt to the dentist.'

Evan Pettyman ignored the Temperance women stationed outside the hotel – '*We keep our homes pure and united, our faith in God unshaken, seek a country free and prosperous*' – and quickly steered Gladys into Young and Jackson. Gladys was not at all shocked to see a painting of a nude woman hanging above the bar. She appeared amused and delighted, and then boasted to Evan that she had studied *The Victorious Athlete* in drawing class. 'It's a picture about strength and power, success and pride, and the skill of the artist in depicting the details of the human body,' she recited.

Evan asked, 'So tell me what this particular nude *Chloe* is about. It is most certainly not about athleticism . . .'

'It's about the beauty of the female body, about being natural . . . unabashed.'

'Free spirited,' Evan said, and winked.

She allowed him to lead her up to the dining area on the first floor, where alcohol was sold, and watched him go to the bar and order a plate of sandwiches and drinks. He was so worldly, so confident. At last someone was treating her as a grown up!

The drink Evan set down in front of Gladys was the first of several he would buy her that afternoon, sweet drinks that made her laugh at first; then she felt dizzy, wanting desperately to sit down somewhere quiet. Finally, the patrons at Young and Jackson saw her sag and crash against her companion's coat.

When she woke much later, sick and confused, she could not recall much of what had happened. It was the Temperance women who had helped her to a tram; she remembered their firm hold as she stumbled and their asking, 'Where do you live, where is home?'

They'd settled her in a seat and must have paid the fare. She clung to the tram seat, the houses zipping past and the smell of horse manure strong. Finally, the grip man shouted, 'Curtain Square, miss.' She clearly recalled tripping, tearing her nice blue dress as she alighted, and then being sick in the gutter.

Mrs Sidebottom ventured to her front window and saw her charge, curled up and fast asleep at the rotunda, her head on Freddy Sidebottom's lap. Mrs Sidebottom went to her room, sat on her bed and cried with fury and humiliation.

Before guiding her across the park, Freddy made Gladys drink water. He wished her luck before he knocked on his own front door and regretfully delivered her into the arms of his pitiless wife, whose disappointment and disgust he found harder to bear than the cold winter nights. He'd thought he had married for love and family, but he found when he returned that he'd lost love and family and, apart from a house, had nothing his wife needed from him. He also realised that somewhere in the Boer War, he had lost all of himself.

Gladys sat for a long time on the edge of her bed, half thinking Evan would come to check if she was alright. She felt so wretched, but she could not convince Mrs Sidebottom that she was innocent. 'I had one drink, the choir secretary bought me lunch – it must have been something I ate.'

Evan Pettyman did not come, and so Gladys wept, saturated in shame. She had known not to go up the stairs with him, even though it was 'just to lie down', and had refused, fought, until someone intervened and made Evan let her go. She was sick and wounded and longed for Molly. Molly would embrace her, soothe her. But there was only Mrs Sidebottom, who banished her to her little room, telling her she would get no dinner since she hadn't been there to make it. Again, she thought of the shouting man, and cried for the tenderness Freddy had shown her.

Chapter 8

A WEEK PASSED. Gladys didn't come to rehearsal, or drawing class, and Molly didn't bother to find out why.

'Something's afoot,' said August.

The following Sunday, the weather continuing warm into March, Molly rose and attended to the chooks, weeded the vegetable patch for her father, turned the compost, and then they all had their baths. Aunt April was in charge of heating the first bucket of water and Molly and her father of emptying the tub after each bath. Afterwards, Molly washed the linen and hung it, then dressed again in her blue two-piece costume with its Poiret lampshade skirt. Aunt April positioned her flag straps and struggled into her rucksack; she buckled up, adjusted her breasts and reached for her posters. The campaign was titled 'Women Who Care', and was organised by the WPA, but it would be attended by anyone upset by anything, as usual.

At the last moment, Miss Berrycloth sent word that she was unable to attend. Something about news from home, so Aunt April would not fly her banner today.

'Once more unto the breach.' She put her hand on her face to ease the pounding. There was a hole where her tooth had been and the dentist offered no solution for the pain, so she consumed almost a quarter of the new bottle of whisky and now had a headache.

August replied, 'Dishonour not our mothers . . . but I think our mother would agree with me that it's not a good time to ask for equality or the vote when your compatriots in Scotland have just burned two mansions.'

'They'd still have their mansions if they gave women the vote,' she replied.

Molly added, 'This campaign is about better support for unwed mothers, preventing violence against women and the rise of matricide.'

They thought of the newspaper report of the poor wretch recently dragged from the Yarra River.

Her father wiped his forehead and left a red and green smear. His sister continued, 'The women of Great Britain are ignored – they've presented over two thousand petitions with over a million signatures to Parliament and all the politicians do is send thousands of brutish police to arrest them. It is just not supportable.'

August raised his arms in surrender.

Aunt April pulled on her gloves. 'We must pursue our possibilities, and though we will be defeated, importantly, we will at least live truthfully.'

'Very good,' said August. 'I'll take my ceramics to the kiln and fetch you later.'

They were surprised to find Gladys waiting at her gate. Mrs Sidebottom shouted at them from the veranda, 'If Gladys ends up in jail, she can stay there. You attack women's freedom in the home!' She pointed to her newest poster:

TEMPERANCE. Children, Kitchen and Church!

'I'm coming today because of men's violence against women,' said Gladys, with greater conviction than they'd ever heard from her. Then, holding on to the gate, she said to Mrs Sidebottom, 'Though some women are cruel to their husbands too.'

Off they went, marching proudly past the humble Curtain Square houses: Aunt April's rucksack a giant wart on her back, their flags flapping overhead, their hems kicking and their banner poles forcing women with perambulators off the footpath.

'Today, I've worn a skirt I can run in.'

'It's lovely to see you again, Glad.'

And then Gladys started to cry, so Molly put her arm around her. Her new gramophone friends had been unkind to her, obviously. Molly tried not to feel pleased.

Miss April Dunnage was familiar to those who worked at the renowned Book Lovers' Library bookshop: she regularly collected *Woman Voter* and Women's Political Association pamphlets to distribute on behalf of their heroine, Vida Goldstein. The library's staff saw the familiar supporter paused at the gutter across the street, an older squat woman, a human sandwich board of badges and sashes. When Miss Dunnage turned to check for traffic, her rucksack nudged the person next to her. Elsie Champion went to her counter, picked up a slab of *Woman Voter* and some pamphlets, and met her loyal volunteer at the front door.

'I'm here to collect the chair,' said Aunt April cheerfully, and removed her rucksack. Elsie headed off to find the chair. April noted that the others in the shop had their backs to her, arranging books on the hefty, tall shelves or standing, reading. She turned to the Philosophy section and picked up *Humankind: A Hopeful Future*.

'Coming,' called Mr Pomfrey, heading towards her with a collapsible picnic chair. He had a big smile. His gums were long and his small teeth chipped. 'How about a cup of tea? Maeve has just brewed a pot.'

'Thank you, Mr Pomfrey, you are very kind, but the city does not facilitate women's bladders.' There was a gasp from someone at the rear of the shop.

Mr Pomfrey carried April's rucksack out on to Collins Street, lifted it so that she could ease her arms through the shoulder straps and stood chatting about the weather while she strapped herself and adjusted her person.

'Once more unto the breach!'

When he stepped back inside, Mr Pomfrey found the entire shop standing at the front window to watch Miss April Dunnage waddle back across the street to Gladys and Molly.

From a distance they saw the crowd assembled again – hundreds of people, mostly women, a colony of penguins in white blouses, dark skirts and sunhats. Molly's spirits lifted, all those women voicing their opinion entirely blocking Flinders Street, the trams, cabs and automobiles at a standstill, and passenger buggies and sulkies trapped along the kerb. There seemed to be a melee around the base of Flinders Street Station again. Opposite, the windows above the veranda roofs spilled workers, and many had climbed out and were sitting along the awnings to see the women milling below. Occasionally a horse whinnied, or a horn tooted, long and loud. The frontrunners, six women in all, held before them a long banner:

WOMEN GIVE BIRTH TO MEN'S BABIES;
EQUAL ACCESS TO CHILDREN.

Behind them, hundreds of women displayed many arguments:

WOMEN SHOULD NOT DIE BECAUSE OF MEN'S ACTIONS.

IT'S NOT THE VICTIM'S FAULT.

LESS THAN 50% OF MEN PROSECUTED FOR RAPE
OR VIOLENCE ARE CONVICTED. IF IT WERE THE
OTHER WAY AROUND IT WOULD BE 100%.

As they pushed through the sightseers, Gladys threw a handful of pamphlets into the air. 'I hope every man in Melbourne reads them.'

Molly looked at her intently. Something had happened, she had been hurt by a man. The person she chatted to last week who made her late for her tram, or someone in the music group. The secretary? Had Mrs Blinkhorn been causing mischief? Whatever it was, Gladys deserved better, women deserved better. 'Gladys, you can tell me anything and I will help you.'

She didn't meet Molly's gaze, just said, 'I know, Molly, thank you,' and unfolded the picnic chair and placed it in the gutter for her. Molly sat while Gladys erected the *Equal Pay & Financial Independence for Women* banner behind her.

'Thank you, Gladdy.' One day, when she was ready, Gladys would tell her what had happened. Molly placed pencils next to her petition and rang her small bell. Two women, a mother and daughter out shopping for the day, turned to see where the tinkling came from.

'We're after *more* than thirty thousand signatures,' cried Molly, referring to the monster petition of 1891, which had asked that women of Victoria be allowed to vote.

'The last one didn't do any good.'

'It showed strength and commitment,' said Molly, pointing to the banners all around. 'We stand for you and for social reform that benefit you and all our sisters. This government won't do it for you, and they're about to fall over anyway, so we support Vida Goldstein's bid for the seat of Kooyong to advocate for equal property rights for . . .' But the women had moved on.

'You can be like that,' she called, 'but we'll fight for you nonetheless!'

The river of women set off, heading up Swanston Street, and Aunt April saluted Molly and prepared to move off with the throng. It was a great glut of women – more had turned up than ever before, all tailored jackets with pretty brooches and white lacy collars tied with satin bows, their skirts falling and their dissent placards like sails above the hundreds of ornate hats.

Spectators heckled, but the women knew the rule – no violence.

Sitting at the edge of the waiting procession, Molly continued to ring her little bell, holding her petition high. In front of her, Gladys, more animated than usual, thrust pamphlets at pedestrians, reciting, 'Appropriate punishment for predatory men . . .'

Molly had just gained another signature from a weary waitress when a policeman came at her and made a grab for her petition, telling her she was obstructing progress.

'No, she's not,' said Gladys. 'That rule only applies to the footpath; she's in the gutter.'

'Where she belongs.'

'As usual, disappointing,' said Molly. 'Not smart enough to think of something *clever* to say.'

Two women peeled away from the crowd to support Molly and Gladys, squaring up to the policeman. He told them to 'Piss orf.'

'You are an ugly brute,' Gladys called.

He shoved her. 'Move, or I'll arrest you.'

Then Gladys did something truly spectacular. 'Bully,' she screamed, clenched her fist and hit the policeman in the chest, then danced around him, her fists raised. The policeman simply picked Gladys up and threw her violently to the road. He snatched her purse full of pamphlets but could not move because Gladys clung to his legs, screaming, 'I hate you, I hate all of you!'

'No violence,' a woman called but Gladys held on. The policeman tore her hat from her head and grabbed a handful of her hair.

Molly begged, 'Please, Gladys, let go, it does no good!'

Another policeman came and grabbed Molly, wrenching her arms around behind her, and she was frogmarched towards the police truck waiting at the kerb.

Gladys, weak and weeping, was helped by the women, who started to usher her into the safety of the crowd.

Aunt April came through the rally, elbows working to shift people. 'Dear, my dear girl, Gladys. Come, this is not like you.'

'No, I usually just do what's expected, don't I?' Gladys stumbled away through the throng. Aunt April looked around for the policeman who had assaulted her, but perhaps something more had upset Gladys, most likely Mrs Sidebottom.

All the way to the truck, Molly resisted, planting her heels and squirming. As they approached, the constable unlocked the door and then turned to admit one more. It was Constable Horatio Farrat, paler than usual but with two rouge-like circles on his cheeks. He looked afraid and far too young to be wearing a police uniform, though it fitted him beautifully.

'Miss Molly Dunnage! How wonderful to see you, truly lovely!' He put his hands to his cheeks, the door swung open and prisoners tumbled out like damp laundry. The policeman holding Molly screamed, 'Farrat, they're escaping!'

The escapees crippled him with a few boots to his shins and bled into the passing crowd while Constable Farrat grabbed Molly by the arm and ran, pushing against the flow towards Elizabeth Street. Behind them, the policeman recovered enough to set off in pursuit of the escapees, but was intercepted by half-a-dozen furious suffragettes waving British flags and yelling, 'Free Emmeline!'

Molly and Constable Farrat ran for a block, then stopped to catch their breath in a doorway with a partially clad nature lover holding a banner: *Stop Automobiles, Stop Roads, Save the Trees.* They smiled and nodded, too breathless to speak.

Behind the glass door, a Chinese man observed the fleeing crowd. The roar grew a little louder. A policeman arrived and the shirtless tree lover fled in his underbriefs and coat tails, the policeman in pursuit. The proprietor opened his door and Constable Farrat and Molly slipped into the shop.

They thanked him, saying how grateful they were. He seemed amused, as if evading authority was something he was accustomed to. They were in a haberdashery shop amid columns of manchester, shelves of crockery and boxes of cutlery, metal kitchen implements and cooking utensils, the walls were bluffs of imported fabrics and brilliant Chinese silks.

'It's like Aladdin's cave,' said Constable Farrat, just as they both reached for a bolt of red silk brocade. They each held it, a standoff.

'What are you going to make?'

'Curtains.'

'Silk for curtains?'

'Why not?'

'It would be more appropriate to make a halter-neck, bias-cut, mid-calf-length dress with a trim around the hip line, three-quarter-cuffed sleeves and a matching hat and a scarf three yards long that can transform into a cowl-backed cloak.' It was a picture she'd seen in a European magazine on her last visit to the library.

'We are behind the times here – you'll have to wait until at least 1920 before anyone will be game enough to wear something like that.'

'I can be ahead of Melbourne's time.'

'I know an excellent market stall where you can get the trim for the hips. What about something in chain links?'

'Chain? How very constabulary.'

The proprietor appeared around the end of the fabrics.

'We like your shop,' Molly said.

He introduced himself as Mr Lau. They stood at the counter with him, and his wife and daughter, watching the crowd dribble away and the noise subside. They talked of fabric, the high cost of import taxes, the wretched state of the Australian goldfields and the fear the family held of being interned if war broke out in Europe. Molly and Constable Farrat offered that there'd be no war, that after the Boer War no one could ever be so reckless.

'And it would be too sad for us as we've only just found your lovely shop,' Molly assured him.

Constable Farrat explained that his mother lived in East Melbourne and was a milliner. 'So I have a natural interest and knowledge of fabric, accessories and garment trims. I will send my mother here.'

On a shelf towards the back of the shop, Molly found a bolt of raw rubber elastic and some elastic cleverly stitched to unwashed cotton, and so awarded the red fabric to Constable Farrat. She also bought herself an offcut of blue silk for a scarf. When they left, both vowed they would return to the shop.

Her father was heading off to the watchhouse to find Molly when she showed up smiling, perfectly intact, and carrying a bundle of shopping. Her aunt was at the stove, her feet in a bucket of water, and while they drank tea they commiserated over the loss of the petition. Then Molly went over to see Gladys. Mrs Sidebottom answered the door and held Molly at bay with a broom. 'Stay back! You have ruined Gladys with your fast ways, I know about the things you draw at so-called drawing lessons. You are *lewd*.'

Molly rested one hand on the end of Mrs Sidebottom's broom and leaned to peer behind her but could not see Gladys. At the gate she paused, 'You have imagined all of that, Mrs Sidebottom, from your own lewd mind.'

Horatio stood before the chief inspector, while all around him various sergeants helped themselves to tea and biscuits, then settled to watch. Between bites of a biscuit, the sergeant who'd been in charge that day explained how Constable Horatio Farrat had left the truck door open then fled with a young female campaigner. 'Aiding and abetting a prisoner to escape.'

Constable Farrat pulled himself up to his full height. 'I gave chase, sir.'

'You let a truckload of the screeching sisterhood go free,' said the chief inspector.

'They crashed through me as I was trying to add another one.'

The chief inspector was curt. 'You proved incompetent at a crime scene, again.'

The accusing sergeant added that the first time, Constable Farrat had cut his finger while inspecting a broken window at a jewellery shop robbery, '. . . then fainted and disrupted the crime scene.'

The chief inspector handed his empty teacup to the senior sergeant at his side.

Constable Farrat defended himself again. 'I recovered when my finger was bandaged and became very useful again, sir.'

The chief inspector ran his hands down the front of his immaculate jacket. 'When used properly the uniform you are wearing conveys authority.'

Constable Farrat smiled. 'On that subject, sir, I am redesigning the uniform so that it is more impressive –'

'We have a factory full of uniform experts who do that. Now buck up or you'll be transferred from Lost Property to cleaning cells. You've been warned. Again.'

Everyone turned back to the refreshment table, and Constable Farrat approached the senior sergeant to remind him that the jewellery thief had been arrested, eventually.

'Noted, Farrat.' It happened that the senior sergeant was a member of the City Aesthetic Society and was greatly enthused by quality of any kind. He turned to Farrat. 'But now see here, your idea on uniforms . . . Make an appointment, we'll discuss.'

'I could bring drawings?'

'Very good.' He'd seen Farrat's small department and was impressed. The umbrellas were colour coded, the gloves and hats arranged according to gender and style, and the safe where the watches and jewellery were stored was hidden behind a painting of a rural scene.

Back in his Lost, Found and Stolen Property, Horatio felt once again secure. And thrilled by the senior sergeant's interest.

Chapter 9

AUNT APRIL'S TOOTH problem did not abate. She returned to the dentist and spoke of the hole where her tooth had been and he said, 'It will heal, or I can stitch it for you. The anaesthetic will cost five shillings.'

'Five?'

'Or I can stitch it without for two shillings.'

Aunt April took her flask from her pocket and drained it, sat in the chair and opened her mouth.

Over in South Yarra, the box waited on the antique Japanese tansu. The package had been there all day. Alathea knew her wedding trousseau would be both pretty and comfortable, but she wasn't excited by marriage. She removed her hat, threw it aside and dug her fingers into her New Woman curls, rubbing luxuriously. Then she removed her collar and undid the top buttons of her blouse, unlaced her boots and kicked them under the bed and finally said to her friend Marguerite Baca, who had also removed her coat, hat and boots, 'Let's open this.'

Being Spanish in faraway Melbourne, Marguerite's and Alathea's mothers had known each other well and their daughters had become childhood friends. Having lost a parent each, the girls saw that marriage wasn't essential in order to live well. They each had access to some money, not a huge amount, but enough. Marriage wasn't a commitment to rush.

Marguerite took the box and drew out a big, soft package, turning it over in her hands. 'Will I like it?'

'I think you will.'

They settled on the bed with the package just as Therese arrived with tea and some sliced pear. She placed it on the tansu and picked up a pamphlet that had fluttered from the parcel to the floor:

Victorian Suffrage Society
   The enemy of Suffrage is the system of patriarchy and if women can support the system of patriarchy why can't men support the cause for equality?

She handed it to Alathea and then started brushing the day's grime from Alathea's hat.

'You can hang Marguerite's jacket too.'

Therese was a reluctant personal maid to Alathea and had been for twenty years. She just looked at her now, her mouth slightly open, as it always was, and her lank, coiled bun puddling on her collar.

'*Please*, my precious companion and wise helper.' Therese sniffed and hung the jacket clumsily.

Alathea said, 'Thank you, dear. You can go now.'

Therese slunk out, taking her time to close the door, her eyes on the package in Alathea's hand.

As she held up the new corselet, another pamphlet fluttered to the floor. While Alathea studied the particularly lovely garment, Marguerite read, '*No votes will be cast by women in favour of a bad man.*'

'True.' Alathea passed the corselet to Marguerite, who said it was *encantadora*.

'Margie, dear, pass me my writing folder, please? I'll send a note to Old Snakelegs and order some for you.'

*

Once she had dispatched Therese to the postbox, Alathea spent the rest of the day in her room with Marguerite and a stack of magazines and newspapers from Europe. By the end of the day, the friends had selected an entire wardrobe for honeymoon travel: four travelling dresses, three evening gowns – a fourth would be her wedding gown with the lace yoke and train removed – three afternoon dresses, three street or shopping dresses, two tailored suits, three light afternoon dresses, matching shoes, a skirt and four blouses, a coat, cape and several shawls. Eight hats, sixteen pairs of gloves and an umbrella. Then they made a list of night attire and all the underwear that would be required to underpin these new garments – drawers, chemises, corset covers and under-vests, stockings, a flannel petticoat or two, handkerchiefs and silk petticoats and her Japanese robe.

'I'll give this list to Molly when I see her.' She placed it in an envelope and put it on her bedside table.

Marguerite settled beside Alathea on the bed. 'I will miss you while you are away.'

'I know. I will miss you, but it's only for a few months and I'll do my best to get pregnant and then it will be over and done with and we can do as we please.'

'What is your husband going to do?'

'We will both do as we please.' They had agreed to be discreet and loyal to each other and to behave like a happily married couple in public; she would support him financially, he would support her entirely. She took Marguerite's hand in hers. Therese knocked and came in, and the resting women smiled at her. 'We are exhausted from making choices.'

'Cook wants to know if you're in for dinner.'

It was her father's habit to spend time in his office when he returned of an evening. Emrys Pocknall would pour himself a nightcap and go through any messages left on his desk. Alathea knew her father enjoyed theatre, opera, polo and trout fishing; he was a man who stayed up late and slept late. Though she was always grateful to enjoy his exclusive company reading in the library – a room that he excluded everyone else from – or over breakfast and on the days she accompanied him to the factory, she had no idea what he did with his evenings and was not interested in that side of men's lives. Tonight, though, she would stay at home and join him in his office to discuss her trousseau – specifically, the size of the cheque. He was a genial man, an adoring father and especially generous with a nightcap in hand.

'We are,' she said to Therese. 'We'll eat in my drawing room.'

Therese shut the door a little too forcefully and Alathea called, 'THANK YOU THERESE, DEAR.'

The sun took a little longer to rise, and the mornings and afternoons turned chilly, so August took to napping. Mid-afternoon, he was woken by shouting – Mrs Sidebottom abusing Freddy for drunkenness, he assumed. But when he moved to the window he found the abuse was directed at his sister, flat on her back on the footpath, her face swollen and her chin lined with dried blood. Mrs Sidebottom cried, 'You people are heathens and drunkards. You ought to be ashamed.'

'Ought we?' said August, opening the front gate. 'I hadn't realised.'

'Would you mind, Augie,' April said, reaching up. He got her to her feet.

Mrs Sidebottom screamed, 'Gladys is ruined and it's because you are a corrupting, germ-spreading suffragette. You will never see her again.'

'Wise, Mrs Bigbottom, keep her for yourself,' said Aunt April. 'Can't let her enjoy life or find a nice boy to marry.'

'I strive to "protect the purity of home life" but I risk my life every time I show up for eggs. And now I find that, like you, Gladys is a drunk and a loose woman!'

Molly appeared. 'Gladys is neither loose nor a drunk and we too risk our lives every day. Each time we draw breath we fill our lungs with the smoke from your copper.'

'How else can I earn a living?'

August offered a solution. 'I hear they're asking for a dishwasher over at the Kent. It would suit everyone in the neighbourhood if you worked there twenty-four hours a day.'

Molly rang the cow bell. Mrs Sidebottom opened her mouth to abuse her, saliva stretching between her top and bottom eye teeth. 'How dare –'

'I'm here to collect Gladys for drawing class.'

'I told you, you won't see Gladys ever again.' She seemed triumphant. 'You are a bad influence on her.'

'As are you.'

But Gladys didn't come out. And Molly was left to face the walk to their class alone, hurting for her friend, who she knew was suffering. Gladys would not come to the side fence when she banged and didn't answer the note she'd thrown over the fence.

'I don't know why she's shunned us,' Molly lamented.

Her father was philosophical. 'Everyone else has.'

'You are no help, Dad.'

Molly's position was now steadfastly next to Horatio's easel. She was perfectly content with Horatio but felt Gladys's absence. At the front of the room was a cloth-covered statue.

Mr King, who some thought was far too quietly spoken to be a teacher, cleared his throat and the class fell silent, craning towards him. He put his hand in the pocket of his green jacket and said, 'We have examined the ankle and the knee, so let us continue to move upwards.'

Horatio whispered, 'Where do you think he'll take us?'

'To the thighs,' Molly said, incredulous. 'Where else?'

Horatio shrugged. 'The abdomen?'

'Oh, yes, good.' It would be beneficial to her corsetry to study the muscles of the midriff.

But it wasn't to be. Mr King said, 'Via a painting of *The Victorious Athlete*, we have witnessed the abdomen and thighs. Let us now see in the round' – he whipped the satin away and there stood a replica statue of David – 'the rather beautiful triceps, biceps and pectoral muscles of David.' Mr King then handed a coloured anatomical picture of the skeletal-muscular system to the first row and asked everyone to study it and pass it on.

'Do we have to attribute an emotion to David's torso?' asked Horatio.

'Remember, David is just about to go into battle.' Mr King sounded a little impatient.

'We know how that feels,' said Molly.

'I think he looks terrifying,' said Horatio, but Molly thought David looked only mildly tense, even resigned.

The depictions of David were mixed, as they always were, but this time Mr King chose a sketch by Mr Tumbler, a stonemason, wretchedly dressed and made obvious by his perennial cough. Mr Tumbler was a fine artist, and Mr King noted that he had depicted David as a little pensive, with a glint in his eye to show a winning spirit and a strength in his person as in his physique.

At the end of class, Horatio waited with Molly until her father came. 'Mr Tumbler, who'd have thought?'

'If he'd been born into another class . . .'

'Yes.'

They moved on to fondly recall the contents of Mr and Mrs Lau's shop and Horatio told Molly that her boater, newly redecorated, was 'Very oriental.'

'Thank you. Miss Alathea Pocknall came to the factory not long ago wearing a rather robust hat made by your mother.'

'I think I know it. Does she look like she's walking around with a palm plantation on her head?'

'That's the one.'

'Miss Pocknall likes to go with the trends,' he scoffed. 'Mother and I prefer to explore our own ideas, especially for occasions like the Melbourne Cup or an important funeral. Mother always says, "There is room for disguise and performance but there must be truth."'

'I'm doing a wedding trousseau for Miss Pocknall. I hope to make more for her honeymoon. I keep thinking about sets, you know, bloomers, corset and undershirt.'

'I think I've seen what you mean on a clothesline.'

August arrived, and was pleased to meet Horatio Farrat. They shook hands, and Horatio's gaze lingered on August's face. The man was unwell.

'Dad's a ceramicist,' Molly said. 'He's been painting.'

'And I'm a little breathless. Your aunt and I have been collecting firewood.' August smiled. He'd been painting something blue.

'A trip to Parkville,' Molly said, explaining that they collected a barrow of firewood from the bush around the zoo from time to time. 'But I'll do it next time.'

'I could give you a hand!' Horatio said.

'That's kind of you,' said Molly, and they turned to walk Horatio to the tram stop.

'You must come for tea, Horatio Farrat.'

'I'd love to.' There was a chill in the air, and so Horatio asked them not to wait with him; a tram would come soon, and they should get home. 'I look forward to seeing you next week.'

On the walk home Molly understood why Horatio had sent them home. Her father's pace had slowed and he was also a little more breathless than usual.

'And what does Mr Farrat do for a living?'

'He's a policeman.'

'Oh dear.'

'I'm certain he's not corrupt.'

'Is he the chap who let you escape the police truck last week?'

'That was just ineptness, truth be known.'

'He might be susceptible, though. You could ask him to get

you out of jail next time without the fine.' August studied his daughter. 'No word of Gladys?'

'No.' She careened between hate, hurt and longing. If she could just speak to Gladys!

'Shame about the bougainvillea.'

As children they would scale the side fence to see each other, Molly to help Gladys with the washing. But then Mrs Sidebottom planted a thorny bougainvillea, which denied the girls access and then, as if in sympathy, had grown also to deny her washing the afternoon sun.

Early the next morning, Molly heard the clatter of kindling and the sound of pouring water next door. She rushed to the fence and balanced on the chicken coop, knowing Gladys was readying the copper before going to the mattress factory. Mrs Sidebottom would light it so the water was boiling and ready for a load when Glady came home.

'Meet me at the cemetery after work, Glad?'

Gladys nodded, then glanced back at the house. She waved and went inside.

It was a clear day, but autumn had arrived, the trees losing their leaves and the sky darkening earlier. Molly was relieved her day at the factory was over. She stopped at her mother's grave, said a quick hello and hurried to their spot, the grave of Cornelius O'Mahony. She waited, and waited, wrapping a blade of grass around and around her finger.

Molly had brought Gladys through the cemetery the first day she met her, on their way home from school.

'This isn't the way Mrs Sidebottom showed me,' she'd said, eyeing the low wrought-iron fences and headstones.

Molly explained it was a short cut, and that their tormentors would be too scared to follow them into the cemetery. 'I told them I open my mother's grave.'

'Do you?'

'I just talk to her.'

Gladys looked at her new best friend. 'I'd talk to mine but I don't know where she is.'

'You can still talk to her.'

Her new friend was wise.

When they arrived at the Dunnages' the girls were speechless with happiness to find they lived next door to each other. It was the first time either of them had known a friend. The Sidebottoms' front yard featured a square of neglected lawn and some sad geraniums; the Dunnage yard was home to banksias bursting from wallaby and spear grass and an army of bellybutton plants, arum lilies and kidney plants pressing over the low front fence. A huge flowering gum dropped its seeds onto the roof, exploding like crackers, which made the huntsmen in their crevices arc up and the chooks squawk and flap back to their coop. Since Aunt April had slipped and bruised her bottom, leaving it like two eggplants, it was Molly's job to sweep the path of slimy leaves each morning. Grass sprouted from the guttering and the whole house needed a coat of paint, but Gladys liked it. The little house was honest and friendly.

'Do you want to play?' Molly asked.

'Yes,' said Gladys, but Mrs Sidebottom rushed from her house, one small boy at her skirts and a baby on her hip and two older boys behind her.

'No!' She bared her teeth, which dipped like a swing bridge between her prominent incisors and reached to the back of her mouth. 'She's a Dunnage, you're not allowed to play with her.'

'Well, I'll see you at school tomorrow,' Molly said pointedly, and waved farewell.

Aunt April informed Molly that there was nothing wrong with being an orphan. 'You must be kind to Gladys because she has no family of her own and there is nothing sadder. And she'll have to work hard for Mrs Sidebottom, who is disappointed.'

'What's she disappointed about?'

'Everything, poor wretch.' For the life of her, April Dunnage could see nothing in Mrs Sidebottom that warranted her superior inclinations.

The cemetery, with its mausoleums and monuments of the wealthy, proved a perfect place for many things, like wagging sport on Friday afternoon or religious instruction on Monday morning. Soon Molly and Gladys were inseparable.

Molly's father and Aunt April encouraged her to 'make more friends', but Molly insisted Gladys was all she needed. 'Managing one friendship is sufficient for us.'

Over time, Gladys grew to be a plain girl with languid eyes and a vague expression. She had always envied Molly for being downright attractive, but she believed, and declared many times, that a rich man would fall in love with her and propose and she would bear him many bonny children. 'My life will be long and happy and I will do as I please in my elegant home.'

'Until you die in childbirth,' Molly always replied. To her, marriage seemed to be about assuming a role of some sort: vanquishing most things about yourself to fit someone else. There were *expectations*.

'Medicine is modern these days, and I'll have many servants who I'll treat very well. But if none of that happens, I'll come to Paris with you.'

The sun had set behind the rooftops when, finally, Gladys approached slowly, a weary and weighted girl now, her wide straw hat slightly askew. Molly waved, cheerfully, thinking that she had spoken of that childhood dream the very first time they came to the cemetery as five-year-olds. And like Molly's dream, nothing had come of them. Yet.

Gladys sat on the ground, her back against the iron rail fence, facing away from Molly. 'I can't stay very long.'

'You could, you know, she doesn't own you.'

Gladys said nothing.

'You have new friends and I'm an embarrassment to you,' Molly began. 'I'm happy to stay out of your social life but don't desert me entirely.'

'They are not my friends, Molly. You've kept me from despair ever since I came to Mrs Sidebottom.'

'We *are* friends, unconditional friends.'

Gladys seemed about to say something and then stopped. After a moment she looked at Molly. 'I'm not meant to tell you . . . I am leaving Melbourne. Mrs Sidebottom no longer needs me, she's searching for another position for me.'

How could that be? How could one person rule another's life in such a way, how could she throw Gladys out after twenty years? Mrs Sidebottom professed to 'preserve the sanctity of family and home'. Yet she was denying Gladys a home. Denying their friend-ship and what Gladys wanted.

'No!' Molly's heart started to race. She suddenly felt hot.

'It's true.'

'She won't cope without you.' Molly battled not to cry. 'Where will you go? I'll come and see you.'

'I don't know where they'll send me but it could be better, Molly. I might be happier.'

'What about us?'

'We'll write. Just don't come near Mrs Sidebottom until I'm gone – don't antagonise her. I want to get sent somewhere good, I need her to say good things about me.'

Gladys's sleepy eyes brimmed with tears. Molly reached for her, but she leaned away. 'I am happy that you are making under-wear for a rich lady, Molly – it's wonderful and I've always felt you'll succeed – but I've grown tired of volunteering at choir and drawing. It has all come to nothing and all I can see ahead is more nothing, just more work.' Wearily, she stood and brushed the grass from her skirt. 'So I'd better go, I don't want to be late.' She gave a limp wave and walked away, swinging her parasol at grass tufts.

It took some time for Molly to find her voice. 'When will you go? Will I see you again? Can I write? Leave the address for me,' she cried. 'You can't just leave . . . what will I do?'

Gladys kept walking, Molly ran after her, grabbed her, held her friend like she'd never held anything before. 'Gladys, remember when we were young and timid? We fought the world together and found a spot. Please, Gladys, write to me. I will keep fighting for us.'

'I'll write when I'm happy.' Gladys disentangled herself and wiped the tears from Molly's cheeks with her hand, dried them on her skirt and looked her in the eye. 'I will write when I am happy. Right?'

'Right.'

She walked away, lifting her parasol aloft, the gesture saying goodbye. Molly felt as if she'd been punched. It couldn't end like this.

She called, 'You will always be necessary to me, Gladdy. I will be happy if I know that you are, wherever you are. Stay my friend, please, I will come and see you.'

When she returned to Curtain Square, the sign in Mrs Sidebottom's front yard read:

ALCOHOL LEADS TO VIOLENCE AND
HARM TO HOME AND FAMILY.

Molly crossed it out and wrote, '*Some people don't need alcohol to be harmful.*'

Then she jammed Mrs Sidebottom's letterbox with pamphlets – '*Equal Pay And Freedom And Financial Autonomy for Women*' – and went home.

She stepped inside the door, caught a whiff of her aunt's room, shut the door, stomped through the house to her cubby, pulled the curtain and lay on her bed.

How on earth would she live without her only friend?

Then she remembered Gladys's plea – *don't antagonise her, I want to get sent somewhere good* – and ran back to retrieve the pamphlets.

She spent the afternoon with her face pushed into her pillow, crying for Gladys, for all her woes, and was joined by August's favourite hen, which flapped up onto her bed beside her.

The smell drew her to the kitchen.

'What on earth are you cooking, Dad?'

August pounded garlic and cloves in a mortar and pestle. 'It's for your aunt's gums, for the antimicrobial properties. You couldn't shout us a bottle of beer, could you?'

'And whisky, dear girl?'

'Aunt, you are drinking a bottle of whisky a week!'

'Your father's helping me.'

Her aunt set off for the Kent, some of Molly's savings in her hand and happy knowing the neighbours were watching and that soon everyone on Rathdowne Street would know that Mrs Sidebottom was right – the Dunnages had turned to drink.

When she returned, they settled for dinner and Molly told them they were to lose Gladys. 'Mrs *FAT*bottom is sending her away to another position.'

'I have a feeling Gladys will be alright.'

'You and your feelings, Aunt.'

Aunt April imagined she could 'feel the future'. Many of her feelings had come true. 'One day people will talk to each other from either side of a continent,' she'd said, and then the telephone was invented. Though then Aunt April predicted that it would kill people: 'It's toxic, made from unnatural materials we know nothing about, and it will transmit germs as well as voices.' She also had a feeling that 'One day they will predict the weather a week away', and then the Bureau of Meteorology was established. Her most famous feeling was about a ship. One morning she said from behind the newspaper, 'In Ireland they're taking three years to build a ship that is unsinkable. It's called the *Titanic*, but the sea is mightier than any vessel.' Hopefully her feeling about Gladys was true, that she would be not only alright, but happy with a friendly, considerate family in a lovely house nearby.

Her father reminded Molly that they could write and travel to see each other – there were trains everywhere these days. 'And you're not alone. You have us!' he said.

'And, of course,' said Aunt April, 'there is always our family friend, Mr Luby.'

'How amusing you are, Aunt.'

Chapter 10

MOLLY ARRIVED AT work and waited behind the crowd of girls at the door. No one said good morning to her. The door opened and she waited until everyone had filed through, coming in last, as was her habit. Mr Addlar often intercepted her and she'd grown weary of being hauled over the coals in front of the entire staff, their entertainment for the day. This time, he threw a small envelope at her. It bounced off her chest and dropped at her feet. 'You will make up for the time you lose, you will finish your quota of corsets even if you have to come back at midnight.' His eyes were cloudy with rage and loathing.

'Midnight? You would have to leave the lights on for me.'

'It is only a matter of time before I drag you out of here by the hair.'

She would have dared him to do it there and then, but for Alathea Pocknall. Like a spider into a web, Mr Addlar moved away between the rows of machines, the threads crisscrossing from the rows of cotton spools tall on thin arms.

The envelope had been opened. Alathea wrote that the enclosed money – which Mr Addlar had obviously pocketed – was fare for Molly to travel to the Pocknalls' home. She had another a project for her.

All day, Molly kept her head down and worked. She ignored an urge to speak up for Sara, who left her machine to use the toilet without permission, and she didn't complain when Mr Addlar left the doors open all day, the chilly wind lifting the fabric and giving flight to dust, flock and thread, rolling the pins on the tables onto the floor. To the thrum of sewing machines and the small sounds of cutting and stitching, she dreamed.

The train moved past suburban backyards, outhouses in the corner and clotheslines hung with bloomers and lifeless shirts. In the streets, boys in shorts and sailor caps and girls with unravelling plaits and trailing ribbons ran and played. As she travelled south, the houses became grand, neater, and the children moved from the streets to play in bigger backyards under fruit trees. It was not a long walk from the railway station to the Pocknalls' home, but Molly saw couture frocks, hats and gloves in shop windows, and sumptuous soft furnishings, exotic grocery shops and sophisticated cafes. Fine carriages were parked along bluestone gutters edging smooth gravel roads. The sunlight finally arrived to warm the beautiful gardens, and she inhaled their perfume, but decided that the warring towers and unused balconies on the mansions behind ornate fences were a little excessive.

The Pocknalls lived on the southern side of the Yarra River, a block from the water, on a wide street in one of the more elaborate examples of Victorian architecture. The house stood on a lush green rise surrounded by a manicured and opulent English garden. It was a wedding cake of a home, with carved corbels, porch posts, dentils and spandrels. The roof was shingled with a turret whose tall, lethal gables and sharp florid ridges punctured the sky. The windows were large and multi-panelled on all three storeys and the balusters edging the generous verandas elaborately detailed – features designed to suit a bigger mansion.

The front gate, a sturdy carved timber frame big enough for just one pony, resisted when Molly pushed, but finally allowed her into a glorious garden. She took the path that led to the kitchen, past a fussy conservatory, with its lush palms and bright flowers, and an aviary, where a dozen or so curious parrots leaned to watch her pass. 'My father would love you,' she said.

Molly

The maid was friendly. 'Please come in, Miss.'

Molly waited, watching the kitchen boy carry in boxes from a delivery cart – sugar, coffee, tea, vast amounts of beer and wine, Champagne, a new electric toaster and even an electric kettle. A shiny new bicycle leaned against the marble pastry table. Wealth was right there in front of her, so different from Curtain Square.

It was a bit like standing in one of the grand buildings in the city. On rainy days you could stand in the doorways or vestibules of the Supreme Court, Parliament House or the Treasury Building; even department stores like Georges let you in if they felt you weren't there just to use the lavatory. In contrast, though, the Pocknalls' house was cluttered. Its ambiance of trying too hard went hand in hand with a Spanish eye for solid furniture. Even so, Molly would give anything to live in a house that was so clean it shone, stuffed with soft furniture, and had tall windows letting in lots of light.

She trailed the maid through the ample kitchen, along the wide halls, passing bright airy rooms, then up two flights of deep, carpeted stairs, her shoulders getting squarer and her chin rising, responding to the sophisticated surrounds. She longed to study the art covering the walls – pastoral landscapes, seaside scenes and portraits of important people wearing elaborate clothing. A huge portrait of Juanita Pocknall – beautiful, raven haired and compelling – took up an entire wall on the third landing. And she passed a library with bookshelves full almost all the way to the ceiling.

Waiting in her room, Alathea was wearing a satin quilted Japanese robe – Japan being all the rage – like pink kelp draped over her frame. She was standing in the middle of a room of Japanese-styled furniture, lacquered stools and benches with upholstered tops for comfort. The chest of drawers – the drawers deep and fat – was tiered so that each drawer acted as a ladder step as well as a small tabletop. Alathea's dresses hung in a separate room behind her bed, which was large and perfectly square, low to the ground and with no head or end. Alathea opened her silk robe to show Molly's corselet and twirled, then bent down and touched her toes. 'It's perfect, Molly, you are so clever. It will wear nicely under my culottes, and I'll be able to go anywhere on my bicycle.'

'Rule number four of the Rational Dress Society: "Grace and beauty combined with comfort and convenience",' said Molly, tongue-in-cheek.

In the corner, Therese rolled her eyes.

'Therese thinks I look like a man when I wear culottes.'

'It's just the outside appearance,' said Molly. 'We're defined by what's inside, or underneath . . . That's my opinion anyway.'

'You could keep it to yourself,' Therese muttered, affronted that a factory worker could speak so boldly to Miss Alathea Pocknall.

Alathea turned to Therese and said tersely, 'It's a tactic. If we look like we're non-threatening we can infiltrate and make changes without much resistance, of all people you would agree it's an effective way to get what you want, Therese?'

'I don't want to do everything men do.'

'Neither do I,' said Alathea, an edge to her voice. 'But I don't want some man to deny me the choice.'

Therese left, taking Alathea's tea tray with her.

'Now see here, clever Molly Dunnage from Carlton, I want you to make me another corselet to go under my wedding gown.' Alathea smiled. 'This is what I am wearing.'

She handed Molly a copy of *Vogue* opened at a Paris creation. It was stunning and Molly wanted to lift it from the pages, study the needlework, smell and hear the fabric and run her fingers over the seams.

'Look at you, you little designer! You just lit up like a candelabra.'

It was a conventional style, for the most part, except that the sleeves and yoke were made of a single piece of sheer net, Magyar styled, so they did not actually bear the weight of the dress. The neck was loose, lightly cowled and detailed with sparkling beads, as was the trim around the wrist. The bodice looked as if it barely skimmed the top of the areolae, and the waist was high – hips would not support the dress. The overskirt was also net, also trimmed with sparkling beads, and underneath were harem pants. Voluminous, made of silk, the cuffs sparkling anklets.

'So you will make a corset to support the garment,' Alathea said. 'And there's something else. I think the same corset will support this?'

It was an evening dress, in oriental colours and style, and, as Alathea said, it was *incroyablement élégante*. The skirt was olive-green silk, the hem only slightly hobbled, and over it the tunic was yellow lace, its hem asymmetrical and edged with a twelve-inch fringe of green, red and gold beads. A gathered overskirt, also with an asymmetrical hem, covered the hips and was anchored by a tassel that dipped to join the lowest triangular point of the hems. It too was high waisted, the bodice basically a thick band of bottle green velvet lined with red, gold and green beads.

She would get to see these dresses, surely she'd be able to fit them to her corset?

'I thought you'd like it,' Alathea said. 'What do you think, blue or crimson?'

'Well, crimson, but your eyes –'

'Blue, I know, which is why everyone gives me sapphires.' She sighed, put her hands back on her hips. 'I'll have crimson, but it will be a combination of reds and crimsons, and I want black beads as the fringe but I want the panel at the front between the breasts to dip, *plunge*, and I want flimsy skin-coloured tulle, or muslin, so the neckline is almost invisible, with the tiniest collar anyone has ever seen. And a corset to hold it all up, so that they think at first that nothing is holding it in place. What do you think?'

'European.'

'Yes, bold. I can't upset anyone so to be married I'll wear cream, a high-necked long-sleeved wedding *gown*.' She winked. 'I'll save the crimson one for the boat and I might even wear it when I disembark in Europe. There are often photographers.' Alathea Pocknall was setting precedents early on in her marriage, but also not destabilising her chance at the future she would inherit, and Molly adored her.

'What do you think?'

Molly studied the *Vogue* images again. A mid-bust corset, she thought, because under-bust corsets accommodate freedom but not exertion. As Aunt April would say, the breasts were easily *motivated*. 'Whichever style we decide, your waist can be where your waist is, but the corset will fit well, smooth on the flesh.'

'You're hired,' said Alathea, laughing. Then, 'Oh! Mr Addlar has told my father that he's not happy.'

'I doubt he's ever been happy. I could work on a Sunday?'

'Your day off. Then you will come here, I'll set up a room for you with a machine. Therese will help you. Be inventive. I'm interested in anything *advanced*, new or groundbreaking. Tell me what you need, and in the meantime I'll buy the fabric. And when that is done, you can make my travelling trousseau. We're honeymooning in America, stopping briefly in Hawaii on the way.'

Molly wanted to leap in the air but, instead, harnessed some courage. It was her right to ask even if Alathea's answer didn't match her promises, so she dived in. 'Miss Pocknall, I will need to . . .'

'What? Measure me? I doubt my measurements have changed.'

'I'll need to be paid.'

'Paid?' It was a word Alathea Pocknall didn't hear much.

Molly kept her expression frank and her gaze steady. 'Perhaps an advance, and the balance when we're finished?'

Alathea shrugged. 'Whatever is acceptable.'

To say that Molly Dunnage was pleased would be to say that the moon was far away.

Therese arrived, breathless, and informed Alathea that Dame Lily Pert was waiting.

'Oh dear,' sighed Alathea. 'Thank you, Therese. Molly, wait a little, I'll see you out. Therese, be a dear and get my dress.'

Therese did not move.

'I said please.'

'No, you didn't.'

'I did, didn't I, Molly?'

'I've forgotten.'

'*Please*, Therese dear . . .'

Molly followed Alathea's mauve afternoon dress all the way back down the stairs, not believing Dame Lily Pert was waiting somewhere. She assumed Dame Lily Pert was waiting at her own home for Alathea to visit. At the bottom of the stairs Alathea's cousin, Norbert Poke, and her fiancé, Clive Woodgrip, loitered. The men didn't even glance at Molly. Clive, his soft fingers around the newel post, informed his betrothed that he and Cousin Norbert were off to the Car Owners Garage to investigate engines, petrol and tyres for the new range of motor vehicles. They would collect her for the dinner dance but would be late.

Alathea shrugged. 'I'll meet you there.'

Norbert and Clive shared a look. Cousin Norbert drawled, 'You're engaged now. We'll collect you. Call it a view of the future.'

Cousin Norbert had been raised and educated in America, then, for reasons unmentioned, packed off to Australia to his maternal aunt Juanita, the late Mrs Emrys Pocknall. Norbert and his flamboyant attire occupied a room on the first floor of the house. Molly thought his cravat too flowery, his collar too tall, his maroon satin jacket too bold and matching trousers too tight. To someone who hated facial hair, with all its wax and dust, food and pipe smoke, his moustache looked like a mistake: it joined his sideburns leaving the lower half of his face bald. All that moved was his lower lip and chin; the rest was a mystery.

'I'll see you at the dinner dance,' Alathea said lightly, touching her fiancé's arm and turning to Norbert. 'Call it a view to the very near future, where women are regarded as people, not pets.'

Norbert remained mute, but Clive smiled. Molly thought she saw a sinister edge to it, but at least he was more reasonably dressed in an unusual dinner suit: the lapels of his tailcoat were velvet and his white bow tie just that, a thick silk ribbon tied in a bow. Like Norbert, he had an air of confidence, and that was fortunate because his shoes were just plain silly – red leather step-in slippers, for dancing.

What Molly did approve of about both men was that they were clean – practically shining.

Alathea led the way out through the front door onto the wide veranda, which was thick with flowery potted plants. There, sitting in an automobile – its roof down to take advantage of the lovely sunshine – was Australia's 'much loved' soprano Dame Lily Pert, in the flesh, and looking very much like a diva. Beside her, an attractive dark-haired woman in a plain black dress held a parasol, its blue colour staining Dame Lily Pert a melancholy hue.

Dame Lily was weeping.

Alathea stood by the automobile. 'What has happened? What is the matter?'

'Luisa Tetrazzini is writing a book,' Dame Lily sobbed. Luisa Tetrazzini was an international superstar. Australia's pride and joy, Our Dame, had failed to woo Europe or America, as both countries had an oversupply of notable opera singers. She was only somewhat famous in Britain – a cruel rumour had it that most people learned to recognise her to avoid her. And her first (and only) review in the *New York Times* accused her of yodelling.

'A book?'

'It's titled *How to Sing Opera*,' said the woman holding the parasol.

Dame Lily wailed.

Alathea patted Dame Lily's arm. 'Well, you can write one too.'

She stopped wailing. 'I am not a *teacher!*'

'Well, then write what it's like to be a famous talented soprano.'

'A memoir,' said Molly. They ignored her.

Dame Lily wiped her tears with her gloves. 'You mean a memoir?'

'What a good idea, a memoir!' cried Alathea.

The woman in the black dress said, 'You tell the story, I'll take notes.'

Dame Lily snapped, 'Penina! I am not retired, old or washed up.' She glanced at Molly, suspecting she wasn't as impressed by the presence of a Great Dame as she should be so assumed a more regal pose. 'Why is she standing there?'

'This is Molly, and Molly is a pioneer in the bygone art of sensible, wearable underclothing.'

Dame Lily grew alert. 'Comfortable undergarments?' She loosened her mantle, revealing a lacy bodice covered in pearl ropes strained by jewelled pendants. 'People are always telling me I am hard to fit. But I need to be able to breathe. They are cruel to me. What exactly do you make, girl?'

'I make corsets that allow movement, and I've made a breast truss that allows rib expansion while containing the breasts. My involvement in choir has taught me much about –'

'Not as much as me – I could teach you a lot more – and it is *men* who wear trusses!'

'I apologise.' Molly's mind was churning through solutions for the regal singer, jettisoning each of them as they rose. The proportions of the woman in the carriage accumulated as they descended, her hips ballooning across the seat under dark brocade and her cloaked shoulders tapering up to her neck and – finally – a tiny imitation crown on her small head. As for most older women, Dame Lily's sense of fashion mimicked Queen Victoria – before her years of mourning.

Dame Lily Pert studied the slim girl in the beautifully cut dress, though the fabric was cheap. 'What would you do for me?'

Molly would first put her on a diet, then remove her in-effective S-bend corset and establish her exact proportions. She would need to start from scratch to build a stay specifically to support Dame Lily's bosom, which seemed, at that moment, to be sitting on the fleshy pier of her abdomen. But when she stood, her bust would certainly shape her posture, and there-fore her breathing. The effort for her to stand effectively on a stage would influence her singing. Molly could help. 'I would make you undergarments that are practical, pretty and comfort-able,' she said sweetly. 'Underclothing with good ventilation and movement, but underwear that also refines and streamlines the silhouette, particularly the upper body . . . but it must be designed to support the exertions that go with singing.'

Dame Lily sniffed.

'You'll come in for a drink, then, Dame Lily?'

'I suppose I could.' She glared down at Molly, so Alathea turned to her. 'Thank you, Molly. I will see you Sunday,' and Molly took the cue to leave.

At the aviary she stopped and looked back. Dame Lily raised her arms, Alathea opened the carriage door and climbed in to help Penina get Dame Lily to her feet. Molly felt a pang of sympathy for her. It was cruel that she was fading without appropriate fanfare – Dame Lily had achieved great recognition for Australia and its singers in the world, but everyone's position is usurped at some point. Still, men didn't seem to fade, only grow in fame. Given the right underwear, and a chance, Dame Lily Pert could soar again.

Aunt April was out shovelling horse manure from the street into a wheelbarrow, her grubby lab coat over her day dress. She looked up to see her niece rushing towards her, all energy and smiling from ear to ear. 'Can I do that for you, Aunt?'

'Thank you, I'm quite capable.' And to prove it she thrust the shovel under the soft khaki balls of digested fibre and chucked them into the barrow. 'Well, tell me, you can't be so happy just because it's a lovely day.'

Molly explained that she had seen her corselet in action and that Alathea would pay her for a trousseau and more corselets.

April paused, placed her forearms beneath her breasts and worked them back up to a more comfortable position, flies buzzing around her. Molly took the shovel and her aunt delivered her usual lecture on fashion, fluid and its importance for elimination, but Molly was thinking about an idea she had for a bust stay.

'A stay that cups the breasts,' said Molly, thoughtfully.

'For some of us a mixing bowl,' her aunt muttered.

There would need to be sizing.

Chapter 11

MOLLY ARRIVED EARLY, and Therese led her to Alathea's room on the north-west corner of the top floor. The table was set up beside large corner windows and Therese instructed Molly not to go into the bathroom.

'There's a water closet down the passage. Do you know what a water closet is?'

'No, please explain how it is used, in detail.'

'Well, it's for –'

'I know what it's for. I make a point of being well informed.'

Therese pointed to the dressmaker's dummy. 'This is the dummy and I've rigged it to Miss Pocknall's exact measurements.'

'So I see,' she said, turning the small knob to widen the hips. Then she turned her attention to the new cutting table, where a bolt of fabric waited. It wasn't crimson, it was magenta, but there was a small bolt of cobalt blue and some black netting and embroidered lace – all for Alathea's going-away dress. Magenta and blue would look good as a trim.

Therese sat in the corner watching Molly unpack her large sewing bag: tape measure, dressmaker's scissors, scissor snips, tapered awl, rotary cutter, dressmaker's chalk, tailor's chalk, hole punch, wirecutter, tin snips, hammer, file, pliers, bodkin, cording and eyelets, bias binding, pins, cotton (many strengths) and needles (many sizes), hooks, loops, precut bones – cane and baleen, busk, flat and conical.

'They look like garden tools.'

'Tools to build a piece of wearable architecture that will last long enough for Alathea's grandchildren.'

'I don't wear them, I only wear a jump.'

'That's because you're like a lamppost,' Molly said, and under her breath added, 'Unlit.'

'What did you say?'

'Nothing.'

Therese stretched her legs out and kicked her boots together. 'You better not mess anything up, the seamstress comes tomorrow to make the red dress.'

She applied her tape measure and adjusted the dummy's chest measurements. Therese banged, letting her boots flop out then bringing them together again.

'What are you using for the shell?'

'Silk.'

'Bit of a waste, isn't it? I mean, no one's going to see it.'

'I bet Clive Woodgrip's keen.'

Therese's boots stopped clapping.

Molly consulted her notes.

Therese resumed kicking. 'You don't preshrink the fabric?'

Molly said nothing.

'It doesn't look like it's been washed.'

Molly snapped, 'Make your feet take you to a room where banging them together is considered good manners!'

Therese's boots stopped. 'I can watch if I want.'

'You're a distraction. If I make a mistake, it will be your fault.'

'You're the one that's doing it.'

'I could stick you with my bodkin, Therese.'

'I'm not scared of you, you work in a factory. Anyway, I've got real work to do.' She dawdled out, leaving Molly studying the picture of the dress and the fabric and thinking that she would write to Gladys and describe this entire day, that's certain! Then she turned her thoughts to her work.

It was a matter of getting the underpinning construction right so that the layers and folds dropped in a way that was right for the fabric, and for Alathea's body. A dressmaker's dummy would do only so much, and then it was up to the dressmaker to match the lines, hobble the asymmetrical hem to the sheer tunic. She played with a scrap of fringed trim and thought about how it would move if she threaded it with beads stitched to the top and bottom of the corset – decorative stitching, of course. Without Alathea, all she could do was spread some coutil, linen, mercerised cotton and the magenta silk on a table, pin samples to the toile and imagine. She cut the basic pattern and pinned it together, but before she tacked, she was drawn by the view from Alathea's top-floor apartment. The third floor was the highest Molly had ever been, and she'd been intrigued by her bird's-eye view of Pocknall's garden. The city was to the north, beyond the Botanic Gardens, and she could see some roofs and, to the west, the bay. She toyed with the idea of walking to the far end of the balcony to get a better view, but Therese was lurking, and on the floors below, Alathea's father, fiancé and American cousin – *there is always a cousin* – swept through the halls and stood at fireplaces smoking.

In the quiet, comfortable room, Molly measured, snipped, pinned and hand-stitched, tacking the corset together. Then she wrapped the toile around the dummy and pinned some fabric to it. The fall seemed good, but she'd prefer to watch how it moved. An impasse reached, she wondered again if she could creep to the end of the balcony to see the bay, when Alathea appeared, coming across the room in her thick quilted Japanese robe.

Alathea pointed to the fabric pinned to the corset toile. 'It is such a pretty shade of crimson.'

'Magenta,' Molly corrected, then reminded herself that Alathea Pocknall did not need to hear her corrections.

'But what do you think of cobalt blue silk for the inlay, and for the sheer tunic, pale blue netting?'

'It'll be startling,' Molly said. 'If you give me the offcuts I'll trim your underwear to match – and add some black tassels.'

Alathea smiled, and Molly blurted, 'I've got an idea for a breast harness.'

'I bet you have, tell me about it.'

Molly had been thinking about the lack of dignity that went with free movement, something forgotten by some fashion dictators, and how she could improve on the idea she had for a bust stay.

She retrieved her prototype from her bag. Alathea took the stay from her and examined it. 'I've seen them. You need a better name – harness is demeaning. The name should be catchy if you want it to sell.'

'I had thought of "breast stay", and mine will have sizing, and I will use elastic.'

Alathea scrutinised Molly's invention, put her arms through the arm holes and laced the draw string around the chest. This was affirmation for Molly; it was a sound idea. Perhaps Alathea would see it as something Molly could do at the factory, but then Alathea said, 'You know you can patent your ideas, though it will probably cost money. You have savings, of course?'

'I have some savings . . .'

Alathea removed her Japanese coat and reached for the corset toile. 'My mother said that all women should have escape money.'

As she fitted the toile, they examined how the fabric moved, the colour, and lowered the front bodice a little, allowing for more netting – and flesh. At the end of their time together, Alathea said, 'Now . . . Dame Lily Pert has a show coming up. You will get a note from Penina, I don't know when. Lily will ask for something Japanese. It's up to you to talk her out of that.'

'Of course.' A kimono would make Dame Lily the shape of a wheat silo.

Alathea handed Molly an envelope. 'This is a letter of introduction to the Dame, though you've met her. I hope she summons you at a convenient time; she is impulsive.'

Molly didn't care if the meeting was at 5 am in Mildura, she would walk if necessary. It was a chance – and what a chance it was – with 'Australia's Darling Dame'.

As she passed the aviary on her way out, she said to the birds, 'See you next time,' and had to stop herself skipping to the gate.

That afternoon Aunt April was attempting to apply the new breast stay Molly had constructed for her when she saw Mrs Blinkhorn. She knew the behaviour: the women stood in the park, their parasols low and their faces to their shoes beneath their hat brims, waiting to skip over and hide behind the posters in the front yard. People didn't want to be seen entering the Dunnage coven but were happy enough to breathe the 'contaminated air' inside to pay insufficient money for superior underwear.

Aunt April, having managed her breasts with her forearms and tied the truss strings at the front, was dressing when the gate finally squeaked open. She heard the timid knock but did not rush. She would leave Mrs Blinkhorn where she was, exposed, hoping many pedestrians passed.

Finally, Aunt April went to the door. 'Mrs BLINKHORN!' she shouted, and Mrs Blinkhorn stepped back into the foliage of the gum. 'AT LAST! YOU'VE COME TO PAY MOLLY THE TWO POUNDS YOU OWE HER.'

Finally inside, Mrs Blinkhorn held a handkerchief over her nose.

'I breathe the air every day, Mrs Blinkhorn, and I'm perfectly well,' April explained, remarking on the weather for a further five seconds, which allowed Mrs Blinkhorn to get a good look in her room and forced her to inhale the lovely stench. On April's desk a crusted scalpel lay next to a blood-soaked blotting pad, its edges curled. There was a microscope, sketching pads, crisp flowers in vases ringed by evaporated water, a Bunsen burner and petri dishes and, along the wall, rows of jars. Some contained creatures wriggling in thick water as the dappled sunlight danced over them, and some had set solid and murky; some lidless containers oozed something foamy yet solid.

When Mrs Blinkhorn had taken in enough of the room, she followed April to the kitchen. In the sitting room – the so-called atelier – Molly Dunnage leaned over her ancient treadle machine, its paint worn under the arm and across the machine bed, the needle plate and thread guides polished. The thick makings of a corset were jammed onto the plate by the needle arm.

Unlike her aunt's room, Molly's atelier was neat, though cramped, everything folded and stacked or in small cardboard boxes, lined up in neat rows, the satin and linen and serge bolts stacked high. Cotton reels and bias-cut tape were colour-coordinated in a basket and Molly's pin cushions and giant scissors were lined up beside her tin snips and pliers, wire and baleen strips, eyelets and a small hammer, string and lace, files and wirecutters. On the dummy, a brilliant corset glowed under the electric globe.

Molly gave a half smile. 'You could have left the money you owe me in the letterbox, Mrs Blinkhorn.'

'I could have.' It was a shame: poor Molly Dunnage, so pretty and clever but never to thrive – unless she married well. But her chances of that were nil.

Mrs Blinkhorn cast her eyes around the kitchen and out to the backyard, where August cleaned his paint pots under the tap, tipping the coloured water into the gully trap. He smiled and waved to her, his stiff, splattered coat lifting like a piece of cardboard.

She pointed to the magenta-trimmed corset, some long tacking marking the machine cords and boning channels. 'That's a startling colour.'

'Wonderful, isn't it?' Molly hoped Mrs Blinkhorn hadn't noticed the elastic. She found her way to the hand wheel, pulled it and pumped the treadle; the pitman rose, gently thudding, and the bobbin in its case shuffled.

Mrs Blinkhorn removed her gloves and fingered the scraps of beautiful fabric. 'Who is that for?'

'A client.'

Mrs Blinkhorn was next captivated by the breast stay. 'The fabric is very expensive.' She picked up Molly's prototype and inspected it, bending in the window light to look at the back and running her fingers along the shoulder straps, which were adjustable by means of small sliding buckles.

'It has elastic. That's very expensive as well.'

Molly abandoned her machine. 'The client pays me in advance for it.'

'Does your *wealthy* client come to this . . . *place* for fittings?' Mrs Blinkhorn removed a bolt of fabric from a chair and sat down.

'No, she pays me to travel to her home south of the Yarra.'

'Do they support your crusades or, like most of us, do they consider their views well represented by their husbands? Mine is of the view that the Christian Temperance Union will end the suffering of women at the hands of drunken men, and, on that note, what do you say about Emmeline Pankhurst's attempt to bomb Buckingham Palace?'

'I have no association with Emmeline Pankhurst and if men choose to oppress women then women will do what they can to get their point across.'

'They use violence.'

'Violence seems to be something a lot of men understand, you just made the point yourself. Why is it that the Temperance Society advocate we remain subservient and mute to their callousness?'

'You make us sound like slaves but I am not a slave, of that I am certain.'

'Did your husband give you enough money to pay for your dress or have you come to beg for more time to pay?' Molly Dunnage held Mrs Blinkhorn's gaze with her sea-blue eyes while Mrs Blinkhorn reviewed her situation. She was certain of her freedom because she was not kept in chains and was perfectly content at home overseeing her maid and laundress. As long as there was food on the table, no overspending and Mr Blinkhorn was kept informed but endured no interruptions, she was allowed to do whatever she wanted. And what Mrs Blinkhorn wanted was cheap attire so as not to raise his attention on the monthly housekeeping ledger.

Mrs Blinkhorn became aware that she was sitting in a smelly house being insulted by an inferior because she feared her husband would reprimand her for spending too much on her clothing. She blinked. 'Well, I think you're lying about your important clients. I think you are making these garments for yourself.'

Molly knew it was bait, but could not help herself. 'My figure is nothing like Dame Lily Pert's nor am I five foot five like Miss Alathea Pocknall.'

'Oh, the boss's daughter.' Mrs Blinkhorn smiled condescendingly and picked up a dress lying neatly across a chair back. 'Is this for her too, or Dame Lily Pert?'

It was a dress Molly was making for herself, plain, the hem shorter, as was the fashion in Europe, and trimmed with cotton tassels which she had also made.

'No, that is for me.'

Mrs Blinkhorn dropped it as if it was hot. 'I don't believe you are dressing Dame Lily or Alathea Pocknall and nor do I, like a lot of women, believe we need the vote. Our husbands speak for us.'

'They deny you a voice and I don't feel superior enough to deny anyone a voice. You owe me two pounds.'

'I don't think I should pay for that dress, it doesn't become me at all.'

'Not even I can make a silk purse out of a sow's ear.'

How Gladys would have laughed.

Mrs Blinkhorn said in an even, thin voice, 'I need to tell you, on behalf of the choir, that we don't want dishonest members or pagans near the group. In addition to Gladys's drunken spectacle, the petty cash box was raided. Someone got in through the window and opened the cash box with a kitchen knife and now the choir has no money to enter the Victorian Chorus Festival.'

'You've had enough fun for the day. Go, before someone recognises your carriage parked around the corner and tells one of the respectable ladies at choir you're fraternising with the local witches.'

'You are very rude for someone in your position.' Mrs Blinkhorn pressed her hanky to her nose again.

It was a very good tale to write to Gladys about, but it made her weary. 'Rude people, like yourself, have taught me. I'll see you out.'

'You took the petty cash, didn't you?'

'Yes! I scaled the brick walls using my fingernails and toes and used magic to unlock those very high windows, and I squeezed in and dropped from that great height onto the floor without turning my ankle, and I found the hidden cash box and opened it with an axe and took all the money, and climbed back up the wall and out the window and dropped to the ground, and then I went shopping. I bought an automobile and a fur coat for Freddy Sidebottom. Do not bring your smelly corset or your shedding prurigo into my home again, Mrs Blinkhorn. Better personal hygiene would help your condition a lot. Good day.'

Mrs Blinkhorn stayed. 'Give me the money.'

August appeared, his sister behind him. 'Leave my house now, Mrs Blinkhorn.'

'She stole money from –'

'She did no such thing, nor would she ever and, unlike you, we pay our debts. Now leave or I shall pick you up and carry you to the park and drop you in the horse trough.'

'How dare you!'

'I'll see you to the door, Mrs Blinkhorn.' Aunt April stepped forward and, with the petri dish, pointed to the door.

Mrs Blinkhorn looked at the dish – which stank and moved as

if it were alive – hovering close to her lapel and turned pale under her face powder.

'No need to be afraid, it's just a common parasite,' said April. 'You're no doubt familiar with them, they derive nutrients off other species, like giardia or perhaps this one was flatworms . . . Oh dear, I have forgotten which.'

But Mrs Blinkhorn was heading to the front door. As August followed her – respectfully – something hit and cracked the front window. On the front veranda they stood staring down at a rotting dead rat. The Dunnages looked to the park, then Molly went to look up and down the street, but nothing moved, no one scampered away; the bushes were perfectly still and no limbs protruded from behind trees.

Mrs Blinkhorn unfurled her parasol. 'I suppose you'll use that rat to throw at passing men.'

'Not this one,' said Molly. 'It'll be dinner.'

While Mrs Blinkhorn hurried towards her carriage, which was parked far away from the Dunnage home, Molly fumed, pacing the front veranda and eyeing the neighbourhood. 'It was *her*,' she cried. 'Old Bigbottom thinks we started cholera.'

August said, 'Now, my dear . . .' but Molly was gone.

Next door she banged on Mrs Sidebottom's door. 'I will keep banging until you speak to me!'

Over the park, the Crosses came from their house to watch and at the rotunda Freddy and his ne'er-do-wells turned to see. Eventually, Mrs Sidebottom opened the door a crack. She was red-faced, perspiring, her apron drenched.

'Your boys threw a dead rat at our house.'

'You belong in an asylum.'

'That's what you did to Gladys, isn't it? You had the minister from St Michael's commit her!'

She saw Mrs Sidebottom's arm flex and stepped back just in time. The door slammed with such force that it unlatched itself again and revealed Mrs Sidebottom standing in the hall hitting her palm on her forehead. Molly found herself feeling some sympathy. Perhaps poor Mrs Sidebottom was the one who could do with a rest in an asylum?

Returning home, Molly flung open the front door, calling, 'They have put Gladys in the asylum.'

Her father and aunt, sitting at the table waiting for the kettle to boil, looked at their flushed and furious girl.

'Daughter, sit.'

Sensing a familiar lecture looming, she plopped down at the table, gearing up to summon as many ripostes as she could.

'Sometimes, arguing is the least effective way to communicate your opinions,' August told her gently.

'Father, mine are not opinions, they're common sense,' Molly retorted.

'Mrs Blinkhorn and Mrs Sidebottom believe the same of the points they make, and you repel them by being so . . . sure. You need to meet them, hear and understand what they are saying and what makes them believe what they say. Bring them with you, don't push them away. If you bring them to you then they will understand your point of view.'

'They are making accusations that aren't true –'

'All the more reason to listen.'

'I don't believe in manipulating people.'

'I know you believe you are incapable of suppressing your responses, but I believe you will make allegiances when you choose to believe you can.'

She opened her mouth but her father raised one finger.

'Think about it,' her aunt said.

And so she thought about listening, and manipulating, but came to no conclusion because of Mrs Blinkhorn's evil accusations. And of course the notion that Gladys had been committed to the asylum. These thoughts kept her awake, but she told herself she must try to stay quiet and compliant. One day, like Alathea, she could have rooms with appealing furnishings, windows that opened onto a veranda, sunshine and fresh air rising from a pretty garden. She would move them all from Curtain Square and away from her badly behaved neighbour and the likes of Mrs Blinkhorn. Perhaps then some would see the unfairness, perhaps they would see the Dunnages and Mr Luby were harmless? In the meantime, she'd make do with Curtain Square, their cosy home, the parkland and its music.

'You have chances before you, Molly, do not risk them,' she told herself, and finally drifted off to sleep.

Chapter 12

BUT SHE WOKE each morning thinking about Gladys, and on Monday, she found a pile of undergarments, tall as a tree, waiting for her. The factory was damp after rain, the sewing machines sounding hard in the chilly swirling air, and sharp under the tall iron and canvas ceiling. Mr Addlar had left the windows open – just for her, she knew, to keep her in her miserable position, toiling away, to make sure she stayed low, where she belonged.

Despite the frigid conditions, Colma and her vassals sat facing the window for the light, heads down, stitching with their stiff, red fingers. Molly had told herself to be content with her pile of work and the cold – *Don't risk your chance* – but it was too uncomfortable, so she closed the windows.

Old Snakelegs wound his way to her within seconds.

'I know you've been waiting for me to do that so you could abuse me, but it's freezing for them, look at their hands.'

'You speak of –'

'Ventilation, I know, but the air is damp and freezing and it hinders our work and makes us ill, and that will slow production.'

He moved towards the windows.

'Please, Mr Addlar, punish me but the others have done nothing.'

He looked at the workers. 'Do you want fresh air or bad health?'

'Risk it either way, don't we?' said Colma, her direct response a surprise to Molly.

Shocked by Colma's bluntness, Old Snakelegs walked away.

And so Molly sat as she usually did, stitching a row of orchids on a silk ribbon edging the top of a white chemise, her thoughts on the challenge of what was under Dame Lily Pert's voluminous skirt. But it was speculation over the exact nature of her breast stay that she found most rewarding, especially sizing. There'd be two sets of sizes, one for chest circumference and the other for the size of the breast. Did small breasts need harnessing? They did. They needed to be kept firm, not gambolling, as Aunt April would say, disapproval in her tone. Molly's breast stays would be practical and an essential item in the wardrobes of all women, but they would be pretty. She would make a special line of wedding trousseau items for those who wanted them.

And so planning kept her even-tempered at work, and drawing prototypes and making toiles filled the gaps in her week where Gladys and choir used to be. She cemented her relationship with Horatio by again taking the easel next to his in drawing class; that week they drew hands – a hand that showed who the person was and 'if they enjoyed what they did for a living'. Horatio drew his mother's hands, pinpricked and soft, content and folded in her lap. Molly drew her father's hands, stained, his nails filthy. The butcher's son drew a left hand only, with two missing fingers. Another left hand with a blackened fingernail belonged to a builder, and there were hands heavy with jewellery, baby's hands, and a traffic policeman's gloved hand, *Stop!*

Molly hoped the class would move on to the main muscles of the back: latissimus dorsi, teres minor and trapezius. Otherwise, it was off to the library to study the book on Myron's *Discobolus* again.

As they waited after class for August to come for Molly, Horatio revealed that he'd been reprimanded again, this time for placing a vase of fresh flowers on the bench of his little office. Molly revealed, in turn, that she'd sent a letter to Gladys care of the asylum.

'You must know, Molly, that as non-relatives, you'll be denied visiting rights.'

'To seek is to find.'

The end of April brought fog, which melted and dripped making the backyard sodden and the house dank and frigid under the tall trees. On Sunday, Molly dragged her clothes from her dresser into bed with her and when they were warm, she pulled on her stockings, garters, undershirt and dress before throwing back the covers. She buttoned her bodice while shoving her feet into her slippers and ran to put her boots in the slow oven. She bandaged herself in woollen cardigans and a wrap, moved the kettle to the hot plate, stoked the fire and put her porridge on to cook. While she washed, the water boiled and her porridge thickened. There was not a sound from the front two rooms, the rest of the house as silent as the frogs in the backyard ponds. She took tea to her aunt and found her knitting.

'Thank you, dear girl. It's the first cold snap so go through your woollens and bring anything that needs darning.'

She took a breakfast tray to her father, who was sitting up in bed in his coat and hat. He removed his gloves to cradle his teacup.

'I can hear the magpies, warbling up and down their scale, but I think to fly is the greatest of all mother nature's accomplishments,' August told her, wheezing a little. 'Do you know starlings and lyrebirds are great mimics? And that the bird of paradise . . . Well, what I'd have given to see one of those. The plumage! I'd have liked to go to the Nile . . .'

Normally, she would have said, 'I would have liked to go to Paris,' but now thought better of it. Her father was pale and rummaging through his life as if it was about to end, and it made her impatient – she wanted to succeed, to accomplish something for him, to lift her father and aunt, make them *more* after a lifetime of less. With all her being, she hoped that something more would come of today. Perhaps today would be the day everything changed.

After lunch, Molly gathered her bag and umbrella, pinned her hat into place, tightened her scarf around her neck and pulled on her gloves. She had said nothing to anyone about Dame Lily: it might all come to nothing and the neighbourhood would say that the Dunnages were liars. She set off for the tram full of anticipation, her sewing kit in her shoulder bag. Her nose was wet and she thought of Gladys, who fretted over her red nose on brisk mornings.

It was known that Dame Lily occupied the main dressing room at the Princess Theatre, even though she was not performing. And it was also well known that this forced other prima donnas to share the cast's dressing room. Sometimes the Princess was forced to hire a room at a nearby hotel for guest musicians.

The theatre, carpeted and upholstered, gilt and crimson-edged through the glass door, was closed, so she knocked until the attendant finally left his ticket booth. She sincerely hoped she didn't smell of Mrs Sidebottom's woodsmoke, though in Melbourne most people smelled of something: horse manure, their breakfast of bacon and eggs, halitosis or a hat that had soured from a sweaty, unwashed scalp.

'Good morning, I am here to see Dame Lily Pert,' Molly said brightly. Dame Lily's soprano voice floated to them through the foyer.

'Dame Lily is not performing this season,' the man replied, moving to close the door again.

Molly put her foot on the step to keep it open. 'I have a letter of introduction. I am her seamstress.'

'No one has informed me that Dame Lily is to receive anyone this morning.' He ignored the envelope she offered but Molly wasn't in the mood for rejection. She put her hand to her ear and listened intently to Dame Lily singing *La Bohème*. '*Così l'effluvio del desìo tutta m'aggira, felice mi fa! E tu che sai, che memori e ti struggi . . .*'

'Do you know, everywhere I go I encounter resistance and it's always from men. If you don't want to be in a world where there are women, then stay at home and let others do your job as it should be done.' She eyed the small, gold-embossed name badge pinned to his pocket.

Glaring at her, he pushed the door closed and snibbed it, and the breath in Molly evaporated as she was taken all the way back to Miss Archambeau's door all those years ago.

But then she was saved . . . by a man. A repairman showed up to test the fly system and when the door was opened for him, Molly pushed past defiantly and headed across the foyer.

From her seat at the piano, Penina watched Molly Dunnage sneak in and sit down at the very back in the dark and signalled for her to stay hidden. Beside her, her back to the auditorium, Dame Lily Pert flicked through sheet music. She was dressed in an elaborate afternoon coat, brown velvet with white fur collar, cuffs and hem, her blouse and skirt underneath also white.

When Dame Lily sang, her voice was lovely, though it scarcely reached the back of the room. Molly knew that because Dame Lily encased her substantial person in an overbust corset, it was restricting her lung expansion and possibly hindering diaphragm function. This lack of oxygen was partly why she was perpetually irritated.

'You are not playing well today, Penina!' Dame Lily abruptly left the stage, rocking as she walked, which Molly knew to be a problem with her hips and knees. She was in pain. Penina, impeccably groomed in a plain dark frock, collected her music, closed the piano lid and beckoned to Molly.

*

Molly followed Penina through the draughty passages and alleys backstage, and it occurred to her that she might never find her way out alone. Dame Lily Pert's room was warm, but smelled fusty. One day Molly would have a warm room. The Dame sat miserably in a soft fat chair holding a cup of what looked like brown tea, waving at herself with a fan the size of an elephant's ear. She had unbuttoned her afternoon coat and her feet were soaking in a dish of warm, soapy water. At her elbow was a pyramid of sodden handkerchiefs.

'Remind me once more exactly what you are doing here.' She spoke softly, pouting and wounded, eyeing Molly suspiciously.

'I make comfortable undergarments.'

'Oh yes.' She let the fan rest on her bosom and gave Molly her full, red-eyed attention. 'You're the girl who makes brassieres.'

'We are distancing ourselves from brassieres – they merely cover the breasts, they don't add control or support.'

Ignoring this clarification, Dame Lily went on, 'As you can see, for a woman in her mid-forties my figure is very good.'

Lily Pert was at least fifty years old and Molly had spotted the edge of the pouter corset hanging off the end of the elaborate quad-fold dressing screen the second she'd stepped into the room. She also saw that the weight of the corset was straining its shoulder straps, proving metal was involved. Here was another chance. Dame Lily's fading voice, also hindered by her lack of ambulatory ability, could be rectified by a personalised corset that fitted rather than garrotted.

Penina turned her dark brown eyes to Molly, and Molly said, 'Yes! Your figure is impressive and I have an idea that will do very well on you.'

'You all say that.' Dame Lily held her cup out and Penina filled it from a teapot, though it smelled to Molly more like sherry than tea.

Molly wondered if she would end up like the Dame, disappointed, dissatisfied and crotchety. She shook the thought from her mind.

'You may measure me and write it all down in that little book you drew from your large ugly sack.'

To stand next to Lily Pert was to stand next to a sherry-drenched hand towel on a warm afternoon. Her powdery complexion featured the traumatised capillaries of a dedicated tippler, which she attempted to hide, but the makeup dried and clotted in the fine creases of her macerated skin, like pink thread, and bits of powder dropped off, filling the tiny whirlpool of gathered creases between her watery breasts.

Molly measured Dame Lily's throat.

'Fourteen inches,' she said, and showed Penina the tape measure. Penina wrote down *Throat, 24'*.

'Bust, forty-five inches.'

Penina looked at the tape measure and wrote, *54'*.

Dame Lily's hips were also recorded accurately, though when Molly said, 'Fifty-two inches', Dame Lily said, 'Oh my, I have lost weight. I wonder if I'm ill?'

As Molly returned the notebook into her large ugly sack, Dame Lily said, 'Show me.'

'I never show anyone my designs.'

Dame Lily's face did not change. Naturally it was her voice, the way she repeated, 'Show me,' that compelled Molly to hand over the book.

Lily did not look at the measurements. She sipped her 'tea' and turned the pages and began to smile. 'You have some surprisingly lovely things in here.'

'Thank you.' Molly told herself to hold steady, show her pleasing side.

'So you drew all of these on your own, from your head?'

'I did.'

'You didn't copy them?'

Molly heard her father's voice. *I know you believe you are incapable of suppressing your responses, but I believe you will make allegiances when you choose to believe you can.*

'There are few people with the rare talent that you have, Dame Lily,' she said, 'and I believe you have been away from your public for too long.'

'Many people think that, don't they, Penina?'

'We will have you back singing very soon.'

The Dame inhaled. 'I would like you to make me something Japanese, a kimono.'

'Of course,' said Molly, cheerily. 'I have many requests for them. They're all the rage, and such a straightforward design.'

Penina topped up her tea again, and said, 'I think you can carry anything,' and Molly agreed.

'Something unique.' She showed Dame Lily a corset that might work for her. 'I think this will make you look . . . it will look wonderful on you and of course you will show anything to its best advantage if you have these underpinnings.'

'True.'

Molly plunged on. 'The breasts need support, but not restriction, and if you elevate the bust it allows the fabric to fall so that the waist area and lower ribs need not be so constrained. And also, by supporting the breasts, the body is made slimmer, the midriff is . . . unrestrictedly minimised.'

Penina nodded to Molly, *nicely put*. Dame Lily sipped.

'Anyway, my design is called a breast stay, but on some figures, it will be made so that it also defines the waist's natural curve.'

'It sounds perfect,' said Lily, her hands rising over her rolling middle.

'Yes, and because you are a singer you breathe up, rather than out.'

'I know that! Just make me something nice.'

Penina squeezed Molly's arm.

'I'm honoured.'

Penina opened the door. Outside, she handed Molly six shillings. 'A down payment, no need to mention it to anyone.' Again, she took Molly's arm. 'We are always very discreet about Miss Pert's

"Pertiness". Lately her public image has been a little maligned but she still performs brilliantly given the right circumstances.'

'I'd love to see her perform one day, preferably wearing something I made for her.'

Penina smiled. 'At the moment, Dame Lily has no shows booked, but I'm working on it.' She gave Molly a card, wrote a time and date on it and thanked her. 'And if her "harness" works, her costumier will be thrilled and we'll get several. I'll get you to measure me up for one as well.'

Before she left, sensing a sympathy in Penina, Molly pushed for one final favour. 'Will you sign my petition?'

'What's it for?'

'Equality, better working conditions, the right to stand for office, better laws about violence against women, a right for divorced women to see their children – many things.'

'You're a suffragette.'

'I campaign for the sake of suffrage.'

'I once had a husband.' Penina signed the petition. 'And I had children. But I was replaced.' She also signed Lily Pert's name, explaining that the Dame was paid less than the men in the orchestra.

On impulse, Molly walked to Myer, as she sometimes had with Gladys. They liked to search through the racks of dresses and try on the hats, and Molly wanted to go there to feel the companionship of Gladys, perhaps even bump into her. She kept an eye out for Gladys everywhere she went – the Rathdowne Street shops, drawing class, when she was off to find a newspaper, or to the library, art gallery, grocery shop – Molly searched for Gladys, scanning the surrounds for her familiar profile, her heavily lidded eyes, anyone with light brown hair curled at the forehead, a figure standing with her elbows jutting out a little, sauntering through a crowd, intent on what she was seeking, any young lady positioned at the centre of groups. 'I will write when I am happy,' she'd said, but no letter came.

*

Molly alighted the Rathdowne Street tram and continued on to her boycotted home – cosy under a forest of native plants, its paint peeling and fence undulating – with her good news. Making underwear for Dame Lily Pert! But she would swear them to silence – anything might happen yet.

Aunt April sat with her friend, Miss Berrycloth, framed by her open front window, a trompe l'oeil of two older ladies taking tea. Around them was April's polluted workbench, furry-haired rotting yoghurt and fungus sprouting from the crack around the window frame. Along the veranda a fan of protest signs leaned against the posts, advertising the Victorian Women's Suffrage Society.

Small, determined and almost bald under her skull cap, Miss Berrycloth had been raised on a farm and stayed for a time when her parents died. Then her brother married, and when the fourth baby was born, Miss Berrycloth caught a train to Melbourne and answered an advertisement for an *au pair*. The position was in an old home with modern amenities, so no water to fetch from a distant well or brown snakes in the woodheap. It also paid wages, so Miss Berrycloth remained with the family and became an *au pair* to their next generation. Of late she had travelled with the entire family to the Blue Mountains. 'Apart from meeting Henrietta Dugdale,' she had declared when she returned, 'it was the highlight of my life.' She'd held up two worn postcards she'd purchased, though would not let anyone take them with their own fingers to study them.

Miss Berrycloth was explaining, as she often did, how she had been 'cast out' by her brother when he brought his bride, Thurma, home to the farm. 'And when Thurma was pregnant, I said that *he* should chop the wood, not poor Thurma, and he cast me out. "You're a rabblerouser," he said, "pack your bags and go." It was the words of Henrietta Dugdale, who I once met, that gave me great strength and still do.'

Her aunt said, 'Miss Berrycloth and I are planning a trip to the country. It's time we went again for the air and sun.'

'And Miss Berrycloth can buy a new postcard,' said Molly, thinking she'd also like to go to their cousins at Yaambul if only for the hot water and bathtubs and someone else's cooking. Thinking longingly of a trip there, Molly imagined how she'd take her corsets and undergarments to the clean country and sew all day, then sit on the balcony and watch the sun go down. August and April's cousin, Eda Mahone, ran a hotel in the quiet and small town of Yaambul with her husband. The hotel was built to cater to the happy beneficiaries of the goldrush and so boasted bathrooms and indoor lavatories. In the past few years, though, holidays at Yaambul had been few and far between.

'And we have been discussing Vida,' said Miss Berrycloth, ending Molly's reverie.

'We think Vida has a chance if there's another election, and I think there will be one.'

They spoke the name Vida as though speaking of an angel.

'I don't,' said Molly, changing the tone. 'She's a pacifist, most people think she's a Labor member and she is too progressive for almost everyone.'

'That's just the AWNL, Molly, and where is your sense of hope today?'

'It's entirely refreshed but the politicians are excited about war already and the newspapers appear to confirm my assessment.'

'It sounds more like you are supporting theirs.'

'It does,' Miss Berrycloth agreed. 'It's those so devoted to King, Queen and Country, but we have a few supporters – some republicans and radicals are against war –'

'Many are!' Aunt April interrupted. 'And we must not forget our Aborigines in the scheme of everything. They won't have to fight for the white man, surely?'

'They are Australian.' Miss Berrycloth removed her cotton cap and scraped back her thin hair.

'They shouldn't be expected to fight,' said Molly, thinking that she had entirely forgotten about them, as had those who were not actively trying to eradicate them. She decided she would write to *Have Your Say* about them, then again, decided she wouldn't. Let them be forgotten in this war, it was not theirs to fight.

Miss Berrycloth said, 'Well, they're too far away, aren't they? They live way out in the desert. I got quite near the desert on my trip to the Blue Mountains – in fact, I believe I saw it from the top of a mountain on our way to Springwood.'

Molly fled to her father in his studio before Miss Berrycloth began the story of the Blue Mountains again. August was working on a serving plate shaped like a fish, and was painting the outline of a flying fish. 'This is *Cheilopogon pinnatibarbatus*. How was your day, daughter?' It was a conspiratorial question; he could see she was bursting to tell someone about something.

'Well, Dad, you'll never guess!'

'True.' He licked the end of his brush and squinted at his fish. 'So you'd better tell me.'

'I have a new client.'

'Do I have to guess?'

'Yes.'

'Mrs Blinkhorn?'

'Try again.'

'Mrs Bigbottom.'

'Again.'

'I give up.'

'Dame Lily Pert.'

Delighted, August embraced his daughter, placed a kiss on her cheek, leaving it slightly purple. 'Molly, such a chance you have now!'

Molly gave her father one last squeeze and disentangled herself. He was very bony under his coats. 'Her assistant Penina runs the show, and she's beautiful so no one believes she's talented or clever. And she's been cast out by her husband. She's plucky but she's good with Dame Lily, trying to relaunch her career. She paid me an advance for a set of underwear.'

'I'm happy for you. But, Molly, did you see the letter?'

'I did.' It was returned from the asylum, but had been opened. *No one of that name here*, scrawled across the envelope.

'But I am sure Gladys is in there,' said Molly angrily, determinedly. 'We have to get her out or she'll be there until she dies. I have a plan. It's a full moon, isn't it?'

'Last I saw.'

It was, and the sky was cloudless. In the quiet parklands around the asylum, their voices would carry up and over the low walls, and the moonlight allowed some visibility.

August wrapped his scarf a little tighter.

'If we aren't back in an hour, we've been captured.'

'Serves you right,' he said. 'This is lunacy.'

'Indeed,' said his sister, heading off towards the Kew Lunatic Asylum.

He watched April and his daughter become absorbed by the parklands as they moved towards the wall in the distance, its vast roof frosted silver, two chimneys leaking smoke into the chilly air.

Predictably, they didn't succeed and would have been lost in the parklands for hours if it hadn't been for August's cough. They paused and listened, following the sound and making intermittent progress until his silhouette appeared nowhere near where they thought they had left him. He coughed again. Their sodden hems dragged in the tall grass and they were flecked with twigs and leaves, and breathing hard.

'What happened?' August coughed.

'It's like Bourke Street – there are dozens of people walking around the walls calling out for missing mothers, hysterical sisters, drunken sons . . .' Molly was shivering in the cold.

'We found it hard to find an unoccupied hiding spot.' Aunt April blew her nose loudly.

'The guards do rounds, apparently, every hour or so. You need to be on your toes.'

'Or else you get thumped with a truncheon.'

'We met one woman who throws ale over the wall to her sister. She visited last week and there wasn't anyone new called Gladys.'

'Right, girls, you have done your best. Shall we go?'

'Yes,' said April. 'Let's get you out of this damp. If you drop dead here, Molly and I might end up the other side of that wall.'

Chapter 13

MOLLY FREED THE chooks and then came in to stoke the fire and move the pot of porridge to the slow plate. Aunt April said she would take the barrow to Royal Park to collect firewood.

'I'll get more on the weekend,' said Molly, and ran, hurrying through Carlton towards North Fitzroy, conscious that she was running late. But when she got to the factory, she found the doors shut and the workers standing looking at them.

'Where's Snakelegs?'

Colma shrugged. 'Sick?'

'Gravely, with a bit of luck.'

She stood with the other workers, all of them very quiet, and still looking hopefully at the factory, today an anonymous shed just like any other.

Eventually, they drifted to sit along the factory wall, the sunshine warming them as it rose and melted the clouds away, their spirits lighter – Snakelegs was dead, surely.

Finally, Norbert Poke, dressed in a black long-coat, striped trousers and top hat, emerged from the factory and walked to a tall, shiny gelding. He had trouble mounting because the horse side-stepped each time it felt Norbert's foot in the stirrup, forcing him to bounce on one foot in circles. Then Mr Addlar emerged from the gloom of the dormant factory and sent the cotton boy to help. The cotton boy steadied the horse, and Snakelegs barked at the girls, 'Get straight to work, and no speaking. You will not speak to each other at all unless I say you can.' But they dawdled, keen to see if Norbert Poke would finally climb safely into the saddle.

As they started working, looks and gestures darted down the lines, from the men sorting and packing corsets to the girl working the torsos and the machine girls. Then all eyes turned to the freight cart driver when he arrived at the loading dock, but he kept his eyes on his job.

Colma nodded knowingly, her mouth vanishing into her toothless gums and her chin rising. 'He knows.'

Finally, from the loaders to the packers to the torso girl to the machinists, the whisper spread.

Emrys Pocknall was dead.

Mid-morning, the flamboyant Norbert Poke returned, solicitors in tow. They did not look at anyone as they ascended the stairs. The staff slowed to watch Snakelegs rise from the desk, allowing Norbert Poke to take Emrys Pocknall's chair.

Colma said, 'Well, if that's not a grab for power I'm a monkey's uncle.'

It went through Molly's mind that Colma would pass for a monkey's aunt, but she bit her tongue. They needed to stick together.

The rivals in the office spent a good deal of time around the desk, shoving and tugging, trying to open the desk drawers. The men moved as one to the locked filing cabinet and Snakelegs went to find a saw. He hurried back up to the office with a tiny hacksaw from the machine engineer's work box, and slapped the louvres shut.

At morning tea, the conversation among the workers was urgent and whispered: what had happened, who would run the factory, would it be Snakelegs, the cousin, or Miss Alathea Pocknall?

At lunchtime, Snakelegs appeared on the balcony outside the office. He stood like the Pope until every curious eye focused on him or, rather, on the middle of his forehead (it was dangerous to look into the eyes of the merciless), and he signalled for the machines to be shut down. In the silence the workers heard the men in the office, grunting, still sawing away at the locked filing cabinet.

Mr Addlar held tight to the handrail and took his time to say, 'It is with the very deepest regret that I inform you that the esteemed Mr Emrys Pocknall has died. It was very sudden, a heart attack at his home, and it is a very sad day for us, for Melbourne, for the country and, of course, a burden for those of us who will take over his great work.'

'I wouldn't call making corsets great,' muttered Colma.

Molly thought, *My corsets will change women's lives.*

Mr Addlar continued, 'It is always important that we meet our production targets, but now we will go well above demand to show that we remain viable, that we have a future.'

Alathea would take over, surely? And she would still need her wedding trousseau. Though her wedding would be postponed, out of respect, she would then take the reins, improve everything? They'd get pay rises, toilet breaks and have a voice, a say in how they would work. Molly would be a designer and improve corsets for back support in labouring work, invent new corsets suitable for waistless fashion frocks, for bicycle pants and driving automobiles, for singers and dancers, acrobats and nuns. She and Alathea would pioneer breast stays for fashionable dresses – practical dresses – and Alathea would see that every girl in Australia wanted them.

Molly Dunnage smiled all day.

Arriving home, Molly saw Mrs Blinkhorn standing out on the footpath reading the election posters and banners.

'At last, you've come with my two pounds?' Molly said blithely.

'There's no point campaigning, you silly girl, there's going to be a war, no one is going to care if Vida Goldstein is alive let alone vote for her, especially for a Senate seat.'

Molly laughed. 'The current government is a shambles, there'll be an election.'

'Oh, so you're fortune tellers as well as black enchanters?'

'Aren't you afraid those people over there will see you talking to the local pagans?'

Over at the pub a crowd had gathered.

'You pride yourself on being progressive,' Mrs Blinkhorn said, 'but you attract people who are less than admirable, like your friend Gladys.'

'You seem to be attracted to me.'

Mrs Blinkhorn gathered herself to deliver something important. 'Your employer, Mr Emrys Pocknall, has died in most disreputable circumstances.'

'So that's why you're lurking?' Molly stepped towards her front gate. 'Only you and your disreputable friends would know something like that.'

Mrs Blinkhorn, bamboozled by what Molly had said, was left on the footpath.

As Molly came into the kitchen, she said, 'Emrys Pocknall is dead.'

Aunt April looked at her brother. 'That wasn't on the wireless, was it, Augie?'

'No, but they might say it on the evening news.'

Molly looked from one to the other; she had missed something.

Her father explained, 'I've been to the Kent – they've purchased a wireless.'

'I suppose it's in the public bar and women won't be able to hear it.'

'In his defence, daughter, Mr Kent opened the windows for them.'

'I feel that one day we will have one ourselves,' said Aunt April, and Molly said that a lot of people already have one.

Her aunt nodded. 'As I predicted.'

In her small atelier, Molly put her hand on her mother's sewing machine and pondered her shaken future. Alathea was a strong woman, she would take over, not Norbert. She was absent from the factory to organise the funeral, to grieve. Norbert was just helping out. Molly would be made designer, Snakelegs dispatched. Alathea would still marry, she would still need her corsets. There was nothing to say Molly should not go on sewing her corsets in good faith. And there was certainly no need to alarm her aunt or father. Emrys Pocknall was the kind of man to leave a clear last will and testament. And if she was dismissed from the factory, or if it closed, then she would find work somewhere else.

The light bulb in the kitchen burned late as Molly worked on Dame Lily's breast stay. Dame Lily would love it, she would ask for more, Molly would make a name for herself.

She went to bed and drew late into the night, replenishing her candle once, and when she woke, she saw that she had a notepad full of underwear designs for Alathea Pocknall and her factory.

Despite the cold and the smoke pall from Mrs Sidebottom's copper, August made the effort to go and get the evening paper. He read it out as Molly ate her soup – it was a substantial notice outlining Emrys Pocknall's manufacturing achievements, of which there were few, though the adjectives explaining them made them seem more.

Molly studied the newspaper photograph of Emrys and Juanita on their wedding day and Aunt April said his most impressive achievement was his marriage to Miss Juanita Martinez, an independently wealthy American. 'Such a shame she perished with the *Titanic*.'

'Juanita . . .' August looked to the ceiling. 'Lovely creature . . . Bit of a handful, though, so they say.'

'Who says?'

'Gossip columnists. If you read between the lines, you get the gist.'

'Slanderers,' said Aunt April.

Molly asked, 'What's a respectable amount of time for wealthy people to grieve?'

'They do have feelings, daughter.'

'If I had money, I could start my own business . . . a line of sports corsets, tennis, badminton, archery, horse riding, cricket. They could be adjusted to accommodate getting in and out of automobiles . . . more like a jump, but with elastic. Elastic will lessen the need for double twill.'

'Rowing,' said her aunt. 'Now there's some tricky torso movement.'

August said she should work out a size guide at the outset. 'You could put an advertisement in the draper's window asking for women to come and be measured.'

The women looked at him as if he'd suggested they move to Siberia.

'That would do wonders for our reputation,' said April.

Chapter 14

EACH MORNING, EVAN Pettyman approached his mother alert for signs that she was breathing. Mrs Pettyman was dangerously thin, a greyhound rather than a human lying in her bed. Without her pouter pigeon corset – rustproof and suitable for the fashionably slender form – the woman had difficulty sitting up and staying there, but removing it did allow her to swallow and digest an entire meal.

Evan whispered, 'Good morning,' and when she roused, he slid his hand behind her, spread his fingers across her scapula and vertebrae, easily discernible beneath her papery skin, gently levered her forward and arranged her pillows to hold her upright. He positioned her breakfast tray and tucked her napkin into the collar of her nightdress.

'I have found something,' he told her.

Her mouth was full of bread and dripping. 'Is that why there is a flower on my tray?'

He smiled.

'It will make me sneeze.' She swallowed some tea. 'I can't read your mind, Evan.'

'A factory, the business of the late underwear manufacturer Mr Emrys Pocknall, is, I am reliably informed, in financial difficulty. Apparently, Pocknall's daughter is his sole heir, but there is a lost will, and a cousin.'

'There is always a cousin. Naturally he'll contest.' She took a scoopful of porridge.

'And given she's a female, he will win.' Evan felt about beneath the blankets for his mother's bedpan. He located the heavy enamel vessel, warm from its cosy night, and removed it.

'Do you think she knows that?'

'She is well educated in the ways of a society hostess and about to get married, my man tells me.' He placed the bedpan on the floor by the door and waited.

'We'd better hurry, then.' She tilted her head towards the window. 'What will you do, Evan?'

He crossed the room silently, his feet bare so as not to irritate his sleepy mother, and to save wear and tear on his socks and only pair of shoes. He pulled aside the sheet tacked to the pelmet and a line of yellow sunshine lit the floorboards and brightened the room. He tried not to look at his mother in the light. 'I'll go and see Father's old collaborator, Mr Hawker, to broker a deal and hopefully he will agree to go into business with Norbert, buy into it and start manufacturing underwear, or army uniforms.'

'No,' said his mother. 'There is too much time and not enough money for us in that plan. We'll work with the daughter. Tell her we'll invest in the factory . . . tell her we'll refinance her and go into business with her; we'll have to borrow the money, of course, so slap a high interest rate on it. She'll have to give us the title and deeds, then we'll do nothing. When the business fails to thrive, you'll put pressure on her to pay the loan back, she'll panic, we'll force the business into liquidation, break it up and sell the assets and chattels, then the land and the building.' Mrs Pettyman scraped the last of the porridge from her bowl with the bread and dripping crusts, and as she chewed she said, 'Borrow the money from Mr Hawker.'

She was right. He didn't want to buy into a failing business with a failure. They'd ignore Norbert Poke. Much better to deal with Alathea Pocknall. She'd be emotionally invested and probably clueless, a pushover. Women were always grateful when someone bailed them out, he'd save her father's life's work while sidelining the opportunistic American remittance man. It could not fail. For a moment he dreamed that he might even get rid of the pointless fiancé and marry her himself.

Mrs Pettyman put the bowl down and burped, softly, her hand on her stomach. 'You'll be one of many trying to buy her out. Any idea how to get to Miss Pocknall?'

'Yes.' Evan looked pleased with himself. 'Coincidentally, I have a connection to Miss Pocknall through choir.'

He left his mother, taking her bedpan with him all the way down the stairs and across the stony, damp backyard to the outhouse.

The glass office louvres behind Mr Addlar cast him black, his hands on the balustrade white, as he looked down on his prey, who today ambled to their posts – common and impudent, all of them – and took their time readying themselves for work. He would not turn on the machines. Let them sit there, uncomprehending and fearful. If he was to run the factory for a week, as instructed, then he would do so in his own way, and he would excel. Norbert Poke was a man of presence, but Mr Addlar knew more of the factory than the American interloper.

'WORKERS,' he shouted, gleeful at their red, stupid faces jerking up to him. He had a good mind to command them all to hear him on their knees. 'Today you will increase productivity. I want seven more corsets on the embroider table by the end of the working day, and tomorrow eight corsets, thirty-five more than usual for the week . . . hopefully forty.'

If they were good enough, and he doubted they were, he'd push them to an extra twenty a day.

'You'll work Saturday afternoon if we don't reach our goal. And you, Dunnage, you will go back to torsos and don't let the switchover lag. And Colma, don't let any mistakes get past your scrutiny or you'll stay behind fixing every one of them yourself.'

He glared down at the women, and then looked to the boy who would roll the crates to the packers to see that he had heard and understood. The boy gave him the thumbs up, but when Mr Addlar turned away the boy swapped his thumb for his middle finger and spat.

The machinists looked to Molly, but she looked to the torsos. It was Colma who appealed, and pointed out that Molly was wasted on the torsos. 'Her needlework's fast and the best, no shop's ever sent her work back.'

'Your wages will be docked a shilling this week, Colma.'

Molly couldn't ignore that; the unfairness was too much. 'Mr Addlar, Colma's just trying to help you.'

'Help me? Insubordinate,' he hissed, and switched on the machines. 'You've just lost a shilling, Dunnage.'

As they returned to their posts, Colma said, 'I've a good mind to put pins in the desk chair.' It was rumoured Snakelegs came in Sundays just to sit in Mr Pocknall's chair.

'And I'll smear pork fat on the stairs.'

They looked at each other: *could easily be done.*

'He'll bring himself undone,' said Molly, and Colma agreed. No one had said anything, but they all knew their days were numbered if Snakelegs took over. Surely Alathea Pocknall would arrive soon to claim her factory.

The girls increased their speed but their frenetic activity seemed to only break more thread and fill the factory with more noise and dust. At lunchtime, Snakelegs summoned them back to their machines early. They were on track to produce only two more corsets that day. 'You are useless. You MUST step up production!'

Suddenly a piercing scream cut above the machinery din. The girls rushed to the cutter, Sara, lying on the floor, wailing.

'It's Sara,' Colma cried. 'Her foot, her foot!'

Mr Addlar elbowed the girls aside and looked down. They had hitched her skirt up, and he saw her leg, soft and pink and draped by the trim of her petticoat, and a fine ankle in a canvas boot – and a pair of heavy cutting shears impaling her foot to the floorboards, one blade sliced through just above her toes. Around the entry point, the canvas of her boot darkened, the stain creeping out and blood pooling. He had a vision of her boot filling and overflowing. A sharp bitterness turned in him, the gruesomeness and the vivid reality of the foot and scissors, ludicrous, bloodied and shocking. He reeled back, his head colliding with Sara's head as he righted himself. The girls looked at him, aghast.

'It's stuck,' Molly said, and grabbed the shears with both her hands. She pulled, surprised at just how stuck it was, how the scissors felt bolted to the floorboards. The girls holding Sara sagged under the dead weight of her.

'You'll have to be the one to pull it,' Molly said to Snakelegs. 'You're meant to have more strength, pull it while she's fainted, she won't feel it.'

Mr Addlar registered that they were all looking at him, those girls, ruddy and damp, pungent bodies under all those skirts. Sara groaned, and someone nudged him. He should do something, but felt weak, nauseous.

He reached down, grabbed the handles of the shears, his hands slippery with sweat, and pulled. The blade moved but didn't come free. Sara moaned again. 'Wriggle it!' It was her again, Dunnage. He wrenched the shears back and forth, and the girl went stiff with pain and yawped, then went limp again, her head lolling back and her mouth open. He jerked the bloody blade back and forth, back and forth with every bit of his effort, and the shears were like a knife in a moist, rare roast, blood oozing. Finally the thing came loose, and her foot was free from the floor, dripping thick blood, though the shears remained firmly through her foot.

Then she was gone, carried away by the humid girls in their thick skirts, and the air was cooler and Mr Addlar felt a breeze and his sticky hand going stiff as the warm, disgusting blood on it cooled. He straightened up, feeling light-headed, his forehead running with sweat, and as he put his hand into his pocket for a handkerchief, a watery weakness swept through him. He took a deep breath, willed himself to stay steady and started to walk, holding the machinery tables and leaning while around him the factory seemed to retreat.

The sound woke him, the bounce of hard footfalls on timber. He saw fluff and thread ground between the worn floorboards, and his bones in his thin body pressed his skin against the hard surface. Every loud footstep thudded in his head, which felt hollow. Inches away, a red-soaked scrap of white cotton smiled at him, and he tasted blood, sweet metallic in his mouth. He understood that he was front down on the floor but was confused as to how he got there.

'You fainted.'

The hem of a skirt circled away over the floor, the cotton flock and thread dancing in tiny whirlwinds at its hem. The Dunnage girl. He felt humiliated, and sick, his body full of something acrid.

Mr Addlar hauled himself to a sitting position, straightened his hair and waistcoat, and looked at his watch, which felt heavy in his clammy hand. Around him the girls were back at their machines, shutting them down, putting the covers on, their backs to him, walking towards the door. Outside the sun shone. No one was looking at him; they'd have let him die there. The injured girl was nowhere to be seen. Then he felt small, stupid, a grown man sitting on his bottom on the floor.

Mr Addlar went to Mr Pocknall's private bathroom and sat for a very long time on the toilet, his hands shaking and his knees juddering while the girls shuffled out, chatting and giggling.

Molly slowly made her way home, threading her way along the streets of low, dark cottages, chimney smoke and dusk gloom, the kids playing cricket with fence palings and newspaper balls, others pushing fruit-box billycarts, women in their house coats standing at their gates, grubby toddlers at their skirts. She was oblivious to all of this and the rotting gutters, instead creating in her mind the undergarments she would make and the life she would have in Paris when Alathea summoned her. She smiled at the thought of Mrs Blinkhorn seeing her name in the newspaper, Mrs Sidebottom speechless with envy watching them load their possessions onto a wagon to move to a better suburb. But what remained was the shocking day. She felt more uneasy than she ever had.

On the corner of Nicholson and Newry streets, she looked up before she crossed the wide road and noted a tall fair man in a slightly dated suit watching for a tram to roll down Nicholson. He had his coat pushed back, one hand in his pocket and the other holding a pipe, his hat tilted and his legs wide apart. When the tram loomed over the incline to the north, the man did not move to hail it. Instead he turned and looked at Molly. It was the choir secretary, Evan Pettyman. She proceeded across the street, and he fell into step beside her while behind them the tram rattled past.

'Miss Molly Dunnage, fancy . . .'

She said nothing.

'I've noticed you've been absent from choir rehearsal.' His demeanour was bolder than at choir.

'I've been busy spending the stolen petty cash.'

'There is no evidence anyone broke in. It was assumed Gladys was the culprit.'

She stopped in outrage. 'Gladys is not a thief, nor is she a liar. I think you, or someone at your music soirees, did something to Gladys to upset her.'

He became serious, and sincere. 'I'm sorry you think so. We found her a friendly and lovely girl.'

'So I am not friendly.' She hastened her gait and he his. 'And you don't approve of me.'

'I always liked you, and I think you have a lovely voice, truly I do, and I think you should be in the choir, you should do solos.'

Amazed, she asked, 'Then why wasn't I given a solo?'

She was quite cross, his approach hadn't started well. 'It's not entirely up to me.'

Molly picked up her pace again and again he hurried along beside her – Aunt April would say he had gall. The path was slippery with autumn leaves under her boots and the branches above them bare.

'But I can help you. I can invest in your ideas. I can get capital, and I will guide you in your business venture.'

They were at the edge of Curtain Square. She stopped and confronted him. 'I haven't the faintest idea what you're talking about.'

Evan clapped triumphantly. 'I rest my case. I'll explain. Mrs Blinkhorn mentioned' – he imitated her high, queenly voice – 'that you are a very good seamstress, and that you are starting an enterprise that involves undergarments for ladies . . . like Alathea Pocknall and Miss Lily Pert.'

'*Dame* Lily Pert, and Mrs Blinkhorn has no right to be proprietary about my life.'

'She also said it was a pity to lose you since you are so cheap.'

She stopped. 'How dare you!'

'I agree, she's an appalling woman. I can help you charge what you deserve. It does no good to undercharge for your skills.'

'Why are you so interested in ladies' underwear?'

'For the same reasons every other manufacturer, wholesaler and retailer of ladies' undergarments is – to build a profitable business. I hear you are designing an invention to allow upper body freedom as well as support. I would like to be part of it – so to speak.'

'I already have some interest.'

'So I hear, but I'm just the chap you and Miss Pocknall need. I've had experience at Melbourne's leading glove shop, which provides accessories to Queen Mary.'

She looked at him doubtfully. 'The Queen sends to Melbourne for gloves?'

'We sold gloves to Queen Mary, yes.'

She held his gaze. 'A queen would never go into a *shop*.'

'Oh, 'alright, you have caught me out trying to impress you. She sent one of her ladies in waiting while the royals were on tour of Australia.'

'That was in 1901, thirteen years ago. It's a fairly tenuous claim.'

'But it remains that at least I have a claim.'

'As do I,' said Molly, triumphantly. 'And mine's bigger. Mrs Blinkhorn is correct, I am currently commissioned to both Alathea Pocknall and Dame Lily Pert and I am designing new undergarments. I'm going into the corsetiere business.'

If she had been looking, if she had not turned to march away from him, she would have seen Evan Pettyman lick his lips with his quick, pointy tongue.

'Well, it's a pity about Miss Pocknall's prospects, then.'

'What's a pity?'

'The Pocknall empire – it's not really an empire anymore, is it? Since Mr Pocknall died in such disgraceful circumstances?'

'Are they bankrupt?'

'Look, bankruptcy is mere incompetence. I meant the way he died.'

He stopped just outside the Sidebottoms' house. '*Please*. Listen to me, I have an idea.'

Molly glanced at her house. She didn't want her aunt to see her talking to a man, but perhaps this could be a chance to help Alathea, get herself a career. She stopped.

'Miss Molly, my mother is looking to invest in something worthy, something to improve life for the common woman.'

'Just as many men are common as are women, Mr Pettyman.'

'Certainly. You're a spirited woman, which isn't at all common . . . but females are common, they're everywhere.' He laughed at his joke.

'Which makes men even more common.'

His smile fell. 'Look –'

'You keep saying that, *Look*. I won't *look*, or *listen*, or anything else you command of me.'

He held her arm, but she wrenched it away. He held his palms out to her. 'I am sorry –'

'I have a friend who is a policeman.'

'So do I. What is your friend's name?'

'Constable Horatio Farrat.'

'*Constable* Farrat.'

She marched off and he followed. 'Would you mind considering, please, that I could finance some part of the enterprise you are broaching with your friend Alathea Pocknall. That factory needs to be put to better use, make it pay for itself, and us. If you could introduce me to Miss Pocknall?'

'Good day, Mr Pettyman.' Molly marched on.

As she shut the gate, he called, 'At least mention my proposal to her, please. You won't get anyone else to support your dream. Think about it. Paris?'

Gladys must have told him about their school-day dreams of Paris.

He dropped his card in their letterbox and walked away whistling, but was distracted by Mrs Sidebottom's posters.

AT 20 A COQUETTE, AT 40 NOT
MARRIED YET, A SUFFRAGETTE.

WHAT IS A SUFFRAGETTE WITHOUT
A SUFFERING HOUSEHOLD?

Molly removed her hat and coat, excited at the idea of her Parisian dream, but wary. What did Evan Pettyman really want?

It took her a heartbeat to notice her father sitting on his stool, his pallor the same dull beige as his surroundings. He was breathing hard, his mouth open and his hands resting between the paint pots and brushes on his table.

Molly looked at his cart, stacked high with carefully packaged crockery, fresh from the kiln. 'Dad, don't do that again. I will fetch the cart and I will take your greenware for firing. Next time, I will come with you, or we will get a cab.'

Her father shook his head. 'It's good exercise.'

His lips were tinged blue, but not from paint.

He unwrapped the fish plate and showed it to Molly, his hand shaking as he held it up, and then he showed her another, a very big smile on his face. It was for the Ornithological Society, a gift that they presented each year for the best photograph of a bird. As commissioned, August had painted an owl.

'Oh my goodness, it's exceptional, Dad.'

'They asked for an owl, but what's one to do with a big cream-coloured face, small beak and brown or grey feathers? So I made it interesting.'

It was a powerful owl in flight, its formidable yellow legs and menacing talons lowered for landing, the branch just visible on the lip of the plate. Its undercarriage was pale with dark grey chevrons and, above, its brown and yellow-edged wings were aerodynamically astute, bent in soft right angles, the feathers symmetrical and tortoiseshell patterned and configured to brake. Molly looked directly into the raptor's black pupils ringed by intense golden orbs, the huge eyes bordered by dark brown plumage, like a mask. Its most acute feature was a gaping bill, hooked and razor sharp, set for tearing flesh. It was beautifully depicted, each feather life-like, as though every single barbule on the vane of the feather had been individually painted with a two-hair brush, the colour of each barb transforming according to the hue of the feather, brown to grey, beige to yellow, from its tip to the rachis.

'It looks like it's about to snatch my hat and fly away!'

'That's the response I most wanted to hear.'

He held a dinner plate for Molly to admire. He'd painted an entire family on it, most of them with ears like wing nuts.

'Where's Aunt?'

'Trapping leeches. She thinks they'll help my blood.'

'You need to rest, Dad.'

'No rest for the talented.' He held a plate up, replacing his face with a bucktooth boy and his equally toothy brother, the same prominent ears and freckles.

While Molly peeled vegetables, she thought of Mr Addlar curved like a snake on the floor, one side of her mouth very nearly turning up to smile.

Aunt April returned, rocking on her bad hips and triumphant from her hunt. After a while April called for more newspaper, which Molly reluctantly delivered. Her father lay in bed with his arm extended over a blood-spotted page of *The Argus*, bulging black and green striped leeches hanging off it. Beside him Aunt April nursed a dish of the creatures, shiny and wet. She pinched some salt in her fingers and tossed it at her brother's arm and the leeches plopped onto the newspaper, curling, leaking red fluid. She rolled it up and gave it to Molly. 'Scrape these into a pond in the yard, will you?' August closed his eyes and looked away.

Molly shoved the newspaper into the stove fire and threw a little kerosene in. Then she went to her room, found her savings, peeled off two pounds, and gave it to her aunt. 'Please take him to the doctor again.'

'He'll say what he always does: rest, fresh air and good food.'

'Well, go to the country! Dad, let Aunt take you to the swamps and creeks of bucolic Yaambul!'

'I don't want to go, the train is arduous, you and April would have to carry my luggage, and the hotel has too many stairs. And there are flies.'

'There are more flies in our yard than anywhere else in Australia.'

'It's a struggle I do not need. You go, leave me in perfect peace and quiet.'

Molly's unease rose and she recognised that something foreboding lurked at the back of her mind. Her father's health?

Chapter 15

SHE WAS A little late but when Molly arrived at the easel next to him, Constable Farrat put his hand on her shoulder. 'So happy to see you.' Molly felt herself blush. She doubted anyone had ever said that to her in her life, not even Gladys. This week, the buttons on Horatio's smock were brown and his tie a yellow tartan.

They stared at the satin-covered easel, intrigued to know what Mr King would reveal. This week it was not a painting, but two statements:

> *'Everything has its beauty, but not everyone sees it.'*
> *Confucius*

> *'The aim of art is to represent not the outward*
> *appearance of things, but their inward significance.'*
> *Aristotle*

And there was also a child.

'This is my son, Oscar,' said Mr King.

The boy smiled and said hello.

'I want you to sketch this child without depicting what he looks like. That is, you cannot portray my boy's physical presence. I want you to present the essence of what it is about him that appeals to you, the essence of what you see in this human. Son, what did your namesake say?'

The boy gathered himself to deliver a rehearsed speech.

'Oscar Wilde said that no great artist ever sees things as they really are and if he did he would stop being an artist.'

'And so, we have three conflicting philosophies. Think about what you agree with and depict it in your drawing.'

The class considered the boy, guessed he was twelve years old or thereabouts, noted his large dark eyes and his smooth and generous face. His expression was confident but self-conscious and, like his father, he was well groomed, though he kept his fists shoved into his pockets.

Some people drew very sweet rabbits, or a bat and ball, someone drew knees with bandages, a fishing line, the rear view of a lad in a school uniform, an old man in a wheelchair. Molly drew a man orating from a beach to a setting sun on the horizon of an empty ocean – no swimmers, ship, whales, just the man saying 'nothing nothing nothing'. Horatio looked at it and said, 'Bleak, Molly,' and showed her his landscape of hills, valleys, deserts and oceans, storm clouds and jungles, with a very long winding road meandering to a far horizon where a sun set.

At the end of the class, after they had revealed the motivation or intention of their depiction, Mr King said, 'Think about what you have heard but most particularly what you have said. Consider what it is in you that makes you see that particular boy the way you do, consider your attitude to life and ask yourself what it is in your culture, the home of your interpretations, that makes it different to that of the person next to you.'

'Shame Mrs Wrench isn't here to heed that,' Horatio said.

As they waited for August to arrive, Horatio asked Molly what it was in her culture that made her depict such emptiness.

'I am too cynical, but that might be because of my gender and economic situation. What about you?'

Horatio said his sketch was both too literal and prosaic. They both confessed they would have to give more thought to what Mr King had asked of them.

'But on the subject of different people to ourselves,' Molly said, 'what do you know about the circumstances around the death of Emrys Pocknall?'

Horatio said, 'Tsk,' and rolled his eyes. 'Scandalous.'

'Tell me, please.'

'Gracious, there's at least one man found dead every week in the Lonsdale Street precinct! He was with a woman of ill repute.'

So, it was true. Poor Alathea, but she felt sad for herself, mostly. 'I'm afraid my future's scuttled again.'

'So is his.'

'Was he murdered?'

'Heavens no! It's always a heart attack. It'll be in the newspapers.'

Aunt April came rocking to them through the fog, heavily coated, a chunky shawl about her shoulders, her curls haloed in the streetlight.

'Good heavens,' said Horatio, 'what on earth is this?'

'It's a dear aunt.' She smiled. 'A woman of earthly passions, a polymath of decay, eternally hopeful, worn of hip and sore of knee.'

'Hello,' she said, her gapped teeth obvious even in the dim lamplight.

'It's my great pleasure to meet you, Miss Dunnage.'

'Your mother makes marvellous hats. I once suggested Molly work for her.'

Horatio's hands went to his cheeks. 'That would have been wonderful!'

'Hindsight,' said Molly, and sighed, though hats were going the way of corsets, she suspected.

They found the factory door shut again. 'Oh God. Sara is dead,' said Daisy.

But Colma retorted, 'I'd pray old Snakelegs is the dead person if I was you,' and they laughed at the thought of him passed out on the factory floor.

Molly's sense of foreboding told her the doors were locked

because Mr Addlar liked keeping them outside in the cold. When he finally opened the doors, he blocked the entrance to deliver a lecture on productivity.

As the day went on, the weather turned even colder and more bleak, the rain coming in through the factory door in sideways sheets. Around Molly the girls did not speak. They kept their eyes to their work, toiling solidly, evenly, consistently as they always had – it was apparent everyone was united in their quiet opposition, their passive aggression, their refusal to risk injury.

She was threading baleen into boning channels when the carriage arrived outside, a single seater with a hood and lamps, sparkling axles and hickory spokes, and a shaft that gleamed. Alathea jumped down from the buggy and strode into the factory. The cotton-reel boy could not take his eyes from her. She was wearing culottes.

Molly's hopes rallied again, but every girl in that factory suspected Alathea Pocknall had already encountered great resistance from her cousin and the board, and would continue to do so. Molly went back to her torsos, moving along the row, inserting the bone and checking laces. She turned to give her stack of corsets to the machinists and found Alathea behind her.

'We are all very sorry that you've lost your father, he was a good boss.'

'Thank you, but oh, Molly Dunnage, you are a sight for sore eyes. Come with me.'

Molly grabbed her bag and followed. Alathea locked the office door behind them and the sound of the factory dulled. Her hair was piled on her head and a sapphire hair brooch glinted from its soft curls, but she seemed shaken.

'You didn't get my note?'

'No.'

She lifted her chin and squared her shoulders. 'I am betrayed, by Therese. She'd never liked being a maid but I couldn't let her go to the kitchen. Cook hated her. And she didn't take to my friends at all, especially Marguerite. I failed to heed it, silly me . . . It's a complicated and brutal story and I will not bother you with the details, but my arrogance has come back to bite me. Molly, please, I'd like to see my new underwear.'

'I've got it! I bring it every day.' Molly held up the bag, extracted the corset and laid it on the table.

Alathea held it up and smiled. 'It's perfect.' Molly gave her some lacy bloomers and a matching slip, which also thrilled Alathea, but there was something else on her mind.

'My father's will is clear, this factory is to go to me. Though others believe differently.' She shimmered with tension and spoke as if she was talking to herself. 'My father also told me that my cousin once threw out a pencil because he didn't know how to sharpen it. Ignorance is enemy only to its owner.'

'I've seen your cousin and fiancé with their ledgers in the office.'

Alathea came across the room quickly and held Molly's forearm. '*My* ledgers.' Alathea turned again to her new lingerie, and held up the corset. 'I know this will suit my gowns, and I know it will be snug, comfortable.' She held it against her and raised an arm, observing how low it was around her side. She bent down, kicked her legs and smiled. 'The hooks and eyes are marvellous. These would sell like hot cakes, Molly.'

Then she was distracted again, worried, and Molly wondered whether she should mention Mr Pettyman. She wasn't sure of the man but didn't want to be responsible for denying Alathea – or herself – a chance at a future.

'You saw Lily?' Alathea suddenly asked.

'I did but I haven't heard since,' Molly replied.

'You will. Like most of us, she is under siege, but she is brave. We must stand up for ourselves. My dream is that one day I will run this place the way I want, but there are complications, some personal, some of them financial.'

Molly decided to be brave. 'As a matter of fact, a man has approached me. He has a business proposition.' Alathea's blue eyes lit up, so Molly gave her Mr Pettyman's card. 'Mr Evan Pettyman and his mother . . . They see an opportunity to help you, so they say.'

Alathea looked at the card and smiled at Molly. As she opened the door, she said, 'I seem to be always thanking you, Molly Dunnage.'

Molly swung her bag as she walked home, her hopes rising, and then falling again when she thought of Norbert Poke and Mr Addlar. They rose again when she saw the envelope leaning against the sugar bowl on the kitchen table. Miss Dame Lily Pert's large pink wax seal secured it, and Molly's immediate future.

Penina had written a brief note on a small square card with Dame Lily's insignia across the top.

Dear Molly, Dame Lily will see you Sunday morning at 11 am.

Again, a new future was almost certain.

Chapter 16

IT WAS EARLY, and despite the cold dark morning August delivered a cup of tea to his sister in her bed then continued on out the front door to find a newspaper. He was overtaken by his daughter, though. 'I'll get one, Dad.' She rushed across the park, her boots still unlaced and her skirt held high above the dew.

His sister rose for the day and as she lowered eggs into a pot on the stove – the chooks had been generous of late – August set about slicing bread for toast. It was time he made another loaf.

Molly returned, newspaper in hand. 'Parliament is dissolved. Another election is called for the fifth of September.' She handed the paper to her father.

'My word,' said April, and had to sit down. She thumped her fist on the table. 'This time, we will see Vida in federal parliament. I'll go to the Book Lovers' Library, they'll be planning a campaign.'

August read a headline: '*Suspicious circumstances surround the sudden death of Emrys Pocknall, Manufacturer.*'

Emrys Pocknall had not 'suffered death' while at home, as reported, but had died earlier at a premises on Little Lonsdale Street, Melbourne. He was in companionship at the time with an employee of the premises, Miss Betty Peddle, a renowned courtesan or demimondaine, whose photograph appeared 'kindly supplied by Miss Peddle herself'.

Molly took the offered page from her father and read aloud, '*Proceedings revealed that a cab was called to the premises in Little Lonsdale Street where two men carried a man, seemingly unconscious,*' *to the carriage. Mr Jonah Tusk, employed by the Little Lonsdale Street establishment for maintenance and security purposes, gained the help of an anonymous passer-by to carry Mr Pocknall to the cab. Mr Tusk had located the billfold of Mr Pocknall earlier to give payment to Miss Elizabeth Peddle, who uses the name "Betty". Mr Tusk paid the fare and gave the address of Mr Emrys Pocknall. The cab driver, a man of many years' experience, declared that he thought the victim was drunk, "or drugged for the purposes of having his wallet stolen".*

On arrival at the address provided, the driver could not rouse him, so summoned a male relative, Mr Norbert Poke, who then fetched the gardener. It was not until Mr Pocknall was positioned on the sitting room couch that it was noticed that he was dead. Mr Pocknall is survived by his daughter, Miss Alathea Pocknall, and nephew, Mr Norbert Poke. His wife Juanita perished aboard the Titanic *in 1912.'*

'Sad for Alathea if her fiancé abandons her because of the scandal,' said Aunt April, 'or perhaps not . . .'

With the wireless stealing customers, more and more photographs were appearing in newspapers. Betty Peddle was a Rubenesque girl. She was draped in necklaces and attempting to look fetching in bloomers, corset and lacy garters. She had monkfish eyes, small and close set, and her teeth crowded.

'Holy mackerel,' said Molly.

Aunt April put her magnifying glasses on and studied the photograph of Betty Peddle. 'Well, I don't imagine Mr Pocknall was interested in her face.'

There was a moment in the kitchen when Aunt April's comment hung, and then vanished. Molly hid her grin under her hand. August just rubbed his cold shins and said, 'My guess is that Alathea will do her best to keep her factory and her marriage.'

'I hope so, no one will hire me after this front-page news, and if I do get another job I'll probably start off on torsos again. I remain a slave to exploitation and torture,' Molly said bleakly.

'Daughter, such attitude.'

'I'm a girl from Carlton so I can't excel and prosper. I am sunk.'

'You have always been a strong swimmer,' said August, and Molly thought of Yaambul again, and the summer days jumping into the friendly creek from a branch of a rivergum. It would be so much easier to live there, better for everyone. Her father was ill, yet smiling and hopeful, and her aunt looked kempt but not polished, not finessed. There was never any money for beauty products or fine clothing.

'Are you both quite content here, or are you pretending?' Molly asked.

There was a pause, one of those pauses in which her father and aunt communicated telepathically.

'We made a pact with life,' said Aunt April. 'We agreed not to accommodate or harbour hate and resentment.'

'Myrtle wouldn't have wanted that.' Her father rescued the eggs, probably boiled brick hard by now, firelight dancing on his face, and Molly saw his expression move from sad, miserable defeat back to pleasant. She lived her life entirely without a mother, but she knew her father moved about the house with his wife, that she went with him for the paper and was as present in his life as the hair on his head.

Aunt April explained, 'Your mother was strong, Molly, but gentle, and she knew that bitterness lasts for generations. It's passed down like the chromosome theory of heredity. Hate threatens and clouds everything. Just look at Mrs Sidebottom. Grief can be a ghost, or a shameful family secret, a mad ancestor in an insane asylum.'

'We made a decision, daughter, about our attitude, like a lot of others. We would do the best we could with what we had. And it has had the effect of making my sister and me authentically happy.'

Aunt April poked another newspaper log into the stove. 'You are all we have, and we agreed that we would work to see you had the best life we could provide. We would have liked to be more worldly –'

'But you are.'

'We were naive,' said Aunt April. 'Our pact didn't factor in life's skirmishes. We didn't anticipate your father's ill health nor did we account for creeping poverty.'

With genuine encouragement, August said, 'Optimism lures us through, you never know, that's the thing . . . you might yet finish the job your mother and aunt started, revolutionising women's lives.'

'Yes,' said Aunt April, quoting from a sonnet by Bella Lavender to Emmeline Pankhurst, '"The cause of women's freedom, once begun, Must grow in radiance, like the rising sun".'

Molly was sure she wasn't growing in radiance, knowing she couldn't change the world. She wasn't even able to change her own life, and that truth felt heavier than it ever had.

'It is you, dear girl, who provides us with meaning, the need for hope. Our lives are about family, love and hope,' Aunt April said.

But Molly wished they could live it with a bit more comfort – at the very least another light in the house. She'd also like a wall with a door to her room, and fewer draughts whistling through.

Just then, with the words *hope, love* and *family* hanging in the room, there was a ruckus next door, a door slammed, and Edna, Mrs Sidebottom's new help, called, 'YOU CAN BUGGER OFF, YOU OLD HAG.'

The Dunnages rose as one and hurried to the street.

Edna tore off her apron and threw it at Mrs Sidebottom. 'I'm not working all bloody day on an empty stomach. I should be allowed to sit down to eat my bread.'

Mrs Sidebottom, standing on the footpath, a wet towel in her hand, said, 'You are an ugly ungrateful girl.'

Edna cried, 'And you look like something a wombat shitted out,' and ran towards Nicholson Street. Because Edna had no teeth, the word came out as 'hitted'.

Mrs Sidebottom was nonplussed, so Molly explained, 'Wombat poo is big and square and it stinks.'

Mrs Sidebottom seemed exhausted, and merely said to August, 'I'll have another dozen eggs if you've got them, please.'

'Right you are,' said August.

Chapter 17

On her way to work, Molly edited the sign in Mrs Bigbottom's front yard.

Women's Potential is in the Home.

Men declare that Women's Potential
is imprisoned in the Home.

Alathea Pocknall, resplendent again in a trousers-skirt and knee-length dust coat, met the girls as they arrived. 'Stop for tea and lunch when it's time, I won't ring any bells.'

So the girls went to their stations and worked. They all stopped for morning tea at the same time and Miss Pocknall joined them, sitting gingerly on the low retaining wall with them in her blue lace blouse with a ruby, emerald and pearl bar brooch pinned to her Prussian collar. The girls looked at her as they would a princess.

'I'll have a cafeteria built as soon as I can. And I suggest you organise a rotating roster so that you are not always stuck at the same task in the same shift.' They were happily discussing the changes when a motor vehicle clattered to a halt at the gate. Behind it, a phaeton parked to the side of the dispatch yard. Cousin Norbert Poke, dressed in a black and white houndstooth suit, his waistcoat striped, jumped down from the carriage and joined the posse of drab men who'd alighted from the motor vehicle.

'If only he spent as much time on his personality as he did pickin' out his waistcoat,' Colma observed.

Mr Addlar emerged from his indent by the clock and bell, grinning – a first as far as anyone could remember.

'They are lawyers,' said Alathea, 'and the board.' She lifted her overskirt and ran, bounding up the stairs two at a time.

Mr Addlar ran to welcome the men but they headed straight to the office in a cloud of trailing pipe smoke, ignoring him. He turned to the workers and hissed, 'Back to work.'

They ambled to their places, their eyes still on the shimmering shape of Alathea through the Florentine louvres.

The American called, 'It's no use, cousin, your cause is lost. I have legal documents declaring that you're unfit.'

'For anything,' squealed Mr Addlar.

Behind the office door, Alathea could smell them, corpulent men with crusty moustaches and wool suits infused with stale pipe smoke and sweat. She bullied an armchair to block the door, grabbed an umbrella and climbed onto the desk.

On the other side of the door, the legal men in their strained waistcoats and silly wigwam towers rallied. They applied their soft bulk to the door. 'One, two, three, heave!' They tumbled, tripping each other, yelping, circling and rubbing the pain from their arms and shoulders.

Alathea watched the door. It creaked but held fast. A general rumbling told her they were regrouping. They tried again, but the door held.

Suddenly she saw a flash of looming dark, a ramming pole, and then louvres smashed and a spray of glass splinters confettied the room. Beyond the destruction, Mr Addlar stood holding a hat stand, smiling. His teeth were small, grey and gapped.

In the quiet, someone said, 'That's the ticket,' and they selected the smallest board member and lifted him through the shattered glass. Alathea swung her umbrella but he slid beneath it to open the door.

She was surrounded.

'You must leave,' said Mr Addlar.

'Get out of my office!' she cried back.

'You are fired,' someone called.

The man next to him said, 'She was never hired,' and they sniggered.

Cousin Norbert demanded her copy of her father's last will and testament. 'I know you stole it from the safe.'

Alathea smiled. 'Mr Addlar will open the safe for you.'

But Mr Addlar looked at Norbert Poke. 'I don't have the code.'

'Oh? Snakelegs doesn't have a code? Then perhaps my cousin Norbert Poke was trusted with the code?'

Norbert shrugged.

'Oh, so neither of you was trusted?'

'Do *you* know the code?'

'Yes, my penniless, grasping cousin from America, I do.'

He held out his hand. Alathea tapped it lightly with her umbrella. 'Thank you, but I don't need a hand to get down. *I'm* quite agile.'

The men started upending drawers and pulling documents from cupboards. Others focused on the safe lock. They badgered and harangued Alathea, and when they could not find a last will and testament or a safe code, they grabbed her, the rancid pack wrenching her down from the desk by her clothing. They carried her, like a corpse from a battlefield, down the stairs, the skirt of her culottes dragging and her hair falling free. On the factory floor they sat her on the ground and left her. The cotton-reel boy, shocked at the men for treating Miss Pocknall so horribly, ran and got her buggy for her.

Though he snarled and spat, the girls did not obey Snakelegs. Instead they rushed to Alathea. She felt them dab her little cuts with cotton and they scooped her hair up and retrieved her hat. Molly pushed the hatpin in and they stroked her hand and rubbed her back and helped her stand, making mewling noises and saying, 'Shush now, pet,' and 'You go on home now and have yourself a sherry.'

Molly cried loudly, 'They have no right . . . they are BIGOTS.'

The girls helped her into her buggy and Alathea Pocknall left, her hand on her hat and her horse moving carefully. Some of the girls sat crying at their workbenches; others filed out of the factory, leaving their smocks over their machines.

As Molly rounded the corner to Curtain Square, fuelled by indignant fury, she was pulled up by the sight of Alathea's fine buggy parked outside Mrs Sidebottom's. Alathea stood next to her chestnut horse with her hand on the mare's neck. Her hat was askew, and she was white with hurt, humiliation and fury. She sensed Molly's presence and composed herself.

'They are brutes,' Molly said by way of greeting.

'My cousin says my father was irresponsible and that I have no capacity to run a business.' Alathea was trembling. 'He says the accounts show that the business will fold, the factory will close.'

'But the factory is yours.'

'It is mine, yes, but if I don't give them control then they will take me to court. I won't give in, I have some money from my mother, but I won't waste it on lawyers. I am a woman, a verdict against me is inevitable.' She stopped, looking at Molly. 'Norbert threatens to use the lingerie you made as evidence of my "moral turpitude", as the Americans call it.'

'Some men commit moral turpitude every day.' Molly remembered Emrys Pocknall's death and was mortified that she had spoken.

Alathea became quite focused. She turned to Molly abruptly. 'Where is your house?'

Molly pointed Alathea towards her house, and she was captured by Mrs Sidebottom's signs:

Molly

LIPS THAT TOUCH LIQUOR SHALL NOT TOUCH OURS.

LOYALTY TO THE THRONE. COUNTERACT SOCIALISM.

A big arrow pointed to the Dunnage house.

'Oh? We're socialists, I hadn't been told until now.'

Alathea grinned.

'Leave your carriage here. Mrs Sidebottom likes horses.'

They secured the chestnut mare and made their way to the warped house snug behind trees and posters. Mercifully, Aunt April's door was shut, a sign that she was out. Molly set about making tea. Alathea removed her gloves and placed her bent hat on Molly's organised but cluttered sewing table. She stared at Dame Lily's huge corset on the table. Molly showed her the wash house to wash and fix her hair, and handed her a clean towel.

Alathea was drawn into the backyard and Molly watched her stand in wonder and move towards August's studio. She stopped along the way to observe Aunt April's stagnating puddles, the compost heap, the vegetables and fruit trees crowding together, and stepped lightly around the ballooning fungi. What an adventure she was having!

Molly thought she saw her father almost bow, a dishevelled vision standing in the chaos of his filthy studio.

'Are you wearing Prussian blue?'

'I am. My name is Alathea Pocknall.'

'Mine's August Dunnage. Happy to meet you.'

'I like your dodos.'

'Bringing them back from extinction,' he joked.

'Good for you,' she said. 'Where can I find them?'

'Crockery shop in Rathdowne Street.'

Aunt April arrived home with a loaf of fruit bread and cheap day-old cream to churn for butter and smiled at the elegant and statuesque woman chatting with her brother.

'Is that Athena your father's chatting to?'

'Alathea, though she'd rather be Nike.'

When the kettle boiled and the tea was drawing, Alathea and August came inside. Alathea plonked down at the kitchen table and sighed. She chatted with the plump-faced older woman measled by badges and slashed with sashes praising Vida Goldstein and told August she thought the crockery section at the big new Myer store would like his creations, adding that she would, '. . . have a word next time I'm there.'

Aunt April mentioned the recent sinking of the *Empress of Ireland* and how awful it must have been for Alathea, who'd lost her mother in the *Titanic* only two years prior.

Alathea looked away. 'She was home in America a great deal of the time . . . but yes, such a loss of life, a thousand people. Poor Mother.'

'Almost four thousand people between both ships.'

'And more to come,' said Alathea, referring to the warring politicians in Europe. They looked at the floor and shook their heads, and Aunt April asked if Alathea would like to observe a war of another kind.

'I think not,' Molly started but Alathea was on her feet and following Aunt April to her room to see some *Campylobacter* microbes wiggling about on a square of glass under the microscope.

'They're very busy,' she said, turning from the table, littered and messy, to the petri dishes and festering jars on top of the bookshelf.

'They'll be dead soon. I'll take a trip to a swamp and replenish stock.'

'How interesting,' Alathea said, sincerely, and quickly led the way back to the kitchen, where a draught provided fresher air. 'Such intriguing things going on in your small home,' she added, and everyone became conscious of their cramped, fetid surrounds.

Alathea tried to smooth the moment. 'Including Molly's lovely undergarments,' and she gestured at the atelier. 'I admire you all.'

She looked at her unweathered hands on the table before her, and Aunt April said, 'Drink up,' which Alathea did.

After tea, while she pinned on her hat, Alathea asked, 'Can I leave something here with you, can you hide it for me?'

'Yes,' said Molly. 'It is hardly the house a burglar would choose.'

'It's not a body, is it?' Aunt April laughed at her own joke.

Alathea said, 'It would be easier to find a spot for a corpse in my own garden.'

'If you have one I'll take a limb and observe its transmutation, if that's alright,' said Aunt April.

August nudged his sister. 'I think Miss Pocknall just wants to hide the murder weapon.'

'I'm keeping my weapon with me, you make it sound exciting and mysterious, but it's just an envelope.'

Molly suddenly said, 'I think you should play them at their own game, those men.'

August cautioned Molly with a 'tsk', but Alathea agreed. 'They think I am stupid, but my father taught me a lot about the world of business.' She drew on her gloves and said, wearily, 'It's greed.' She looked at Molly. 'And to fight, I need to find a way to be at ease with all that comes from that.'

'There's a difference between justice and what is just,' Molly replied.

Alathea handed over an envelope, large and fat, and August said he had the perfect hiding place for it. They followed him to his library-cum-bedroom, where a jar of leeches sat on his bedside stack of books, and he removed the skirting board and brought out a tin cash box containing an old fob watch. He placed the envelope inside. 'I used to hide my savings there – when I had savings. The watch was my father's, but it is broken.'

The neighbours – men, women and children – were admiring Alathea's immaculate buggy waiting in their somewhat unkempt street. On the front veranda, Mrs Sidebottom watched the Dunnages emerge from their hovel with elegant Alathea, who ignored everyone, climbed in, raised the step, gently closed the little door and thanked them. She drove away, her sleek chestnut dainty on its hooves and the slim wheels raising very thin dust. The horse had left quite a mess on Mrs Sidebottom's footpath.

Mrs Sidebottom called to April, 'You'd be wanting that manure.'

'I will respect the intentions of the horse.'

Chapter 18

MOLLY WOKE, AS she had for five years, her first thought of Pocknall's factory. It was another rainy day: water trickled from the umbrellas leaning by the door, and the factory smelled fusty and cold. It was like working between cold wet sheets.

Somehow Molly felt this was her last day at Pocknall's.

It started after morning tea. First the accountants arrived, then the sour board members gathered in the office, pipe smoke oozing out the door. Then Mr Addlar walked between the tables and machines, stopping first behind Molly at her torsos; he drew a cross on her smock with chalk. He moved along the tables, stopping to draw a cross on the older women and those who had spoken out in the past, those who had asked for time off, and those who had left early to take a parent to the doctor or to bury a grandparent. Then he stopped the machines and stood above them on the balcony outside the office. 'Those of you with a cross, leave now.'

'What about our pay?' Molly cried.

'You, Dunnage, get out of my factory now.'

She removed her smock.

'It was never your factory. You are a man who long ago reached his pinnacle . . . as a minion.'

'Leave before I throw you out.'

She folded her smock and draped it carefully over her machine. 'What about our pay?' she repeated.

He came down the stairs and eased up to her, but she stood her ground, looking into his awful eyes. His top lip twitched.

Molly didn't flinch. 'You owe us pay.'

He took her by the arm, his grip surprisingly tight. She resisted. He tugged. She held on to a torso. It fell, the line of scantily clad black plaster figures toppling like dominos.

She grabbed Snakelegs, her fingers around his skinny arm. 'You need to pay us.'

He tried to prise her from his arm but she clung on with her sewing fingers, her cutting, threading, tugging fingers. The girls left their machines and tables and came closer.

'You never understood that you're here merely to do management's bidding and you were chosen because you have no creativity or spirit, no soul.'

She saw nothing in his eyes, no flicker of anything, not even loathing. He just pushed with his body, swayed, tried to shake her off, but she stayed, danced with him, a slow, fierce waltz, entwined and foolish, pulling and shoving and their fingers digging into each other's flesh, their bodies resisting and wrestling backwards and forwards again and again, making their way towards the door, past the cart man, through the circle of girls and Eric the cotton-reel boy, willing her to hold strong. From the balcony, the board members looked down, not moving to help, amused. Mr Addlar could not give up, though he was short of breath and pink-cheeked, and his careful fringe unsettled across his creased brow.

The girls started yelling, 'OUR PAY, YOU NEED TO GIVE US OUR PAY.'

Molly called, 'You have mismanaged it, haven't you, Mr Addlar? You have lost it all? Is that why you're not paying?'

There was a rumbling from the men on the balcony.

He tried to summon the strength to propel her out into the rain but she held fast to his arm, his lapel, the skin on her fingers raw against his coat, so he tried again to shove, then drag, but she dug her heels in, pushed back, and he was weakened so she manoeuvred him through the water falling in sheets from the leaky guttering. He gasped from the cold, and still she clung. He could not scrape her from his jacket, and his fury became desperation, humiliation.

Molly's arms were tired, her hands pinching, but all her disappointments and letdowns, all her frustration and every slight, insult and sneer fuelled her grip, and they circled further out into the rain, slipping in the mud. His coat was sodden now, his fringe dripping stinging pomade into his eyes. And still, he could not scrape her from him. She would not give up, she would not be defeated, she'd had enough of defeat, setbacks and drawbacks and regrets.

'Let go!' he demanded.

'Never. I have always let go but I'm not going to anymore. I'm going to *plough on*, Mr Snakelegs, and you can just carry me to the gate like a corpse, like you did to Alathea Pocknall, like they will do to you as soon as you've done what you're told for them, finished their dirty work as you have always done.'

She felt him tense, saw his lips purse, his eyes fill with pomade tears. He levered back, mustering all his energy to headbutt her, she saw, so when he was far back, she let go, and he stumbled and fell to his knees, and the girls watched that horrid man kneeling in a gutter in the pouring rain, a small man, drenched as a wet rat and trying to gather enough strength to stand, trying not to topple into a puddle, and Molly Dunnage standing above him.

Her dress was hanging long, her curls sinking, and her blouse sodden, but she smiled at her co-workers standing at the door, at the rotting, draughty factory with its corrugated-iron walls and high windows, its leaking downpipes and drains full and sluggish water and a shallow lake pooling under its floorboards and seeping up, and the air foggy with damp cotton flock. Someone started clapping, and soon the applause was louder than the rain and the girls with crosses on their skirts came to her with her bag and coat and they laughed at Mr Addlar as he gasped for air, his suit ruined.

Molly said, 'You have succeeded at nothing, Mr Addlar, except dumb brutality and violence.'

Sara kicked him with her boots, steel-capped since her scissor injury. He yelped. The girls turned and walked away, arm in arm.

Molly branched away from the girls at the corner, turning to wave goodbye. She didn't want them to see her cry. Her odd little family was now without the income they needed so much, and she would have nowhere to go to, no daily escape walk, just a 'bedroom' out the back with the chooks. She would be trapped in the crowded home she shared with elderly people who would need her more and more as the years passed.

She had a good mind to burn the factory to the ground, let something better emerge from its ashes. She indulged in the image of the burning factory, beams and rafters collapsing and sparks ballooning, and in it all, a blackened man, Mr Addlar, thrashing around in pain, his flesh melting and his bones cracking, his skin crackling and spitting like bacon in hot lard. The image stopped her shaking and crying, her rage stilled, and she set about reasoning with the surges of anger, then feeling grubby but languishing in the bursts of joyousness.

Stopping at the cemetery, she sat on the grave of Cornelius O'Mahony, Gaelic scholar and Fenian, and rested her hand in the drizzle that pooled on the slab. Her hands were her best asset, along with her mind, her imagination and life force, and they would never take those from her.

She was swamped with joy, a sense of freedom. Nothing was fair, that was true, and people were selfish and callous. But she wasn't. Molly was clever and strong, she had not been defeated by Mr Addlar. She smiled, stood up in the rain, and headed home.

The Pocknall family solicitor, Mr Oliphant, was a cheerful man who winked and tilted his head at the same time. He used this friendly affection to say hello, farewell, to agree or disagree, compliment or obfuscate.

As a school chum of Emrys Pocknall, he'd helped him spend his wife's money to build a small empire, and, for her sake, he'd risked his reputation to save the rickety empire when insolvency threatened. And all because Charles Oliphant had fallen in love with Juanita Pocknall the minute he saw her. When he told her he loved her, she put her hand on his arm and said, 'Well, that is a great shame,' and turned away. It wasn't a flat refusal, he decided, and even now, he still loved her. And each time he saw Alathea, he thought for a moment Juanita had been helped into a *Titanic* life raft – (upper class) *women and children first* – and saved, after all.

Alathea had known Mr Oliphant as a personable and generous man her entire life, an unofficial godfather. She knew the trick to his door handle and how many steps there were to his office and could interpret his winks. He was tall and lean and slowly canny, and she enjoyed the smell of him – he did not smoke or cultivate a food and mucus trap under his nostrils – and through Mr Oliphant's knowing eyes she had learned the truth of her father.

Alathea was entirely at ease in his office, so after recapping events, her first question was, 'Can I do anything about their accusation of my "immoral behaviour"?'

'You say they only have underwear, no evidence of –'

'They've distorted my friendship with Marguerite. Can I sue for slander?'

'Those sorts of rumours stick, that is true, but if you sue for slander . . .' Mr Oliphant leaned forward in his chair. 'As a woman, should you pursue such an accusation in legal terms, your disingenuous fiancé would see a gauntlet and sue for breach of trust and intent to deceive and, as we know, he and your lurid cousin will find someone to say they saw something. You have not located Therese?'

She shook her head, her eyes downcast at the thought of Therese's betrayal. Alathea had been good to her, kept her on despite a resentful manner and forgetting her station. But two days prior, Alathea had found Therese's room empty, of everything – the bedlinen, the bedside lamp and wash bowl. She would no doubt sell them.

'There is a potential investor, a Mr Pettyman. Have you ever heard of him?'

'Never. I'll ask around.'

The lawyer sat back in his chair and looked right at her. He always made her feel *heard*, appreciated, and she knew he was about to tell her the true measure of things, and she in turn would tell him of her plan.

'I have no doubt you could run that place and do very well,' he started, ' . . . despite the "investors" and "advisors" that, as a woman, you'd likely have to endure.'

'I understand that, yes.'

'That said . . . *some* businesspeople happily succumb to unscrupulous investors, who, for example, gamble on the risks involved in investments. It sometimes gets these bad business-people out of trouble . . . they lose the lot, their debt as well.'

'On that note, there's something I'd like to mention to you. Just you.'

He winked; *something confidential.*

'My father told me many things.' Emrys Pocknall liked to share with his daughter gripping stories about inventive short-term investors who took advantage of changes in the financial market, and each other. She liked to hear those stories. They were always vivid tales with villains and goodies, coincidence, accident and deception. And there were heroes, naive fools who ultimately outsmarted entire companies and big banks, and there were also yarns about 'likeable baddies' who drew outsized returns on investments that were not sound. Her personal favourites were the tales about grandmothers who robbed banks and women who swindled their husbands, sometimes even their dastardly siblings, or perfectly lovely parents – every different variety of female rogue. Sometimes she'd ask him to repeat specific stories.

'There was a story my father told me about, an investor, Mr Vulture, who appeared to be sympathetic to a failing business carrying a lot of debt, he basically paid them an amount to reinvest and restructure, enough to gain control. He'd promised he'd save the company; management were against it, but he knew the owner was gullible, desperate to save the family company and against advice, she accepted the sympathetic investor's offer, even with the hefty interest rate he demanded. She insisted on a cheque made out to her lawyer, it wasn't much of a cheque, but more than Mr Vulture wanted to pay, though he was certain he'd get it back. But he underestimated Miss Wily.'

'The factory was worthless, of course, failing to meet the needs of the changing times?'

'Yes.'

'But Miss Wily could have manufactured something else, like uniforms, durable shirts, rucksacks, hospital gowns.'

'Yes, and many will make money from violence, but some believe it's wrong to profit from war over greed, power and real estate.'

'What if the ownership of the factory was . . . not strictly, legally, speaking, Miss Wily's?'

'That doesn't bother people like Mr Vulture. Those men don't care, they only see money, they don't think of consequences for anyone, even themselves, so if it went wrong he'd claim he was lied to, that he had no idea the sale wasn't legally binding . . . he was swindled by a conniving *female*. All he'd get from the legal profession is mercy and leniency.'

Mr Oliphant stood and looked out his window. A miserable geranium in a pot on the windowsill opposite would thrive if it had sunshine and rain.

'I don't mean to be rude, Mr Oliphant, but the courts are notoriously slow . . . and in my case, the axe handle in the spokes is that my contesters can't find the will, deeds or title, so it will take a long time before any progress is made and it will be slow progress at that.'

He turned to her, and winked very slowly. 'Quite, the process of contesting a will is cumbersome, it takes time to amass all official documentation around the business, especially if some of it can't be found, and so this is often seen as an advantage to *keen* investors, the Mr Vultures of the world.' Mr Oliphant sat down again. 'I'm about to retire, so I won't be around to see what happens in the end.'

'Quite, you won't know the truth of it unless I tell you, but that said, if things don't look like they'll go as I anticipate, I'll settle quietly out of court . . .'

He waved her words away. 'Even the best lawyers are sometimes bamboozled. When do you hope to travel?'

'I have a ticket for the end of the month.'

'That should be enough time. Let's go ahead with your plan, I'll investigate this Mr Pettyman and alert you if I find he's not the man for the job. Keep me informed, and I'll quietly put things in place for you to go abroad.'

Alathea extended her hand. 'Thank you, you have been most reassuring.'

He stood and gave her a fat *that's my girl* wink. 'Do not hesitate to contact me if there's anything, anything at all, that I can help you with, Alathea.'

She winked back.

Out in the street, as she closed her solicitor's glass door, Alathea saw the man's reflection between Mr Oliphant's emphatic gold lettering. She approached him and pushed his newspaper aside. 'Good that you waited. Norbert will be pleased. I have finished my meeting with my solicitor.'

He feigned disbelief, misunderstanding, confusion.

'You might as well be playing bagpipes naked as wearing that silly hat you've got on.' She reached up and removed the stalker's tall wigwam hat. 'I saw you waiting outside my front gate this morning and you were behind me all the way down St Kilda Road.'

He reached for his hat but she hid it behind her back.

'Tell Norbert and Clive that they are, like yourself, grasping, opportunistic and magnificently inadequate as men.' She told him that, as a woman, she knew her struggle for what was rightfully hers was futile, that the magistrate would reject her plea despite the fact that Norbert had no ability, that she would be labelled disruptive and unstable and thus awarded a meagre stipend she'd be expected to be grateful for.

'Have you finished?'

No, she was not at all finished, but she just smiled and left, taking his silly hat with her, giving it to the urchin begging on the street corner who held the wigwam out in his small grubby hand.

From the corner of his eye, August Dunnage detected something moving in the house. He put down his paintbrush and sipped his afternoon cup of tea, a weak purple stain sliding down the side. His daughter emerged and sat on the back step. He watched her wrench her soaking boots from her feet and make her way slowly to his studio, her hair flattened by rain and her skirt sodden.

'Molly,' he said, watching her slope around the studio. She had been crying, but she picked up a tall vase, a dodo, and mumbled, 'That's nice.' He had started to paint its plumage blue grey, the tip of its beak red.

'One more resurrected!' He chortled, but Molly did not.

She sat on a stool and looked at her lap. August put down his teacup and sighed.

They heard the front door shut, the thump of her aunt's rucksack in the hall, a pause while she threw her hat and bag onto her bed and propped her *Vote for Equality, Vote for Women* placards against the wall. As they fell in a clatter, April came puffing down the hall towards the outhouse, discarding her League of Women Voters sash, her face flushed. As she passed the table she left pamphlets – *A Vote For Vida Is A Vote For Progress* – and some mushrooms she'd picked on her way through the cemetery. She burst from the back veranda, eyes only on the lavatory.

She was washing her hands when she looked up at the studio and saw Molly and August.

'Put the kettle on again, will you, sister?' August called.

They came into the kitchen and Aunt April noted the atmosphere in the room. It was Molly, and her clothes heavy with rain. Tellingly, she was dramatically downcast. April looked to her brother, who explained to Molly, 'Your aunt and I are experiencing a moment of déjà vu.' They were remembering a similar rainy afternoon, when Myrtle had arrived home early, also wet, downcast and guilty, and announced, 'I have been sacked . . . because I am pregnant. But I will sew from home and clean houses.'

Molly shared her news from the factory and sat up straight. 'I'll sew. I'll tidy the house, I'll advertise my sewing, but I'll also keep trying for another job. Or Mr Luby might die and I'll set up shop. It's a good position on that corner, and that way I can care for you both. And the venture with Alathea Pocknall might proceed, and I am seeing Lily Pert on Sunday. Unemployment is a temporary situation.'

'You could always ask Mrs Sidebottom if she needs help.'

'That's not funny, Dad. I am destined to live in my draughty room with a few skinks for my entire life.'

'And a few fluffy huntsmen,' said her aunt. 'I found a *Delena cancerides* only last week.'

Molly burst into tears again.

'There will be some yearning, some searching. You will find a way, my dear niece, keep on doing what you do and your daughter will have a better life than you.'

'I won't have a daughter.'

'I have a feeling you will.'

Molly rolled her eyes but her father reminded her that her aunt's predictions had a habit of coming true. She wanted to cry out, 'Being so hopeful and positive has got neither of you anywhere,' but instead said, 'I realise now that my life is not about achieving, it's about settling for what I can get.' She wanted Gladys, she needed her friend to listen, console and cheer her, have a *serious* whinge without being proper and appropriate or ashamed as she was compelled to be with her aunt and father. Why hadn't Gladys written? Had she left Molly forever?

'You must never give up hope,' August warned.

'People need strength to have hope.'

'Which is why,' said April, leaning and pulling herself to her feet, 'a good strong tot of whisky with tea is in order.'

Chapter 19

SHE THOUGHT SHE was feeling the everyday dread then remembered she did not have to go to Pocknall's, so rolled over again but couldn't stay there with her thoughts about unemployment and the day before, Mr Addlar's face so close to hers.

Over the washbasin, Molly examined her face in the mirror. She was another year older. Twenty-five! The capillary-like lines around her eyes would deepen. She couldn't find any grey hair but in a matter of days it would turn white, she was sure, and the faint droop at her jawline would fall, like Aunt April's. Gladys once told Molly her eyebrows were like awnings and she had a point, so Molly tidied them up and spent some time experimenting with her hair.

She went to buy a newspaper and it told her nothing of what the girls at Pocknall's had endured the day before. Instead, she read that Mr Norbert Poke had – in the company of Mr Clive Woodgrip – mounted a challenge to dispute the last will and testament of Mr Emrys Pocknall. Mr Poke declared that neither Mr Emrys Pocknall – pictured standing regally next to a potted palm – nor the board felt that Miss Pocknall's scant business instincts were up to the job of resurrecting and running a factory, let alone an entire business. The article went on to say that Mr Norbert Poke had been employed for some years, first as a clerk, and that Mr Emrys Pocknall had made him muse and counsel with a view to a more substantial role to help see the factory thrive into the future.

'Such malicious nonsense,' said Aunt April.

'It also says that Miss Alathea Pocknall objected,' Molly added, 'and was happy to go to court to argue the matter.'

The Dunnage women agreed they would be on the court steps with their banners when the time came. August said he doubted that would help.

Throughout the day Molly sewed, though not with any real conviction because she really needed to find a job. After lunch, when the dishes were washed and the food in the meat safe in the garden, her father and aunt lingered. When August rubbed his hands over his knees, she anticipated a 'talking-to', so paid attention.

'Molly, dear.' Aunt April moved her folded arms to adjust her person to a more convenient position. 'We brought you up to be entirely secure within yourself, and we are pleased that you show outwardly that you are inwardly liberated. You are not easily daunted.'

Her father raised his finger. 'The world, as you know, is dominated by men but happily, you remain secure in yourself.'

'Though you could exercise a little more introspection,' said her aunt.

Her father said, 'We will get to that, sister, I am on a track –'

'I'll pipe down.'

'Where was I?'

'You said that I remain secure, and rational,' Molly offered, 'and up until today, I had not sunk to *their* level.'

Her father rubbed his knees. 'Dammit, I've gotten off track.'

Molly and her aunt remained still while August looked at the ceiling.

'As you know all too well, you don't have to do anything you don't want to do and the extension of that is, of course, that other people feel the same way, and so we can only *try* to change other people's beliefs . . . especially when they feel compelled to do as society dictates.' Her father was struggling to find his way to the point.

Aunt April sat forward. 'If you try to change the old ways then you might only succeed in remaking the old ways in a different form because thousands of years of habit means thousands of years of knowledge and that's a lot to change. You must take things slowly. To make something new, do it in such a way as they don't know that you're changing anything.'

August was now resting his head in his hands, his elbows on his knees. 'I had a very good point I was trying to get to.'

Molly and April waited in respectful silence.

'The thing is, Molly-Myrtle, my dearest daughter, you are in danger of becoming your own worst enemy. You are forthright, which is good, but you are forthright to the point that people become fearful –'

'Not that they are afraid of you –'

'Not at all, but they fear change, even when they think they don't.'

She looked at her so-called guardians. Her father's brow was creased and appealing to her for affirmation and understanding, and her portly aunt looked pleased with herself, her spinnaker at rest.

'You are telling me that if I want a new job I must temper my bold nature and you're admitting that it's your fault that I am entirely secure in my capabilities and that you fear you have nurtured me so that I will never fit into this particular society and therefore I won't progress.'

'That's it,' said Aunt April, slapping the table, and August clapped his hands, thrilled with himself.

'But I can set an example and if I lose because of it, then that is the price I must pay, and that price will pave the way for better outcomes in the future.'

They were nonplussed.

Molly continued. 'So . . . in my lifetime I will not be entirely free or equal, but I can make sure my daughter is more free than me, so that her daughter will be even more free. And I am free within myself: I can freely choose to live in a way that I am not hounded, and if I am hounded then I will take it on the chin for going against society. Or I could remove myself from society. I don't mind my own company.'

Aunt April looked a little doubtful. 'I'm almost certain we have made our point.'

'Now, daughter, you'd better pack.'

It was quite a jolt. Was she being sent packing onto the street?

'I'm almost packed,' said her aunt.

Her father explained, 'There is localised heavy rainfall in the Upper Yaambul catchment area. You will go next week.'

For a moment Molly could not speak.

'A flood?'

Aunt April clapped. 'Yes, a once-in-a-lifetime chance, we cannot miss the pathogens or, of course, the molluscs. There's been an invasion of freshwater molluscs and our native species risk being outnumbered.'

'I can't really afford it.' She would not get her hopes up, anything could happen.

Then April and August started singing, quietly at first and then jolly, belting out the song. Molly imagined Mrs Sidebottom at her copper, hearing them bellowing, 'For she's a jolly good fellow . . . which nobody can deny' and Bigbottom disagreeing entirely.

'Happy birthday,' the siblings cried and placed an envelope on the table.

This was why they had delivered a lecture on how to behave. Now was the time for a new beginning.

'You thought we were awful parents, didn't you?'

'Thought we'd forgotten your birthday!'

'You are wags.' She opened the envelope. It was a train ticket to Yaambul.

She would work, and she might find Gladys, who was from that part of the state, and her aunt would collect specimens and leeches.

'But we can't afford this!' Molly cried.

'The crockery shop has commissioned more of your father's dodo jugs. They've already sold two,' Aunt April told her joyously.

'A four-pint capacity and a six-pint. And I think the value of this particular excursion outweighs the cost of it anyway.' Her father was beaming at her. 'A birthday gift for our dear Molly.'

'I have things to design for Dame Lily Pert and I have a business proposition,' Molly protested, her mind whirring.

'You are seeing Dame Lily on Sunday and Alathea Pocknall has not even buried her father, and there is a legal process. Nothing bad will happen in a week.'

'I have a feeling something good will happen,' said Aunt April.

Molly said, 'Tsk,' and rolled her eyes, but something like hope was brewing in her too.

Evan Pettyman watched the house from the square. First the older aunt, stout and determined, charged out the front door, her breast polka-dotted with badges between crisscrossing sashes: crosshairs, he thought, for a bullet or an arrow. She looked up and down the street, shrugged her rucksack into place and set off, rolling along on her bung legs, stopping to put pamphlets in letterboxes as she passed.

Then the father appeared with a wheelbarrow, Molly with him. There was a discussion until finally he left, a little arched by the weight of his barrow despite the very small load of what appeared to be grey and white birds, actually greenware off for firing.

Evan slipped from behind the rotunda, hurried through the young elms and crossed the gravel road to knock on the door. Footsteps, firm on the timber, approached and then the door opened wide. Molly Dunnage was wearing a very pretty blouse that was translucent around her shoulders. She was holding a cup of tea and had not done her hair yet and for a moment she didn't register who her visitor was. Then she stepped back, closing the door a little. 'What do you want?'

'To help you or, at least, my mother does. We heard about the dismissals at the factory. Mother would like to meet you.'

'Generally, we only take callers Sunday afternoon. Please leave a card.'

'How very eighteen-hundred.'

She closed the door.

Evan shouted for the entire neighbourhood to hear, 'It's not as if you have anything else to do.'

'I have garments to make,' she called back, knowing that curtains up and down the street were twitching.

'Imagine all the things you *could* make if you had a firm business plan and financial support.' He slid his mother's card under the door and said, 'There is an address on the back, we expect you for tea. And we will be joined by Miss Alathea Pocknall.'

A handwritten letter from Alathea appeared under the door next to the calling card. Molly read it and opened the door.

Evan held his hat in his hands. She decided he looked better wearing it.

'We are entirely and eternally grateful to you, Miss Dunnage, for passing on my card. Miss Pocknall and I have corresponded and as a result, you are requested to join us this afternoon at three o'clock.'

Molly's hands shook as she held Alathea's note. Evan Pettyman was guilty of being forthright, but so was Molly – and, crucially, he might just represent the next opportunity. It was right to bravely seize the day; out of ruin her future would come. If Alathea Pocknall was prepared to trust this man, then why let her down?

*

When Molly arrived, there was no sign of Alathea's smart buggy outside the house, an impressive double-storey terrace, though the small front garden needed attention. When Evan Pettyman opened the door, he was expansive and welcoming. 'Molly, the girl with the ideas! Come in.'

The house was dim – an attempt to disguise its shabbiness. There were no pictures on the walls, the ornate staircase was neglected and, without carpet, when the door closed behind her, there was a faint echo, as if the rest of the house was empty. The sitting room was sumptuously furnished, though eclectically, and it was chilly.

Alathea Pocknall sat in the corner of the room on a small floral couch between two pot stands, the plant pots empty; the room was too dark for anything to survive. Alathea wore a small hat, the spotted netting lifted back and sitting on the brim like a black cloud. She smiled cheerfully, 'Hello, Molly.'

In the middle of the wintry room, a crone leaned on a parasol, around its knob her veiny hands were brown-speckled and white-knuckled. She was emu-shaped, a victim of her pouter corset, and her face thrust out from a flounced, high-necked collar, her thin hair a crown of stiff, upswept curls. Molly noted her hobble skirt had once been a full skirt – altered – and that her knees pressed against the fabric. She looked at Molly without curiosity then moved her parasol forward and shuffled towards it. She stopped, moved the parasol another pace and shuffled towards it again, repeating this three-legged hobble until she reached her stuffed easy chair beside the small couch occupied by Alathea. Evan steadied his mother as she lowered her insubstantial bottom, and rested his hand on the back of her chair. Mrs Pettyman held herself upright by leaning on her parasol. 'Begin,' she commanded.

The three people were looking at Molly, anticipation on their faces. Suddenly, she realised it was all about her and her designs, which she was reluctant to share, but she dug into her shoulder bag and brought out a corselet and a breast stay. The sketches for Alathea Pocknall stayed in her bag. 'I'm creating designs for the future as well as some underwear for established clients.'

Mrs Pettyman passed the breast stay to her son and reached for the corselet. 'We are interested in underwear for the common woman, mass produced as they do in America.'

Evan smiled at Alathea. 'We'd also like to offer a bespoke service and a line of delicate undergarments for the trousseau. Convenient undergarments.' Evan winked, though Molly had no idea why. Alathea ignored him.

'There is a war coming, Evan,' said his mother coldly.

'And possibly a rush of weddings.' Evan imagined Alathea in her boudoir dressing, wearing only the breast stay. 'This one is pretty – is it comfortable?'

'Yes.' Molly took the stay from him. He was paying deep attention to the smell of the fabric and running the lace between his fingers.

Alathea said, 'If there is a war we will make sensible underwear for sensible dresses women will wear to work.'

That was, Molly thought, *her* idea.

'Is this corset comfortable? I have not found one yet that is, though they advertise that they are.' Mrs Pettyman tossed the corselet to Alathea, who caught it and looked at Mrs Pettyman with disbelief.

'Corsets should be simply *reassuring* to wear,' said Molly, politely. 'And that's entirely possible if the horizontal circumference of key points and the location of the vertical measurements of the torso are determined accurately. Comfort also depends on the waist size' – she looked at Mrs Pettyman's waist – 'actual and desired.'

'And, of course, what the client wants for her finished look,' Alathea added.

'How do you know so much about all of this, Molly Dunnage?'

'I make them, Mrs Pettyman.'

'In a factory.'

'Yes, we make a lot of them, all designs and sizes. I was taught by the corset hygienist; she has a certificate in Anatomy and Hygiene of Corsetry, and I also make the patterns. I know every stage of the process.'

The Pettymans exchanged glances.

'And she is very good on the floor,' added Alathea. 'The girls are in awe of her.'

In awe of her? They disliked her. 'For my private clients, I make bespoke garments that suit the individual's needs and torso. Compression is achieved but the seams are not restrictive.'

'What is the point of a corset if it is not tight?'

Mrs Pettyman was getting on Molly's nerves: another Snakelegs. 'Women can wear whatever they choose but fashion dictates, and at times fashion isn't artful or practical. Take for example the S-shaped corset which distorts the body by changing the points of pressure. Happily, that design is redundant these days.'

Alathea interjected, hoping Mrs Pettyman hadn't noticed Molly had insulted her out of date taste in corsets, 'What Molly means is that she is making a corset designed to alleviate the problems caused by tightlacing. And it's symbolic.' Alathea glanced at Evan. 'Emancipation of the female, if you like. That's the sort of advertisement I'd like to see.'

Mrs Pettyman took no notice of Alathea, continuing to glare at Molly, but Molly was undeterred. 'My designs are based on stays that smooth the torso and allow it to conform to more of an eighteenth-century silhouette, which, like the Victorian S-bend, is also dated, but the tubular or conical shape is less constrictive. And modern fashion doesn't need to support petticoats or heavy layers of outer clothes. Unnaturally small waists and big dresses have gone the way of crinolines and bustles, we don't *need* corsets, but stays do allow the mature woman her security given her muscles are wasted after years of contrived support. And, of course, I am pioneering a corselet which will allow women greater choice in what they wear, and no steel.' Molly had read that one year's worth of corset steel could build at least one battleship. Men were happy to free women from corsets to build ships that destroyed their brothers.

'Your thoughts are bold and tell me that you know nothing about fashion,' Mrs Pettyman said.

'You're the one wearing the S-bend corset.' Molly heard her tone, knew her father would want her to temper her spirit, but Mrs Pettyman doubted her and she was pressed by the power of her convictions.

In the gloom, Alathea Pocknall looked at her lap, hiding a grin.

Mrs Pettyman said, 'I do not think we can work together.'

'I am a corsetiere. You ask me for advice and then baulk at it. I'm the one who can see the particular physical attributes of each wearer and how the corset will interact for the best-looking and most comfortable result. My skill is in making and fitting a corset. Your skills, I'm led to believe, are in business.' Molly looked pointedly at the threadbare rugs and cushions worn to a slant. She stood up. 'Good day to you.'

Evan Pettyman stepped in front of her. 'You have a secret ingredient, don't you?' He didn't want Alathea to follow her out.

'I have experience, skill and talent.'

'We can't prepare legal matters until we know what we are signing for,' said Evan.

'You'll have to take me at my word.'

'But how can we?' He was indignant.

'How can I?'

His mother squeaked, 'What is important, Evan, is what Miss Alathea Pocknall thinks, and if she thinks she will retain her factory, which is ideal for all our needs, then we are forced to put our faith in the girl as well.'

That was the truth of it. Molly's future with these people meant she would always be striving, proving herself. But it might just be a chance, a start. She would proceed with caution, but she knew she could be a designer, she knew she could work with Alathea.

'My lawyers assure me that the factory remains mine, technically, until the courts say otherwise, and my lawyer feels a compromise will be reached. What I want is to retain the factory and offer us all a viable, profitable business with a sound future. And I have a good working relationship with Molly, and if there is a war, we will take advantage of that.'

Evan supported her. 'Of course! Now, I'd like to explain to you the basics of a business overview. We'll start with an executive summary and operations plan.' As Evan talked, a woman arrived carrying a tray with tea and cake.

Mrs Pettyman did not attempt to serve tea, and Molly thought the cake looked dry.

Molly listened, and sitting in that dank room with dusty drapes, she decided that the Pettymans were parsimonious, as some wealthy people were, and thus possibly shrewd businesspeople. But she would certainly look out for her own interests. She interrupted again. 'I want commission for every piece sold that I design.'

Evan coughed, disguising a scoff. Alathea shifted on her couch, and Mrs Pettyman said, 'That suggestion wouldn't find a happy reception in any business, particularly a fledgling one.'

'One thing I would say,' said Evan, drawing himself up for praise, 'is we will save money on the goods carts. The initials painted on the sideboard won't need to change.' He laughed. No one else did. 'The initials, EP, Emrys Pocknall and Evan –'

'Pipe down,' snapped Mrs Pettyman.

Finally, Alathea drew on her gloves to leave.

Mrs Pettyman raised her parasol. Molly was surprised to see Evan flinch, but his mother was merely pointing to the door. 'See her, and Miss Dunnage, out, Evan.'

At the door Molly said, 'I'll think about your offer.'

Evan said kindly, 'Yes, think it through to the best of your ability, it shouldn't take too long.'

Alathea headed in the opposite direction. Molly ran after her.

She turned, showing Molly her hand, *stop*. 'I'm being followed.'

Molly glanced about but couldn't see anyone. 'Tell me what you think.'

'The Pettymans want my factory. Norbert and Clive are working very hard to seize it and others have approached me. They are scavengers, but it's basically all to my advantage. I will take Mr Pettyman's money and hope that in the end, everything works out well for me and you.'

'I'll go along with you, us girls have to stick together.' Though she wasn't sure how long she'd be able to stick with the Pettymans. She almost gave Alathea her book full of sketches, designs for all manner of underwear, but decided to wait until she was at her design desk in the renovated and refurbished factory.

Alathea smiled. 'You are strong, Molly. I'm certain that if this doesn't work as you expect, you'll recover and establish a life for yourself regardless. I'll contact you but give me a week or so, I have legal documents to attend to.'

Aunt April took the short cut from the Royal Parade tram through the cemetery: such a peaceful, pretty place, and very occasionally foxes left the remnants of dead wildlife behind. She wasn't surprised to see her brother in the distance but was rattled by his complexion. He was very pale and lying on his wife's grave, gazing up at the sky, his hat sitting on his chest.

'Yoo-hoo,' she called, and August raised one arm, pointing to a hovering falcon.

For April, the day had been mixed. She met Miss Berrycloth in the city for morning tea, always a delightful event. They ordered the deluxe plate between them – sandwiches and sweet biscuits as well as a bowl of trifle, with two spoons. As they sipped their tea, Miss Berrycloth said, 'I am returning to the farm.'

'Did you say you were returning to the farm?'

'I did say that.'

April put her cup down. 'But he called you a rabblerouser, told you to "pack your bags and go". You can't chase sheep anymore –'

'My brother is unwell.'

'But where is Thurma?' Aunt April's tone was indignant, hurt and cross.

'Apparently Thurma died several years ago, some sort of seizure.'

Chastised, she said, 'Oh. That's very sad.'

'My present charges are all off to boarding school so I will be dismissed soon. I think that's why they took me on their trip to the Blue Mountains, a reward, *such* a highlight, like when I met Henrietta Dugdale.'

'But what if your brother recovers and casts you out again?'

'He won't recover.' Miss Berrycloth looked out to all the happy people passing, going about their business while her brother, her only sibling, lay dying. She took a breath. 'So much time has been wasted. My niece wrote to me – it's a chance for me to secure a home and some semblance of family. I am getting old, but I'll still be useful.'

'I'm sure you will,' said April, raising her cup to her lips, disappointed to be losing her only friend. 'When do you leave?'

'Oh, not for weeks, my employers need me to stay until the youngsters are safely in their new schools and then they'll be off for their European tour.'

'Europe? But the war?'

Miss Berrycloth shrugged. 'If there is a war, all the better for me to be safe in the country.'

'I wish you all the very, very best. It sounds ideal for you.' But it wasn't ideal. It meant that her friend was compelled to compromise, again. Miss Berrycloth, financially dependent spinster, would merely cease doing the bidding of her employers to have to do it for her nieces for security in her old age. April's cup landed a little heavily in its saucer. When would things change for women?

After morning tea they had a marvellous day together at the bay, though it was a cold day. April removed her boots and coat and tempered her quiet fury chipping mussels from jetty pylons and catching creatures in her jars. Bravely, Miss Berrycloth dog-paddled near the shore, her cotton cap high in the water. She had lost more hair under her cap but wasn't perturbed. Henrietta Dugdale advocated short hair – good ventilation cooled the brain, short hair lowered the risk of catching a chill after washing and saved women hours dressing it each day. When Miss Berrycloth emerged from the freezing water she declared herself 'invigorated'. All April saw was a skinny, child-sized woman, her nose blue-tipped and runny, shuddering in layers of dragging, dripping wool knit stiffly trudging towards the beach boxes.

As they parted at Flinders Street Station, glowing and with salty, windswept hair, Miss Berrycloth said, 'We have one more campaign together, April, one last push for Vida. And then we'll write and you must come and see me. They grow pigs. And there are dams and a creek.'

Dams *and* a creek. Aunt April felt a little restored, but her heart was sluggish, and the wound she carried for Hurtle yawned and turned.

As she approached her brother, he sat up and leaned on Myrtle's headstone so that his sister could sit next to him. She shrugged off her rucksack, the specimen jars tinkling, and there was a smell . . .

'Augie, be a good brother and take my sack, will you?'

August held the fat thing until his sister had unthreaded her elbows. It was heavy. 'Had a successful field trip, then?'

August coughed. It was not a cold; it was his chest and, of course, polluted air.

'Some of it was marvellous, thank you. The billabongs along the estuary are inspiring – stagnant but teeming with truly colourful ecology . . . and, even better, I ended up with an entire compartment to myself for the trip home.'

'I see.' He could smell dead fish and rotting seaweed. 'I think some of your specimens are leaking.'

She looked at the rucksack's darkened canvas. 'I thought my back felt wet, but I assumed it was exertion.'

They bade farewell to Myrtle's headstone and wound through the graves towards home. At Curtain Square, exhausted from carrying the rucksack, August paused.

'I could do with a cup of strong tea.'

Suddenly, they heard a call and turned to see Molly running at the edge of the square, waving her hat.

'We are saved,' she called. She ran towards them, elated, her skirts bouncing up, and people turning to watch the young woman belting along in public. She stopped in front of them, held their hands, puffing and pink-faced. 'It could be said that I, Molly Dunnage, am obnoxious, a spinster, and won't find a suitable job with like-minded people. But I *will* have a future! My creative future is being planned as we speak.' She was bursting with hope and energy, beautiful with her wide smile and her sea-blue eyes, and happy, which in turn made her father and aunt very happy. She turned and ran towards home, calling that she'd put the kettle on.

'I wonder what all of this is about?' said August.

'Indeed.'

Chapter 20

EVAN PETTYMAN FELL into a large leather chair opposite his lawyer, who was drinking whisky and smoking a cigar. At Mr Hawker's club, the chairs were stout and occupied by smoke-seeping men, others snoring, some frowning at the tiny writing in broadsheet newspapers.

'I've got a proposition for you,' he said.

Mr Hawker said warily, 'I'm all ears.'

At the end of the conversation, Mr Hawker was upright and beaming, his cigar forgotten. It was an 'unmissable opportunity': the plan to invest in Pocknall's folding business could very well work, as long as Evan made sure that Norbert, or anyone else at all, didn't get wind of it. The last thing they wanted was for someone to advise the heiress. He agreed to lend Evan the money from his clients' funds to negotiate the deal on the condition Evan repay every penny, with interest. 'If things go wrong, I'll try to keep you out of jail, but only so that you can repay me. You might have to get a job.'

'I'll see if I can get one in a bank, or I'll find a rich spinster, even a widow,' Evan joked.

'That's not a bad plan either,' said Mr Hawker.

Evan looked about for the waiter and signalled for a drink.

Mr Hawker reached out to the crystal ashtray and rolled the ash from the end of his cigar. His coat folded back to reveal a flourishing tummy and a sweat stain that reached halfway to his waist. 'Do you know the lawyer for Poke and Woodgrip?'

'A Mr Miškinis.'

Miškinis. An immigrant. Mr Hawker leaned back, almost joyous. 'And Miss Pocknall's lawyer?'

'Mr Oliphant.'

'Never heard of him,' said Mr Hawker, but he had. Mr Oliphant moved in munificent circles, he'd be the kind of solicitor not savvy to swindles of any sort.

Pettyman could go ahead and give Miss Pocknall a sizeable cheque that ensured Evan and his mother had control of Pocknall's. Oliphant would advise Alathea to invest the cheque straight back into the business, almost certainly. To be safe, Mr Hawker would cancel the cheque the very next day. Evan would sell the machines and fabrics, the tools and stock, the chattels in general. He would pay back Mr Hawker, and while Alathea was busy overseeing the new line of white frilly things, Evan would locate a 'developer' to buy the land and factory, bully Alathea out of it, liquidate the business, take the money and give Hawker his cut. All very straightforward as long as the timing was good.

Mr Hawker and his friend Mr Pettyman didn't bother to shake hands, each wary – and admiring – of the other's capacity for treachery.

Mr Oliphant winked hello and poured a glass of bottled water while Alathea settled into her seat. She was wearing culottes, a riding jacket and a top hat. She removed her leather driving gloves, and unfolded and smoothed a piece of paper with her notes.

She cleared her throat. 'I'll take the initiative concerning my undergarment business and those interested in taking it from me.'

Mr Oliphant placed the glass of water in front of Alathea. She was so much like her mother, with her stoic temperament, but she'd also inherited her father's tranquil mien.

Alathea sipped her water and continued, 'Despite the challenge from my cousin, the fact remains that the out-of-court agreement is not yet properly drawn up therefore the assumption is that I am still legally owner of Pocknall's.'

He smiled. 'The legal system is very slow.'

'And so business suffers. It seems counterproductive to me. My father should not be ignored. He does not deserve to have everything – such as it is – just *taken*, and nor do I.'

'Bear in mind the courts might find your cousin has no grounds to contest.'

'He will find a way. But while he searches for the deed and titles, the legal processes grind on, and I will proceed with what I think is just. Norbert Poke does not deserve my factory. I'd rather see it ruined than let him run it further into the ground or make a fortune manufacturing soldiers' uniforms or sell it and keep the money for himself. So, if you will, Mr Oliphant, I am instructing you to draw up a contract today handing over a large percentage of Pocknall's to Pettyman Enterprises for a sum of money.' She handed him the piece of paper to study.

'I can do that for you, with the understanding that I advised you not to sell because there were procedures being carried out and with the warning that I won't be around to help you if things go awry.'

'Agreed. I'll be far away by the time anything should go awry. I'd like a cheque from the Pettymans and I want it made out to me.'

'I doubt you'll get that – let's get it made out to me, I'm company lawyer. You're sure of the percentage?'

'It's a figure they'll agree to.' She started to weep, then told herself it was just a medium slum factory, making garments no one required anymore, and that somewhere a different life could be lived and a new, better enterprise waited.

'Ah, yes! You've written here that Pettyman's lawyer is the inimitable Mr Hawker. I see what we have here. You have made an excellent choice.'

'You're certain they believe you?'

'Yes, and they are certain I believe them.' It would not be

Alathea who was left penniless and bankrupt. And then she added, a little ruefully, 'The only one who believes all of us is Molly, who makes the whole thing seem sincere.'

'The lackey?'

Alathea flinched at the word.

'Set the handover up for the Friday before I go, can you?'

Mr Oliphant placed the piece of paper on the desk and winked from his right then left eye. 'I take it you know where the lost Pocknall's titles and other appropriate documents are?'

It was one of the first things she'd done, gone to her father's factory office, opened the safe and removed everything of importance – the wages, documents, birth certificates and bank statements, titles and deeds – pulling back her overskirt and stuffing it all into the deep pockets of her culottes. 'They are hidden.'

Alathea wiped a tear from her eye with her gloves. 'See you at the funeral. You've written the eulogy?'

He winked again. *You can rely on me.*

Chapter 21

ON SUNDAY, MOLLY, in her tasselled dress, stopped at the letterbox to button her warm coat and headed off in the still icy morning carrying her 'large ugly sack'. She was looking forward to seeing Dame Lily, if only for her warm room.

The second she opened the backstage door Molly heard the wailing, which drew her to Dame Lily's door. She knocked. Something hit the back of the door and smashed. Dame Lily screamed, 'GO AWAY, PERSECUTORS.'

Seconds later, the door opened a fraction, and Penina looked out, her eyes darting to check for burly men. She opened the door. 'Look, Dame Lily, it's Molly with your lovely new garments!'

Dame Lily was crumpled on her lounge, like a marionette. Her makeup was melted, her pinnacled hair had collapsed into balloons around her plump neck, but she had pinned the small crown into place atop her head anyway. Her blouse was stained, her skirt screwed into creased clumps, and she clutched a shoe with a fine tapered heel.

Penina explained that they had been told to vacate the dressing room. 'They need it for a production of *Orpheus and Euridice*.'

'They're using that witch with the stupid name! She is a talent-less ham and has risen "via management", their couches, that is, favours to talent scouts all over Melbourne. I ROSE WITH THE POWER OF MY OWN VOICE!'

Penina said quietly, 'Miss Elsa Stralia –'

'Elsie Fischer!' Dame Lily threw the shoe.

'. . . is to play Euridice.'

'I hope they use a taipan!' The Dame took her other shoe off and held it at the ready.

Molly handed Penina the package, which Dame Lily snatched and tore open. Without looking at it, she flung the breast stay back at Molly, snarling, 'You have the cheek to expect payment for *that*?'

It was as though Dame Lily had cleaved her happiness with an axe, but Molly simply gathered the garments and folded them as best she could. If she'd been fully employed, secure and independent in her work, she'd have told Dame Lily Pert that she'd never allow her garments or herself to be associated with an obsolete bedlamite, but the Dame was a chance, Molly's future dangling before her. 'Always interesting to see you,' she said, through gritted teeth, and Dame Lily raised her shoe to throw. But Molly was gone, Penina following.

'Molly, I apologise.' Penina gave her a cheque for the underwear. 'I've organised for Australia's treasured *soprano suprême* to teach a class at the conservatorium and her visits always include an impromptu performance. And she is always immaculate when there's an audience. We'll have the newspapers there, to announce a tour of the rural provinces featuring "everyone's favourite arias".'

'What are our favourite arias?'

'Good question. Dame Lily has confirmed "O mio babbino caro", "Libiamo ne'lieti calici" and of course, *Madame Butterfly*'s "Un bel dì, vedremo".'

'*Madame Butterfly*?'

'*Madame Butterfly* is popular, that's the point. There's a war looming, people don't want anything serious, and she sings it so well. I'll pick a time to give the new garments to her, she will love them.'

'If she sees them, she will want them?'

'Yes, to go with her new costumes, which she has yet to choose, and this might depend on the corset you come up with.'

'It will.'

Penina wrung her hands. 'She wants to sing "Queen of the Night".'

'"Queen of the Night"?' Molly was incredulous.

Penina sighed. 'Yes, I think she will, for better or worse.'

'If the costume is good then they might not notice –'

'She will carry it off, she is a professional. But it will help if she looks spectacular.'

She thought of Paul Poiret who'd made a costume for the actress Gabrielle Réjane. 'Can I make something to go with her corset?'

Penina shrugged. 'You can try.' They shook hands. 'Give me a week or so,' Penina said. 'I'll send a note when Dame Lily's a little less unsettled.'

Outside, Molly scrutinised the cheque; tea, sandwiches and cake were in order, then she would go to Mr Lau's to purchase elastic, muslin, calico, cotton, linen, lace, binding, ribbon, buttons, hooks and eyes, and drawing string. With what was left, she would pay the house tax.

She would make a corset that allowed Dame Lily to inhale fully, let her diaphragm rise and project her voice to the highest theatre ceiling in Melbourne. And she would make a costume so startling that the audience would be speechless, a spectacular costume that housed the Dame's astute theatricality, a costume that made her the Queen of the Night.

Horatio Farrat swung down Newry Street on Sunday afternoon wearing a striped suit, beret and cape. He carried a small suitcase containing the police uniform he had designed.

'It's a toile,' he said, importantly, holding it up for Molly, April and August to admire. 'They'll make it from slub, as they do, but the design is good, much better than the one we endure currently. And it's a good colour: blue suits me particularly well.'

'It's beautifully cut, and I like the pocket flaps,' Molly said.

'They can be worn tucked in, or out, and I kept the clerical collar because it keeps the rain out and, of course, any fluids that civilians throw at us, but it itches, so I have lined it. And I changed the buttons. They were too workman-like, and when captured criminals struggle buttons tend to pop off, and there are eight of them, including the epaulettes, so it's far too busy, especially when medals and rank stripes are added.'

'Indeed,' said Aunt April, admiring the lining. 'Do you think pink is a good colour for the lining?'

He looked at her. 'It's more of a red, I thought, but I'm open to comment.'

'Well, pink was a masculine colour when I was a tot but these days it's more for baby girls.'

'Very well, I'll make the lining sky blue.'

'No,' said Molly, 'it'll get grubby. Black's good.'

Horatio screwed up his nose. 'You're right, but sky blue is such a spacious colour.' He held the pants up. 'Our trousers bag at the knees and we all look like we've got a possum clinging to our leg so I've machined a crease and double-stitched the seams for a more *plat couture* effect. I think it gives the whole outfit a sharpness, don't you? More like the well-pressed Navy Commander's britches.'

August cleared his throat. 'How do you think your superiors will react?'

Horatio frowned. 'It's a much better design, anyone can see that.'

'You'd assume people would be interested,' April said, warming to the topic. 'Nothing pleases me more than time spent on microbiology or parasitology, anything to do with the study of waterborne pathogens in different climates, or different landscapes, rural, desert, coastal . . . and urban, even our little park across the road. But people aren't interested at all when I show them things.'

'How disappointing,' said Horatio, a little insincerely. 'I've got an appointment to show it to my senior sergeant soon.'

They wrapped themselves in coats and took a rug and a picnic and found a patch of sun right down the front near the rotunda. A chaperone wasn't necessary as Horatio was so much younger, but Molly knew the neighbours would gossip anyway. Horatio was bemused to see some in the small crowd pick up their chairs and move a little further away.

Molly explained, 'We don't spend days polishing our stoop and they say we put curses on people.'

The choir arrived and assembled on the rotunda. They were to perform their piece for the Victorian Chorus Festival. Mrs Blinkhorn was standing importantly at the rotunda steps but was of no apparent use. The secretary, Evan Pettyman, wasn't anywhere to be seen.

After the mediocre performance – Fanny's voice evaporated into the treetops – the crowd applauded and drifted away, while Molly and Horatio stayed, talking of Yaambul.

'We are off tomorrow. My Aunt Eda has a bathroom with hot water.' Molly went on to explain that they had gone every year when she was at school, but she hadn't been for years.

She thought of the kids she'd known there, how they were fair when it came to games – often numbers were short for cricket or football, so girls got a go. There was a horizon that the sun melted into and rose from. This trip would give her days of perfect peace while her aunt puddled, and she might even have a room of her own with a door and a window that opened. 'I'm going to finish some undergarments for Alathea Pocknall,' she said, not daring to tell him about Dame Lily. But as she walked him to the tram she found she couldn't keep it to herself, '*And*, design a costume for Dame Lily Pert for "Queen of the Night".'

Horatio stopped, amazed. 'How intriguing, Molly! I've heard she's an old bat.'

'Penina believes she's still capable of commanding the night.'

'I'll see you in a week,' Horatio said, flinging his cape around his shoulders and walking towards the slowing tram. She waved him off, his toile on his lap, and went home to finish packing.

Chapter 22

THROUGH THE GAP in her curtains, Molly saw her aunt walk carefully past, her potty in her hands; it was time to rise and face the woodsmoke and grit, the noise and ostracisation of the world. But it was also time for Yaambul. She pulled her clothes into the bed and dressed under the covers, then washed, ate breakfast, dragged her suitcase from the studio and started. No tennis in June, so no need for sporting attire. Warm clothing was required, though there would be sunshine and warmth in the middle of the day. For hiking and rambling her bicycle pants would be perfect, and in case they were invited to tea, she folded her tasselled dress carefully into her suitcase. Then she packed a box with a complete sewing kit, fabrics and offcuts, paper for patterns, sketch pad and crayons, watercolours and brushes, and put it all in the hall next to Aunt April's suitcase and box, adding the dressmaker's dummy.

August came into the house carrying a crumpled newspaper, coughing.

'You should be coming to Yaambul for your lungs, Dad.'

He ignored her, because the truth was, they could not afford to lose him and his meagre pension to a waterborne disease. He surveyed their combined luggage.

'Why do you need to take her?' He pointed to the dressmaker's dummy.

'I have gone to a great deal of bother to pad her to the size of Dame Lily Pert's decidedly un-pert shape.'

'Just use your aunt.'

Molly

Aunt April raised her chins. 'I won't pay for a seat for a dummy even if it is Dame Lily. She can go in the baggage compartment.'

The cable tram groaned to a halt and the grip man watched the Dunnage family struggle on board. It was good etiquette for ladies to occupy the comfortable enclosed trailer, but the Dunnages sat outside with their luggage, squashing along the seats of the dummy carriage, the old woman perched on the edge because of her rucksack and holding on tight. August clung to the wide waist of the dressmaker's dummy, which Molly had carefully dressed; Aunt April had refused to be seen with a man carrying a naked figure through Melbourne. The grip man, who thought himself a wag, said he should charge them for the dummy.

'It would have to be a worker's fare,' Molly said.

They rolled gently down Rathdowne Street and, nearing Elgin Street, the grip man rang his bell and cried, 'Hold on!' They braced for the westward curve towards the city then turned again abruptly into Lygon Street. It was at this point that the dummy's base slipped from the running board, left August's grasp and rolled into the gutter. The grip man braked and August retrieved the dummy, dodging bicycles and an automobile, but its base was snapped off. She would not make the journey to the Wimmera.

And so August left them to return to North Carlton, lugging the broken dummy, quite satisfied that they would find a porter to help them with their luggage. He would have liked to go – Yaambul was a second home – but the morning's fuss had sapped his energy and he was keen to get back for a cup of tea and rest. He thought of the quiet, his studio, his paints and the birds – a week without a soul to bother him. He would finish the dodos and go back to the shoebills and magpies, birds whose song (or clatter, in the case of the shoebill) would play in his mind as he painted. If only Molly – everyone – appreciated birdsong. It was everywhere, all the time.

*

Once the steam had curled away, there was the view, the winter glare and a horizon. And when the sound of the train was absorbed by distance, Molly and her aunt took a moment to adjust, standing with their luggage on the siding, sunshine bouncing off sheets of water across paddocks all around. They heard only wind through grass and trees and two magpies chortling at them from the Yaambul sign. No other passengers had alighted. Aunt April began to count their boxes and suitcases, but Molly remained with the peace of it all, the great void, the blindingly bright sun as it made its way down, the smell of mud and sour floodwater.

They were standing in infinity, a 360-degree horizon dividing the unframed space in two; above, miles and miles of clouds and patches of blue stretched out over plains and paddocks and met at the earth's faraway edge. A zephyr whistled around under Molly's hat brim, and beside the water tank the windmill blades tried to turn, a single cheerful clank at each gust. To the east, a giant cliff of wool bales waited to be taken to a mill somewhere. It had been a bumper year and they had seen, waiting at stations all through Victoria, many great stacks of bales, one as big as Georges Emporium, and wheat sacks piled like bodies under huge tarps.

Down the road from the siding, the small settlement of Yaambul gathered around an intersection. The scene was dominated by a green football oval and a water tower a short distance from a creek, the solid line of dull trees marking its presence. Small bays of floodwater reached out across the floodplain. On one corner, the hotel waited. It was faded weatherboard, two-storeyed and their view was of the back of the building, the timber fire escape and several shuttered windows and vertical downpipes. A figure appeared at one of the windows, waved and closed the window.

Aunt April said, 'Good-o, there's Rìan.'

Soon they saw the horse moving up the muddy road towards them, dragging a tall flatbed wagon with one bench seat. It stopped at intervals, Rìan slapping the reins along the horse's back so that it moved off again, either side of it the low, one-storey houses leaking chimney smoke. The sharp winter sun lit slashes of rain-water in the cartwheel ruts, and just a few people and a couple of horses attached to carts moved along the backstreets.

A breeze pushed Molly's skirt against her knees, and she inhaled, the tension across her shoulders and neck releasing as if someone had removed a lead scarf.

Rìan, middle-aged and coatless despite the cold, called, 'Good to see you again, April, and who is this great beauty?'

Molly rolled her eyes. 'Hello, Uncle Rìan.'

He tipped his hat at Molly. 'Miss Molly, all grown up and the jammiest of jams.' He reached for her, but she knew Uncle Rìan well, and quickly bent down to brush something from her boot so that his arms closed around thin air.

'And she's quick!' he cried, and loaded the luggage onto the cart. They followed, carrying what they could down the siding steps, thick green puddles threatening their hems.

For Aunt April, the climb into the cart was a battle. Molly helped her get her foot onto the bottom step, levered her up and steadied her aunt's large, warm bottom while Rìan dragged her by the collar. The horse smelled like a wet country horse. Molly sat with the luggage. After a few yards the horse stopped, as it always did, having pulled a milk cart for the first twenty years of its life. It stopped for the last time at the hotel veranda steps and Rìan helped them down and unloaded their luggage.

Cousin Eda Mahone came in from the orchard carrying apples in her apron. 'How marvellous to have you back again, April, and you've brought Molly to row you about?' Eda was sun-burnished and windswept, and spoke loudly.

Molly felt her soft dressmaker's hands grow damp; she had no intention of floating about a wet, insect-infested swamp all week. 'I was hoping to do some work.'

'Work?'

'Yes, my sewing.'

'Sewing?'

'Yes, sewing.'

'You'll need my machine,' Eda yelled, and turned back to her cousin. 'The boat's already out there, got it all set up for you. Rìan's cleared the laundry shelves for your jars.'

Eda reminded them that they didn't allow animals in the rooms. Aunt April checked if the rule included insects and molluscs.

'I don't like finding leeches in the bath,' said Eda.

'And my yabbies did escape last time,' said April, contrite.

Eda pointed at Molly. 'And she didn't catch them all. My God, the smell!'

'I apologise, again.' Aunt April hung her head.

'I gave you a room each.'

'Oh no, Eda, we don't have the funds –'

'No one else is coming because of the floods. And if they do, we'll move you in together. In the meantime, we're happy for your company.'

Molly felt a surge of joy. Her own room! With a door and a window.

Eda thrust an apple at Molly. 'Here, put a bit of pink in your cheeks, a few worms but I'd rather you eat them than the bats.'

'Thank you,' she said graciously, but was happy for the bats to have her share of both apples and worms. Why couldn't anyone grow fruit without grubs?

Rìan dumped Molly's box in the middle of her room. 'We're cut off from the farms the other side of the town – a bit of the bridge got washed away – but I bet there'll be a lot more blokes in the bar when word spreads about you.'

When he had gone, Aunt April said, 'Rìan is harmless.'

'And annoying. But he recognises I am a great beauty.'

'You sound like Gladys.'

One day soon, she might find where Gladys was.

'You use the bathroom first, I need to settle my feet.' Aunt April flopped down on the bed and put her feet on the dressing table to ease the swelling so that her boots could be more readily removed. It was not unknown for her to sleep in her boots after a long day with no one to pull them off.

Outside Molly's window two women walked with shopping baskets, trailed by two boys dragging sticks and one girl reading as she walked, her stocking cowled at the top of her boot. Beyond the low rooftops the plains continued flat, one side a windbreak of pines and fenced off into uneven paddocks as far as the eye could see. Ponds of water glistened silver in the afternoon sunshine and some trees were knee-deep in muddy water. In the town, all the west-facing walls were illuminated and the shaded east walls dark. Molly had forgotten how compelling the picture could be. Already she felt joy, her thoughts tidied and her confronting dismissal from Pocknall's fading. Anything was possible – good things came from bad.

She unpacked, thinking about her meeting with the Pettymans and Alathea. And Dame Lily would sing 'Queen of the Night' in the costume Molly would design and make, and every singer in Victoria would choose her as their corsetiere, and progressive women would use her for corsets that accommodated their unconventional fashion needs.

She draped her clothes over every surface and occupied the bathroom until every bit of travel dust and damp grime was sponged away, eyeing the bathtub. Before bed, she would soak for a very long time. As she shoved the final hairpin into place, the dining bell chimed and she said to no one, 'Good, I'm ravenous.'

There were no other people dining, confirming Molly and her aunt were the only guests. One table was set for four, so they made their way to the kitchen and helped Eda bring out cold roast lamb, pickles and salad, bread and butter, even wine, and there'd be a slice of fruit cake with butter for dessert.

Eda shouted, April talked, Rìan and Molly said nothing. Molly was thinking of the long, uninterrupted days of creating ahead, and then Rìan interrupted her contemplations. 'What are you going to do with yourself?'

'Create.'

'Lotsa ladies set off with an easel and paint but they soon come back – flies, wind or snakes.'

'I'm going to sew.'

'She'll need my machine,' said Eda again, and Rìan said she could use the dining room. 'No one's coming and if they do, they can eat in the ladies' lounge.'

Rìan went for the machine and Eda and April began to clear plates, still chatting.

April had started talking about immigrant molluscs, so Molly asked if she could have a bath.

Eda stopped. 'I strongly recommend cleanliness. No shortage of water out here nor wood to heat it.'

Molly filled the bath almost to the top – such a luxurious miracle that taps and pipes brought hot water to a bath. She stripped off, took an extra second to stand naked in a warm room without fear that someone might walk in, and lowered herself into the water, steam dancing on the surface. Then she sank, looking up at her hair floating across the surface. It was far superior to squatting in a tub by the fire in the kitchen.

Clean, warm and dry, Molly visited her aunt, who had thrown herself onto the bed. She'd managed to discard her dress. Her hair resembled a salt bush and in her yellowed undergarments, she looked like a giant squash. Molly removed April's boots, plumped the cushions behind her, and handed her a fat textbook which she used to balance a glass of whisky and water.

'Eda is deaf.'

'Not at all,' said her aunt. 'She's accustomed to shouting above the rowdy bar.'

On her own bedside, Molly found a lamp filled to the top with kerosene, and considered reading *A Doll's House*. She was keen to see if Nora would stay, because she had decided that the husband, like Nora, was not really authentic, just pretending at marriage and life. But instead, she snuggled in to watch the endless sky through her window as it turned from purple to pitch black, enjoying the short surges of joy, which she realised had been arriving since the suburbs ended and the countryside took its place through the train window.

Her mind was already shedding city clutter. She wanted to wake early, start her day, her new life, so she closed her eyes to sleep. She soon found them open again. She remembered the sky, and there it was, twinkling stars dusting the great black dome from horizon to horizon, not like in Melbourne, where it was dimmed by woodsmoke and smog and framed by rooftops. She began to relive the vast landscape as it passed her train window from Spencer Street Station to Yaambul, rolling away from the platform and jerking across tracks in the shunting yards and sliding past the backyards and clotheslines as far as North Melbourne . . .

She woke to a sunshine-filled room, the odour of horses and the sound of talking men drifting up to her. From her window, Molly looked down at a tray wagon stacked with fencing materials. A farmer stood talking to Rìan at the head of four Clydesdales, beautiful animals of bulk and muscle, his hand on the neck of the lead horse. She went to the bathroom, found evidence that her aunt had been there before her, and then dressed in her culottes.

Aunt April was by the stove, her dress pulled up to warm her cotton bloomers, and was working her way through a slice of toast. She pointed her crust to the pot of tea on the table next to a newspaper.

'What a glorious day!' Molly exclaimed.

'Chilly,' said her aunt, 'but things are heating up in Europe. Germany has declared unconditional support to Austria-Hungary against Serbia.'

'It's getting complicated.'

'Yes,' said Aunt April. 'The French will not like it at all, nor will Italy or Britain.'

Their cousin appeared carrying more apples and helped Molly make a packed lunch. When asked, Eda told Molly that she had not heard of anyone called Gladys moving to Yaambul, though there was a Gladys who'd married and moved away. Rìan arrived and said he would ask in the bar. Eda barked, 'No one in your bar would know a respectable young lady.'

The sun was not far into its rise when Molly and Aunt April set off for the swollen billabong by the river, Molly dragging the fruit-box billycart containing lunch, drinking water, specimen jars and nets. The landscape, soggy though it was, still pleased Molly and she felt that surge of joy again. But it was a different matter rowing a small boat in the sunshine, her palms rubbing under her gloves and her bottom damp and itchy.

'Row with both arms at the same time, Molly, I need to get to the middle.'

'It's the same water.'

'It's not, it's different.'

After some time rowing in circles – 'Left! Left! Pull your left oar and you'll go right!' – their argument got louder and carried to the group fishing over on the river, who scowled at the two women, their hat nets polka-dotted with insects and their boat disturbing the reeds in the billabong and frightening the fish. Aunt April occupied the forward thwart, her hem sodden, her boots shrinking on her wet feet and her cheeks the colour of ripe apples. Molly's good humour evaporated.

'My hands will be ruined and I want to draw and sew! Why don't you get Rìan to row you about?'

Her aunt was frowning at a jar full of tea-coloured water. 'Can you imagine a day confined to a boat with Rìan? All I ask is one day, Molly, so now that you are here you could take an interest, swing the net about for something flying past, or search for molluscs in the reeds.'

Molly sighed, irritated. But she told herself it was only day one; there was plenty of time for her to achieve what she intended.

Eventually, the shadows shortened, the surface of the flooded billabong became a mirror reflecting the burning orb overhead, and Molly's coat rested on the centre thwart beside her. The biggest flying insects were out and about, bussing and fluttering around the boat, and the fishermen had long ago packed up and gone, without a fish dinner. Molly rowed towards the shore. 'I'm abandoning you.'

'I'll come with you.'

After a tricky disembarkation, Molly and her aunt retreated to the shade of the gums where Molly set up the picnic. She spread the rug too close to an ants' nest and her aunt insisted they move. The butter in the sandwiches had warmed and tainted the cold lamb, and the drinking water was beige. Aunt April eyed it and then tipped it out.

Molly stood up and brushed off her skirt. 'I will happily pay Rìan to row you about tomorrow.'

Her aunt, her face damp and shiny, said, 'You are a dreadful disappointment and dreary company.' She held her hand out and Molly helped her to her feet. They wandered towards home each thinking of a tepid bath.

Nearing the edge of town, at the intersection of two dirt roads, a young man sat on the platform of a windmill high up in the glare of the midday sun. Behind him, the wind wheel was stationary given the nearby dam was overflowing. It was hard to see him clearly in the sun but, as they approached, he threw a grain sack with a piece of fabric attached from the top of the windmill. It landed in some scattered hay below with a deep thud, the fabric fluttering and settling beside it.

'Aerodynamics?' called Aunt April and the young man looked around, startled. Below him, in the centre of the intersection, two women looked up at him. The older one's face was obscured by insects attached to the netting falling from her hat brim, and she carried a rucksack on her back. The other one was young and wore ankle-length bloomers under a skirt, which was hitched up and tucked into her waistband. Beneath her wide hat brim, her face was pale, her cheeks pink. She was dragging a small cart with some tins made into buckets by way of a wire handle. There was also a picnic basket. They did not look as if they belonged to this particular landscape.

'It's what's called a parachute.'

The young woman called, 'The first one ever was used by a woman called Georgia Broadwick. She jumped from an aeroplane over Los Angeles in June.'

'Actually, there's been a few, Captain Albert Berry jumped from an aeroplane in 1912. It was in the paper.'

In the awkward silence that followed, the young man conceded, 'Perhaps Miss Broadwick was the first woman to do it.'

'I'd say that's it,' said Aunt April, and Molly had to agree.

He scratched his head. 'The parachute's meant to open and break the fall . . .'

'But it doesn't.'

'No.'

He climbed carefully down the foot pegs and glumly inspected the wheat sack in the hay. The two women approached and for a moment they, too, studied the wheat sack in the hay.

The young woman asked, 'You're interested in flight?'

'Not anymore. Broke my arm, which is what led me to parachutes.'

Not many people showed an interest in his parachute, and he was intrigued that these two women were curious. The older woman seemed educated, probably self-taught, and there was something about the younger one too; she was fair-skinned and quite beautiful, with a small gap between her two front teeth. Her mouth was generous and her eyes blue – turquoise blue – and she seemed to be deep in thought.

Molly was thinking she had asked a stupid question, wished she hadn't, and wondered how she could make amends and prolong the conversation when her aunt said, 'My passion is pathogens, and we are here to study swamp ecology,' which Molly thought was an even more stupid thing to say.

The young man asked, 'Why don't you just do the puddles in the city? They'd have some very impressive diseases, I'd say.'

Molly liked him; he was straightforward.

'Indeed,' said Aunt April.

'What makes you think we're from the city?'

Then he turned and looked at her. His eyes were brown behind gold-rimmed spectacles, and she felt a small tingle, like an ant crawling over her heart. 'You're not dressed like country people,' he said, and for a moment, Molly regretted her culottes.

Aunt April continued, 'I can research waterborne disease in my own backyard or my front gutter, but any contamination's usually something to do with horse manure or micturating men, so, you see, the natural swamp is more pleasant.'

Molly wished her aunt hadn't mentioned micturition, but the young man didn't seem fazed. And then she realised who he was. He was the dark-haired boy she had played with as a kid.

'I have returned to Yaambul for the molluscs,' her aunt explained. 'An invasion of freshwater molluscs, which likely arrived in seedlings illegally brought in from Asia, was found in waterways associated with the Great Artesian Basin, and that discovery reinvigorated wide interest in molluscs, specifically molluscan diversity and organic evolution. Scandalous . . . Common species are diminishing.'

'That's not good news,' said the young man, but his thoughts had returned to the girl. He remembered her; she was from Melbourne and related to the people who owned the hotel. He recalled a durable girl with a spirited presence. And she had grown up to be small but strong. 'You're Molly.'

'And you're Leander.'

'Leander?' said Aunt April. 'Are you a strong swimmer?'

Molly said, 'I bet everyone asks that.'

He was pleased that they knew the Greek gods. 'I don't swim in bad weather or at night.'

Molly asked him about the parachute fabric and so he moved his mind back to parachutes and wheat sacks.

'It's a silk blend.' He picked it up and offered it to her to feel. 'Our local draper sent away for it and Mum showed me how to stitch the rods into the hems.'

She dropped the handle of the cart. 'You sew?'

'Yes, you need the rods to unfold and keep it open. But . . . I don't quite know why it doesn't stay open.'

'It's very light,' Molly said, delighted that she had met another man who sewed – she would tell Horatio. She handed the fabric back to Leander.

He lifted his hat to run his fingers through his hair, which was dark and wavy, and she knew she'd seen him do that as a boy. The band of his hat featured a shiny dark blue feather. Her father would like it.

'What sort of bird is that feather from?'

He didn't get a chance to answer her because, again, Aunt April interrupted, suggesting the wheat bag was too heavy.

Leander scratched his head again. 'There's forty pounds of wheat in that sack, and the parachute weighs ten pounds. It should work.'

'That's heavy.' Molly thought he must be very strong, but he explained that he raised it with a pulley, his horse walking away to pull it up. 'That's clever,' she said, knowing it wasn't, that everyone used their horse to raise and lower things. She wished she could say something intelligent.

Her aunt suggested that perhaps the flow of the fabric was wrong and he'd catch more air with a bigger piece of fabric.

'Or thicker,' Molly cried, a little too loudly, 'like calico?'

'Those are all very useful suggestions, but I suspect the whole experiment needs more height and speed than I can get around here.

The force has to burst the parachute open. I've even tried from the top of the silos but it's not enough.'

'It needs to be like a kite, catch the wind.' He didn't hear Aunt April. Leander was looking at Molly again, so Aunt April offered her hand. 'By the way, I am Miss April Dunnage.'

He turned back to the older woman, musing over the fact that he'd never forgotten Molly; he'd always known her. 'Pleased to meet you, Miss Dunnage, and it's nice to have someone to offer suggestions. I'm trying to improve, or perfect, Franz Reichelt's design.'

'What's wrong with his design?'

Leander grinned. 'He plunged to his death in 1912.'

'Well, then, it'd be good if you worked out how to improve it,' said Molly, and they chuckled. 'Try Tiny Broadwick's design,' she suggested, and he said he would go home and do that right now. She appreciated that he had heard her, noticed her – not just a girl, but *her* – though she wasn't sure why she felt that way.

They looked at each other for longer than they should have.

'Any rate, it's time I got home.' He picked up the sack, which didn't seem to be much of an effort for him.

'Where's home?'

He pointed to a house half a mile or so across the paddock. 'That's our house. The building to the side is my mother's, she grows orchids.'

'You must get a lot of insects?' Aunt April asked eagerly.

'My father's done a good job with wire netting.'

To Molly's delight, Aunt April said, 'We'll sit on the veranda tonight. The stars are so lovely, you're welcome to join us.'

'Thank you,' he said, and was gracious enough not to point out that he saw them most nights from every window in his house. He went to his horse, tied the sack and chute to the saddle and cantered away, raising his hat.

Molly watched him until her aunt cleared her throat, and they set off again. 'What a well-dressed, well brought up boy,' her aunt said.

'A boy with a dream.' She sighed.

'Not the usual type at all. Did you know that some molluscs are hermaphrodites, so they are capable of forming both sperm and eggs? Sexual reproduction is achieved by the formation and fusion of sperm and eggs, or gametes in individual molluscs, but those with separate sexes reproduce sexually. Females are fertilised when the male sperm are drawn into the female bivalve through her siphons, but in humans, penetration is needed and the sexual act, an entirely natural urge much maligned by the conservative class, but then of course women's menstruation ceases, and they get tired, nauseous and bloated, but first, the female hymen must be broken, but that is a brief discomfort and the path to a secret –'

Molly put her fingers in her ears and heard no more.

While her aunt sat in her petticoat by her window, an eye to her microscope, her murky bottles lined up and sketching pad and coloured pencils at hand, Molly set up her sewing apparatus and feeling inspired – invigorated! – she spent the afternoon committing to paper ideas for the 'Queen of the Night' costume.

They ate their evening meal sitting on the veranda, watching Yaambul life. Drays and oxen and carts loaded with farm animals moved towards the railway station while others came past loaded with goods – including newspapers – from Melbourne and the world beyond. Molly was struck, not for the first time, at how easy it was simply to board a vehicle and disembark sometime later at another destination, a whole new world and culture. It would be easy to travel, when she finally did. She also noted that in Yaambul, the women dressed simply but fashionably, and many visited the library and art gallery just down the road. But as Yaambul progressed towards nightfall, Molly lost hope that Leander would somehow come across the paddocks to join them.

Her aunt said, suddenly, 'The trees, Molly, the proximity of many trees with large trunks means that out here I don't have to plan my day's activity around the only two public toilets that exist for women in Melbourne.'

'That must be quite a relief for you.'

'How amusing you are, Molly.'

When the sun had slipped out of sight, they bathed and, from their beds, watched the stars appear, and fell asleep as the night sky lit in a bright gritty arc from horizon to horizon and meteorites shot fiery trails through space.

The next morning, after a struggle to get her damp boots to slide over her heels, Aunt April ate a hearty breakfast, reading a newspaper spread on the kitchen table beside her, with Eda slicing worms from apples and chatting boisterously. 'We'll lose a lot of men to the war. All our farmers will go and then who'll harvest the crop and send the lambs to slaughter? They'll all be off to be slaughtered themselves.'

'Eda, dear, so brutal.'

'It certainly is. But if there wasn't an enemy they wouldn't have to go. We need defending, that's certain.'

April turned a page. 'I'm not certain. I can't see that it's got anything to do with us all the way down here at the bottom of the world.'

Eda kept talking. 'It's the right thing to do, and we all have to make sacrifices.'

'We will have to make some sacrifices but asking a young man to go and fight and perhaps die is too much to ask, I think. It is all too terrible to contemplate, especially before nine o'clock in the morning.'

As Aunt April left, she dropped in on Molly, who was tacking cotton undergarments together in the dining room. 'You'll give Eda a hand with the dishes, won't you?'

Molly nodded gingerly, holding pins in her teeth.

'If I see Leander, I'll ask him to join us for a picnic.'

Molly spat the pins into her hand. 'Good, Aunt, any day will do.'

As she wandered down the soft clay track towards the river, pulling the billycart, Aunt April thought that she had not seen Molly so vibrant in years, almost shimmering. Hurtle Rosenkranz came to her thoughts: those lovely afternoons drinking beer in his big timber bed, around them textbooks on pathogens and astronomy, molluscs and clams. And, oh, the lust. Hurtle so fervent, and the tender violence of their union, the textbooks thumping to the floor. They adored each other, were one in mind and, startlingly, in body as the efficiently well-designed human anatomy was tested successfully over and over, the marriage between physiology, sexual desire, love and science explored by two enthusiasts to produce such emotions.

She sighed, feeling hopeful for Molly, for the future.

When the shops opened, Molly dutifully set her post a respectable four yards from the local ladies at their church fundraising street stall. She would have preferred her aunt take on the locals, but the belief that her cause was true and right steeled her to the smiles – grimaces – from the street-stall ladies. She opened Eda Mahone's folding chair, sat down and adjusted the sash across her chest – *Equal Pay & Financial Autonomy for All* – before hastily pulling the skirt over her culottes to look more conventional. People paused and read her sash but did not consider the petition she offered.

The ladies at the street stall watched, and then the woman with the fifteenth-century plaits wrapped around her head said, 'You are staying with Eda Mahone?'

Molly used her most friendly self. 'I have been to Yaambul a lot, in my youth. I like it here.'

'So do we.'

She gestured at the surrounds. 'So much space.'

The second woman, a redhead, said, 'Tsk,' and the others smiled condescendingly. Molly asked if they knew anyone called Gladys Sidebottom. The thin one, whose hat featured gumnuts and wheat heads, said that the only Gladys they knew had moved to Patchewollock.

The plaited woman explained loudly, 'It's over near Walpeup,' and her friends gazed at Molly as one would to someone who was terminally ill.

'I understand,' said Molly, knowing they thought her inferior, and mad.

A girl of about fourteen, her plaits as fat as black snakes, approached with great purpose. 'Eda Mahone says you sew nice things.' Her skin was very fair and her eyes dark brown.

The women at the street stall were suddenly interested, the decorations on their wide-brimmed hats jolting as they turned abruptly to the stranger wearing galligaskins.

'I make lots of things, my speciality is underwear for ladies,' Molly said. 'Do you make things?'

The girl nodded. 'Meals. I make breakfast and dinner, Mum does lunch because I'm at school. Will you make me a dress?'

'I would like to, but do you have fabric and a pound to pay me?'

She looked at her boots. 'No.'

Molly felt she had looked into the girl's eyes at some point, but perhaps she just thought she knew everyone in Yaambul. She handed the girl a pen and the petition just as the girl's father arrived.

'Not many people around here get paid much, full stop,' he said. He was a scholarly-looking man in a three-piece suit, carefully groomed with soft hands. A banker or schoolteacher, perhaps?

The girl scribbled her signature. 'I'm going to be a New Woman when I grow up. Are you a suffragist?'

'Proudly so.' Molly told her Vida Goldstein was going to stand for parliament.

'Has she got a husband?'

She wanted to say 'Husbands are not compulsory to a happy life', but suddenly realised this was Helena Behan, the baby sister she had seen many years ago with Leander, who had been unfazed by the other boys jeering at the sight of a boy pushing a pram. 'Not at the moment,' she said, brightly.

'No one will marry me if I'm a suffragist,' said Helena.

And again, Molly stopped herself saying what she really wanted to say, and said, 'We have many men supporters.'

'Not many around here,' said Mr Behan, taking his daughter's hand and leading her away from the city woman wearing trousers under her dress. She hoped she'd meet him again and give a more conventional impression – for Molly, an unconventional hope.

In North Carlton, August woke late, and wished he would one day wake feeling rested and refreshed, as he once had. He put his coat on over his pyjamas and liberated the hens, collected their eggs, cleaned out the stove, scattered the ash onto the vegetable garden, then set and lit the fire. He cooked and ate breakfast – an egg on toast – stoked the stove, put a bucket of water on to heat and brought the tub in. When he had enough hot water to take the chill off the rainwater, he soaked for longer than usual, adding hot water as the kettles and pans boiled. He dressed in clean underwear, taking stock of his blue-tinged legs and short-ness of breath before going back to bed for some time, drained and depleted, struggling to hold yesterday's newspaper. When he had recovered strength, he dressed and strolled down Rathdowne Street and found a current newspaper. Then he brewed coffee and read again and spent an hour in his studio painting – the crockery shop had received a request for another shoebill vase.

When the brass band struck up at the park, he picked up a kitchen chair and wandered over. Mr Luby waved from his balcony. The band was playing 'It's Nice to Get Up in the Morning' and

Molly

August tapped his hand on his knees and hummed along. He steamed vegetables for dinner and thought a nice piece of steak would go well but didn't have the energy to walk to the butcher's. In bed early, his thoughts turned to Myrtle, as they usually did, and then they turned to their daughter, and the problem of her future. Molly would survive when he was dead, but he would like to see her happy. August knew what true happiness was, and that being blissfully happy, even for a short time, could sustain a lifetime. If only Molly could find the right chap.

Molly chose and occupied the biggest table in the dining room, and worked facing the windows so that she could see the street and anyone approaching the hotel, but what really occupied her was the 'Queen of the Night'. In the end, it was the song and the lyrics that settled her ponderings on a fabulous costume for Dame Lily. She created a basic dress pattern, then opened her mind to the subjects of queens, creatures that were at home in the night, evil and power. She closed her eyes and, holding her pencil tight, drew. When she opened her eyes, she said, 'Crikey.'

Half an hour later, Molly turned to her pattern paper, tore the tape measure from around her neck and started measuring and drawing, moving her pencils and curved rulers all over the page.

Most days, the newspapers were only a day or two late, and April boasted that the Kent Hotel had purchased a wireless.

Rìan suggested he could purchase one for his own bar. 'We could *hear* the news.'

April described the crowds across the park at the Kent and everyone agreed it would boost business. 'But put one in the ladies' lounge, won't you?'

'I'll turn it up loud for them.'

Finally, *The Age* arrived and over lunch in the kitchen, it told the Dunnages that Alathea Pocknall had agreed that the challenge to her father's will, which clearly left everything to his daughter, would be settled out of court, and that matter remained in the hands of lawyers.

'Nothing more ruinous than a public spat,' said Eda.

Aunt April and Eda agreed that to drag Miss Alathea Juanita Pocknall's name through the courts would be devastating to a woman who had lost both her parents in tragic circumstances, and to the family's reputation and even its business affairs.

'And her prospects for an advantageous marriage,' said Eda, digging damp salt and pepper from condiment shakers.

'Alathea's story would be a good drama, a moving picture,' said Molly, and asked if Yaambul planned to build a motion picture theatre. But no one had heard of such a plan, which was disappointing. It would have made Yaambul perfect for everything Molly enjoyed. Eda said they were a waste, just a passing fad, and Aunt April said she had a feeling that one day there'd be one in every suburb and town.

Molly read on, relaying that Alathea's lawyer had asserted that she had resources to rectify the business model. '. . . *much evidence was presented to confirm that ledgers, notes, letters were overseen by Norbert Poke and that it was his sporadic and imprecise accounting skills that saw the factory financially corroded.*'

Aunt April said, 'Nonetheless, being a woman, Miss Pocknall won't gain anything – they'll most likely deem her without capacity. Her only solution to avoid Norbert Poke being awarded complete stewardship of the factory is an agreement of mutual benefit.'

'Yes,' said Molly, 'but it would be to the mutual benefit of the men concerned.' She wandered out to the main street to see who was about. Leander Behan wasn't like those men, surely.

Chapter 23

FEW PEOPLE TOOK any notice of another well-turned-out young lady in a fine buggy and Alathea steered up into the bush by the Yarra River, her horse ducking the low-hanging branches. She secured the brake, left the mare to the appetising grass and headed to join the many other fashionable young ladies, upright and deportment-pert, at the tea house. She was dressed demurely: a sombre green, high-collar, single-breasted hip-length jacket over an ankle-length overskirt that hid her culottes. As she crossed the veranda, she guessed he would not stand up to greet her and was content with that – neither wanted to draw any attention. Evan Pettyman signalled the waitress and Alathea sat with her back to the crowd and did not raise the net fascinator falling from her small-brimmed hat.

'I have taken the liberty,' he said, 'of tea for two.' Evan knew that young ladies like Alathea rarely ate cake.

She did not remove her driving gloves. 'There is very little time . . .'

'For either of us,' said Evan, opening a notebook.

Alathea handed him an envelope containing a draft contract of sale. Evan browsed the document, running his pencil down the side of the page.

Even in the gloom of the front parlour it had been obvious that the Pettymans were not really monied or successful, and in broad daylight, while he appeared impeccably groomed, his suit was weary and his cuffs soft and on the brink of fraying – like Clive Woodgrip's. Most likely Mr Pettyman managed his own investments and possibly speculated using credit or borrowed capital. Today's meeting confirmed for her that he didn't have his own funds, that Mr Hawker was most likely his partner, and that financial engineering was what the Pettymans and their lawyer did, to lesser success, apparently.

The waitress arrived with the tea. Alathea thanked her and waved her away, though she did not see to pouring the tea herself.

Evan folded the documents and put them back in the envelope. 'As traders, Mother and I are pleased with this draft. It confirms that at this point, you remain the legal heir to the company, the factory, its goods and chattels.'

'Though it is subject to a pending agreement. A date is not yet set to discuss the agreement or when it will take effect.'

'Very good,' said Evan, and he assured her that he and his associates agreed to the proposed purchase price, that the sum allowed him a large enough percentage of Alathea's company, '. . . to take control of the restructure, something your cousin will be delighted to be part of should he be successful in his bid to seize it from you – but I think once we're up and making a profit, the courts will look favourably on you.'

Alathea simply nodded. 'The future will decide what role my cousin might take in the business, if any.'

'If any,' Evan agreed, and gestured at the tea tray. Alathea said she would not have tea, thank you.

'We expect to hear from our lawyer and bank within the next two days,' he said. 'You'll be informed when the formal handover will take place.'

'I understand that most lawyers don't have a sense of urgency about the process . . . but I hope to have our agreement finalised within the next week or so.'

'It will be,' Evan assured her.

She stood, as did Evan.

'I look forward to our ongoing enterprise, Miss Pocknall.'

He did not offer a handshake – neither wanted anyone to see them shaking hands in agreement – but she felt Evan watching her all the way to her buggy. Other eyes watched her too, she knew, so was even more sure-footed and straight-backed than usual and did not turn to acknowledge him. She hitched her overskirt to climb up into the seat and took the reins, confident Mr Pettyman believed her to be entirely gullible, and that she trusted he would rebuild the factory.

The buggy she drove was very smart, a fine vehicle pulled by a fine horse, but Evan thought an automobile would be nice. His mother would not allow him money for a motor car, of that he was sure, so he dedicated some thought to who he might inveigle into giving him more money. Once, he had mortgaged a house that they rented . . . but he would not tempt fate at this stage.

Steam curled from the teapot's silver spout and the milk was impossibly white in its small crystal jug. Evan called to the waitress, 'Here, girl!'

He pointed to the tray and she poured the tea and he drank the entire pot and polished off the milk as well. Why they thought they could run their own lives when they had to be told to pour tea was beyond him.

Leander came through the hotel kitchen to deliver potted orchids for Eda's reception desk, their spikes bent with fat buds promising many blooms. He found Eda in the kitchen.

'Oh my,' she cried, embracing the orchid, 'tell your mother I am grateful. I'll look after it well.' She cut him a slice of pie. 'Take some apples home, will you, son? I got far too many.'

As he ate the pie, he wandered to the dining room door and pushed it open a little. He had seen the machine on the table through the window and, as suspected, there she was, bent over the table.

'Hello, Molly.'

She jumped, spun and stood protectively in front of the underwear.

'Good morning.' He smiled, and came towards her in her small clearing between the heavy dining tables, all the chairs up.

'Hello.'

He glanced at the bloomers and breast stays. 'What are you making?' He took another bite of pie.

'A costume.' She thrust the picture of Dame Lily's costume at him and scraped the white fabric and lace into a pile.

'So,' he said, 'I suppose you wear things like this all the time in Melbourne?'

'Only when we go grocery shopping.'

He put his plate and spoon down on the service sideboard to look more closely at the sketch of the 'Queen of the Night' costume. 'Gosh, I'd like to see this when it's finished.'

'Perhaps you will,' said Molly, thinking of Dame Lily's regional tour. Leander was more attractive than the day before and, though she had to look away to take a deep breath, she felt entirely comfortable with him.

He handed her back the drawing. 'You had the petition at the street stall?'

'I didn't see you.'

'News spreads. You got signatures?'

'Some, yes!'

'Helena told me.'

'I thought it must have been your little sister.'

He remembered his hat and took it off. 'She believes in equal pay for equal work, as do I, in theory, but girls aren't as strong as men –'

'We have endurance, though.'

'So do we.'

'Exactly, and you get paid for it. Some tasks need to be specific, I agree, but we should get paid the same as the man next to us for the same job for the hours we work, don't you think?'

'It seems only fair.' He looked at his hat in his hands.

She knew she was harassing him, so took a different tack. 'Did you change the weight in your sack?'

'That's why I'm here. I want to try it again.'

She smiled and stepped towards him. He didn't step away. 'I love heights,' she said, far too enthusiastically. 'I've seen Melbourne from three storeys up.'

'Where's your aunt?'

'At the swamp, of course.'

'Of course. Do you think she'd like to see the next version of the parachute?'

'She would.' Molly would crawl through stinging nettles to go anywhere with this young man.

He nodded, unsure of how it would work, if they could step out together, or if it was not the right thing to do. What would people say?

Eda Mahone walked in.

'Do you think I could walk to the creek with Leander, perhaps take a picnic?'

'You could take lunch to your aunt. I'll give you a basket, make it official. But you'd be the only two people who want to go for a picnic on a flooded creek.'

So they made a picnic for three. The air and sun again made Molly's fingertips tingle and her feet itch to be free of her boots, but she was walking with Leander Behan and his horse in the beautiful countryside and so slowed her pace to talk. She discovered that Leander's mother sold her orchids locally – the churches got them for free – that his father was the school principal, and Leander worked as a teacher. For a brief time he'd studied for a qualification in Melbourne.

'I wish I'd known,' said Molly. 'I'd have asked you to tea. My father was a teacher too.'

'I'd have come to tea,' he said, adding that teaching was an admirable profession, 'though the pay could be better.'

Molly told him her job had ended when Mr Pocknall died, but that she had some private clients that would keep her going until she found another job. She explained that she had invented a new, better corset, and that it would take over as the women of the world threw the old ones away.

'That makes you clever,' Leander said, 'which isn't always appreciated.'

Each had silently observed that the other hadn't mentioned friends, or a particular social group, and were quietly comforted.

The swamp had receded a little, yesterday's tide mark visible on the small levee the water had created. The swamp stank like a swamp and the floodplain was muddy, and Leander took Molly's elbow to steady her as she lifted her skirt to trudge through some sodden patches. She felt his touch for some time after.

Aunt April was propped against a gum, her face under her netting flushed and her culottes hitched for ventilation. Her head was bent forward, concertinaing her chins and swallowing her mouth, and she was snoring softly through her nose.

Molly called softly, 'Yoo-hoo.'

Her aunt's eyes opened and she looked suspiciously at the ground before realising where she was and raising her head. 'Did you bring lunch?'

'You look like a tomato.'

Her aunt ignored her and thanked Leander for carrying the picnic basket.

'It was the horse.'

'Do extend my thanks.'

They sat down in the fallen bark and sharp grass and Molly hoped no spiders crawled into her clothing.

Aunt April studied her sandwich, chewing with the few teeth she had.

'Cold rissoles,' Molly said.

'Rather tasty.'

'The relish makes them so,' said Molly.

'Has your morning been creative, Molly? Are you planning a trip to Paris?'

'First, Aunt, I have to dress two customers in Melbourne and then revolutionise the female form in Australia, then I'll be able to afford Paris.'

'I'd like to throw my parachute from the Eiffel Tower, when I've made it perfect. I was wondering if you'd care to see today's parachute fall, Miss Dunnage?'

'I would, but only if you will row us about on the billabong tonight.'

'Oh yes,' said Molly who, a day ago, hated the idea of water at night.

Leander said, 'I'm more than happy to.'

The parachute didn't open, it landed and burst, and they left a splash of poor-quality wheat grain on the ground for the parrots: small flocks of pink and grey, pairs of red and green, lumbering black and red cockatoos and the noisy sulphur-crested cockies. Molly would tell her father all about them when she got home.

'I'll be back at dusk,' Leander said, as he left them. 'It will be cold tonight.' And they said they would dress accordingly.

Molly watched him walk away, noted the width of his shoulders and his calves against the back of his trousers. And she was watching again from her window when the buggy came up the road that evening, taking in everything about her new friend. His boots and jacket, the thick jumper that had replaced his waistcoat. He drove a three-seater pulled by a big grey gelding. She retreated from her spy window and called to her aunt, 'He's here!'

Molly ran downstairs and out onto the veranda. 'I'll get in first for Aunt, I'll pull, you push,' but Aunt April arrived with Eda, who carried the hotel stepladder so Aunt April's ascent was not difficult. Eda handed Leander the ladder and Aunt April squeezed onto the seat next to Molly. She had never sat so close to a man before. The country way of living was very agreeable.

It was a clear night, no clouds, so the cold was crisp, clean and thorough. Leander carried a hurricane lamp on a pole, holding it high to light them to the creek, insects flitting about in its glow and Aunt April swinging at them with her net. Crawling into the boat, he took Molly's hand and she was grateful for her gloves – her palms might have been damp – and for the dark, because she blushed when he reached to steady her.

Leander rowed them all over the billabong, manoeuvring where he was told, dropping Rìan's fishing line in whenever he could, the lamp propped against the bow. Molly wielded the insect net while Aunt April lowered her ladle into the murk and brought up freshwater creatures.

'I imagined I'd find the elusive creatures at night,' she lamented.

Molly was freezing and tired and hating the boat but she would endure – would agreeably sit there for a week – because she was sitting beside Leander. Around them the billabong was loud with frogs and flickering insects and above them the sky was a riot of twinkles. Small insects buzzed; little white darts were haloed in the beam of Aunt April's head torch. Occasionally a fish, or something, splashed, and Leander identified the plaintive cry of a barred owl and the trill of a screech owl. Aunt April filled the quiet with metaphors about swamps, how they create their own immune system and support all their many populations, how they all *swim* together, 'if you get my drift.'

She laughed, pleased with her wit, then fell silent, deciding that the quiet youngsters in the boat were coming to terms with heightened hormones and dopamine influxes.

Finally, Aunt April declared herself content with her efforts, and Leander rowed them through the mist to the shore. As he landed them, April toppled and tumbled softly onto the damp grass, making a sound like an orange rolling over a paper bag. Leander was alarmed but Aunt April was not fazed; she shushed his apologies and rolled back onto all fours, her head torch catching a spider busy constructing a web in a rotted sheep skeleton. They all watched the animal diligently build its web in the rib cage, its furry body lit by a sharp-edged spotlight, which turned it into a sparkling creature dancing in a frosty maze.

'It's beautiful,' said Leander, and Molly felt what a joy it was to be with someone new and different.

'Female,' April said, 'and given the size of it, well fed.'

They helped the older lady to her feet and walked towards the buggy, Leander between them, all following the dim light of Aunt April's head torch and the high lantern, April's basket clinking with specimen jars. They found the Southern Cross, and what they suspected might be Mars, and thought they saw Saturn and Jupiter. They heard a fox cry and, startlingly, had to freeze when a pack of fleeing kangaroos passed, just yards away, a thick rush of *phuf-phuff* and the quiet whoosh of bounding animals, sprightly but heavy, making a small, swift wind as they blew past.

When the time came for nature to cease occupying them on this enchanting night, Leander left them with a big redfin he'd caught. 'See you tomorrow,' he said, and Molly's hand went to her heart: *tomorrow.*

They watched Leander's lamp move away from the town, Aunt April breathless and red-cheeked from effort and cold, and Molly elated, though her fingers and toes were numb.

Leander hummed all the way home, happy he'd had a redfin to offer. He never thought he'd meet a girl like Molly, especially in Yaambul.

Aunt April peeled off her hat and fell onto her bed, fully clothed, her hat net on the nightstand crawling with captured insects and full of anticipation for what the jars would reveal in sunlight. Molly removed her aunt's wet boots and gave her a glass of tank water.

'People are so nice here.'

'They are, dear girl.'

From her window, Molly looked again for Leander's lamp, a very faint glow, hardly moving, in the distance. It was the most magical evening Molly had ever experienced.

At the intersection, Leander stopped to look back at the faint light in the upstairs hotel bedrooms.

Something had changed; there would be change.

Chapter 24

FROM HER ROOM, Molly saw Leander looking at the window of the general store opposite. As it was Sunday, it was closed. Above him, the sky was cloudless but pale and there was no wind, a splendid day for a walk, and Molly felt a kind of ease. If Gladys had been sent back to the Mallee, or wherever Mrs Sidebottom had sent her, she hoped that she was at least as happy as Molly felt in Yaambul. Away from Carlton, there would be happiness for Gladys too, surely . . .

She called out to Leander, liking the sound of his name, and he turned and smiled.

Next door, Aunt April flung back the covers and waddled to the window to see Leander. She flung her towel over her shoulder and headed for the indoor water closet and bathroom, amused at Molly's footsteps bolting down the stairs as fast as her culottes would allow; April was pleased to spend another day as a chaperone.

Today, Leander had brought a big farm vehicle, a flatbed cart, but the same horse, a dirty grey thing with a bent ear.

'I thought we could go for a drive, is your aunt up?'

'Almost.' The horse turned and stretched his nose to Molly. 'Hello, horse.'

'His name's Tiger.' He put a glossy dark blue–purple feather in her hand. 'And this is from a satin bowerbird.'

It was lustrous, like moiré, and Molly was bewildered. 'But how –'

'Helena's cat brought it home, sadly . . . so I harvested the feathers. Beautiful, aren't they?'

'Beautiful.'

'I've got a jar full, you could have them for your sewing.'

'What a bowerbird you are.'

His smile broadened and, again, Molly was elated because of this new person in her life.

'I thought we could go to the island?'

'I'd love to!' She could have been a little more restrained but didn't care. 'I'll get Aunt.'

'I'll come with you, you'll need to pack lunch.'

'And make a thermos of tea.' She clapped, then turned and ran through the lobby. Aunt April was not in her room, or in the bathroom, so she thumped back downstairs again to the kitchen, where she found her aunt buttoning her bodice and leaning over a newspaper, a glass of stout in her hand.

'Aunt! A buggy ride to the island.'

Aunt April closed the newspaper solemnly. 'Lord save us.'

She informed Molly and Leander that Archduke Franz Ferdinand of Austria-Hungary had been assassinated by a Serbian nationalist in Sarajevo. 'It happened back on the twenty-eighth of June. Two lines at the bottom of the article mentioned, as an incidental fact, that his wife, Sophie, Duchess of Hohenberg, was also murdered.'

'Assassination? That's horrible,' Molly said, but was uncomprehending of what this violent action actually meant, so Aunt April went on, outlining the situation in Europe. 'The politicians have signed many treaties trying to prevent hostilities and resentments, but the Serbs feared the Archduke was visiting to seize power, to turn Serbia into an Austro-Hungarian outpost, so someone has pulled a trigger. There'll be trouble. Thousands of young men could die. Families would be ruined, animals exploited. There'd be disease, untold suffering and starvation, and the wrong people would make money out of the entire tragedy.'

The grief of April's lost love, Hurtle, surfaced, and she turned away to let it wash through her, and to come to terms with what might be in store for Molly and Leander. They didn't know yet that they were meant for each other, that they were about to have something that would make their lives meaningful, and were actually already in love. It was as clear as sunshine to Eda and April, and up until now April had been excited that they'd know the ecstasy that she and Hurtle had known. But the assassination . . . they had no clue what threat the Archduke's murder brought for them, for everyone. Aunt April knew the loss that would come if England got involved, if a war came.

'Would you like to go for a ride, Miss Dunnage?' Leander asked, hoping to lift the mood.

'She would,' said Molly, 'but let's finish breakfast first.'

Leander had already eaten breakfast but ate more of Eda's apple pie, and Molly admired the way he held the slice in his big hand and ate it in four bites. Aunt April didn't eat her toast and went to the bar for more stout.

Leander had not stopped thinking about Molly Dunnage. He woke wondering about her, what she was doing, and imagined seeing her every day, walking with her in the mornings or as the sun set, going on adventures with her. For the first time the prospect of settling down, marriage, raising a family, providing a home and a steady income – *responsibility* – seemed real. He'd even confronted his fear of going bald like his father – but any wife worth her salt would love him anyway. Right at that moment, sitting in the kitchen of the dilapidated pub, he knew Molly was the right girl and that his prospective elderly aunt drank stout at 9 am.

When he was about twelve, he'd sat with her on a low branch by the creek, Helena in the pram at their feet, and he'd picked a dragonfly from her hair. As he reached over, she leaned towards him and, for a moment, his arm sought to rest on her shoulders. He should have felt some sort of shame, he supposed, for touching her, but he didn't. It felt normal; from then on, he was more aware of girls. It wasn't something he'd ever articulated or even formed a thought over, but he had always known that life would either bring her back to him or someone whose imprint was similar. Now, he could see Molly Dunnage was the most engaging woman he'd ever come across; he belonged with her.

While Aunt April readied herself, Molly and Leander sat on the veranda looking at the old grey horse, whose ear, Molly noted, was frozen like a small antler. Tiger was an ex-plough horse, Leander explained. 'But he enjoys a trip to town, and I take him to school with me sometimes. The children like him, he's very patient with them.'

'Do you like the children, are they good for you in class?'

'I quite like children in general, you?'

'They're alright, I suppose, but I don't know many. You must like your job?'

'I do more administration work for Dad than teaching. My job's really teacher's assistant, but it's the best job in the world because I get holidays off. Without pay, though. I do the nursery with Mum during holidays and I'm required to read and know many things so that one day I'll be a qualified teacher, though my dream is to study agronomy, advise on soil and the like.'

'What about snakes?' She sounded like Gladys, but it was the only thing she could think of to say.

The snakes, Leander explained, fled like brown lightning when they felt anyone coming, but occasionally a dog or a horse was bitten. 'It's always a great sadness to lose an animal.'

She felt it was her turn to say something about her life but also felt it was too soon to tell him the truth about Pocknall's, or Gladys and their Carlton neighbours.

Leander pointed to the plains around Yaambul and told her that the vegetation changed little with the seasons; the soil was mostly sandy loam, and the high points crossing the landscape were sand ridges. The thin bands of river red gums were all that remained of the woodlands and forests that had been cleared for farming. 'We have lots of grey box gums, though,' he added, identifying the positive, and Molly thought it was the most interesting topic she'd ever listened to and that Leander was wise and knowledgeable. She decided her natural inclination to be impatient with lectures was childish, and from then on she'd be interested in everything.

When her aunt emerged, her rucksack in place, Molly said, 'Leander has told me all about the landscape.'

'Indeed?' April had been telling her about soil and trees and grass since she was born.

They set off for the wriggly riches of the river near the island in the flatbed wagon pulled by old Tiger, Molly sitting between Leander and her aunt, Leander's body against hers, his arms brushing hers as he steered.

Molly and April stood in the shade of a tree and watched Leander climb the windmill and drop the sack. The parachute opened, but only in the last two yards before it thudded to the ground and as the fabric settled over the sack, Tiger opened his eyes and chucked his head and went back to sleep again.

Later, as they each cautiously ate worm-ridden apples, Aunt April said, 'Your parachute could be used for warfare, couldn't it? It could drop young men into enemy territory.'

'It's occurred to me,' he said, and looked to the sky, imagining how glorious it would be to see dozens of young men floating down, but stopping his imagining when he saw them floating towards thousands of upward-pointing enemy guns.

Molly quickly changed the subject. 'I don't suppose you know a girl called Gladys?'

'I went to school with a girl called Gladys. She married and moved to Patchewollock.'

'Oh yes, over near Walpeup.'

Hunger got the better of them a couple of hours later and they drove home, leaving Tiger and the cart right out the front as they went into the hotel.

Aunt April made a dash for the lavatory, and while she was gone, Leander and Molly made tea and took it to the hotel dining room, and when Aunt April returned and Molly left for the lavatory, Leander gestured towards April's rucksack.

'What do you do with the creatures in the jars, the results?'

'I put the animals back when I can, sometimes I must throw them out, but I always throw them in a vicinity where other animals can eat them, or they can decompose in a friendly way.'

'Molly says you copy them into a book.'

'Yes, I copy them into a book along with my findings and then I check with the known texts and rectify, or attempt to rectify, anything I find that isn't in those texts, or defies their "truths". Often I'm compelled to dispatch a letter and accompanying drawing to the University of Melbourne Bioscience Department.'

Molly arrived and poured herself tea.

'They must be very grateful to you.'

Aunt April shook her head emphatically, her fleshy throat, like a spinnaker, wobbling. 'They ignore me and dismiss me as a crank. But I've found a couple of *my* discoveries in their magazine. I am forced to be satisfied that my knowledge has been stolen to develop biological solutions that sustain, restore and improve the quality of life all over the world for animals and humans. It helps plants too.'

'You can't accuse them of plagiarism?'

'Not a chance. I have no qualifications. I expect nothing, but I'm still always disappointed. Change is slow.'

'All the odd bods at the same looney table,' said a passing local. The comment cut through their happy gathering.

But Leander said, 'Evening, Jim.' He turned to Molly and her aunt. 'Ignore him.'

'Is he the town bully?'

'Not really, Jim just pretends. His father died and his mother took him from school very young to work.' He shrugged. 'We all have to rub along together out here.'

Molly was impressed that Leander could be so generous, but Molly was impressed by everything about Leander.

Aunt April worried. It was all tragically wrong timewise; she must voice the obvious and so cleared her throat. 'Will you go to war if there is one, Leander Behan?'

'No. War is *wrong*,' Molly cried.

Leander agreed that it was 'a horrible thing that solved nothing.' But he hadn't allowed it any real thought. 'I'm not keen on violence, but my conscience might push me to go. I'm considered to be a small "someone" in the town, being a teacher, a principal's son, and an example to my students . . . it would be hard to stay here while the others go.'

Molly put her hand on his arm. 'You could work in an army office of some sort.'

Or he could help the scientists, April suggested. 'The Boer War advanced medical practice enormously. We have better vaccines and drugs, medical evacuation systems, chlorination – all important beyond the carnage that inspired them.'

'Well, that's what I'll do, then.' He nodded. 'I'll save lives instead.'

Molly clapped. 'Bravo. And we'll campaign – no! We'll protest, against any conflict at all.'

'We will,' said Aunt April, and thumped the armrest with her fist. 'I bet Vida's already painting her banners.'

Molly walked Leander to the veranda and down the steps to Tiger, who was waiting patiently, and Leander put his hat on and then took it off. 'Molly, I must ask, can you explain exactly what it is you campaign for?'

'Well, I'm not a suffragette. But I believe in Vida Goldstein.'

'Vida Goldstein,' he repeated, and she looked at his waiting expression.

'You need to explain me to your parents, don't you?'

He nodded. 'Yes, I'm sorry.'

'Well, then.' Molly squared her shoulders. 'Basically, I believe that society should be fair. Suffrage says that women are human beings and therefore equal – we should have the same civil, political and social rights as men. We should all have equal rights but women are still treated as less; we are not truly valued by society, which is run by men, even though we're half the population. Those men make certain that we are kept inferior by denying us our right to make choices about our own selves, it's men who make laws and therefore most decisions for us and by doing that they keep us in the kitchen and doing as we're told, and so most women don't even know that they could have personal liberation, that they could be allowed to decide what they want. Most women don't even *know* what they want because they've been dictated to all their lives, as have their mothers, and most of us have always endured a kind of psychological oppression. But that said, some women know what's best for women but can't get purchase into the hierarchy to make change. Vida tries, the suffragists try but most of us have lost our spirit because the culture prevents us expecting anything of ourselves beyond marriage and reproducing and so no one else expects anything more of us either, not even our sons, who are brought up according to the norm and so assume their mothers are less.'

She was ranting but couldn't stop.

'We've never been allowed to be who we could be, determine what we want for ourselves. But we're getting our nerve, and when all of us know that we can change everything, then everything will change. But we are still the exception in decision-making and when we are at least half of it then we can change things for all women. And men. Until then, we still have to ask a man for everything, basically. It's not fair.'

Leander nodded. He'd read these things, but none of it had ever meant a lot to him until now, and he reflected on his mother and sister and their roles in his small family.

The girl he thought he'd like to marry kept talking, mentioning equal education, family violence and the economic gap, prejudice and bigotry and the Aborigines, and finally, as she petered out, war. 'I think war is a crime. Everything needs to change to make it fair.'

He said nothing.

'What do you think?'

'I think what you want is fair, I'll be mindful of it, and I'll try to explain.'

'Good, because I'm going to keep campaigning.'

He nodded again.

'The way the world is . . . It's not really your fault, a lot of men don't understand us or the way it is, so I won't hold it against you.'

'As far as I'm concerned, you can be yourself, Molly.'

She wondered if he'd still say that once he'd talked with his parents.

August was in the dank little kitchen by the stove when someone knocked. He'd been thinking about his sister and daughter and Yaambul; he would suggest they move there when he died. There was something wrong with him, something spoiling him, but he didn't know what and couldn't afford to find out how to stop it.

Warily, he made his way towards the front door. It was possibly the debt collector from the water board or an angry Mrs Sidebottom, or perhaps some children scampering away leaving a poor dead shingleback on the door mat. But no – it was Alathea Pocknall, a startling figure, tall and angular, pale, elegant and *clean* under a low umbrella . . . quite out of place on his front veranda. She brushed past him, quickly, lowering her brolly but not lifting her fascinator. How beautiful wealthy people were, with their fine skin and healthy diets, sumptuous fabrics and fragrances, and how shabby his worn and affectionate home was by contrast. He was relieved April's room had aired a little in her absence.

'Could I trouble you for the envelope, please, Mr Dunnage?'

August fetched the envelope and handed it to her with his paint-red fingers.

As she pocketed the envelope, she turned back to him with another in her hand. 'Can I also leave this remaining envelope with you? Is that alright?'

'It is.'

She shook his hand and thanked him, saying, 'I'll see you again.' And then she was gone, floating down Curtain Street with her head bowed, hiding beneath her brolly, the innkeeper across the road pausing to watch her. August peered into the envelope, which contained many opened letters. He opened one, and read, but then quickly folded it, replaced the envelope behind the skirting board, and went back to the stove.

When he came the next afternoon after school, neither mentioned the war, campaigns or suffrage, and over the next three days they went to the river, or the billabong, unchaperoned and uncaring about what others would be saying about them, and still didn't speak of anything that would interrupt their happiness. They had fallen in love. It was terrible that their time together would end, unthinkable that war would take Leander away. They fished and fried the redfin or cod on the kitchen stove for Rìan and Eda and Aunt April. They collected mussels but found them muddy and gritty, so gave them to the chooks, and as they did, April said earnestly, 'Did you know, Leander, that molluscs have a foot?'

He managed a straight face. 'I did not. I'd ask why they don't have two but I think you'll tell me anyway.'

Molly got the giggles and had to move away.

Her aunt continued, 'They only need one and it's retractable.'

'Retractable?'

Molly put her hand over her mouth and moved further away, her eyes filling with tears, but dear Leander listened and learned how molluscs moved around and the various ways some molluscs use their foot.

Later that night, Eda found them sitting at the kitchen table, bent in half, laughing. Eventually, Leander was able to say, 'Molluscs use their foot to catch prey. It's a weapon.'

Molly said, 'A club.'

'They have a club foot.'

Eda watched them holding their stomachs and laughing. 'I don't see what's so funny.'

They laughed even more.

On their happy afternoons with Aunt April, they followed her all over the paddocks as she collected water from rain-puddled hoof prints and even to the cemetery once, where she updated their dead relatives on world events. Leander brought his binoculars and they spotted birds as they went, which Molly sketched for her father. They even harvested the last of Eda's orchard fruit for her and, over tea – stout for Aunt April – they read the newspaper. Molly thought everything lovely and people beautiful, kind and generous. She discussed with Leander her plans to be a designer and corsetiere, and shared that she didn't think she'd get to Paris but if Madame Weigel had reached the world with a journal and paper patterns, so could she. He agreed. She confessed to him about Pocknall's, Snakelegs, the slow rain dance and her dismissal, and he smiled. 'Good on you, Molly. Tyranny's an evil thing. I think you're brave.'

Her new contentment was something she'd not had since childhood, and she was entirely comfortable – except when the tentacles of reality reached in to her happiness, when thoughts came to her of going home, to the city, Mrs Sidebottom, her cramped dressmaking room, her freezing to oven-like cubby, and the prospect of everyday suburban life. The next day, April and Molly would leave Yaambul, and she condemned the treachery of every passing minute that brought her closer to Carlton and took her away from Leander.

Chapter 25

MOLLY AND LEANDER stood at the edge of the paddocks watching a new moon, gleaming more brightly than it should, ascend to dull the stars. The crickets and frogs were loud, and the crisp air smelled of earth and she fought to quell a swelling ache. It was their last evening together, but she longed for it to go on forever. 'I like you,' she blurted. It was the truth.

Leander looked at her like no one else ever had and walked towards her. She loved the way he walked and could have wept with happiness when he said, 'I know. I like you too.'

It was the promise of something in the future, an understanding, a bond that she'd hoped for.

'What will we do, Molly?'

'We'll write.' She would say what she felt in written words and he would respond, and it would keep their relationship alive.

'And, school holidays, I'll come and see you in Carlton.'

'Even better.'

They went back to eat their evening meal in the dining room with the Mahones, drinking beer and a little wine, knowing what had been declared between them. They moved to sit around the fireplace and Aunt April read poetry aloud. 'This is my brother's favourite, Sir Philip Sidney's "My True Love Hath My Heart". *My true-love hath my heart and I have his, | By just exchange one for the other given: | I hold his dear, and mine he cannot miss; | There never was a bargain better driven. | His heart in me keeps me and him in one.*'

They couldn't look at each other, the truth so loud in the air, but Leander said, 'That's perfect,' and for Molly, breast stays and corsets and prima donnas and heiresses all paled.

'It's your turn,' Molly said, part of her wanting him to recite a love poem, yet hoping he wouldn't.

'I only know poems about birds and trees.'

'I like trees,' said Molly.

'And I birds,' said April.

His face brightened. 'I know! Emily Dickinson. *"Faith" is a fine invention / For Gentlemen who see! / But Microscopes are prudent / In an Emergency!'*

He received a standing ovation from Molly and Aunt April, and then Eda stood up and said, 'Well, there you have it.' It was time to close the pub and get to bed.

Leander said he would see them before the afternoon train tomorrow, and all Molly could manage was, 'Yes, tomorrow . . .'

As Molly removed her aunt's boots she suggested they could stay on, send for August.

'Indeed,' said her aunt, 'we'll tell him to abandon his beloved garden and pack up all my experiments and his crockery and paints and the chooks and bring it all with him on the next train.'

Another opportunity for Molly to enjoy her life was lost. She felt stung, and then her aunt said, 'We will come back to see Leander. In the meantime, write to him. He might invite you back. You could visit his farm.'

Molly's hopes were affirmed. They would come back, but in the meantime she would deal with her new emotional state, her restlessness and anxiety: the heaving joy and immediate twinges of sadness, the elation when she thought of Leander and even the 'Queen of the Night' costume she had created – the best thing she'd ever made, and it was because Leander had said he'd like to see it finished. She would invite him to Melbourne to see it when

Dame Lily performed. She was flabbergasted by the sudden bursts of frustration, the lurch back to fury and then the climb, once again, to happiness. She hoped the rise and fall of emotions would pass, leaving her with only the feeling of Leander's proximity, of bliss, forever. But how to maintain it through letters, mere *words*?

She packed, slowly, methodically, and was astonished at what she had achieved. She had worked in a focused and sustained way to be free at the end of each day for Leander. Should her secret dream of life in the country come true, she had no doubt she'd be productive. Life had changed. For seven days she'd sprung out of bed to hope and love –unemployment, dashed hopes and war pushed aside. For once, the fractious state of her small world and the world at large were really of no consequence to Molly Dunnage of Carlton.

She woke on her last morning and looked for the last time across the plains, the dew bright under the sunshine, and there was Leander, dressed in a nice jacket and tie, walking along the road towards her. She watched him, wished that he would walk to her like this forever, and then as he disappeared beneath the veranda roof, she noticed that he'd polished his boots . . . to come and see her. Her breath was suddenly insubstantial. She ran to the toilet and then to the bathroom and tidied her hair and met Aunt April on the landing.

'Leander wishes to take you walking.'

'Are you coming?'

'This is not a walk where I am required.'

'Not required?'

'Molly, there's an intention behind the walk.' Her aunt was struggling to hide her happiness.

It dawned on her. 'He's asked to take me *walking*?'

Her aunt nodded. 'My dear, you look as if you have seen a unicorn. I told you this would happen one day, that the right boy would come along. This one came from the sky.'

Molly

There was a sound like the sea in Molly's ears, and she reached to steady herself on the wall. 'But I'm not ready.'

'No one ever is. Now brush your hair.'

'I just did.' She skipped down the stairs, pushed through the hotel door out into the morning and there he was, smiling at her, a neatly constructed, physically robust young man wearing a suit jacket and spectacles, his hair clean and teeth sound. He was the most beautiful thing she'd ever seen. Molly Dunnage understood then that she'd known this was going to happen, she'd known since she was ten and sitting on a tree branch with Leander. He was meant for her and she for him. Finally, there would be reason for everything that came and everything that was. It would all bounce off them and find a place in their world, or not.

'I'll sit here and keep an eye on you,' said her aunt, glancing up and down the street.

Molly pointed to Leander. 'It's *him*, not a bushranger.'

'Well, when I was your age —'

'When you were my age it was 1884.'

And for a moment Aunt April was back with Hurtle and they were not merely walking together — but she couldn't allow her niece to be so bold . . . though there was a war looming, and Leander might have to leave her.

Molly took Leander's arm. 'Let's go.'

People watched them walk across the street and perch on the horse trough outside the store, while Aunt April sat at a table on the veranda with her morning stout so that Yaambul could see her at her chaperone duties.

'Well,' said Leander, 'like you, I'd like to see a bit of the world . . . perhaps that Eiffel Tower.'

'Me too,' said Molly, though Paris evoked the idea of Europe, and war. He was strong; she knew that. There was a firm, even sharp, side to him. But she also knew no one could endure war and forget it.

Leander had faltered, focused on the dirt between his boots.

He was stuck.

'I was hoping for a pledge,' he suddenly blurted out.

'A pledge?' Not a proposal.

They sat there, looking at each other, coming to terms with their future, which was before them, but uncertain, and they were unsure of what it would end up being.

'Because there might be a war, I find I can't expect you to promise me anything.'

'But I do, I promise, I want to promise.'

He looked up and down the street. 'The entire street thinks we are engaged now, but we can't be engaged.'

It took all of her control to say 'Very well,' but she was furious, anger coursing through her like never before. She was hot with prickling disappointment, could hardly swallow for the swelling hurt in her throat and was filled with hate, though she wasn't sure what it was she hated.

'I'm sorry. I do want to marry you, and we will one day, but the war . . .'

'The war.' She nodded.

Love was found at last between her, an ambitious and independent city girl who wore pants, and him, an unaffected, enthusiastic country boy who sewed, and he was being *considerate*? Her chin tremored a little and one very small tear escaped, soaking the soft area just below her left eye. She couldn't stand it anymore. Her fists clenched and she stood up. 'I don't understand . . . if two people –'

'I know! You don't know how sorry I am.'

'Then why? It's your parents, isn't it?'

'They're very conservative in lots of ways.'

'But you're an adult, times have to change. You said I could be myself.'

'I know, but that doesn't mean I'm without responsibility, and consideration for them especially now.'

She turned away, crying now.

'If there's a war . . . if something happens . . . well, you might be left in a predicament.'

He made a sound that made her turn back. It was hurting him, too much, and she knew that his parents were behind this idea of a pledge, not him, and she hated herself for making it worse for him. But she was tired of disappointment, and this was the worst hurt of all. It was like a sock in her throat and she didn't think it would ever go away. But to lose him would be worse, he was hers and she his and there might not be a war and everything would finally be hers. 'A pledge, you say?'

'It's really a proposal of marriage, Molly, we just can't tell anyone yet.'

'Aunt will be disappointed.' But not as disappointed as Molly.

'I will make up for it when we're married and she's living next door.'

'Oh gosh, won't that be fun?' She said it sarcastically, but it eased the tension a little.

They stood there for a while, waiting for the misery and pain to abate, and then he said again, 'If you'll have me, Molly, we'll get married. But we need to know what's going to happen.'

'I know it's sensible and I should be gracious, but I think you have just told me that if there's a war you will go and that I'll have to wait.'

'As will I.'

As they walked back towards the hotel, Leander said, 'So, next school holidays are in September. I can come to Melbourne and you'll come back to see me?'

She said nothing, she had never felt so let down, though she hadn't known she expected anything.

'Mid-year exams are soon,' he urged. 'Senior students get a week off to study but they mostly help out at their farms. Anyway, I'll come to Melbourne.'

'We can go to the bay, there's a tram that goes straight there.' She hoped she sounded cheerful, while inside she was crushed.

'A tram and a plan.' He nodded. 'I can't stay to see you off, I'm sorry, I'll be at school.'

She wanted to bawl. 'That's alright, you'd just end up carrying Aunt April's smelly rucksack.'

Aunt April watched them walk towards her, and let the newspaper crumple in her lap. 'You're going to let the wretched war stop you, aren't you?'

They nodded.

Aunt April cast the paper aside. 'Life is . . .' She stopped. She was going to say 'short', but thought better of it. 'Life is for living and, for what it's worth, I think you should make hay while the sun shines. I hope you change your minds.'

'I'm truly sorry,' Leander said. It was obvious that she was cross, that she felt wretched for them, especially for Molly.

And so the parting was easy, disappointment drowning any other emotion. Molly and Leander just looked at each other, half smiled, said, 'See you soon.' Molly committed to memory Leander's face, his brown eyes and the small smear on his spectacles, and he did the same, her clear blue-green eyes and her soft, silky hair, though his mother would have called it 'lively'.

Eda sent them off with sandwiches and apples – 'Careful of the worms' – and Rìan delivered them and their bags to the luggage car. He said farewell – 'until the next flood or sooner' – and reached to give her a hug. She let herself be held. Her uncle smelled of beer, tobacco and the cold wind on his neck.

So Molly left Yaambul, wretched with sadness and resentment, and very disenchanted, though there was a sliver of light, some hope. As her aunt said, it was as plain as a horse that he loved her. She turned her thoughts to her father, and her future as a corsetier.

Chapter 26

A LAMP BURNED in August's window and the garden smelled as it always did, of moisture and eucalyptus and wattle. The front door stuck, which meant there'd been rain. The house seemed small, and Molly made a mental note to rectify all the pictures, none of which seemed straight . . . or was it the walls?

There was one letter for Molly propped against the sugar bowl. It was from Dame Lily Pert, and Melbourne life, which had been so far away, came rushing. But all thoughts of her clients ceased at one look at her father. He was at the stove, smiling at them, holding the teapot. Her aunt put her hand to her bosom, 'Augie, oh . . .'

Either August had withered in the days they were away or they had been too accustomed to him, always too close to notice. He was beaming, though, delighted to see his family again. He'd seen a wren in the backyard that morning, enjoyed having the stove all to himself. 'So, it's been very good here, no one has died. How was Yaambul, tell me about the trees and the plains, are they the same?' He coughed, a rattle in his lungs much worse than they'd ever heard before.

'You look like a weathered scarecrow.' His sister put her hand on his forehead.

'Now that you're here I'll recommence daily grooming.' He smiled weakly. 'And I might have caught a bit of flu.' He was unwell – it wasn't necessary to pretend, even to himself. Coughing was exhausting, walking was arduous. 'Did you find your alien molluscs?'

'No, but we found a great deal more, didn't we, Molly?' Aunt April reached into her knapsack and drew out a jar, leeches stuck to the inside like tar, some waving their heads about, searching. 'But first, homegrown vegetable stew and Chinese herbs.'

Molly collected vegetables and, while the soup cooked, they told him of their adventure. Aunt April announced, 'Molly has news.'

Her father saw his daughter's sheepish smile broaden further than it ever had, the kind of smile he had not seen for some time. She had changed: she seemed more vibrant, less fierce.

'I have a new friend.'

'I would say Leander was more than a friend.'

August's eyebrows shot to the top of his brow and his sister nodded to him: *At last!* Molly explained Leander Behan and his parachute. 'But he might be able to tell you all about it – he says he's coming to Melbourne to see us.'

On the journey back, she had come to terms with her pledge. She loved Leander, he was worth waiting for.

August's hands went to his face and his eyes filled with tears, which was not unusual for him.

His sister said, 'Yes, it is lovely news, brother.'

Then Molly added, 'But nothing formal has been agreed to.'

'Yet,' said Aunt April, spreading toast with dripping.

August wiped his eyes with his hanky, and as Molly talked of Leander she came to believe even more that it was true – that he loved her, and that they would be together – and the happiness she had felt when she was with him returned.

Chapter 27

HER AUNT MADE different kitchen noises from August's. Her father coughed as he went about breakfast, a familiar sound now more immense in the house, while her aunt broke the kindling more decidedly before shoving it onto the hot coals, and was less temperate generally. She banged things. Soon the fire crackled and spat, then Molly smelled bones boiling and heard the spoon scrape the pot. She stayed in her bed, knowing that Aunt April needed to 'do' for her brother, that she had been to see him in his bed even before she'd run to the lavatory, had found the butcher at the back of his shop sawing meat at dawn, and was now bent over the saucepan, cooking soup with tears dripping into the brew. Molly would not interrupt that. Her aunt set a tray, poured soup, grilled bread with dripping and flupped up the hall in her slippers.

As she cooked herself porridge, Molly heard the siblings talking in low tones. She knew her aunt was apologising to August, saying she should never have abandoned him, and she heard her father's mumbled response, consoling his sister.

Molly retreated to her bed with her tea and porridge and thought about Leander until her aunt and father had settled into their daily routine. When she had fed and liberated the chooks, chopped and stacked firewood, and washed and hung the laundry, she made her way to the letterbox, sweeping the path as she went. But there was no mail; it was far too early for the postie and any letter from Yaambul would have had to travel on the same train as Molly. But there was a pamphlet, from Mrs Sidebottom.

The AWNL supports the white man's lonely outpost in the Eastern Seas, and we recognise that the hordes from the mysterious, crowded lands of Asia above us are poised to come South to desolate everything before them. Australia can never remove herself from the protection of Empire.

Inside, Molly paused at her father's door. He was lying in his bed with one arm flung across a newspaper, thick shiny leeches hung from his thin arm, and there were small circles of blood on the newspaper. Her aunt picked one leech from the newspaper and tried to drop it back into the jar which sat on his bedside table on top of a stack of library books. She dropped it, bent down to pick it up, knocked the books and the jar containing several engorged leeches and the books fell. She sighed, 'I'll get them next time I sweep.'

'Oh God,' said Molly, and went to her cubby. She could not fathom why her aunt, so knowledgeable, believed in such a medieval practice. It had never done any good. She found her savings and peeled another two pounds from the wad and pressed it into her aunt's hand. 'Please, Aunt, take him to see the doctor.'

After August and April had left, Molly sewed, prepared lunch and checked the letterbox again. She told herself her dear father would be strong, that he would thrive, that her aunt's remaining teeth would hold and that she would get everything she wanted. Somehow, she would get everything she wanted, finally.

On her journey to see Dame Lily Pert that afternoon, Molly considered the woman: she was an artist, a stellar opera singer, temperamental because her star was fading and therefore she suffered little consideration. There was no need for Molly to be nervous; she would be gracious.

Penina opened Dame Lily's dressing-room door and smiled, the smell of sweet sherry the first thing Molly noticed. Dame Lily was quiet and composed.

Molly handed over the new breast stay and Dame Lily said, 'I suppose you want to see me *déshabillée?*'

'*Avec encore moins de vêtements,*' Molly replied, and was sent outside by the flick of the Dame's contemptuous wrist.

When finally she was readmitted, Dame Lily stood in the middle of the room, pleased with herself, and pushed back the robe to display her ample bust, which was secure in Molly's breast stay. It was a mid-bust design, supporting and enhancing the breasts to draw attention away from the waist, which would not be as constricted as vanity would dictate.

'You are in luck,' said Dame Lily. 'I have made this garment work on me.'

'Wonderful,' said Molly, and Penina smiled a conspirator's smile. 'But it is the corset I am most concerned about.'

'As are we.'

Again, Molly left the room, then was called back into the warmth to find the Dame standing in the middle of the room in her corset. Mrs Blinkhorn's butterfly cakes came to mind, sponge wings sprouting from the whipped cream on top, but it was doing its job in all the right places. Molly kept her distance until the Dame indicated she could approach. The length went over the hips to the thigh, giving a streamlined effect; the rubberised elastic at the seams allowed a lot of movement, and the general silhouette appeared smooth. Her costume would hide her fleshy arms and unsteady cleavage. Molly walked around her, inspecting her work; it was a glorious construction, a large cylindrical brace, but pretty rather than industrial with lacy edging and the shell, lining silk and the stitching all decorative. The clasps were coloured gold, as were the lacing string and eyelets. She had not made it with waist tape – it was double boned – but the side channels were reversed, sewn on the outside to reduce the chance of irritation.

'There are a few bumps.' Dame Lily ran her hands over the flesh-coloured stay, revealing no bumps at all.

'Do you feel any creases between the construction and the flesh?'

'I do, you will need to fix them.'

'I will.'

'It's not very tight.'

Molly had made the back measurement smaller than the front at the chest and hip, allowing the corset to 'breathe' with the lungs. 'There is compression through the seams and edges but no boning channels that will restrict, so for –'

'Singing, yes, I know!' Dame Lily looked doubtful. 'But it's not tight.'

'It's made to accommodate a costume that uses certain principles, a close fit, V neckline or a feature to draw the eye . . .'

Penina was gesticulating behind Dame Lily's back, *Stop talking!*

But it was too late, Dame Lily's good nature had vanished. 'I know all of that! Who do you think you are?'

Molly stepped back. Dame Lily threw her bound and substantial body onto her lounge and buried her face in her hands. 'It is all too, too much, I am treated so badly, people are so unkind.'

'It's Luisa Tetrazzini,' said Penina. 'She has stolen Covent Garden from Dame Lily.'

'My artistic home!' screeched the Dame.

Penina exclaimed, 'And worse! Luisa is coming out to Australia.'

'But Dame Lily's show will sell out,' Molly offered, 'it always does. You are greatly loved, Dame Lily.'

'Of course I am, what a stupid thing to say! Just go, I need peace.'

Molly took the parcel from her big bag. 'I brought a gift, I'll leave it with Penina.'

'Is it something for me?' Dame Lily composed herself a little.

'It's a costume . . .'

Her grief evaporated and she lunged for the parcel but fell, face down, then managed to curl over onto her back, face to the ceiling, like a dropped eiderdown. Penina made a fuss of the carpet saying she'd speak to the manager about trip hazards, but Dame Lily's eyes were on the costume, which Molly had unfurled.

'It's for the "Queen of the Night".'

Dame Lily raised one arm. 'Give me that.'

Molly and Penina helped Dame Lily heave herself up, quite easily as the corset held her firm, but allowed her to bend and help herself a little. Her eyes had not left the costume. 'You made this for me?'

'I did.'

'I didn't commission you.' Dame Lily didn't want to pay for it.

'No. It's yours, if you'd like it.'

The Dame held the costume against her substantial body. It was outwardly a plain but beautiful dress, bat-shaped, thinning towards the hem. The Dame's breath became shallow, her eyes shone and she struggled to contain her glee. Penina winked at Molly. Dame Lily held a cuff and the Queen of the Night raised her arm, unfurling translucent, bat-like wings. The net was shot through with veins and capillaries darned in red and blue.

'It's bold,' she said, embracing the gown. 'Not the *best* costume I've seen, but I'll wear it as a favour, since it is a gift.' She paused. It was Molly's cue to be grateful, and so she gushed her thankfulness, which Dame Lily waved away.

'What fun!' cried Dame Lily, her composure again lost. 'Oh, Penina, won't the audience be astounded when I raise my arms!'

'And when they hear your voice!'

Dame Lily started to sing the aria from *The Magic Flute*. Penina quickly cautioned her, 'You haven't done your warm-ups . . . the high C.'

'"Der Hölle Rache" does need preparation.' Dame Lily grabbed Molly's arm. 'Luisa Tetrazzini's middle voice is thin.'

'I've heard so,' said Molly earnestly.

Dame Lily sang – very softly, and a little off-key – '*Un bel dì, vedremo, levarsi un fil di fumo, sull'estremo, confin del mare,*' but as the notes got higher she stopped suddenly. 'Well, off you go!'

Molly stood and curtsied, though she wasn't sure why, and Dame Lily was lost in her reflection. But as she opened the door, Dame Lily said, 'It's very good, Molly Dunnage.'

Molly stepped out onto Spring Street a new woman. She would be invited to opening night, of course, and wondered what she would wear, and what they would all wear. Her aunt must absolutely wear a breast stay.

August and April fronted up at the hospital, as instructed, and spent the morning in their underwear, holding hands across the gap between their gurneys and connected by rubber tubing inserted into their forearms. As April's lifeblood poured into her brother, their ageing doctor left them with the enamel bowls and sterilised dressings and serrated clamps and lurking nurses, and wandered off to have morning tea.

When the procedure was complete, the kind nurses provided tea and a biscuit, and instructed them to take a cab home.

In Carlton, April shuffled her brother through the front gate and straight into bed, then took to her own bed, her boots resting on the bed end.

When Molly came home she took one look at them, heated the soup and fed them, propping up her aunt and tucking a napkin under her chins. She sat with her father, tempting him with a spoonful of shank stewed with garden vegetables, but he prodded the bandage around his arm, a spot of blood where the cannula had been. 'Tell me, my dear daughter, what about this boy, Leander? Can he swim?'

August was pleased with his joke, and Molly smiled. 'Like a leech, Dad.'

'Leeches are banned forever. Apparently, I need all the blood I can get. I hear he's a teacher? I found teaching a good steady profession, though there are risks: low wages, headlice, childhood excretions and disease. Will this man support you and your dreams?'

'He will. But we are just friends, Dad.' It had hurt to say that, but she knew they were more than friends.

Molly would keep aiming for everything she wanted, despite the world and its war.

Chapter 28

HORATIO ARRIVED THE next day, parading across Curtain Square in a dark three-piece suit, the band on his hat matching his tie, and swinging a brass-handled cane.

'You here to do some tap dancing?' Molly asked.

He pointed the cane at her. 'It actually shoots poison darts.'

'That's handy. You do look lovely, though. What's in the box?'

'Mother has made you a new hat.'

'Why?'

'Because the one you wear is more amusing than you intend.'

She took the box, put the hat on and smiled. It was a burgundy felt cloche, with a fine red cotton grevillea moulded to its side, exquisitely made.

Horatio stood behind her, looking in the hat-stand mirror. 'That's better, isn't it?'

'Is my current boater really that bad?'

'Mother is making some rather nice hats for the Spring Racing Carnival.'

'What's the trend?'

'Despite what Europe dictates, here they still want the biggest hat, but we know the bigger the hat the smaller the husband's income. It's going to be hard to get ostrich feathers if there's a war.'

They took two kitchen chairs to the rotunda and sat at the back with a picnic basket and, rather boldly, a bottle of wine. There was such news to catch up on: Alathea, Dame Lily, Yaambul. Molly described the landscape, fishing and collecting mysteriously populated water and molluscs with a local boy called Leander, tugging yabbies and leeches from a sheep shank. Halfway through their second glass of wine, the band started up: 'It's a Long Way to Tipperary'. They moved further away to talk.

'Tell me more about the country,' he said. 'Was it dusty? Did you sneeze a lot?'

She told him about the weather, the hotel, the view, the sky, the stars, the friendly people who were not ready for equality for women, though the women did more of their fair share on the farms and in the homes. She boasted that the rail system was efficient and the post office very modern, and she mentioned her expeditions to the windmill to try out the parachute.

'Is there a social life?'

'Football.'

'What about a band or an orchestra?'

'Cousin Eda says two chaps play fiddle and squeezebox on special occasions. And when I was having tea with Leander I saw a pamphlet on the hotel noticeboard for a footballers' ball.'

'Marvellous,' said Horatio sarcastically. 'I suppose if you wanted more friends you could try church.'

'Less threatening types at the pub, I'd say. But as I mentioned, I found a friend up a windmill.'

'Yes, you mentioned . . .' He looked to the band, who were now playing 'Ode to Thee'. They listened for a while. She was about to announce that she was bored and leave, when he said, 'I'm teasing you, Molly, I know you're bursting so you'd better tell me all about this boy.'

'Well, he doesn't play football and he's quite different, though he's still just one of the locals. Everyone knows everyone else's strange ways, it seems.'

'There are degrees. Some of us are *too* different. Intriguing that his name's Leander?'

'Yes, Leander, and he's a good swimmer.'

'Molly, your face flushed pink and misty when you spoke his name!'

'I hope that one day you will meet him. Mind you, it might all come to nothing.' He was meant to write, but he hadn't yet.

'Are you going back to the country?'

'One day, but he said he was coming here.'

But she had no letter to say exactly when, and still swung between irritation and yearning, surprised that she even wanted to get married. It was something she hadn't considered seriously up until last week, and now she wanted nothing less than life with Leander.

'I have news too.'

She hadn't really finished talking about Leander but could see it was thrilling news, so gave him her full attention.

Finally, Horatio was to present to his superiors his uniform design to improve mobility and athleticism and the presentation of the entire police force. 'I'm to take drawings and a written description, but I will surprise them with the actual prototype. It's more efficient and effective to show them, they'll see that the uniform will be admired by the general public, and this in turn will boost morale. They like initiative.'

'What does your mother think of your new design?'

'She says my upright superiors will send me to the provinces immediately.'

'Will they?'

'Well, if they do, life has taught me to make the most of what is allowed me.'

The following day, Molly gasped when she saw the pale square envelope through the slit in the letterbox. But it was not written by the lovely boy from the endless plains beneath the endless sky – it was a cheque from Penina, with a note that said, 'With gratitude, Dame Lily adores her costume.' And there were six tickets to *Your Favourite Arias* opening-night show – but no request to return for the final fit for the 'Queen of the Night' costume, nor for any further garments. The devastation Molly felt was brief and sharp. She decided the six tickets were compensation, a 'thank you and goodbye', that there were surplus tickets because the Dame could not fill the theatre; this concert was her swansong, her career over. Then her vengeful thoughts gave way to despair, and finally cautious cheerfulness: it wasn't necessarily the end of all opportunity, her costume might appear on stage, it still might be a start to something and this would cheer her father, so unwell.

It was clear now, she would dedicate herself to building her business at home and help care for the older people in the house . . . until they all moved to Yaambul, for that seemed like a good thing to do for everyone.

'We're all off to hear our favourite arias,' she called, sounding joyful.

Her aunt moved her magnifying glasses to the top of her head. 'Holy mackerel.'

'We have six tickets.'

Her aunt beamed. 'We could take Miss Berrycloth – a farewell gift?'

'Let's,' said Molly, thinking she'd have taken Gladys. Still, it would be a better experience than a brief handshake with Henrietta Dugdale or herding children around the Blue Mountains. Miss Berrycloth could tell everyone at the farm that she had seen Dame Lily Pert; that would give her more gravitas than a worn postcard.

'Where's Dad?'

'He's gone to enlist.'

'How amusing you are.'

She found him in his studio, where he always was, and he was dumbfounded. 'The Princess? Opera? *Live* opera? I have nothing to wear.'

'I'll make you something.'

*

Molly was heading home with spare ribs for dinner when Evan Pettyman's face loomed at her, startling in the passing faces by the Kent Hotel on Rathdowne Street.

'Did you follow me?'

He was taken aback, for he *had* followed her. 'Coincidence, that's all. But now that we're here, I should tell you that if we're going to be partners, then we must inform you of the exact financial situation and in light of that, we need know a bit more about your very progressive and interesting ideas.'

'I will tell you when there is a contract for me to sign and a factory waiting.'

'Did you know that corsets are being abandoned in Europe?'

'Yes, left in doorways and on orphanage stoops all over the continent.'

He ignored her joke. 'I'm keen to see our dream of making underwear for women come true.'

Molly replied that people would always need underwear.

'Let's discuss all of this like civilised, grown-up people?' He pointed to the pub behind her.

She thought he was joking. 'What, in *there?*'

'There's a nice dining room and we can have a refreshing cranberry drink while we discuss some general points of the business plan.'

Mrs Sidebottom could be watching her, and she thought about her Temperance Society ideals, her fury over Gladys and her lie that Gladys was a drunk. 'Very well.'

He pushed the door open and steered her towards a table. She felt the warmth of his hand in the small of her back and pulled away. That gesture was Leander's right alone. Evan pulled the chair out for her and snapped his fingers at the waitress, who was taking an order at a table across the room. Molly thought of Snakelegs.

'She'll come when she's able,' she said.

'And now she knows where to come.'

When the waitress did arrive, Evan ordered a drink Molly had never heard of, then proceeded to explain his connections in the business world, and the world of justice through his lawyer, Mr Hawker, and what he expected of a work ethic. He reminded her that he had knowledge of retail, given his job at the glove shop, at which point Molly interrupted to ask about Alathea. 'Have you seen her?'

'We have met to discuss the exchange of money.' She saw a gleeful flicker in his small, intense eyes. 'Has she told you?'

'I have been in the country for the past week.' And everything changed in that week: a lifetime of events collided and made her future.

'The country? How are things in the country?'

'Much more pleasant than the city, if I'm honest.'

'Well, while you were holidaying, details have been discussed and contracts are prepared for signing. But you haven't mentioned this to anyone, have you?'

'Just my parents. Is something wrong?'

'No! Good Lord, no! You are more useful than you know to our enterprise.'

The waitress arrived with a drink each and Evan raised his in a toast.

'Are we celebrating? Shouldn't Miss Pocknall be with us?'

'Miss Pocknall is securing our new venture.' He began to speak, quickly, and Molly was baffled by his discourse on 'profit' and 'expenditure'. He pressed her to drink, but it did not agree with her. It tasted sweet, yet bitter. 'What we want from you next, apart from detailed drawings and designs, is some sort of input, or guarantee.'

'Guarantee?'

He laughed. 'My dear girl, we have funds, but not enough. This is a big enterprise – it simply *can't* fail – but we need more funds. We need to show people that we are progressive, a company with a name and assets, not just a cart horse and dray!'

He laughed. Molly did not.

'Women are discarding corsets by the minute. We need to present as a viable business – for example, we need a motor vehicle with our name on it, to transport and advertise product to shops and the modern woman, and we need those things quickly. You have drawings, ideas?'

'I do, but they are mine.'

'There's not much point having them and not wanting to invest them into your own company. You have a savings account, surely?'

'I am female, I can't do anything without a man's permission.'

'Which is why you have me.'

She changed tack. 'About the possible war . . .'

'Manufacturing will boom, there'll be demand for uniforms and linen, and good-quality clothes for women who will need to do their share, work without the restraint of whalebone and steel . . . the steel will go to the war effort . . . *if* there is a war in Europe.' He moved a finger towards her glass, *drink*.

'I have no savings.' She took one more sip and put the drink aside.

'You could help us borrow, use your inheritance.'

Molly shook her head, confused.

'The family home as security.' He took a form from his pocket and put it on the table in front of her.

'That's impossible.'

He moved his hand near her drink, his fingers touching the base of the glass, but she didn't pick it up. 'We just need to show the bank, it's just a bit of paper. If I thought our homes were at risk I wouldn't advocate we sign them over. Explain to your family that this venture could change your lives. You could learn to drive an automobile, Molly Dunnage, and you could be rich.' He placed a fountain pen beside the piece of paper. 'Your own business . . . if you invest.'

She didn't even look at the form or pen; she was suddenly quite weary and needed to get home. It had been a heady few weeks, and the thought of being a businesswoman at that moment felt overwhelming. She gathered her coat.

'You're going to waste your drink?'

'You have not offered me anything firm, you have simply asked me for more. It is all just talk.' The floor beneath her undulated, so she steadied herself with the help of the chair.

Mr Pettyman put the form in her hand. 'Molly, you are not thinking clearly, it will all be settled this time next week. This is your chance to invest and make *money* rather than just wages.'

What she needed was air. There was alcohol in the drink, much more than the smallest nip of whisky she was used to. She was almost at the door, and he hovered in case she stumbled, but she didn't.

'Well, at least I tried to help you, but you have the form . . . just fill in some of the detail, just in case, we can always sign it later.' Or he could sign it himself.

She squared her shoulders and left. Evan sipped her drink and put it down, grimacing. He had not got anything from her; his hand hadn't even brushed against a breast or pressed the inside of a thigh; there had been no stolen kiss. She was tricky, this Molly Dunnage. He half admired her. Probably best to not try wooing her again until he had a signature. Evan slunk away, heading towards Princes Hill down Rathdowne Street so he could pause to admire the ladies' white underwear in the apparel shop.

August and April watched her walk across the square, slow and steady, and were pleased when she pushed through the gate and settled on the veranda bench between them. They were waiting for a hearse to pass on its way to the cemetery.

'I think it's going to rain.'

'No newspaper?'

'No, Dad, none to be found.'

Next door Mrs Sidebottom came to her front gate, her hat

sitting on top of her piled-up hair and her umbrella unfurled above. She looked like a railway signal. Mrs Sidebottom was leaving home early to secure a spot close to the grieving relatives, and she also liked to get a good look at the coffin, gauge how much the family spent on it. She nodded to the Dunnages and remarked, 'It will be a big funeral,' as if the number of mourners indicated the point of life itself.

'She'll be pleased,' August replied, the comment was lost on Mrs Sidebottom.

'It was typhoid,' she said, accusingly.

'Typhoid is from bad water,' Aunt April replied. 'Or bad food.'

There was silence, then Mrs Sidebottom said, 'It's Mrs Blinkhorn, you know?'

'It was in the paper,' Aunt April replied sweetly.

Molly wanted to say that Mrs Blinkhorn still owed her two pounds but found she wasn't in the mood for sparring. She felt a little woozy, and she had not heard from Leander, or Alathea, and this made death seem less remarkable.

'She was a very upright woman,' said Mrs Sidebottom, pointedly. 'Well respected, and as I say, a very big funeral.'

Wearily, Molly said, 'Well, that's something you should aspire to,' and looked up at the low, dark clouds. The air turned chilly and damp and smelled of rain,

'She was in your house not long ago.' Mrs Sidebottom's tone was now hateful.

'Thankfully, she didn't pass her typhoid on to us,' spat Molly.

There was a thunderclap and suddenly hail fell like rocks, cracking on the roof overhead just as Mrs Blinkhorn's hearse rounded the corner. Hail gathered on the flatbed of the cart and shredded the corsage on top of her casket, petals sliding down. Mrs Sidebottom hurried after it, hail bouncing off her umbrella and striking her bustle, the back of her skirt turning dark with rain.

Sitting by the fire later, Aunt April said, 'That's two.'

It was a well-known fact that people died in threes.

August looked from his sister to his daughter. 'I refuse to be number three.'

'I'd take either of your rooms,' Molly said.

'Just know that the minute you've moved to Yaambul we'll rent out the living room and take ourselves on a holiday to Paris.'

She laughed, but thought again that she'd had no word from Leander.

Chapter 29

ALATHEA HAD BEEN out for the day with Marguerite and some of the girls. She was starving, so stopped in the kitchen to make herself supper. As she headed up to her rooms with wine, cheese and fruit, they blocked her.

'We need to talk,' said the American cousin.

'Not now.'

Clive took her arm and guided her into her father's favourite room, the library, a room they'd rarely entered. 'Please,' said Clive, 'sit down.'

Sitting would mean her back was against the wall and they would stand in front of her, blocking the doorway. 'I'll stand.' She put her tray on the baby grand and popped a grape into her mouth.

'We know you have the deeds to the factory and house.'

'How do you know that?' She pushed the pips out onto her hand and scraped them onto the tray.

Norbert said, 'Your actions have stopped the legal process until copies are located or new deeds drawn up. We think you know the safe code and that you have the deeds and the will.'

'You can think what you like.' She picked up the tray.

Clive stood in front of her. 'Your relationship with your "friend" Marguerite Baca is inappropriate and illegal.'

'Oh,' she sighed, '*this* tactic again.'

Norbert held up a pamphlet and read it aloud, '*The enemy of Suffrage is the system of patriarchy.* You don't like men, you prefer women.'

He did not read out the last of the quote from Molly Dunnage's pamphlet: '. . . *and if women can support the system of patriarchy why can't men support the cause for equality?*'

Norbert continued. 'You have already been warned. We will expose your lewd behaviour with Marguerite. You won't be considered fit for anything, or anyone.'

'And then you will have me committed?'

'We hadn't thought of that,' said Norbert and he turned to Clive.

'I'm not surprised given you are a man who has not yet mastered riding a horse.'

Clive looked askance at Norbert, 'Really?'

Norbert said, 'I doubt we'll have any trouble finding a doctor to certify you, cousin.'

'Nor do I.'

There was no lewd behaviour. Marguerite and Alathea's relationship was friendship, they were children together and now women who sought refuge with like-minded women in an oppressive man's world. Alathea and Marguerite were affirmed by their mutual ideas, emotional support and rewarding discussion. She appreciated Marguerite and in turn Marguerite saw who Alathea was and responded.

'You take part in violent and illegal demonstrations with suffragettes.'

'I don't, but you will find someone to say I do, for example, Therese. Anything else you need to say?'

'Plenty,' said Clive, but then found he didn't have anything at hand.

They watched her stroll out and up the stairs to her rooms, then strode across the landing to Emrys Pocknall's office, certain of their victory, buoyed by their superiority, and greatly encouraged by the supportive backslapping from their chums who waited, drinking and smoking.

Alathea wished she'd brought the entire bottle of wine, but was consoled that she'd soon be out of it all, off to find a new future for herself. And she thought of her father's factory, her poor mother's fortunes sunk into it – and wasted – and heard her father's voice: 'Strong reasons make strong actions.'

She found her bedroom door wide open. The lock had been forced and her room looked like a bull had been dancing in it. The contents of all the drawers had been upended, her bed stripped, the linen thrown into a corner and her mattress upturned. Paintings had been taken from the wall and dropped onto the floor, her jewellery was sprinkled across the tatami and her writing case pillaged for evidence of an inappropriate relationship. They'd even searched her wardrobe, leaving her dresses like corpses all over the floor. She laughed at the fact that her cousin and fiancé were driven in circles by their frustrated search.

Later, Clive Woodgrip pushed the door open and stood looking at her, his fingers in his waistcoat pockets.

'I am withdrawing my offer of marriage.'

She continued brushing her hair. 'Well, see it's done properly. Have lawyers make it official.'

'Of course.' He left, then turned back. 'But if you would just return the ring.'

She swept her hair to the side and reached for a hair clip. 'You find it.'

He kicked through some trinkets and but could not bring himself to get down on his hands and knees to search through the mess.

Later, on her way to see Marguerite, she stopped at the aviary and opened the door. She looked at the birds, all Australian natives, and said, 'The sky is yours, I wish you all well.' Over the next few days, the people of Melbourne were delighted to see galahs, lorikeets and cockatoos – black, white, grey gang-gangs – corellas and cockatiels, rosellas and grass parrots flapping across the sky and sitting on telegraph poles, many species perched together, as if they were friends.

Chapter 30

AUGUST DUNNAGE LABOURED his way across Curtain Square, a tall lean man carrying a newspaper, listing, mouth agape, his stare fixed on the ground before him. He was conscious of the frosty grass crunching under his boots, his wet socks, his numb toes sliding about in his boots. Freddy Sidebottom's feet protruded from beneath the rotunda stairs and August peeped under the structure, but Freddy was asleep. He had stuffed newspaper up his sleeves and down the front of his overcoat and August felt for Freddy Sidebottom's frost-bitten extremities. He took the business and sports sections of *The Age* and laid them on top of Freddy's lower legs and feet.

He checked the letterbox as he passed, though his daughter was wearing the broom to a stub, sweeping her way to it every ten minutes. April was expecting a reply from Miss Berrycloth, while Molly was hoping to hear from Alathea, as well as from Yaambul. Molly was also eager to read about news of Dame Lily Pert's concert, or Alathea's court proceedings.

He threw the paper onto the table and said, 'I just saw a pair of eclectus parrots sitting on Mrs Raven's apple tree. Quite wonderful.'

The newspaper said much to flag a coming war: 'Australia To Stand With The Mother Country'. In an election speech at Colac in Victoria, Mr Andrew Fisher, leader of the Australian Labor Party, had declared that 'should the worst happen, after everything has been done that honour will permit, Australians will stand beside the mother country to help and defend her to our last man and our last shilling'.

'The worst should not happen,' said Molly. She found what she wanted below the engagement notices. It was a small article, but significant . . . a 'Breach of Promise' notice between Alathea Juanita Pocknall and Clive Robert Woodgrip. Mr Woodgrip had 'ruptured the engagement by asking to be released from vows which could never be met in marriage.' There were no costs to be reimbursed, no gifts to be returned, and no payments for breach of promise were to be made.

Molly cut the piece out and placed it on the hot plate. She watched Clive Woodgrip's name turn brown, curl and disintegrate, a thread of smoke disappearing up into the chimney blackness.

'Something awful happens to that poor woman every week,' she said, thinking of her own pledge, possibly broken.

'Sometimes,' said Aunt April, 'things happen for a reason.'

Her father agreed. 'Woodgrip was likely not an honest chap at all.'

'Opportunistic,' said Aunt April, pouring tea for her brother. 'Mind you, it does take effort and fortitude to deceive and betray.'

Molly almost winced. Surely Leander hadn't deceived her? Why was there no reply to her letter? How could a week be so exciting and then life become so devastatingly disappointing?

August added, 'And it hurts terribly when you once thought the betrayer was your friend.'

Molly took herself to her cubby to fret. Tomorrow, she would write to him and ask for a formal clarification that their pledge was broken. Like Alathea, she had been cast aside. Leander Behan was insincere; she was a mere dalliance – or perhaps he had been kidnapped, or drowned? It had been almost a week and she had received no reply to either of her letters. He was discouraged by the life she described, or his parents had changed his mind for him. Was it his mother? His father? Or Mrs Sidebottom was stealing her mail, or Leander had written the wrong address. She contemplated sending notes to every house on every Curtain Street in Melbourne. Or had there been an accident? A train derailment that stopped all mail? Perhaps the government had cancelled exams and he had to teach?

She wondered how Alathea coped with the lies and deceit of her cousin and fiancé. She thought of Evan Pettyman. He would save them, but then she was dubious about the meeting at the hotel, the drink, and felt a little sick. Would Alathea have any part of a devious man? Or was he honest? Opportunistic, or a liar? Or was her reason tainted by her sadness, the rejections she felt? She must write to Alathea.

Aunt April sat with her toes in the slow oven, knitting new gloves for the family. August sat beside her and she made room in the oven for his feet. 'Winter's going to be grim.'

'Yes.' He wasn't sure he would make it through the winter but would press on. 'Do we have a spare blanket for Freddy Sidebottom?'

'We'll find something.'

August inspected his shoes. The stitching along the side had burst on one and there was a hole in the sole of the other, mere insole between his foot and the frost. He found room for his sad boots at the back of the slow oven.

Molly shoved her way between her aunt and father to get to the stove. She picked up another log – a dried water-soaked and rolled-up newspaper – and poked it into the coals.

'I should order more wood,' said August, and Molly knew the point of that statement was that she should either go and collect some or increase her contribution to the household budget.

'If there is a war they will need needle girls.' She tried to sound cheery, but going to work sewing in a factory was not a future to relish when better dreams floated before her. Her father turned the page of his newspaper and there, smiling at them, was Dame Lily. The headline read, 'Our Dame Lily Returns'.

Dame Lily Pert was to retain her rightful place at the Princess due to support of the Australian prima donna's enormously popular show, *Your Favourite Arias by Dame Lily Pert*. Tickets were selling fast.

A single line at the bottom of the article mentioned that Luisa Tetrazzini had cancelled her tour 'due to the worsening conditions in Europe'. Luisa did not want to be stuck in Australia when war broke out.

Mid-morning, Molly checked the letterbox and found it empty. She aimed her hurt at Mrs Sidebottom. Her poster read:

A WOMAN IS SUCCESSFUL BECAUSE SHE HAS SELF-
DETERMINATION AND THE RIGHT TO BECOME HERSELF.

Molly added, '*Except that men prevent us from being so.*'

Then the sun rose above the trees and the house started to thaw, though Molly's fingers remained itchy with cold, which meant she wouldn't sew just yet. And then she wondered why she bothered to make anything when she had no current commission; no one would want the corset she was making, no one would ever know about her bust stays, and apparently all of her customers had sufficient practical bloomers and linen jumps. No project was worth her effort. She had lost her impetus, was miserable, and decided to go back to bed to finish *A Doll's House*.

And then there was a knock at the door.

Aunt April wondered aloud why anyone would drop in before lunch. August assumed it was either the debt collector or Alathea Pocknall again.

'It'll be Mrs Bigbottom come to snarl,' Molly said.

'Well, you can sort that out since you're the one who upsets her.' Her aunt kept knitting, not prepared to move from the stove, and her father decided to attend to the chooks.

Blowing on her cupped hands to remind her aunt that she too was cold, Molly peeked out to the veranda. It was a man, though she could only see the arm of his coat. It must be one of the Sidebottom twins, Aubrey or Manfred, arrived to abuse her.

She flung open the door. 'Go away!'

It was Leander, taller than she remembered, more handsome, and beaming at her. There he was, in the flesh, a live person smiling at her, a magical beautiful face that sent a rush all the way to her fingers and toes.

It was true. He was real. He did love her.

His face fell and he took a step back.

'Oh!' she said. 'I thought you were Aubrey or Manfred.'

He took another step back and she reached out, grabbing his coat lapels and dragging him in. 'Don't go! Stay! Come in, come in, please, you misunderstand, they're neighbourhood boys, childhood chums, my friend Gladys's cousins, I thought you were them.'

He let himself be dragged into the house by Molly, relieved that it hadn't been his imagination. She was as lovely as she was a week ago. Then she put her arms around him and squeezed, just for a moment, before remembering herself and stepping back.

'Sorry.'

'Don't be,' he pleaded, reaching for her.

But Aunt April cried, 'Oh, how lovely! Leander, do come in, please, we are thrilled to see you.'

He was looking at Molly, longingly; such a feeling, like a flame, in that one brief impulsive cuddle.

Aunt April took the bewildered boy's arm and pulled him down the hall towards the kitchen. He felt the need to stoop a little under the low ceilings and was pleased by the pictures covering the walls, which he could see only partially hid the cracks. Yaambul was there! Depictions of the land and scrub around his hometown – in all seasons, including harvest. He found the sculptures a little unsettling, until he realised they were pots, vases and figurines that had failed in the kiln. He felt large in the small messy house, though it was homely.

'Sit,' Aunt April said, wrenching his rucksack from him and pointing to her chair by the fire. 'Molly, put the kettle on, please.'

She was staring.

'*Kettle*, Molly. Leander, have you eaten? Would you like some bread, fruit, or perhaps some toast? We have soup. Bone soup.'

'Don't go to any bother –'

'It's no bother, you have travelled far. Please. Tell us about your journey.' She snapped her fingers in front of Molly's face to break her trance, for she was staring at Leander as though he was King George taking a bath by the stove.

Molly saw to the kettle and sliced some bread, her hands shaking, while Leander marvelled at Melbourne. 'I'd forgotten how many people live here and how fast and modern it is, so many automobiles and cabs, and trams . . . And Flinders Street Station, so grand. Nice clock tower.' Then he paused. 'I hope it's alright that I'm here, I was trying to surprise you, I thought you'd be happy –'

'I am!' yelled Molly. 'Aren't we, Aunt?'

'More than you'll ever know.'

'And who would you be?' It was August, standing in the doorway, wearing a knitted cap and his painting coat, his smile a pale lemon colour.

'This is Leander. And this is Dad,' said Molly. 'He's painting a yellow pot. Obviously.'

'I'm a ceramicist.' August reached out to shake Leander's hand, beaming at him like he was a tall wad of hundred-pound notes. 'So happy to meet you, so happy . . .'

'And I'm happy to meet you, Mr Dunnage.'

'Call me August, please.' There was a silence, so August sought to fill it. 'You're here for a holiday? Business?'

'I'm here because, well, um . . .'

Molly saved him. 'Dad, Leander's a teacher, it's exam study week.'

'Honourable job. Molly, you must take Leander to the bay.'

'Yes. The beach!' Aunt April clapped.

'We can all go,' Molly said. 'I'll make a picnic.'

August and April looked at each other, thinking of the wet weather, the wear and tear on their boots, their painful chilblains, the effort to enjoy dry sandwiches while sitting on a wet rug and the taste of lukewarm thermos tea. 'We've been many times,' said August.

While Leander ate lunch, Molly sat next to him or circled him, and then she took him for a tour of the backyard and showed him her sewing room. August's paintbrush went stiff as it dried yellow and Aunt April sat so long with her feet in the oven that her chilblains thawed.

Finally, lunch over, Leander said he 'must head off'.

'Where to?' Molly asked, alarmed.

He reached for his rucksack. 'I wondered if the hotel across the square took guests.'

'Nonsense,' said August. 'You must stay here.'

'Where?' said Aunt April and Molly, in unison.

'Molly can sleep with Aunt April.'

'Never,' said Molly, and Aunt April closed her eyes and shook her head slowly, her chin scraping across her collar.

Molly stood beside Leander, leaning a little so that her arm touched his, wanting very much to take his hand. He was so handsome, his brown eyes so soft and his hair so thick and shiny, his face clean shaven and his teeth well maintained. And he had a noble profile, Molly decided. And then she considered that she might run into him on her morning dash for the lavatory and knew that it was too awful, far too soon for such an encounter.

'How long are you staying?'

'Well, there's a weekend coming and then study week, and I'd go after that, if that's alright. I'll stay at the hotel.'

Eleven nights! Molly could scarcely contain herself.

'We expect you back here for breakfast, lunch and dinner,' April told him.

'Whenever you are awake,' Molly said.

August backed them up. 'Come, I'll go to the Kent with you, but I'll bring you back as soon as you're settled, we will plan your Melbourne adventure.'

From the front window Molly and Aunt April watched the men walk through the square to the Kent Hotel, a spring in August's step and their breath visible in the wintry air. As they passed, the men glanced down at Freddy Sidebottom, still sleeping in the doorway under the rotunda, a magpie raiding the sole of his boot.

Molly was back at the window watching for them when they came back across the park. The magpie hopped away and the men paused to speak to Freddy. Then Leander leaned down and touched Freddy's leg and stood up quickly.

Something was wrong. Still watching, Molly cried, 'AUNT!'

April came quickly, and they hurried, Molly calling, 'Will I go for the doctor?'

But August shook his head. 'Thank you, daughter, no. It's too late for that.'

Her first thought was that Gladys would come back to attend his funeral and she could tell her about Leander, and of this Molly was ashamed. Her second thought was that Leander would be accused of being one of them, a magus dropped in from the sky to kill Freddy. And third, she didn't want Leander to think Melbournians were barbarians who let their frail old neighbours die in parks.

They all stood for a moment in contemplation, the potency of what had actually happened dawning. Why, in this day and age, did a man die of exposure in a park?

They were too bound up in their own selves.

August and Aunt April stayed with Freddy while Molly and Leander went to fetch a policeman. No one thought it their job to inform Freddy's wife, especially since she would accuse them, and so it was Mr Kent who finally went to fetch Mrs Sidebottom. The policeman and the Dunnages stood well back as she marched across the square with the copper stick still in her hand, wet from stirring the sheets. She looked at her husband. 'He hasn't been my responsibility for a decade, he left me penniless.' She left, her face as expressionless as a saucepan lid.

Molly wanted to call out, 'But you had a home he bought for you . . . for you and your love of war,' but Leander was beside her, so she said, 'Freddy never recovered from the war.'

And so Freddy Sidebottom was wrapped in a tarp and waved off by his rotunda friends, a dishevelled guard of honour around the flatbed wagon nursing bottles of rum and port under their coats.

At home, by the fire, Aunt April nudged her brother. 'That's three.'

Later, Aunt April started work on a new sign for her front yard:

FAIR COMPENSATION FOR WOUNDED WAR
VETERANS AND THEIR INNOCENT CHILDREN.

PATRIOTS MUST PAY FOR THE PATRIOTISM OF
EX-SERVICEMEN AND THEIR CHILDREN.

While the Dunnages and Leander ruminated over the inequality of the world and the fate of those with no one to turn to, the gap between the privileged and poor, Mrs Sidebottom stood at her wash trough, her feet in mud, quite alone. Beside her, towels turned in the boiling copper and a sheet, stalled in the ringer, dripped onto the dirt floor. She reached to turn the handle, remembering the young man she had married, eager and optimistic as he went off to the Boer War. His adventure would bring better wages and a new house far away from Curtain Square and the uncouth neighbours. But her eager, happy husband came home spent, and the wages went to the hotel opposite, and because he was not considered 'of good character', he was declared ineligible for the service pension, the invalid pension and the old age pension, meagre as they were. All around her people seemed almost as poor, even poorer, but still content, even happy. How?

She turned the ringer handle, the sheet cascading slowly to the wicker basket like a flat python and her mouth yawning with misery for herself.

The Dunnage family were accustomed to a certain way of moving around each other, observing an unspoken protocol surrounding the stove and warmth distribution, who had right of way when it came to dodging each other in the hall. But Leander was a new entity in the small house and Molly and her cohabitants became less territorial. In the kitchen especially, Leander's shoulders seemed broader than they did in big country rooms and he occupied a lot of leg room under the table, which pleased Molly as she felt her knee resting gently on his. And he pressed against her from time to time, and she against him, when someone squeezed past the table or approached in the passage.

Molly was sent to the grocers with a pound from her savings and ran, all the way there and back, pausing on the veranda to catch her breath before she sauntered down the hall to make a poised entrance to the kitchen. August exceeded himself with their late evening meal, poaching parsnip in herbs and wine, mashing the potatoes with cream and chives, steaming the silverbeet with garlic and butter and, for dessert, sliced pear with nuts. Because of the rain, the general greyness and the cold, they remained together at the stove all afternoon, talking. It was an easy conversation, freckled with laughter, and some male company allowed

August to shine. Leander showed interest, and Molly learned details about her father's days at school, how his family had been 'generally moderately comfortably off', but that was no longer the case.

'Indeed,' said April.

He talked about his teaching career, how he met Myrtle when she delivered a letter mistakenly sent to her address.

'I opened the door and looked at her and knew at once I'd like to marry her.'

Aunt April smiled at her brother, who was taking full advantage of his platform. He went on to speak a little longer than required about his joy in art and nature.

After dinner, August asked Molly to fetch the whisky and April reached for four glasses. Molly told Leander, 'You'll need this before a walk across the park on a freezing night, but not too much, you don't want to fall down.'

Leander laughed, stopped and apologised, as they thought of Freddy Sidebottom, but April and August laughed for joy and happiness and their new, small family – and joy for Molly, the cheeriest she'd been since she was a small girl and had found her friend Gladys.

They said good night to Leander and the guardians stayed by the fire while Molly walked her beau to the door, where he held her hand and said he would see her in the morning. Molly wanted to see him every morning until she died.

She peeled off another pound note from her savings and found her father in his studio, rinsing the brushes and pushing lids onto paint tins. 'Do you think of Mum often?'

His hand stopped. 'You see, they don't leave, they stay with you. Your mother is a presence when I do anything.'

'A presence.'

'Yes, like snug shoes. You're not entirely conscious of them but you know they're there. Sometimes I consciously think about how Myrtle would have done certain things – ask myself, what she would think? And lately I feel that she is here to reassure me while shepherding me gently to her.'

Next time she went to the cemetery, Molly would ask her mother not to hurry him. 'That's comforting,' she said.

'It is.'

The next morning, when Aunt April asked if he had eaten breakfast, they understood why Leander had arrived wearing a frown.

'I've had porridge,' he replied.

'Molly will make breakfast, won't you, Molly? Scrambled eggs?'

His face brightened. 'Lovely, thank you.'

'How did you sleep?'

'Very well, despite the noise from the bar.'

Molly wasn't confident breakfast would be perfect, but she did her best with scrambled eggs and homegrown mushrooms on toast. Leander left few crumbs, accepted seconds of toast, complimented August on his jam, and then August and April cheerily waved the two youngsters off for the tram stop, huddled under an umbrella. It was too cold for the seaside, but they wanted to be somewhere other than a cramped kitchen with chaperones. They visited the library, where Molly returned *A Doll's House* and collected *The Custom of the Country*. Then they paid the electric light bill, delivered August's invoices to the crockery shop on Rathdowne Street, and wandered through the cemetery and streets, looking at gardens and talking. Molly Dunnage could not define how happy she was, she could not think of the words, but thought perhaps that she might have everything she wanted walking beside her.

Molly came to her aunt's room and sat on the bed looking out at the Kent Hotel opposite. Her aunt said, 'If he said he will come back for dinner, then he will come.'

'He said he would be ten minutes.'

'He might have gone shopping.'

'To buy what?'

'Souvenirs?'

She headed back to the kitchen and then he knocked, and she rushed down the hall and opened the door and he was looming against the fading day with a sack of firewood on his shoulder. He carried it down the hall and dropped it on the hearth, then produced two bottles of stout and some flathead fillets.

'I don't have sea fish very often,' he said.

After fish and chips and a glass of stout, April and August went to their rooms and Leander and Molly were left by the fire. Leander asked about August's health.

'Bad blood.'

'The fish will do him good.'

'Your presence here has done him good. He doesn't get to talk to boys much. Actually, he doesn't get to talk much at all.'

'Do you think he'd like to watch a football game at the MCG?'

'No. He'd find it very tiring, and he's not a loud crowd sort of person.'

'Neither am I, I just want to go so that I can tell Jim that I've been.'

'We'll catch a tram there and stand outside,' said Molly.

'Could we?'

'We can sneak in at three-quarter time.'

He took her hand. 'This is a very good holiday.'

The next day, Saturday, Molly and Leander announced they would travel to the city.

'By tram,' said Leander eagerly.

Molly looked very stylish, Leander thought. She was wearing a homemade cream cotton dress, high waisted with a wide red and blue tartan sash, the neckline V-shaped with a lace edging and a muslin infill. The sleeves were elbow length and trimmed with lace, as was the narrow skirt. Her cloche would not match, so she had redesigned her boater with a wide red and blue tartan band.

Leander watched how she confidently purchased tram tickets – two adults, one a non-worker's fare – and how efficient she was choosing a good seat, and he learned to stand to let the grip man know to apply his brake.

Their first stop was the Book Lovers' Library where Molly collected pamphlets while Leander stood holding his hat, taking in the ceiling-high shelves of books and souvenirs, the suffrage badges, sashes and placards. He turned a world globe and ran his finger from Melbourne to Paris, and then wandered to the science section, where he found books on aerodynamics. He was served by a shop assistant – fashionable, efficient and friendly – and was impressed that the man who came to empty the till knew Molly and asked after Miss April Dunnage.

'My aunt is well, thank you, Mr Pomfrey. I'll tell her you asked after her. I see you are advertising Dame Lily Pert's concert?'

'Yes, would you like some tickets?'

'Thanks, no, ours came in the post last week.'

The shop assistants kept their eyes to the shelves but she knew they heard, and that they probably inwardly scoffed, so added, loudly, 'We've been invited to opening night.' Molly took Leander's hand and left the shop without a backward glance.

On the streets, Leander asked, 'Is that true?'

'Yes.'

Leander looked afraid.

'You can wear Dad's old suit.'

'Dame Lily Pert, *the* Dame Lily Pert?'

'At the Princess Theatre.' She pointed east towards Spring Street.

'The theatre?'

'You can tell Jim.'

As they walked through the city, she noted various styles and accessories all around them. She found it enchanting that Leander seemed to listen to her: when she explained that the trend continued away from bustles and fat sleeves towards a more tailored look, that Poiret had featured his more theatrical designs on runways this year and so the women parading around the city wore variations of his designs. She pointed out lampshade skirts and geometric cuts, as well as draped skirts under tailored jackets, and told him that Japan was all the rage and pretty caps were popular, that both women and men were fashionable in boaters but her burgundy cloche was the most fashionable. 'I'll wear it tomorrow.'

'You made what you are wearing?'

'Yes, and I feel entirely adequate.'

'I think you look entirely wonderful. Let's have morning tea, my shout.'

They found a lovely tea house for coffee and cake. It was grander than she'd ever experienced and crowded, and she suggested they find somewhere less expensive, but Leander opened the door for her and asked the waiter for their best table, please.

They were seated to the rear where the waitresses lined the wall, too far away to be able to watch the passing fashionable people and close to the kitchen's swinging doors, but the coffee was not bitter and the cake and the cream were fresh. She smiled at the weary waitresses and her feet throbbed in sympathy with theirs.

'I'm having a very head-turning time, it's great fun,' Leander said. Then, after a moment, he added, 'But I wouldn't want to live here.'

'I'm always happy in Yaambul,' Molly said, unashamed that she was being forward. 'In the city . . . because I don't have much money, my enjoyment's a bit curtailed. Theatres cost money, you need dresses and shoes for dancing, dining's too expensive, the library and art galleries and museums are wonderful but the noise of the place, the smell and the crowds: it's not for everyone. In the country, there's nature and space, and with space comes imagination and time.'

'We'll be happy, Molly.'

'We will.' And they both thought of their whole future spent as companions. It was too wonderful to have found each other.

She had eaten most of the cake, methodically, lingering on each mouthful, and watched Leander taking time to study the patrons. 'What do you think?' she asked.

'I can't see these customers lining up for apple pie in Mrs Mahone's lounge.'

They laughed, and Molly gathered the last two mouthfuls of fresh cream, icing and cake on the corner of her small plate. Before she could lift it to her mouth, she was struck by a great weight and knocked from her seat; the room upended, and the teacup clattered onto the floor beside her, the last of her tea splashing across the floor. Shoes and boots rushed over. Leander lifted the weight from her, which she then saw was one of the waitresses. The poor girl had fainted. The image of Mr Addlar, drained of colour, damp with sweat and sprawled on the factory floor, came to mind and she felt a little sick, but then she wondered about Sara and if her foot had healed. And all of those unemployed girls from Pocknall's, what had happened to them?

Leander lifted her back onto her chair, replaced her hat and wiped the coffee from her skirt with a napkin. The proprietor and the pastry chef rolled the waitress over and dragged the poor girl out to the kitchen. Molly looked at her plate, the last two scoops of cream and pink icing and sponge waiting. She reached for it when the proprietor said, 'I'll see she is punished.' He was wearing a suit that he had grown too big for.

'No, she can't have helped it, she must be ill.'

'Then she should have gone home.'

'Would you have let her? Are they given food and drink and a rest break?'

The proprietor sneered at Molly. 'I picked you as one of *them* the minute you walked in. You've just come to cause trouble.'

'It isn't me who works my waitresses until they drop. And if she'd gone home you wouldn't have paid her for the half day, would you?'

'It is you who should go home now, miss.'

Molly looked back to the last of the delicious cloudy pink and white confectionery on the pretty plate. 'I haven't finished my cake.'

The proprietor grabbed her elbow and whipped the spoon from her hand.

Leander said, 'Leave her alone,' but the proprietor pointed to the door. 'Sir, escort this nuisance from the premises.'

'She wants to finish her cake.'

The proprietor picked up the cake plate and handed it to a passing waitress. Leander sat back down in his chair. 'Sit down, Molly, we'll order more cake,' but the proprietor pulled Molly by the elbow towards the door. The floor was slippery and the customers stared as she was dragged, Leander following but unable to reach her in the crowd, all the big skirts and hats in the confined space.

Molly cried, 'This man is a bully, he's assaulting me!'

He propelled her onto the street. 'Just bugger off!'

'My handbag,' she said, and headed back towards the door but the woman on the cash register arrived with her bag and threw it at her feet. The proprietor and the cashier were both forced to stand in the doorway while Leander blocked their passage, the entire tea house turned to them, the room silent. Leander said, 'You exploit your workers. It's discrimination towards the weaker sex who are in truth, not at all weak, just bullied by men and women like you. You feel entitled, but you are not.'

Out on the street, Molly said softly, 'Now you know what I am really like.'

'I've never seen such a thing! You were manhandled.'

Inside, the customers turned back to their cake and cream and teapots and conversation but Molly no longer cared – Leander's arm was around her shoulder, enfolding her, supporting her.

'Where will we go? Do you want more tea?'

'No, thank you, I'm good now.'

She reached into her bag and handed a pamphlet to a woman passing, who glanced at it and put it into her purse. She offered more to passers-by, but it was Leander who removed the menus from the small wire frame against the teashop door and replaced them with Aunt April's pamphlets. Then he too started handing them out to passers-by – 'Equality means that whatever conditions are guaranteed to us, in the form of rights, shall also in the same measure be guaranteed to others, and that whatever rights are given to others shall also be given to us.'

The proprietor returned to shoo them away, but Leander just stepped towards him, smiling down at him, and he retreated to harass the waitresses instead.

On the trip home, Molly next to him and a little shaken, Leander deliberated on the anger shown to Molly. He'd seen the other side of what the newspapers reported, what people subsequently believed. His own parents disapproved of 'protesters', yet he'd never heard them discuss what they stood for, or why.

Molly felt Leander's contemplative mood and worried that he would not cope with her as she was, but she felt he would. It would be better soon; they would sit by the fire together and the bruising parts of the day would fade. Molly checked the letterbox as she passed, and there, smiling up at her, was an envelope. It was addressed to Miss Molly Dunnage. The postage stamp was indiscernible under the blue stamp stains of every post office from Alice Springs to Darwin, Brisbane to Melbourne. It had come a long way southward, very slowly, and the dust and the burnish of many hands had made it soft. Aware of Mrs Sidebottom close by, she hurried inside, tearing it open as she headed to her room.

Molly

Dearest Molly, I hope this letter finds you well. I told you I would write when I was happy.

She stopped, reached for her pillow and held it over her face, stifling her sobs. Gladys was happy.

Mrs Sidebottom sent me back to St Michael's and they found a position for me. I am in the Northern Territory near the top of the state. It took me three weeks to get here by sea, trains, coaches and I even had to ride a horse. It was a very rough and bumpy journey but I can ride a horse now and I am learning to drive the trap. I am engaged to a farmer named Albert, a widower, and I have servants to help me with the children. I told you I would. There are four ranging from ten to three, and Albert's wife is buried here in the family plot. She was bitten by a snake. We see her every day and talk to her like you and your mother. The maids are local Aboriginal girls, they are my only friends out here, apart from Albert. It is very hot and dusty and we wash the linen in the creek & sometimes I go with them on walks through the bush. The cook, Ella, is very good and Albert is a nice man and good to me and I will be alright here with him. He works very hard with his cattle but it is peaceful here, there's a lot of time to do things, or nothing at all. It would be wonderful to see you again one day, Molly, but it is a long way from anywhere and a difficult trip that takes weeks. I am happy now, Molly. Albert and the children are best for me. Please write and tell me of your corset empire and your life. We don't wear corsets here, and we get mail every six months. Always your friend, Gladys.

'A happy ending for Gladys,' said August, who was painting another set of dodos – the crockery shop had commissioned more – and so was not stained as colourfully as a lorikeet today.

Molly thought of Gladys, calmly making her way through a crowd of brawling women and thrashing police, waving signs and fluttering pamphlets, then changed the image to Gladys strolling through the bush around Ayers Rock. Gladys could rest, and so could Molly. They would write, perhaps only two letters a year, and she wondered if Gladys wore her pretty dresses out there. Culottes would be just the thing.

Aunt April went to the wall map and put her finger on a spot. It was in the far north of the Northern Territory. The area was coloured pale yellow, with no discernible hills or mountains, and there was one tiny river, the size of a capillary wiggling through the nothingness.

Aunt April put her magnifying glasses back up with her curls. 'She did mention it was peaceful.'

Looking at that remote spot on the map, Molly knew she would never see Gladys again. It was the end of their story in Carlton. But she would always have Gladys, simply because, like everyone, she could never erase the first act of her life's story. Carlton would always be in Molly: her school years and her youth with Gladys, dancing together to the rotunda band, behaving badly at choir, taunting the neighbourhood, arguing with Mrs Sidebottom, factory work! How could they ever forget Mr King's strange drawing class and its startling revelations – especially of *The Victorious Athlete* – and finding Horatio and then, finally, escaping to something better. Molly could not be happier for her true friend. She had what she'd always said she wanted. If Gladys, who chose not to waste energy tackling staircases, could endure horseback riding in the desert and find happiness at the end, then Molly was certain she would get what she wanted too. She wept into her pillow for a little while longer, then splashed her face and tidied her hair, and waited for Leander to walk down the hall and sit at the stove with her.

Chapter 31

NORBERT POKE FOUND Clive Woodgrip in his 'rooms' at the Victoria Hotel, shaving at the sink with only a towel tied around his waist. He had come in from the so-called sitting room, actually just a doorless wardrobe with a fancy standard lamp on a sideboard. He settled on the edge of the bath with a glass of sherry, cautious of the cold murky water and the tiny islands of soap gathered around its rim. 'She's up to something.'

'Ah, my ex-fiancé.' Clive rinsed the blade. 'It's a shame, you know. I did admire her.'

'There are plenty of marriageable daughters in Melbourne, most of them amiable.'

'And who still have money.'

Norbert said nothing.

'Anyway, what's she up to?' Clive was approaching his moustache in the journey around his face with the razor.

'Cousin Alathea is calm, somehow resolved to it all, not as sad as she should be . . . which makes me think she's up to something. You've still got time to sue her for breach of trust or something. She must have a bit of money somewhere, her mother was rich.'

Woodgrip paused, then shrugged. 'She decided to settle out of court, so she might have already signed, Miškinis will tell us all.' Clive saw the look on Norbert's face. 'Stop worrying. What's she going to do? Swindle us? It's all under negotiation, Oliphant knows that, and he doesn't have the legal right, nor the titles or the deeds.'

'She does.' Norbert was morose.

'And soon they will be yours.' Clive washed and dried his face, and combed, waxed and styled his moustache. 'Stop sulking. Oliphant will do the right thing by the business. He's saved the company more than once – it's a big part of his income.' He inspected the collar and cuffs of his shirt, sprinkled some white talcum powder on them to hide the wear, and dressed. He did not put on any underwear and replied to Norbert's puzzled expression. 'Good underwear is expensive. Come on, let's cheer ourselves up on Pocknall's account.'

As they ate a leisurely lunch at a fine restaurant, they discussed with Miškinis the slow progress of the deed and title copies. Miškinis, a plainly dressed man with a slight accent, agreed to send a message to the stalker, get him to take time out from tailing Alathea Pocknall to have a go at lockpicking the factory safe.

'If he fails,' Miškinis said, 'I'll ask around for someone else.'

Clive put his hand on the lawyer's shoulder and said, 'Ponas Miškinis, a superior example of the successful immigrant, the sort who gets here, sees a niche and works efficiently to fill its potential – sometimes using tactics from the old country.'

'We all have our tactics,' Miškinis said pointedly, and reminded them how hard he had worked with Miss Alathea Pocknall's lawyer to persuade her to settle out of court, though in truth it hadn't been hard at all. Some women knew their place. 'Soon you will be CEO of Pocknall's, Mr Poke. You will be responsible for everything.'

This news didn't lift Norbert's spirits. The finances were a mess; he suspected he'd have to sell everything. So they went to the factory to sit in the office, looking down at Snakelegs as he bullied his new staff. Surely the stalker would arrive and he would open the safe and finally they'd have the deeds and title, and hopefully they'd find a lot of cash.

Leander and Molly planned to spend Sunday at the zoo, where Molly decided she would hold his hand. What she really wanted, though, was to be kissed. Gladys surely would have been kissed by Albert, and so by the end of Leander's stay, Molly *would* be kissed, of that she was now certain.

As it was Sunday, Leander asked if they would have visitors, and Molly said none were planned. But then someone knocked. August opened the door to find Horatio, his police uniform pressed and crisp and his hair scrupulously tidy, but he was slumped against the doorjamb, bereft.

'Dear boy, what has happened?' August ushered him to the kitchen table and directed Aunt April to give him whisky. Horatio introduced himself to Leander, who thought his handshake weaker than Molly's.

Aunt April asked, 'Is it your mother?'

Horatio hid his face in his hands. 'I am to be sent to the country.'

'Where?' said Molly.

'Wherever they tell me.' He blew his nose noisily, folded his hanky and put it in his suit pocket, then buttoned the flap and smoothed it. 'The chief inspector said they have a place that's suitable for someone *like me*.'

'What are you *like*?' asked Aunt April, moving her magnifiers to her hair and squinting at the young man.

'The chief inspector said that they have perfectly workable uniforms, there's no benefit from changing anything, but they particularly didn't like the fact that it was *me* who had designed new uniforms. They were all under the assumption that my mother had designed them, and in hindsight perhaps I shouldn't have modelled my prototype. They were all alarmed when I opened my coat to show them the lining.'

'The lining?' Molly sat down next to him.

Horatio whispered, 'The chief inspector said I was "perverted".'

The chief had become a statue, grey and rigid, though it was clear he was boiling inside. His voice was flat and acidic. 'We don't want your type in our force, we don't want to see you or know about you. Now, get out of my office before I have you thrown in jail for sodomy and perversion.'

The people in the kitchen empathised, and were saddened for Horatio and what he had been accused of. Molly put her arm around Horatio's shoulder, August poured him a whisky, Aunt April called them 'wretched so-and-so's,' and Leander said, 'It sounds to me that you were only trying to do something good.'

Horatio continued. 'I am to be sent somewhere far away. Every man they've ever sent there resigns mere days after getting off the train. Apparently it's cheaper and easier if we just resign.'

'Why did he hate the lining so much?'

'I couldn't get black, so I used the red, which I now see could be interpreted as pink.'

'Indeed.'

'But it's such a friendly, warm colour! I thought it might calm some of the more callous policemen. I joined the force because I wanted to make a difference. I thought I could influence the general constables not to be suspicious or cruel to people who . . .' he trailed off.

'Who don't conform,' August said.

Horatio nodded. 'I am not allowed to knit while at work anymore.'

'What were you knitting?'

'Bed socks. I get chilblains.' He did not mention he had found a pink dress hanging in his locker at the station, nor that he'd taken it home and tried it on. It was far too small.

'People make terrible assumptions. We collect mushrooms from the cemetery, they grow so big there, but all of North Carlton thinks we sneak into the cemetery to steal corpses for our spells,' Aunt April explained, trying to be helpful, but Constable Farrat was shocked.

'*Corpses?*'

'I know!' said Molly. 'Any witch will tell you a hex works better if the victim's heart is still beating when it's torn out.'

Horatio smiled at his friends: August's mouth green-tinted; Aunt April's hair a veranda of curls above her ears; Molly, pretty and wide-eyed. All of them innocents accused and completely conversant with being treated appallingly. Leander explained that the locals made bird noises at him because he spent his life 'trying to fly.'

As Constable Horatio Farrat waited for a tram home, he felt restored and confident that he was liked, a respectable human being with friends, a new friend in fact, since Leander had been sincerely sympathetic. And his friends assured him that a country town would be a place of very little crime, lots of fresh air, a harmonious community and a regular modern railway system. He could subscribe to all manner of magazines from all over the world; there'd be a library, possibly tennis or golf.

'You'll be able to live apart from your charges, in a house of your own, with ample time to indulge your hobbies when you're not playing your role as law enforcer.'

Molly completed her father's idea: 'Just think of your uniform as a costume; you can be yourself after hours.'

First thing Monday morning, Evan Pettyman brought his mother to the office. It was quite an effort for her to ascend the two steps at the stoop – the fault of her hobbled skirt – and she became quite breathless. Mr Hawker pointed to the staircase to the first-floor office and suggested they do the handover and signing in the reception area; it would likely get them out of the place quicker. 'Dressmaking prevents the lady from climbing stairs.' He smiled – women would not be able to walk about at all when the fabric restrictions of war kicked in.

The group of five agreed to remain in the downstairs reception area. Mr Hawker sent for the necessary papers, a pen and ink bottle. Alathea produced her contract, the deeds and title, still in the grubby envelope she'd retrieved from the hidey hole behind Dunnage's skirting board.

It was quiet while they signed, just the sound of the nib scratching across legal papers. Mr Hawker glanced at his fob watch often – it was getting close to lunchtime – and Evan was almost emotional as he received the deed, title and key to the factory. Mr Hawker snatched the paperwork from him, and made a point of handing the cheque to Mr Oliphant, rather than Alathea. She might do anything with it, buy a new hat, even lose it, and Oliphant would see it was used to reinvest in the factory, almost certainly.

Evan suggested they should celebrate.

Mr Hawker said it was a capital idea.

Alathea declined the invitation, instead shaking their hands – Mrs Pettyman's was blue and cold – saying she looked forward to a prosperous and happy future.

'Hear, hear,' they said, applauding happily.

But Alathea was happiest of all, she would soon be gone, and Norbert would be answerable for an insolvent business and possibly even bigger debt than he thought he had, and would spend the rest of his life suffering for it.

The Pettyman party departed for a nearby hotel where Mr Hawker ordered a dozen oysters and a bottle of French Champagne. Mrs Pettyman said she couldn't stomach oysters and ordered corned beef. Evan chose the roast of the day and asked if they could have dessert.

'Most certainly,' said Mr Hawker, knowing he would add the bill to their debt. For the rest of the lunch, as they ate and drank, they discussed the details of the sale of assets. Mr Hawker would meet the potential purchaser in his office the next day. 'He is keen,' he said. 'He thinks there'll be a war, he'll use the machines to manufacture uniforms, or shirts, cook's aprons . . . anything anyone needs, really.' Miss Pocknall would learn of the new arrangements in good time.

*

There was no sign of the stalker either on the footpath opposite or along Bourke Street, east or west. Mr Oliphant even checked the windows above the awnings either side before he crossed the street to meet Alathea for a farewell lunch. They commiserated – Mr Hawker and the Pettymans were a heartless bunch.

'And witless,' Alathea said, happily.

Mr Oliphant laughed. 'So much so that they don't comprehend that they are.'

Both were relieved that this vital part of the deal was over, the cheque in hand. The process would soon be complete. Alathea's new business partners would know of the real situation in good time.

At the bank Mr Oliphant asked the teller to fetch the manager and, while they waited, he studied Alathea: a dignified and commanding figure under an impressive lightshade hanging from a tall ceiling, blending in with the dozen or so other wealthy customers. He had stayed on, just for her, and was more than happy to get away from it all now. But not so pleased to be losing the opportunity to spend time with Juanita's daughter.

Alathea watched the bank manager, a meticulously groomed middle-aged man. He nodded to Mr Oliphant, who handed him a cheque, and they exchanged a few friendly words while the teller deposited it and recorded the transaction. Then the teller, as instructed, gave Mr Oliphant an envelope containing a great deal of cash and recorded the withdrawal.

Standing on the footpath outside the bank, Alathea said, 'I am very grateful for everything you have ever done for us.'

'We've reached a worthy solution, I think. Your father would be proud that you have saved his business from your cousin and that you have saved yourself. And now I aim to catch a trout every day.' Mr Oliphant handed her the cash-filled envelope.

'Here is half the money, Alathea. The rest will stay in an account until you need it. Just write to me and I'll see you get it when you are organised.' He winked. 'Don't lose the envelope.'

'It will travel with me in my secret pockets and if the ship goes down it will go with me, back down to Mother.'

'You are very much like your lovely mother.'

They embraced, briefly, like uncle and niece, and she assured him they would stay in touch.

'I might even sail over to see you one day.'

'I hope you do.' She raised her hand, and a cab drew up before her. She'd opened the door and was settling into the seat by the time the driver got down to help her. 'Please take me to Rathdowne Street, Carlton.'

Chapter 32

Mrs Raven said that the girl at the crockery shop had told her that the Dunnages were given free tickets from Dame Lily Pert herself to see her show, *Favourite Arias*, because Molly Dunnage had made a costume for her. Mrs Cross said they must have put a spell on her. And Mrs Sidebottom said it was all a lie because no one had been to their house since they had killed Mrs Blinkhorn. Just then, a cab drew around the corner and pulled up beside Mesdames Cross, Sidebottom and Raven. A gloved hand came through the open window to open the door and a fine skirt tumbled onto the small step. It was Miss Alathea Pocknall. She ignored them, just walked up the Dunnages' uneven path to their worn front door and knocked.

'So beautifully dressed,' said Mrs Raven.

Mrs Sidebottom sniffed. 'Nothing Molly Dunnage would have made her, that's certain.'

The gossips stayed to see what would happen next.

April Dunnage was buttoning her bodice when she spotted Alathea push through the front gate. She wished she'd put on her new breast stay, for Molly's sake, at least. When she opened the door, Alathea smiled, and stepped swiftly past Aunt April's room. 'Is Molly at home?'

'Yes.' She had a feeling Alathea was the bearer of bad news. 'She'll be pleased to see you, possibly . . .'

Aunt April followed the guest down to the kitchen, and while

Alathea waited, April removed the jar of slime from the table and threw her grubby lab coat into the firewood box. 'We weren't expecting anyone.'

'Yes, it's early to intrude on anyone.'

Molly was picking parsley when she heard Alathea's voice, and was suddenly aware that she might, in a moment or two, have to choose between Leander and her career. Did she want to continue this adventure with Alathea Pocknall? She looked at Leander, stepping through the backyard puddles with fresh eggs in his hands, and at that moment knew she would choose him.

August left his studio and Alathea watched the three of them come in and stand around the table, straight-backed and smiling in formal greeting. August resembled a calico sack, and Molly beamed beside a young man with spectacles and a lovely head of dark hair. Alathea smiled at him. He said, 'I'm Leander, a friend of the family.'

'He's from the Mallee,' Molly said, and wished she hadn't.

'Yes,' Alathea said, noting his rural clothing. 'You grow a lot of wheat out that way.'

'Some do,' Leander replied.

'Would you like a cup of tea, Miss Pocknall?'

'No, thank you, Miss Dunnage, I have just popped in to ask for the last envelope.'

Alathea moved to warm herself at the stove, and when August returned with the envelope, he brushed an earwig from it and rubbed it on his chest to remove the dust. She lifted the hot plate, shoved the envelope into the fire and stirred the coals with the poker as if it she was folding meringue. Replacing the lid, she then put the poker back in its spot and clapped the soot from her gloves.

'I'm grateful,' she said, smiled at them all, and left, her skirts gently swishing as she walked.

Molly followed her. 'Miss Pocknall, I need to know what's happening with the factory? I was going to write to you, but I want to say that Mr Pettyman asked for . . .'

Molly

Alathea opened the door and lost her footing on the veranda step.

Molly steadied her. '. . . for the factory?'

'Is that your young man?'

'Yes.'

'True love is the lightning rod for life force, Molly.' Alathea held Molly's arm and seemed to study her, 'You will be alright.'

Presumably, Alathea Pocknall had been too preoccupied to really consider the rumours of war. She didn't realise that Molly's 'lightning rod' – or any young man for that matter – would be sacrificed. It was clear to Molly that her hopes of becoming a designer would also be sacrificed and that Alathea didn't understand the weight of that either.

'Did you lose everything to your cousin?'

'Not everything.' Alathea looked briefly at the trio of women watching from across the square and, her voice unsteady with emotion, said, 'There is a Japanese word, *mottainai*. It's a term that means a sense of regret for something good when it's not fully utilised, like the waste of one's natural value, or talent. I'm determined never to regret anything so I'm doing the best I can with what I have.'

'You owe me some money,' said Molly.

Alathea opened her purse, took out a ten-pound note and handed it to her. It was sufficient for her work, but only just. 'Molly, you might have ended up making military underwear or uniforms for the next five years, and I don't think anyone should profit from war, nor be forced to condone it through their job.'

She walked away, leaving Molly standing and the women across the road watching, so Molly waved to Alathea, a friendly farewell. As the cab pulled away, Alathea dabbed the corner of her eye with her glove.

It seemed it was over, there would be no factory, she would not be a designer. What had happened? Had the cousin swindled them? But Molly felt no pity for Alathea Pocknall.

She felt nauseous, but hope remained – Leander Behan was standing in her kitchen. She used the friendly passage wall for support and arrived into the kitchen composed, her eyes on him. She would focus on her current happiness; the days were speeding by . . .

'From what's left, it looks like they were letters,' said April, peering into the stove.

'They were from Marguerite someone.'

They stared at August. He looked slightly ashamed. 'Well' – he shrugged – 'they could have been something dangerous, or illegal, so I peeked. I didn't read them, I just wanted to know what I was hiding.'

Leander said, 'Molly, your business venture?'

Molly shrugged. Alathea had not said . . . but it didn't seem likely, and she would wait to hear from Evan Pettyman.

'Oh dear,' said Aunt April.

But Molly sounded cheerful when she asked, 'Do you know the term *mottainai*?'

'Yes,' said Aunt April, and got that melancholic look she got when she thought of Hurtle Rosenkranz or *Mycobacterium tuber-culosis*. But Molly was thinking about herself, her talent, and the odds accumulating against the future she had dreamed of.

She looped her arm through Leander's. 'If Madame Weigel can do it, so can I.'

'So can *we*,' he said. He meant he would help her, of course, but she couldn't escape the fact that as a man, he had more rights and more privilege, and she would need him for financial and legal transactions, but would she need his permission?

She felt the ten-pound note in her hand and thought about her savings. There was still enough in her roll of notes to contribute to her future and, for the time being, there was an opening night to attend.

*

So, on Wednesday, Molly and Leander went shopping. At the exchange shop, where thrifty ladies bought used clothing, Molly purchased a warm coat for herself, a coat for her father, and a shawl for her aunt. She wanted to buy Leander a shirt and he chose one, but paid for it himself. Then they spent the afternoon in the kitchen, Molly sewing, Leander reading old newspapers to her and drinking tea. Long minutes of contented silence passed.

Leander imagined the house he would build for her on the corner of the small farm close to the town, a sturdy and spacious construction with deep verandas but plenty of light. It would have a studio with a pergola to grow grapevines for shade in summer and light in winter. Like the house, the studio would be positioned to capture the best of the sun's rays in any season, and it would have an enclosed change area next to a fireplace for her clients. Molly would keep it as neat as she did herself – except for her hair – and he would honour her way of being by putting things where they belonged. He would go on working with his father, while stoic, capable Molly would make apparel for ladies. Her independent, forthright side would make it a success, though he wondered if clients would adapt to her. She'd most likely rub some people the wrong way but there were no secrets with this girl, no performance. What you saw was what you got. And she might also sew his parachutes. Above the letterbox he would put a sign, *Molly Behan, Corsetiere and Dressmaker.* He would live with her, build a life with her and watch her hair go grey, greet each new crease in her lovely face, and see her smile for every grandchild who came to take their place.

Chapter 33

IN ALL PROBABILITY, this would be their first and last concert, Dame Lily's last tour, and the height of Molly's career, since Dame Lily hadn't commissioned any more garments and she was certain she'd seen the last of Alathea. Molly wanted to utilise her potential, avoid *mottainai*, or at least try. She wanted the triumph of this night to be passed on, perhaps in newspaper, and to her child if she had one, or at least around the neighbourhood.

Molly had got this close to the evening of theatre and was grateful nothing had stopped her, as it often had. No one died, or got sick, sacked or banished. If Dame Lily Pert failed to appear, she would simply sit in the grand theatre with Leander and her friends and family for at least an hour. Tonight would be a perfect dream and, with its memory, she would face whatever was to come.

Aunt April sent the men to the yard to buff their shoes again, then they gathered in the cramped kitchen to do a final check. They straightened each other's ties and hats and brushed each other's coats with a new sisal palm brush purchased for the occasion. August's new coat was a little big for him, but aside from that it was almost as good as the one Emrys Pocknall had worn. It was a modern cut that covered the hips, and its silk lapels reached to the button at the waist. Molly had pressed his wool trousers with a wet tea towel and iron, hot from the stove, then wielded a lead pencil to cover the small tears and stains, and Aunt April had soaked his collar in starch and ironed it until it was better than the Pope's. Happiness made August's cheeks pink and his eyes glitter.

August's old suit jacket was too small on Leander, so he left the buttons undone and kept his shoulders back. Boldly, Molly had sewn a strip of matching ribbon down the seams of his best woollen trousers. It was a subtle effect but lifted his trousers from day wear to evening wear, and the fat, pale scarf draped around his neck completed the look: tall, slim, handsome, broad-shouldered and suitably 'theatrical'. He'd initially removed the scarf, but Molly placed it around his shoulders again so he knew to leave it there.

Aunt April could not take her new shawl off because the only way she could fit into her best dress was to leave the middle section unbuttoned at the back, but Molly had made an overskirt trimmed with a scrap of bottle green satin, which she also used around the hem, giving the skirt a dressy edge. She'd used the satin on the bodice and neckline too, but it was the shawl that crowned her entire outfit. It was wide and made of pale green lawn trimmed with an abstract design of bottle green silk thread, and it fell across her shoulders and elbows like a waterfall. Her hat was black velvet, an oversized tam-o'-shanter that she had seen Mary Pickford wearing on a motion picture poster, which Mrs Farrat had kindly donated. The effect was striking. 'I feel quite bohemian,' April said, and Leander thought she looked very well; not even the ladies of Yaambul would disagree.

Molly took a great deal of time to do her hair, wetting it then twisting it in rags and rushing around the house and yard to dry. And when it was dry, she stood by the fire using a warm hair wand to fold her New Woman curls. Leander held the mirror for her and passed the small hairpins with tiny white ribbons tacked to the end. She wore her newish linen two-piece, the waist high and the skirt narrow, a white Japanese silk blouse with heavy white guipure trim, and her new cape, which was more of a coat, circular and Japanese-inspired. The shoulders were dropped and the three-quarter sleeves very wide. It reached just beyond her knees, and was made of black moiré lined with pale blue moiré, so was reversible. The collar was rabbit fur, dyed blue, and it stood tall around Molly's neck. She would have looked at home attending the Paris Opera.

Leander looked at his new family, and was pleased, especially with Molly. He could not find the words to tell her how lovely she looked, her small white gloved hands clasped to hold her big coat close. He would hold that image of her for the rest of his life.

Aunt April made Molly check twice that she had the tickets, and then off they went to catch a tram, far too early, so they might secure a quality position to view Society as it arrived.

Mrs Sidebottom hoped it would rain on them, all four of them prancing up the street as if they were somebodies. But there were no clouds in the sky, and they looked very smart indeed, almost unrecognisable. April Dunnage appeared to be wearing a new shawl, better suited to a twenty-year-old, and Molly was almost invisible in a huge shapeless coat. What things to wear to the theatre to see Australia's own Dame! But Mrs Sidebottom was wretched. Her sons were out and about and didn't seem to need her anymore, and she couldn't find anyone suitable to do the laundry. It was galling that Molly Dunnage, young, fit and strong, was next door and in need of work, but gadding about with a young man for everyone to see. Mrs Sidebottom had even lamented the loss of slothful Gladys, ungrateful and pretty as a mudbrick wall. Here she was, left alone in her small house, a widow with a great pile of other people's soiled linen to wash and not enough money earned from it to buy new bootlaces.

'It isn't fair,' she said, and thought for just one moment that the suffragettes might just have a point about equal pay and widows' pensions.

But her sons would go to war; they would return heroes. Mrs Sidebottom would be a proud mother of decorated soldiers, and she would work hard for good causes. When the time came, hers would be a big funeral attended by many mourners with only nice things to say about her character: a humble, hard-working woman, always tidy and sensibly presented, true to her latest placard: *Aspirations Are For The Worthy And The Worthwhile.*

It was the wonder of electricity that the lights shone from three blocks away, all those electric globes under the portico lighting up the dipping, mingling crowd outside the Princess Theatre. Oh, the crowd! And so much buzz, and all nodding top hats and white scarves and tails, vast flowery hats and elaborate hair and jewellery and fine lace and netting and dresses, brocade and satin and silk. It was a rainforest of velvet and lace and net and sparkling jewellery and long gloves gesticulating from fur; coats, capes and shawls.

Leander and August looked at their polished shoes and laughed – they'd thought their shoes dazzling until they saw the glittering slippers the men wore. Molly and Aunt April said they'd return to watch an opera crowd in summer, when the ladies' diamond bracelets, necklaces and gowns were not hidden under coats.

Constable Farrat was conspicuous but not out of place in a top hat and cape, his shoes sparkling and his cane resting on his shoulder, its flamingo head looking down on the feathered hats. He was smiling from ear to ear and running a critical eye over the carriages drawing to the kerb, the gentry disembarking from substantial landaus, barouches, buggies and cabriolets, the grooms kept busy opening and closing carriage doors, at the ready to catch a tumbling passenger. Everyone was smiling: a few with glee anticipating Dame Lily's swansong – 'Oh, another fare-well!' – some with adoration for the return of Australia's favourite daughter, and those who would profit from war excited by the coming event. And it was Friday, and an evening of culture and amusement for the privileged.

Horatio caught a glimpse of the Dunnage family at the edge, paused to gather the courage to plunge through the crowd, so he waved and pointed his cane back to a phaeton. They turned to see Norbert Poke and Clive Woodgrip step onto the footpath in the company of two overdecorated ladies. The foursome walked straight past Molly. She was tempted to put her foot out to trip them, but she couldn't risk ruining her one and only red-carpet experience. She scanned the crowd for Alathea but found instead Miss Berrycloth, nudging her way through a layer of elbows in her cotton cap and lace collar, lit up like a waif with a gold coin. She reached them, unable to speak, her small dark eyes ringed by their whites. August offered her his arm, Horatio offered Aunt April his, and they led them proudly up the wide marble stairs, one step at a time, Molly and Leander at the rear.

The air was warm and perfumed, and the decor soft beneath bright chandeliers. Horatio felt at home, as if he visited the Princess every week. In the gilded, ornate and milling upper foyer he purchased six programs, and the others followed him into the roomy, ornate theatre, the carpet lush underfoot. Constable Farrat wasn't disappointed to be shown seats towards the back of the stalls, which swept downwards – they could see the entire stage.

Leander gazed around the balcony and boxes, studying the domed ceiling and wondered at the length of the curtains edging the tall proscenium arch. He set about deciding exactly how they'd built the place but couldn't identify the famous retractable ceiling.

It was a dream come true for Molly, a perfect evening – she was at the Princess Theatre with her handsome beau – but she was also itchy with anticipation and her jaw tight. Would Dame Lily wear her costume? Slowly, she opened the program: *Head of Costume; Mistress Theodosia, with contribution for 'Queen of the Night', Miss Molly Dunnage.*

Her name was in the program, spelled correctly, in bold letters.

She pointed it out to Leander, who opened his program and looked closely at her name. 'You're a bright and shiny star.'

Aunt April said, 'Indeed,' and August showed his daughter's name to the man sitting next to him, who turned away.

Leander squeezed her hand; *his bright and shiny star*.

Molly felt a deep longing for Gladys, to describe every detail to her. She would write a very long letter.

The theatre wasn't full, and Molly was able to watch Mr Slutzkin, underwear manufacturer from Flinders Lane, arrive and settle into his seat. She had a good mind to find him in the foyer later and show him her name in the program.

Bells rang, there was a flurry of people to their seats, and the Dunnage group took the cue from Horatio and assumed a 'so now encase me in wonder' expression.

The lights dimmed, the whispers and murmurs subsided, there was applause, and the oboist sounded the note for the orchestra to tune. The conductor held them to attention, his arms wide, then swept them into the notes. The music ballooned, all the way to the back of the theatre to the Dunnage family. Goosebumps rose on Molly's arms and Leander squeezed her hand again. And after what seemed like a very short period of time, a spotlight illuminated Dame Lily Pert standing regally on the stage. The crowd applauded, their greeting a little perfunctory.

Dame Lily Pert bowed and smiled, a practised reaction. To Molly, the Dame looked taller, stronger, a star completely at home on the stage. Mistress Theodosia had made an elegant gown that followed exactly the contours of the Dame's corset – Molly's corset.

Dame Lily adjusted, her chin rose almost imperceptibly, her head turned a little and her lips scarcely opened, but the sound that came out was smooth and strong. Immediately Dame Lily was Carmen, singing a saucy 'Habanera'. *'Love is a rebellious bird that nobody can tame, and you call him quite in vain if it suits him not to come . . .'*

The applause after 'Habanera' was better, more confident, louder. Dame Lily's rendition was faultless, technically perfect, and she bowed demurely to accept praise from a relieved audience.

'What was that about?' Leander asked.

Molly said, 'The flighty nature of love, I believe.'

He nodded, and looked at her, *That's not our kind of love.*

'O mio babbino caro' came next and the crowd, now reconciled, allowed themselves to be enchanted in the glorious surrounds, mesmerised by Dame Lily, who, they had to admit, was in good form. A consummate performer, emotion in every word, each one fat with meaning and emphasised occasionally with the perfect, understated gesture.

It was moving, and Molly felt Leander moved too. This time, the applause was ecstatic and some members of the audience stood to show their love for the song, and for the Dame. After several bows and ongoing applause, Dame Lily became Madame Butterfly and sang an impassioned 'Un bel dì, vedremo'. The crowd swayed, moved by every familiar lilt, and handkerchiefs were dug from pockets and purses, people adoring the popular song, some singing along, while the orchestra moved with the notes they played. At the end, the crowd rose: the applause was deafening, the foot-stomping rumbling and the floor juddering.

Then she left.

The applause went on, but Dame Lily kept walking, she didn't return to bow or even glance back. When the clapping eventually subsided, the crowd was quiet for a few seconds and then the chatter erupted. It was the sound of a happy appreciative audience. Some people had remained still, holding the spell.

The Dunnage group stayed in their seats to savour what was left on the stage, and interval looked too difficult; all that shuffling and craning just to turn around and come back again. August and April sat quietly and seemed a little shocked from the emotion of the performance and the sheer drama of the evening so far. Miss Berrycloth quietly wept. The sentiment of the songs moved between Leander and Molly through their clasped hands. Molly felt fulfilled, and happy. And as the crowd filed out, the chatter amplified and then a very English voice said, 'Well, that was wonderful, but those songs are not that difficult.'

'She won't pull off the "Queen of the Night".'

'"Der Hölle Rache" is too difficult.'

'We saw Luisa Tetrazzini in London, now *she* can sing!'

The mood around the Dunnages was punctured, people behind them had ruined their joy and they began to doubt their own responses.

'She will not come back,' the English voice continued.

'She'll either surprise us again . . . or she'll make a mess of it.'

Molly watched her family demur, their smile changing from joy to 'Oh, perhaps I got that wrong . . .' She said very loudly, 'She was wonderful, wasn't she?', recalling the mood. The Dunnages agreed enthusiastically.

Leander reclaimed his hand from Molly, and rubbed his palms together, talking gleefully about the orchestra, particularly the percussionist. 'Such precision, and very dramatic.'

The room was warm and plush and the people-watching entertaining, and they thought through the songs again, but soon the bells rang and the crush returned, people fumbling and stalling in the aisles, trying to remember where they sat. It seemed everyone was less eager than when they had left. A poison had filtered through the crowd, just a word here and there, a patron-ising smirk, a question: 'Really, is that what you thought?' The mood had changed, and anticipation of failure had stolen the delight. Why were people so quick to appraise? Molly's hands began to sweat. She looped her arm through Leander's.

As the lights dimmed, the audience leaned forward, inquisi-tive, scrutinising – jubilant for the coming humiliation . . . stage death.

The proscenium and all around it was pitch black, silent, perfectly still, and then the sound of the string section, quivering and then dramatic thrusts and Dame Lily's voice cut the dark, *'The vengeance of Hell boils in my heart, Death and despair flame about me!'* It was note perfect.

And then a downlight lit the Dame from directly above.

She was standing in a low swirling cloud that flickered with lightning, her arms encasing her like a resting bat, a sparkling chrysalis, winking tiny stars. Her eyes were black rimmed and her lips crimson, her cheeks made sinister with white powder and grey shadows, her features elongated in the throw of the overhead light, her face sneering. The Queen of the Night was armed and ready to pitch anyone to hell.

The audience was perfectly still, not even a cough.

Dame Lily inhaled, and as her lungs filled, easily, with the power of her soprano voice her chest rose and her rib cage expanded in her breast stay, and her diaphragm, secure between its elasticised verges, propelled the notes, loud and authentic, and straight into Molly's heart. Goosebumps rose on her arms.

'. . . the pain of death, You will be my daughter nevermore . . .'

Leander patted Molly's hand. 'Your costume!'

At a caesura in the music, Dame Lily raised her arms and there were gasps when her bat wings suddenly unfolded and she was transformed, a tall and frightening villain, her spiked pinions reaching high and her wings spread, fanned, long and translucent above her.

The costume was a work of art, as she'd imagined. Tonight, the Queen of the Night was a black and crimson spike-winged creature standing in a low storm, a sharp dagger poised to strike in her claw; the digit bones of her wings were backlit, web-like, with spider's legs of tendons, and the many veins and arteries vivid in the thin fabric. And it was because of Molly. She had confronted doubt and shone.

The spectacle took her breath away and Molly was stunned, grateful and proud.

'Disowned may you be forever, Abandoned may you be forever . . .'

Molly

The Queen of the Night lowered her appendages a little to focus and they hung like angel's wings, her pinions retracted, and Molly wanted to cry; the costume was a triumph, but for a devastatingly short time before the end of her career. Right there on stage what might have been was folding as Dame Lily climbed. The audience braced, and Dame Lily took on the impossibly difficult and very staccato, stratospherically high Fs. She held firm, not a waver, her energy palpable, driven by vengeance for her ill-treatment, the lack of faith from her public. The hairs on the back of Molly's neck tingled and she felt the power of the composer, his imagination, the notes he'd assembled moving her, frightening her . . . Dame Lily Pert knew what to do with those words and notes and understood how they would move the audience, she knew that they'd *feel* the music, and she knew what to make them feel. She had served them for decades and they had walked away from her for something merely new. She'd given a career to many journalists and now they were bored, or tired, and had written unkind, ungenerous reviews.

It was them, not her.

But they had lifted her to the high Fs; she was powered by management, the bureaucrats and poseurs at the Princess, drunk on piffling power, businessmen who wished to throw her into the street after years of bringing the streets to them.

As for Luisa Tetrazzini and Elsa Stralia, plain old Elsie Maud Fischer, well, she would not hate them – as their requests for appearances stalled, they would hurt for Dame Lily Pert.

She continued, magnificent, accusing the audience, pointing her red talons, her wings sweeping, her lips curled; she made blades of the vocal athletics of 'Der Hölle Rache', her words a darting menace. She was attacking the audience as they drank her in, amazed, thrilled, sitting there in their chairs with emotions coursing through them that someone else had made for them, delivered to them.

'Destroyed be forever, All the bonds of nature . . .'

It was revenge at work, fuelled by the breath denied her by corsets her entire career.

'If not through you, Sarastro becomes pale! Hear Gods of Revenge, Hear a mother's oath!'

The Queen of the Night thrust her wings high again, lightning flashes of coloured lights behind her, her pinions long, black and sharp at the edge of her flimsy appendages. And then Dame Lily's coup was over, but her conquest was held by Molly now, forever.

The audience seemed shaken, stunned, and after applause that lasted five full minutes, Molly's hands hurt, but the diva was long gone. Again, she didn't stay for the applause. She turned her back and left the stage. She did not come back for her flowers; she did not come back for an encore. Dame Lily went to her dressing room and shut the door.

'I knew she could do it,' said the English voice behind them, and a woman replied, 'Of course she could.'

The Dunnages sat in the warm theatre and watched the last of the orchestra dribble out. Leander said, 'That was magical, I'd never thought . . . And your costume, Molly, what an extraordinary person you are.'

No one had ever told Molly she was extraordinary. Sitting there in the atmosphere, both electric and exhausted, while the crowd – oblivious to her – left, she knew she was.

They'd imagined they would go to a club or for supper afterwards, but managed only one glass of Champagne at the bar, exclaiming about the performance, the costume, the orchestra, and Aunt April got wistful. But it was clear that August was worn out and Molly knew that Aunt April needed to remove her shoes, so when the path outside was empty they moved into the cold and waited until a lazy horse dragged a cab around the corner for them.

Leander and the Dunnage family travelled home feeling worldly and sophisticated and tingling with inspiration. Horatio flung his cape over his shoulder and raised the flamingo head high, strolling off into the night, a beaming Miss Berrycloth on his arm. As they walked, she told him, 'I have met Henrietta Dugdale and been to the Blue Mountains, but I think tonight was the highlight of my life.'

Leander Behan would never forget this night with Molly Dunnage on his arm. He'd caught an image of himself in that theatre, a mirror reflecting a tall man behind a modern girl, all dressed up with little white flowers in her hair. She looked very fine in that crowd, not like anyone else, and she was quick as lightning and smart, no shrinking violet – a rose, in fact, and oh so creative. He would swim for six weeks through mud to catch a glimpse of her. They drank sherry and ate biscuits around the kitchen table, though August went straight to bed, and they talked for an hour about the theatre, the people, and most especially, the Queen of the Night's costume, and Molly was pleased at how well the disguise made her sing, how the Dame had become an especially wonderful Queen of the Night.

August was asleep before his head hit the pillow, but an orchestra played in his dreams. And later, in her rank little room opposite, his sister sat up in her bed and relived a night with Hurtle Rosenkranz, the night they saw J. C. Williamson's production of *Orpheus and Euridice* at Theatre Royal, all flowing capes and draped gowns, a snake made from rope and Persephone's voice with an irritating warble. Hurtle had bought her Champagne at interval, and it was delicious; its bubbles really did tickle her nose. Sitting in that theatre with her true love, every note became magical, festering with meaning. Portentous, in hindsight. She would happily descend to the land of the dead to retrieve dear Hurtle whenever it was asked of her.

Molly saw Leander to the front door, and when she saw the light go on up in his room, she shut the door loudly. Her father didn't stir, and her aunt chastised though she knew it was to startle Mrs Sidebottom.

Snuggled in her bed, Molly told herself that nothing would come from Dame Lily's performance for her, that no one knew of Molly Dunnage and a war would prevent them ever knowing her. But she had this night to treasure forever.

Chapter 34

Mr Addlar rose at 6 am, as usual. Then things started to go awry.

While washing, he dropped the soap, had to rinse the cake then start again, and all of this set his schedule back by at least a minute. He shaved, but rushed, so it wasn't as close at he'd have preferred, then he stumbled while putting his foot into his trousers and thought he heard some of the stitches in a seam rip. Usually, he arrived at his table just as the landlady placed his boiled egg and toast next to his teapot, but this morning the egg and toast were already waiting, slightly cooler than they should have been.

He managed to leave home promptly at 6.45 am but was unsettled as he set off along the footpaths of Abbotsford towards Collingwood, though you could hardly call them footpaths, just worn tracks in the dirt. Behind him the sky was tinted grey and pink, and ahead of him was a whole day – it was Saturday, a half day, but he would stay on. There were letters to write on behalf of Norbert Poke, military uniforms to research. His spirits lifted as he remembered that soon he would have the great pleasure of sacking the embroiderers, those of them left, and then he'd employ tailors – men. A new venture, a patriotic endeavour, and a contribution to the war effort – it was thrilling.

Mr Addlar rounded the corner, his gait smooth and his key in his hand, and found the padlock hanging free and the gate wide open. He sped to the factory door, which Norbert Poke had left ajar – sloppy; he'd mention it. For a moment he was disoriented. There was no one there, just a draught and a vast, deserted space. It was like standing at the bottom of an emptied sea.

Then it all started to sink in. It was the right factory but was entirely vacant apart from a pile of unfinished corsets lying at the base of a straight line of nude torsos – 'ideal midriffs of the ideally shaped woman'. Every machine was gone, every bolt of fabric, every bin, table, stool, even the scissors and tape measures were gone, as was his desk – although his bell, hanging from the wall, still chimed softly as it moved in the swirling draught. He steadied it, cupping it fondly.

The floor was covered in documents: someone had stood on the balcony and tossed the contents of the desk drawers over. Above, ceiling windows were open and Mr Addlar felt cold, yet hot, and was about to faint; he reached for something, but there was nothing, and so he staggered to the stairs and sat with his head between his knees. He thought he could hear his blood rushing about his body, searching for a place to settle.

When he finally dragged himself up to the office, he found it stripped bare: the desk, chair, globe and filing cabinet were gone. The safe remained but it had been shuffled to the middle of the office, leaving scratches like reptile tracks in sand. It had proved too heavy to steal and remained locked.

What to do? There was no chair, no pen, no paper, not even the hat stand for his fedora, no desk to sit at to think.

Someone called and he moved to the louvres. The cotton-reel boy was standing beside the line of torsos, smiling. What a comeuppance! Snakelegs sent him to fetch the police, and Mr Poke.

Mrs Sidebottom saw the flamboyant chap reading her posters as she crossed the park. He was one of them, a friend of the Dunnages, and she wondered why he thought a fur-collared coat over a three-piece suit and knee-high boots was acceptable in

Carlton on a Saturday morning. She looked about for a tree big enough to hide behind, but he waved to her. 'Good morning!'

She ignored him, conscious of how undignified she looked, a middle-aged woman dragging a huge sack of soiled linen through a public park, her boys out and about and not helping her one bit. She felt most disrespected, but she had to give them their freedom before they went to fight for King, Queen and Country.

Then Molly Dunnage opened the door and she, too, waved to Mrs Sidebottom. 'Morning! You'd have heard us come home after the concert; it was truly a wonderous evening.'

Mrs Sidebottom ignored her, though she was always alert for the thump of their front door.

'Poor woman,' said Horatio as he handed Molly his hat, but Molly pointed out that she would have scowled at people enjoying themselves and waved a placard condemning Champagne.

Horatio handed August a pile of newspapers, and he then presented Aunt April with a box of chocolates, which she held, before putting them gently on the table. Not even Hurtle had ever given her chocolates. Horatio's fair hair was undressed, parted off centre, and fell over his youthful forehead. He draped his coat around Molly's dummy, then he settled at the table next to Leander and the discussion of Dame Lily's concert resumed. August made coffee, put a plate of jam fancies on the table, and went back to stuffing a pumpkin with breadcrumbs, herbs, nuts and diced carrots, parsnip and a sprinkling of currants. Aunt April smoothed the chocolate box on the table before her.

Horatio ate a jam fancy. 'I think Miss Berrycloth could do with a new hat, don't you?'

'It would have to be a sun hat,' said Leander, and they looked at him. He shrugged. 'She's moving to the country.' He turned the page from the rural report to read the political pages. Every article wrote of the looming war.

Molly, seated next to him as she always was, read aloud the arts section: '*The Argus* says "An Emphatic Return when a Mediocre

Farewell was expected. All were surprised to hear Dame Lily back in top form after years of competent but lacklustre presentations"; "Dame Lily dazzled in her dramatic costume, her voice reaching to the heavens"; "Dame Lily came onto the stage to rapturous applause wearing a striking costume that would find a perfect home in a production of *The Magic Flute*"; "We were treated to a stellar performance, Dame Lily's voice sounding stronger and richer, confidence underpinning her every note and gesture, a voice that came to us better than it ever has. Her instrument was not strained or vexed."'

She lowered the paper. 'I am a success here in the kitchen in Carlton.' They duly made a fuss of her for all of a minute.

'I wonder, if you made us all one, if we could sing like Dame Lily Pert?' said Horatio.

'I already can,' said August, wielding the stove poker and singing 'Der Hölle Rache' very badly. Aunt April joined him, her voice astoundingly deep, as did Horatio, gesturing a little too dramatically. Leander put his fingers in his ears and Molly ignored them, silly as they were, but if Leander wasn't sitting beside her, she would have joined in.

With the aria over they settled back to the papers. Horatio scanned the social pages of *The Argus*. 'Alathea Pocknall is wearing one of Mother's hats. She only recently made it for her.'

'Oh, show me.'

And there it was, in black and white. The hairs on Molly's arms stood to attention. It was a photograph of Alathea Pocknall boarding an ocean liner. The caption reported Miss Pocknall was travelling to family in America.

They all leaned in to see the page. It was a small photograph but told them everything. Alathea Pocknall was standing on a gangplank, her hand raised to wave, and she was laughing. Her hat was quite lovely. It was unadorned, the crown deep and the very wide brim oval shaped, its trim matching the full band, which obviously worked as a chin strap, or fascinator. For her triumphant farewell photograph, Alathea wore the hat band as a scarf that sat elegantly around her fine throat and fell tranquilly over her shoulders. She was wearing the magenta gown and, presumably, Molly's corset.

'She's absconded, how very bold,' said August. It was his version of fury.

Molly checked the date of the newspaper. 'She sailed away yesterday.'

The room was quiet, all of them confused about the true implications of Alathea's surprise departure.

Finally, April said, 'She's obviously been paid out.'

'They were to settle out of court, weren't they?' Leander said.

'Or she's made off with the money,' said Horatio, and pennies dropped all around the table.

Molly could not respond, was grappling with the facts that she knew.

It was Leander who held her, his lips at the temple, his breath warm. She was amazed, and speechless. Her career had been over for weeks . . . was never going to be. Why had they led her on? Why would Alathea do that to her? At that moment, every disappointment, big and small, arrived, splinters all around her, pointing.

'I think,' said Aunt April, one hand still resting on her chocolates, 'that you were the bridge, Molly, or perhaps a doorway might be a better way of explaining it.'

She was a decoy, a ruse. Alathea never really intended on going into business with anyone. Molly buried her face in Leander's shirt front, his watery intestines loudly processing his coffee and jam fancies, and his arms holding her. When she glanced up again, their anxious faces studied her – Leander, Horatio, her aunt and her father – and she felt pitiful.

But Molly Dunnage was not prepared to be defeated yet. 'They were insincere people. I have dodged a bullet. It's best she is gone to America.'

Finally, Horatio asked, 'Do you think Evan Pettyman knows? He might have been in on it, taken half the money.'

'Or he has just read it in today's paper like us and realises he'll have to deal with Norbert Poke and the legal system.' August sounded sorry for the man but there was part of Molly that was gleeful – did fancy clothes-wearing cousin Norbert know?

'I'll see if I can find out exactly what's happened,' said Horatio, though no one imagined the disgraced constable could ask questions anymore. Sensing their doubt, he explained, 'My job lends itself to spectacular scandal and rampant gossiping.' He looked at Molly. 'So, what now?'

'This won't stop me. I think I always knew, but it still hurts to know that all along it was just a contrivance.' Again, she wondered what part Evan Pettyman and his dreadful mother had played.

'We'll go to the football,' said Leander, as though it would solve everything. 'And we'll have lunch somewhere nice. Are you coming to the footy, Horatio?'

Constable Horatio Farrat thought of the games he'd attended in his capacity as police officer, the unruly drunks, the profanity and noise. 'Thank you, Leander, kind of you to ask, but no.'

'I don't like it much either but I'm keen to go to the MCG.'

'It's Collingwood and Carlton,' said August, as if that meant it was a compulsory event.

'I should go home,' Horatio declared. 'There's a book I must read.' It was the latest *La Mode Illustrée* catalogue sent from Paris for Horatio's mother.

While the conversation went on around her, Molly remained incredulous, still staring at the photo of Alathea Pocknall, laughing, and wearing Mrs Farrat's lovely hat.

Evan Pettyman was whistling as he rounded the corner to the house but slowed and crept to the front step. He removed his shoes, hat and coat, quietly opened the door and tiptoed to the kitchen, put the packages on the bench; newspapers, a roll of corned beef – his mother's favourite – onions, vinegar, peppercorns, bay leaves, cloves, sugar and even an orange. The cheque in his pocket had survived his night of celebration in the grime of Little Lonsdale Street with drink, merriment and the kind of women he liked, those who did as they were told, or would for the right price. While the tea brewed, he placed a knob of butter and a scoop of strawberry jam on a pretty plate beside the milk jug. It was usual for them to have dripping on their toast, but today was a celebration. He patted his top pocket, heard the faint sound of paper against cloth, and was reassured again, knowing the cheque from the sale of the factory goods and chattels was his.

At last, relief from grinding poverty and his mother's unhappiness. She would be proud of him, finally. It was now just a matter of depositing the cheque, hiring the milk cart and moving his mother and their meagre possessions to another location. He touched his pocket again. The cheque would repay Hawker his loan, Evan would have his fee, and Cousin Poke would be pursuing Miss Pocknall – wrongly – for selling everything from under them. He had the deeds and title, he would eventually sell the factory, possibly to someone interstate, or overseas. Sorting the mess would take years. By then, the money, Evan and his mother would be long gone.

He leaned the cheque between the toast and the boiled egg on the tray, his whistle echoing in the stairwell as he ascended to his mother. Mrs Pettyman raised her arms and Evan gently levered her into an upright position in her meagre bed, placed pillows to support her and settled her old fur around her shoulders against the chill. She reached out her hand. Evan moved to cup her hand in his, but she snatched it away. 'I want the cheque.'

He pointed to it resting on her tray. 'Are you pleased, Mother?'

'I've been waiting all night.'

He apologised, poured her tea while she studied the cheque,

front and back, and he knew she was planning exactly how to spend it. Evan hoped he'd at least get a new suit and a spare shirt.

'It'll be deposited first thing Monday.' He handed his mother the Saturday papers.

'It would have been far more efficient had you sold everything during the week, we could have banked it that very day.'

'We can blame the manufacturer who purchased the assets for that.' He found her night pot, which he carried downstairs and emptied into the lavatory. Then he started on the corned beef in the kitchen.

Like everyone in Melbourne, Mrs Pettyman took in the front-page headlines then read on through the pages, slowly, taking in news of the threatened war, the railway and mine workers strike in the UK and the tedious campaign promises before the federal elections in September, and was relieved to get to the social section.

Evan heard the bang of her cane on the floor. He kept loading vegetables in with the boiling beef, but she banged. And banged. Apparently it was urgent.

As he entered the room she lifted up the photograph of Alathea Pocknall on the ocean liner gangway.

Evan felt fear, so familiar to him, and nausea. His buttocks started to sweat and he fought an urge to flee.

'She has sailed to America and I'm assuming Mr Hawker's money is in her suitcase. You failed to convince her, you failed to see that she was smarter than you, you didn't see that she was prepared to dupe her greedy cousin and ruin her own factory rather than lose everything. You have been hoodwinked, Evan.'

Evan began to shake.

Because he slept late – the afterparty at the Princess had been somewhat muted without a star to ogle and shine her light on everyone, so they took their lady friends out elsewhere – Norbert did not hear the cotton-reel boy knocking two storeys below, then leave via the orchard, stealing a pear and a pomegranate on his way. And because his cousin had let Cook, and everyone else, go, when Norbert finally got out of bed he had to brew his own coffee and make his own toast, which he was quite proud he had mastered. He considered riding his horse, but couldn't face trying to saddle the unmanageable animal, let along try and get on it himself. And anyway, annoyingly, he had to get a newspaper from somewhere.

On the tram en route to the city Norbert read his way through the headlines; Germany was secretly preparing for deployment, Germany would declare war on Russia, in Echuca, hotel drinkers refused to drink German beer. But no wars anywhere would affect Norbert, an American in Australia. Finally, he turned the page to the social section, read that a new automobile shop was opening and someone he knew had recently married, a big flashy wedding. At the bottom of the page, he caught sight of someone familiar. It was his cousin. Boarding a ship. The toast and coffee turned acrid in his stomach, and he felt the need to piss.

In the city, he ran to Woodgrip's hotel and found him still in bed.

'Norbert! You're early.'

'She's gone, sailed away, I told you she was up to something.' He threw the paper onto the bed. 'She must have money, where did she get money?' Norbert made his way to the bathroom, unbuttoning his fly.

'She used the passages we purchased for our honeymoon,' said Clive, scanning the social pages for an event he could attend, a debutante ball or perhaps even a wedding where bridesmaids would be intoxicated by bouquets, veils and the prospect of a husband. If he didn't find a wealthy fiancée, he'd have to consider enlisting. Then he studied the photo of his ex-fiancée again and felt a pang of hurt. 'That's her friend in the background, isn't it? Miss Marguerite Baca?'

Norbert shouted from the bathroom, 'We are due to sign and settle . . . she hasn't been paid off yet, surely?'

'You sound like a horse pissing, Poke. The lawyers are slow, you have not signed anything therefore you haven't agreed to pay her –'

'*She* was slow, it was her, the BITCH – she stole the deeds and titles, she stalled on signing! Now she is gone. It will all have to be done by post . . . though we could give America reason to send her back.' He barged back in, buttoning his fly. Clive noted he hadn't bothered to wash his hands.

'She can't have done anything too drastic, it is all under legal negotiation.'

'Women can be cunning.'

'Men can be ruthless,' said Clive, himself opportunistic and hardnosed, and Norbert missed the reference to his own behaviour.

'Pity it's Saturday,' he replied. 'Where does your friend Miškinis live?'

'I've no idea. And we can't do a thing until Monday anyway.'

'This will take years to sort out, all those letters to and from America. But we'll see her in jail eventually. Or perhaps an asylum. Are you hungry?'

'I could do with a drink.'

Over a long lunch the men discussed their next move and decided that they would give the safe a crack since everyone else had failed. They would search every single piece of paper for the code, look for hiding places – under floorboards, in secret drawers, even old Pocknall's flash new indoor toilet. And so it was well after lunch by the time Norbert Poke and Clive Woodgrip caught a cab to the factory, intent on finally opening the safe, but they were flummoxed to find the gates wide open and the staff loitering outside. Mr Addlar stood next to his bell, his hands idle, watching policemen wandering around the shed. A plain-clothed detective made notes.

Norbert confronted one of the policemen. 'What's happened?'

'Who are you?'

'I am the owner of this factory.'

The policeman looked around the shed, at the papers all over the floor, and gestured at the disrobed torsos. 'Looks like you've been robbed to me.'

Mr Addlar, who seemed on the verge of tears, explained that the neighbours saw the thieves load up the sewing machines, the fabrics, the tools, the desk, chairs . . . everything.

'Why didn't these observant neighbours send for the police?'

'They were under the impression the place was being repossessed or sold to pay off Miss Alathea Pocknall. They follow the case in the newspapers.'

'Why didn't you send for me?'

'I did, I sent the cotton-reel boy.'

'He never came back,' said a toothless crone standing with the waiting, wondering staff.

'You can all fuck off,' Norbert said, but they stayed where they were. 'Why don't you go, are you donkeys? Find another job.'

The sharp-chinned crone thumbed in the direction of the office. 'What about our pay? We haven't been paid since Mr Pocknall died.'

'I don't have your pay.'

'It's in the safe.'

'I'm not in charge of pay, Addlar does all that.' Norbert turned to Addlar. 'Is there insurance?'

'Of course.'

They all looked to the floor and the papers from the office strewn everywhere, walked on, torn and dancing out the doors on the breeze.

'Well, then, Addlar, find it.'

Addlar looked to Colma and pointed at the floor, but Colma turned away. 'We need to be paid.'

'We can't pay you today, though, can we?'

'Why not?'

Mr Addlar, a little more in control of himself, snarled, 'We'll write to you.' He did not know the code to the safe, Mr Pocknall had not trusted anyone with it, and so he would not be paid either. He told himself he had a stable career behind him, much experience, he'd find employment again, though he was terrified just thinking about any sort of change.

Colma pointed to the papers on the floor. 'But you might not have our addresses no more.'

Norbert bellowed, 'For Christ's sake, someone deal with this woman!'

In the end, it was Snakelegs who got down on his hands and knees to sift through the papers. Colma set about writing everyone's addresses on a piece of paper – not many of them could write. There was no prospect for work, even for those who could. Colma, like some of the others, would end up on the streets, begging. Hopefully she'd get enough to pay for a room or a place on someone's floor, at least for the winter.

'It's her, that fucking bitch,' Norbert roared.

'She won't get away with this, whatever she's done. Oliphant's the man we need.'

It was the knock at the door that saved him. Whoever it was, the police or Mr Hawker, it would be better than standing there in front of his mother, waiting until she told him to take his trousers off, knowing he would have to bend over in front of her so that she could wield her cane.

From the window he saw that it was Hawker. As he scurried to the door he snatched the cheque from his mother, who screamed, but he left her helpless in her bed.

Mr Hawker was looking at his new automobile parked outside the house, one tyre cleaving a mound of horse manure. 'In shit,' said Mr Hawker, pointing to the wheel of his car. 'I knew the second I saw her goodbye photograph in the newspaper.

A photograph! She must have organised it herself – no one gets a photograph in the paper unless they're a criminal or royalty.'

'I'm sorry.'

Mr Hawker pushed past and into the drawing room, puffing cigar smoke. Evan stood before him, his trembling hands clasped tight and conscious that his mother was perhaps struggling to the landing to listen. 'I don't know what to do –'

'Obviously not.' Mr Hawker sat in Mrs Pettyman's chair. It was like sitting on a throne in a dark medieval dungeon. 'My wife won't approve but I'll try to keep you out of jail if it comes to that.'

'I'm grateful.'

'I checked with my man, she withdrew on the cheque the day we paid her. You should have stopped it.'

'I'm sorry,' Evan said, but in truth Mr Hawker could have done the same. 'The deeds and titles –'

'They are no use, Norbert will make a fuss, we won't be able to sell, and the police are probably searching for you as we speak. Though I won't get my clients' money back if you're in jail, will I? But if you put one more step wrong, I'll see to it that you do go to jail, for a *very*, very long time.'

'Thank you, Mr Hawker, I'm so very –'

'You need to find some way to pay me back the hundreds of pounds you owe.'

'Alathea Pocknall owes you –'

'I lent it to *you*! You're the one who underestimated her, you fool.'

'I cannot tell you how grateful –' He stopped, the hairs on his neck prickling at the tap of his mother's cane on the floorboards, then the pause as she shuffled forward, another tap.

Mr Hawker glanced at the staircase. 'Did you at least sell the machinery?'

Evan handed over the cheque; it would go some way to paying back the money he'd borrowed from Mr Hawker to buy into the factory, he hoped.

Rosalie Ham

It was all so humiliating. To be deceived by a woman.

They heard the tap upstairs again, another shuffle shuffle, tap.

Norbert and Clive found Mr Oliphant's offices closed, the sign on the glass door scraped off, small curls of gold lettering on the footpath sticking to their shoes.

They enquired at the tailor shop next door. 'Retired,' said the tailor. 'Cleared out on Friday, moved to the high country somewhere, he's going to breed Dorking chickens, I believe.'

Evan followed Mr Hawker to the gate and stood briefly, hoping to find an escape, but knew he would have to face her, sooner or later. He stepped back into the antechamber and that's when the first blow landed. His mother struck him violently in the groin with her walking stick. He doubled over, holding himself, a hot boulder of pain in his stomach, legs, everywhere. He could scarcely breathe while the agony came, then abated, and returned, his mother standing over him.

'Why did you not see that she would escape with all our money? We are in debt forever.' She struck him across the back. His neck smarted and his shoulder blades screamed as he curled tighter.

'She is devious, a liar, Mother! Please stop.'

'You have failed once too often.' She swung the stick again, and he felt the sting in his bones. Such a small woman, but fierce when driven by anger.

'Mother, please,' he whimpered, but it was only when his mother was breathless, flushed and gasping that she ceased and leaned on her stick.

He looked up at her from the floor, tears streaming, his mouth a silent scream. She was wearing only her blouse and coat, her legs beneath her bloomers skinny and mottled. 'I cannot hobble about in that wretched skirt anymore, Evan, I cannot live on boiled potatoes while you feed your musical friends and play gramophones, and I can no longer live like some pauper in a miserable freezing hovel.'

'I will help you, Mother, I have a plan, please stop . . .'

'You always have a plan, Evan, and none of them have ever fed or clothed me. What sort of man are you? I keep telling you, if I am to rely on you then you must be reliable.' She moved her stick and went to step away but was anchored. Evan had a hold of her ankle. She raised her cane, and as Evan tugged on her leg, she overbalanced, stumbled and made a sound like a dropped bag of golf balls when she landed sideways on the floor.

Mrs Pettyman lay still, her eyes wide with pain.

Evan rallied, wiped his face and gathered himself. He looked at his mother lying beside him. A small yellow flow of urine wound its way to the skirting boards. He stood quickly. 'You are hurt, Mother?'

She reached out, feebly, her face ashen. 'Something has broken,' she breathed. 'My laudanum, please?'

Mrs Pettyman's bones, frail as wheat stalks, had snapped and her hipbone was lodged in the soft matter in her pelvis. She was in agony, but so was he. He was sick of trying, and failing. And he was hungry. Evan went to the kitchen in search of food, found the boiled meat ready to eat, then took a short nap. When he woke, he knew what to do. It was them, those women. Molly Dunnage and the whore Pocknall, they had double crossed him. He would find Dunnage and confront her.

In his mother's room, he kicked the mirror from the seaman's chest and found her skirt, felt for the pound notes she kept rolled in the hem. He tore them from their narrow nest and, as he left the house to go shopping, he nudged his mother with his shoe. She moaned faintly.

*

Molly wore her new coat to the football, though it was a little dressy. Leander felt proud with her on his arm. The general din and the sudden roar drew them towards the MCG and the crowd of joyous and upset people, the roar rising and falling away to swell again. Outside the oval, the next wave of thunderous noise gathered speed and volume and overwhelmed them, a tsunami of passion mushrooming over the top of the grandstands, a physical sensation swamping them.

They stood at the gates, hand in hand, the dank ground littered with posters and rubbish, streamers and discarded newspapers and half-eaten sandwiches, the tides of hullabaloo looming and receding. Then people started flowing out of the gates. It was three-quarter time so the score must have already decided the outcome. Molly and Leander went in and stood between the grandstands, on either side of them two big vases of people waving and milling at the railings, rising and falling; on the big green field before them, the goal squares were a quag-mire and the men filthy and splattered, red-faced and running, chasing, and all the while the noise gathering then easing.

The final siren sounded and Molly and Leander turned and ran, ahead of the fleeing fans, most heading straight for the pub. The emotion had caught them; they felt alive again, as they had at the concert. Leander stopped. 'One day,' he said, and took both her hands, 'on a day like any other, there you were in the middle of a country road under my very own windmill.'

'And to think I might not have gone with my aunt that day.'

'I was meant to play football but they found someone who could actually kick the ball.'

'Last night, when we were sitting close together in the cab, I wished we'd never reach home.'

'I feel the same.'

She thought he might kiss her there, under the grey sky, oblivi-ous to the noisy crowd splitting and flowing around them, but he just kept looking at her, longingly.

'You know I'm not always an amiable person but you make me more pleasant,' Molly said. 'I would normally have stewed for months over Alathea Pocknall but I'm not angry because you're here.'

Leander shrugged. 'I'll make a deal with you. If you don't change for me, I won't change for you.' He raised her hand and kissed her palm. She hoped it wasn't sweaty, and she hoped he would kiss her properly soon. Leander would be the only man she ever kissed, the first and the last person in life to kiss her. But though he was prepared to love her as she was, she still feared, having briefly met his father, that she might have to change some things about herself.

The manufacturer who'd purchased the machines looked at the police and swore, hand on heart, that he'd thought nothing of taking delivery of the entire contents of a factory in the middle of the night. 'They told me it's best because of peak hour, the crowds and traffic.'

'They were right about crowds and traffic.' The fervour of war was in the air, uniforms and patriotism and medals, and footy finals were approaching so fans flocked to every training session and stood at the boundary shouting advice. The pubs were full, the streets crowded.

The clothing manufacturer assumed an expression of a duped, innocent man. 'Can I get my money back?'

The dealer, so-called 'Mr Evan', was known to the police. They started at real estate agents. 'He's fair, red-faced, beady-eyed, and his mother looks like a praying mantis, the kind that eats its family when she's hungry.'

Many agents knew the Pettymans, and the third agent they asked said, 'They've got a house over in Princes Hill. I'll get you the address.'

The police found no one at home, the house dark and silent. There was always tomorrow.

Inside, the knocking roused her. She could not move for the pain and cold and she felt her shoulders hard on the floorboards, the wind slicing under the door, cutting her side, and with each breath shards of pain shot through her.

'I will die,' she thought, her eyes on the doorknob so high, so far from her reach.

Chapter 35

LEANDER WOKE IN his cold hotel room and looked out through his grimy window. Molly's house was snug and smoke leaked from its chimney, lingering before finding a way up through the branches. Before he left Melbourne he would prune the trees to let in more light. He bathed and shaved, noting someone else had used the hand basin. Another guest had moved in. He dressed and checked again that his collar was clean.

As he came down the stairs, the barman called to him, 'News for you, son,' and Leander joined him beside the wireless. The news told them that Germany was preparing for deployment. War was declared on Russia and, because of Germany's actions, France had mobilised.

He stared at the polished box, its cloth-covered speakers and bakelite knobs. 'No,' he said, unfazed. He had Molly, his life was set, the governments would sort it all out, they would negotiate, Germany would back down. 'England has the sense to stay out of it.'

The barman shook his head. 'Not a chance, cobber, Britain's got an empire they want to hang on to.'

On his journey across Curtain Square, Leander felt something was different. He looked up for buds or a fresh spring canopy, but the trees were still bare and the sky still a winter sky. It all looked the same, and it was very early but there were people gathered in small groups, talking . . . of war. He squared his shoulders, walked on towards Molly. He should marry her and be with her before he left, because he would have to go. 'Enlist early,' his father had said, 'secure a position that you want rather than be drafted into the infantry and end up on the front lines.' This all made sense, but he disliked the advice that followed: 'Don't marry the girl. If something happens, we'll be responsible for her and any children that might result.'

His father had a way of being pragmatic, but Leander knew love didn't comprehend pragmatism. He wanted her, and he wanted to know that when he came back, she would be with him; he wanted assurance.

August Dunnage was in his front yard, still in his dressing gown and slippers, a scarf around his neck, his hair unbrushed and sticking up at the crown. He was removing one of Aunt April's posters.

WE DESERVE THE RIGHT TO SOCIAL, POLITICAL
AND ECONOMIC EQUALITY FOR WOMEN.

Someone had crossed it out and written:

SOCIAL, POLITICAL AND ECONOMIC EQUALITY FOR
WOMEN SEND THEM ALL OFF TO THE FRONT LINE.

'Good morning.'

'Leander, son.'

It was the second time that morning he'd been called 'son'.

August gestured at the graffiti. 'We're accustomed to ridicule and ostracisation, but this decoration is a little violent.' His voice was weak.

'Germany has declared war on Russia.'

'Yes, a lot of squabbling. The newspaper's been telling me diplomacy is no use, it has all gone too far. Germany will most likely declare war on France and all of this will upset Britain, so . . .'

As Leander put his hand on the doorknob, August said,

'I cannot tell you how sorry I am, son. We might have done better for our youngsters.'

Molly had woken lamenting that he hadn't kissed her properly. There was only one more night left – tomorrow was Monday and he would catch the train back to Yaambul. And now there was going to be a war.

She was sitting at the table, a hanky scrunched in her hands, her face pinched and her eyes swollen. 'You won't go, will you?'

'The war's nothing to do with me, I know, but . . .'

She nodded and smiled, *I understand*, but it was not convincing. She moved the kettle to the hot plate and reached for the eggs.

They spent their last morning together by the stove saying not much at all, holding hands and watching the flames. August made himself scarce, fussing in his studio and reading in bed.

Molly baked damper and made soup. Towards lunchtime, they heard Aunt April come in, the squeak of her bedroom door opening and her rucksack hitting the floor, then her poster dropped and clattered and she came heavily down the hall, paused at the kitchen table, breathy, urgent, her hat askew and with what they thought was a whiff of her bedroom odour trailing. But it wasn't: Aunt April had been pelted with rotting fruit and vegetables. Her dress was polka-dotted with decayed tomato, streaked with slimy silverbeet and pieces of shell clung to egg yolk on her shoulders. It was the potatoes that stank the most: pink potato flesh all across her sashes and what looked like guano dusting the rim of her bowler. A large badge pinned to its band read, *Send the Politicians to War*. She dropped a box of pamphlets on the kitchen table and a new edition of *Woman Voter*, and rushed towards the lavatory, calling, 'You should have seen it! Patriotism is at fever pitch.'

'So is hatred of the pacifist campaigners,' said Molly.

August wandered in, noted that the headline on the *Woman Voter* pamphlet simply said, *PEACE*. He decided he would roast some vegetables for lunch.

Aunt April returned from the outhouse, her cheeks a shade lighter.

'Were you hurt?' Molly asked.

She smiled. '*Roughage* doesn't hurt, but I'm grateful no one spat on me. I managed to bat most missiles away with my poster, even managed to send back an apple or two.' But she would have been better off with Miss Berrycloth at her back. Miss Berrycloth was terrifically accurate with missiles.

While her aunt changed, Molly took the filthy dress and soaked it in the laundry trough, her tears dripping into the soapy water. She had never felt so wretched.

Aunt April arrived back in the kitchen in her dressing gown. 'Vida's anti-war position will affect her chance at election.'

'Surely,' said Molly, 'we don't have anything to do with such stupidity down here at the bottom of the world.'

Aunt April scoffed. 'Thousands have volunteered already in Britain.'

'But we are too far away,' she cried.

Aunt April repeated that Leander shouldn't have to fight *any* war if he didn't want to.

Leander shook his head. 'How can I *not* go?'

'You can object. All men are brothers. You're not the type to kill anyone, let alone your brothers. No one should even ask you to,' said August, assembling potato and pumpkin to chop.

'It won't do any good for anyone if I object.'

'But you shouldn't be asked to risk your life.' Molly felt she was losing her grip, about to succumb to utter desolation, and Aunt April, too, was struggling to contain her emotions. The kitchen seemed colder than usual.

'You must decide what the *right* thing to do is rather than what you *should* do.' Aunt April loved this young man; he was their happiness, Molly's future.

'I see that,' Leander said, 'but there's everyone else . . . my parents and my sister.'

'They don't want you to go, surely?'

He stood and walked in a small circle. 'They have to live in a community, everyone else will go.'

'Now see here,' said August, exasperated, 'whatever any young man finally decides is bound to cause great heartache to those who love him. Any decision at this time will upset somebody.'

Aunt April saw that they were not helping, but was furious. Patriotism was forcing personal happiness aside for the sake of King and Country. Fundamentally and instinctively she did not believe violence was anything other than violence. 'War is wrong,' she said, and no one could disagree.

Leander needed to go home; his family would be fretting.

The afternoon was solemn, and after a dinner of little conversation, Aunt April opened her box of chocolates and everyone was allowed to choose one; then she put the lid back on and took it with her when she went to bed. August also went to bed, and Molly and Leander rugged up and walked to the square, where they sat on the bench under the one gaslight where the two paths met, his arm around her. A possum on the rotunda studied them.

'I'll see a bit of the world,' he said, and Molly cried.

Leander stood, and helped her up and gathered her in his arms to take her home, but she clung to him and he felt her shaking body and held her close and she felt him pull her, crush her against his woollen vest, her nose squashed against his throat. They were as one, their bodies pressed together, safe, his breath on her hair.

'Don't, Molly, please don't cry. You'll make it even more sad. It is a rotten old world.'

'It's cruel,' she sobbed. She howled for her disappointments, her mother, and Gladys, the adversity of Mrs Sidebottom and the neighbourhood. She howled for her poor sick father and her stoic aunt with her precious chocolates and Leander held her while she hated people for not seeing their generosity and naivety, hated that others were blind to the resilience, bravery and warmth in their snug little house, and hated Alathea Pocknall for her betrayal and her superficial sincerity. She hoped that posturing, grasping Lily Pert would lose her voice. She finally gave in to the obstructions and sheer bad luck and unfortunate timing and let herself be wretched for her desultory life. She sobbed for herself.

'It is rotten, but I think all of the things you want, or at least some of the things you're campaigning for, will come to you because of this war. Women can't be ignored. Who else will make the ammunition and drive the cable trams?'

'And when the men come home, we will all have to relinquish our jobs and our gains to care for you all. I'm sorry I'm so glum when you are going to war and nothing is as rotten as that will be for you. I'm sorry, I'm selfish.'

'You are perfect, and I love you with all my heart and I always will.'

'I feel the same. I'd sit through an entire cricket match as long as you were there.'

Leander kissed her for a very long time, drew breath, and kissed her again, and Molly Dunnage thought she would melt. Her body did not seem to be hers, it was just a mass of tingling nerve endings, and she was grateful for her boots, strong and flat and supportive halfway up to her knees, keeping her upright.

She would not miss out again, she would not get close only to have what she wanted taken from her again. She took Leander's hand and led him back to the house, to her room.

In his room at the Kent Hotel, Evan Pettyman sat on his bed. He was dressed in a new suit, shirt and underwear, and very pleased with his view across Curtain Square to the Dunnage house. He'd watched the young man and Molly Dunnage sitting together on the bench, seen them kiss, and on the doorstep they had embraced and gone inside. He was still watching when all the lights in the house went out.

He didn't see the young man come back across the park, nor did he hear anyone come up the stairs or open and close a door in the night.

Chapter 36

WHEN EVAN ROUNDED the corner late Monday morning, dressed in the smart suit and carrying his bag of new clothes, he was stopped dead by the scene at his house. Two men stood at his front door; one held what looked like a dressing case.

'Sir!' The man carrying the small case called. 'I am a doctor of medicine and we are wondering if you can help?'

The other man moved to stand close to Evan. 'You live in this house.'

'No, not anymore, but I visit to check up . . . I haven't been here these past couple of days.'

The doctor said, 'It looks like there's been an accident.'

Evan was wondering if he should run or stay. 'What do you mean by an accident?'

He put his free hand on Evan's shoulder. 'You're related to the woman in this house, aren't you?'

They had called it an *accident*. 'She's my mother.'

'I'm from the estate agent,' the other man said. 'A woman has died in this house.'

Evan reached for the fence to steady himself. The men watched distress wash across his face. They saw that he was working to take everything in, weak at the knees, incredulous. 'She died?'

'Our condolences,' said the doctor, and both men looked sombre for a moment.

The agent explained, 'When no one answered, I used my key – she was behind in her rent . . . and then I sent for the doctor.'

'It appears that she fell,' the doctor explained. 'She may well have tripped down the stairs, her injuries were serious.'

While the doctor and the agent stood awkwardly, Evan Pettyman sat on the front step, his face in his hands, crying tears of joy. The tension lifted and he felt he was floating. It was the end of tyranny and a lifetime of persistent dread. 'She was unsteady on her feet and needed her cane to walk.' But she was the stubbornest, most miserable and vindictive old cow on earth. 'I'm sorry, I didn't know she was behind in her rent . . . I would have helped.'

The agent handed him the letter. 'Ignore her notice of eviction, of course, but the balance will need to be settled.'

'Settled, yes,' said Evan.

It started to rain, sudden fat drops, and the men moved to the porch to shelter.

The doctor put his hand on Evan's shoulder. 'Would you be able to identify her, to be certain?'

He nodded, tried not to smile. He'd love to. He'd been looking at her pitiless face his entire life; he knew every clogged pore and whisker. And he needed to be certain.

His mother was wrapped in a waterproof sheet, lying on her back on the floor where she had fallen. The doors and windows were open but a faint odour seeped. When the doctor peeled back the sheet, one of his mother's curls flicked out and Evan flinched. The doctor steadied him.

Her skinny blotched hands lay flat on her bony sternum. He nodded. 'I am certain.'

Evan accepted the card naming the local funeral parlour but declined their offer, gratefully, to stay with his mother while he went to fetch the undertaker. He said he would spend some moments with her, alert her friends, who would help prepare her and say farewell, and once the rain had stopped . . .

'Of course.' They said goodbye and that they were sorry for his loss, they'd be in touch, there were procedures.

He closed the door to them and stood looking at the water-proof sheet which looked like an unexceptional hillscape. Then he busied himself; he used soap and water to prise the ruby and diamond rings from her stiff fingers, unhooked her brooch, earrings and gold necklace. He even took the tortoiseshell combs from her hair, and then he wrapped her again and ransacked the seaman's chest. He pocketed her laudanum, gathered her trinkets, her official letters and her will (though she no longer had anything to leave anyone). He held his father's watch and cufflinks to his breast then attached them to his new suit and shirt. He slipped the silver sleeve garters up his arms, tied the silk bow tie around his collar and admired his reflection in the small mantlepiece mirror.

Evan gleefully roved through the empty rooms of the house, checking for anything else of value, then turned his attention to the photographs. He threw the photos of his mother onto the floor and jumped up and down, up and down on them, pounding her until her face was just mottled grey and white paper, then burned them in the fireplace along with his mother's underwear, brush, comb and foundation powder and any remaining general detritus. After a bite to eat – corned beef again – Evan went to see the milkman.

He paid to hire the horse and cart and drove to the city morgue, where he unloaded his stiff mother.

'This woman was my tenant, a widow with no family, and a pauper, as it turns out. I found her when I went to collect the rent.' He gave them some pound notes, climbed back onto the cart and was gone before the workers at the morgue had divvied up the notes between them.

When she finally heard movement in the house, Aunt April walked noisily but carefully down the passage. She did not take her eyes from the night pot but as she passed through the kitchen, she said, 'Good-o, Leander, you've stoked the fire.'

'I've made tea,' he said, a little too exuberantly.

'Weak black with three sugars, please,' she called as she proceeded out to the lavatory, passing Molly, who was splashing about over the wash trough.

They sat at the table and drank tea, as they usually did, and August and April glanced knowingly at each other.

Leander noted that no one asked anyone how they slept the night before, and neither Aunt April nor August mentioned that they hadn't heard him leave the night before . . . or come in early. Molly's skin was all fluttering nerve endings and she felt mature, grown, because she knew a great secret, and beside her, Leander felt the same. They held hands under the table, as they usually did, but there was a different message in their grasp now, it held a knowing, a secret bond, a *first*, a truth and a pledge.

Her aunt and father saw there was a glow about Molly. She was serene and pensive, and didn't leave Leander's side. They moved about the house as if they were joined, looking up together when anyone mentioned either of their names and gesturing at the same time. They finished each other's sentences and anticipated when the other needed another egg, the salt or a knife. Something had been completed and was settled.

And then it was time for Leander to go.

August and Aunt April took charge of the mood, acting as if Leander was leaving for a brief adventure. 'I will have found a solution to eradicate the rogue molluscs by the time you return,' April announced.

August said he'd make them a dinner set. 'What bird would you like on it?'

'Surprise us,' said Leander.

He went for his rucksack, and as he crossed the square he considered his parents, what he thought he knew of their marriage up until then, but understood now that it was far more. He had just learned a wondrous quality about the love he had with Molly and was certain that his life would be with her, he would have that night of passion for the rest of his life.

When he stepped into the hotel he saw the men of Rathdowne Street and Curtain Square gathered. It was too early to serve beer, but the doors were open, the bar crowded but quiet as a painting, the wireless blaring. A very British voice was informing them that Germany had declared war on France and wanted to invade by going through Belgium. Belgium refused to let them, so Germany declared Belgium an enemy and, fearful that the Germans might take over the world, Britain declared war on Germany.

The world would go to war.

He'd been certain of his future happiness, but now his future didn't belong to him. Up in his room, Leander reached for his rucksack and stuffed clothes into it, tears dripping down his nose, furious at the cruelty of it all and knowing that he was in love and always would be with Molly Dunnage.

When he returned to the house, he hugged Aunt April like she'd never been hugged, and looked August in the eyes and said, 'Thank you, sir, for Molly. She has made me the happiest I'll ever be.'

August said to him, 'You'll marry her one day, won't you?'

'I will, sir, as soon as I can.'

They shook hands and embraced, patting each other's back, as men do.

Leander turned to Molly and held her. What carried between them was beyond words. Molly knew what her mother had felt for her father and understood how Hurtle Rosenkranz remained for her aunt. She understood what it was all about, and now Leander would go home to his family and then to training camp, and then to war. They would not have their happiness. Not yet, at least.

'I'll write,' Leander said simply, and he walked away.

'Love is the most important thing,' said her father, and put his arm around his daughter's shoulders. Leander would keep her strong, even when he was not with her.

*

Molly

Evan Pettyman watched Leander Behan walk away down Curtain Street, and saw Molly Dunnage stand at the gate, watching the man until he disappeared around the corner.

It was her, the Dunnage girl; she'd conspired with Alathea, always knew the bitch would set sail with his money . . .

That night Molly found a card under her pillow. It was a picture of a house on a slight rise in a lush garden with smoke coming from the chimney and children playing in the street, and it said, 'With all my heart, Molly, my love.'

On his long train ride home, Leander relived every hour of his time in Melbourne, and every second of that last night together. It was a miraculous thing.

Chapter 37

WITH NO ONE to cook or clean for him, Norbert Poke was miserable. The lawns at the house were already ankle high, coffee and toast were not at all fulfilling and he was powerless to do anything until legal matters were settled – until they found Alathea. He tried to think of anyone who might lend him money to set up again, but he hadn't seen much of his chums of late. He looked at his horse, contentedly chewing its way through the long grass beside the empty aviary. He would have to either eat it or sell it.

Norbert moved through the big house and sat at Emrys Pocknall's desk. He opened his top drawer and found some unused chequebooks and a box of cigars. He lit one up and considered what more there was to sell. He'd sold the automobile to pay a few bills. He could sell the paintings, beds, the electric toaster, the refrigerator – this would keep him alive until they found his bitch cousin and settled matters, but he could never replace those fine things, and he liked them. If he was to keep on he needed a decent house. And the bicycle was easier to ride than the horse. It could take years to settle things. He needed a nice house to live in, for the foreseeable future anyway. And there was Miškinis to consider; Miškinis had agreed to sort out the mess of things, 'at a fair price.'

What was Miškinis's version of fair though?

Woodgrip, handsome devil, had found a girl to pursue, so he hadn't seen him for days. Perhaps she had a sister, a wealthy friend?

Norbert thought of going back to America, but embarrassingly would return as he had left: a disappointment. And how would he get money to live?

Sitting there in his dead uncle's office in a cloud of cigar smoke, he wondered what he was supposed to *do* from now on. And where was it in his life that things had gone awry, and why?

He gazed through the doors into the room opposite, its shelves solid with hundreds of books, all manner of novels and non-fiction, plays and all of Shakespeare, atlases and encyclopaedias, history, all the Greeks, Romans and Russians, even some stuff on Japan and China, dictionaries and texts on philosophy and science, and rare books too.

He sat bolt upright, marched across to the library and looked in wonder. He could get at least five shillings each for these books, more for some of them.

Dame Lily Pert sat up on her day bed, a blanket over her knees and a cup of sherry in her hand, secure within the brick walls of her little womb-like dressing room. She was admiring her disguises – her colleagues – the masks of paint and powder and the costumes, characters made of silk and satin, cambric and lace, spot delaine, sateen, renaissance lace, Japanese silks and guipure, lawn and muslin, embroidered bodices and glittering necklines, diaphanous sleeves and beaded cuffs all draped over furniture or hanging on the walls around her.

A note had come that morning. Due to the war, her *Favourite Aria* season had been postponed until further notice. Dame Lily's response was swift. Management's decision was 'preposterous', her people needed her . . . music was the blood of life, songs the breath.

The Princess Theatre agreed, but added that there were many singers and musicians breathing meaning into the beating hearts of a great mixture of people and they had an obligation to respect the right of all to see all brands of musicians.

Dame Lily locked her door and pushed her chaise longue against it and Penina was now begging from the other side – there were maintenance staff waiting to break down the door.

'They have saws and sledgehammers,' Penina called, 'and a wheelbarrow.'

Dame Lily tore every string from every corset in the room and started lashing herself to her chaise longue.

After several hours of imploring, bribing and threatening from Penina and various stagehands, the fire brigade arrived and applied their axes, splintering the door. Dame Lily merely pulled her blanket up over her head. When they removed the blanket, they found she had laced her torso and lower limbs to the leg of the lounge and backrest with knotted corset string. Someone fetched scissors, and as they approached with the shears, Dame Lily hit a high C, holding the note for over twenty seconds. The men retreated, shaking their heads. When they returned, she became the Queen of the Night and blasted them from her room.

More strong men were summoned, equipped with ear plugs, and eventually the Dame was lifted on her chaise longue. They then discovered that her chaise longue would not fit through the door, so they set about securing the Dame's safety, padding her with pillows and wrapping her in her furs before proceeding to knock bricks from around the door frame. Once it was wide enough, they barrowed the bricks away and approached their precious diva under her dust-covered protection to remove her from her feathered, sequined and diamante-sprinkled room.

Penina said quietly, 'There are four more doors before the foyer's double entrance.'

From under her brick-dusted tent, Dame Lily commanded Penina to send for dinner, blanquette de veau and Champagne from the French bistro around the corner. The men worked on, deeper into the night and early morning.

Chapter 38

SPRING HAD ARRIVED: overnight, it seemed. Lively recruitment posters started appearing all over the city and, while he hid, Evan Pettyman passed the time sitting on the edge of his narrow bed, watching the square. He wasn't so captivated by the people who arrived with rugs and picnic baskets to enjoy the sunshine, or the kiddies who played with balls and were embraced and comforted by their mothers when they fell. Nor was there any allure in fathers playing kick-to-kick footy with their sons, helping their wives carry groceries and babies.

It was the Dunnages' narrow, overgrown house he watched. No visitors came calling. Molly Dunnage wheeled goods in a barrow while her father followed, slowly, breathlessly. The old woman wandered off – cheerfully – and when she returned she was greeted at the door by her niece and helped with her ruck-sack. The bullish neighbour came out at night with a candle and read the signs and returned with a pot of paint and a brush.

In their quiet home, the Dunnage family were feeling lonely, and their friendly, crowded walls of landscapes and animals seemed a little childish. Molly was aware their home was more of a shelter than a secure, well-maintained house, that her atelier wasn't as appealing as it should be. But she turned her attention to the newspapers. She needed a job that she could endure. One after-noon, her father was taking a nap and her aunt staring into the stove when there was a knock at the door. They looked at each other, then at the doorway to the hall, neither of them eager to leave the kitchen and walk all the way down the passage to find something less than welcome waiting. It could be Leander, though he'd written from training camp.

When Molly opened the door, she found Constable Farrat, with newspapers and a bag of fruit. 'These are loquats, grown by Miss Peachy, our neighbour.'

'Horatio, you are a sight for six sore eyes.'

He was dressed in full police uniform, pressed, the belt burnished to match his immaculate boots and the buckle and buttons on his coat gleaming gold.

'You look very smart,' Molly said, but he apologised, said that he felt sad, though he knew they had their own troubles.

August, hastily tying his dressing gown, said, 'We are here to help, tell us what's up.' The old man was the colour of a mushroom and thinner under his coat.

Horatio pinched the bridge of his nose. 'I am to go to a place called Dungatar.'

'Never heard of it,' Molly said, and led them to the kitchen where Aunt April had put the kettle on to boil. She asked if Dungatar was by chance in a tropical area? It wasn't. What creek was it established on?

Constable Farrat had no idea. 'It's a one-man posting, with a fortnightly train service to Melbourne. It's only two days away.'

'Two days?' Molly thought of Gladys way up in the Northern Territory, the time and distances her journey had taken her. The long letter she'd written wouldn't reach Gladys for months yet.

He was trying to console himself when he told them that he would find reading unsettling on such a rocky vehicle, so would knit, and the journey would be his transition from city to country, or country to city on his annual visits to his mother. The trip would allow him to realign for each new set of expectations.

Aunt April mentioned that Miss Berrycloth had written to say she was enjoying the plains and farmwork. She milked the cow and was expecting many lambs this spring.

'How lovely for her,' said Horatio, flatly. 'You are kind to try and cheer me.'

'Dungatar,' said Molly, rolling the name around in her mouth.

'It's a very small population. I think it's best I don't let people know much about me.'

'Maintain the distance, be separate and keep the authority,' Molly agreed.

'Know thy enemy,' said Horatio.

Aunt April made and poured tea and Horatio said, 'There is a small reason to celebrate.'

'Oh?'

'If I stay in Dungatar, I will be made sergeant.' He placed his hand to his collar where the insignia ribbon would go. 'It should be senior sergeant, but that might come in time.'

Molly folded and set aside *The Argus* to make room for their tea, and Horatio asked if they had seen the article about Dame Lily.

Molly found the photo on page five. 'Oh my,' she said. 'Dame Lily has been evicted, finally.'

The photograph showed the prima donna being carried out of the Princess Theatre on her day bed, her eyes kohl-rimmed and her lips black with lipstick, her face sneering. On her head was the Queen of the Night's trident headdress, and her arms were raised, her spiked wings unfurled as she clutched the dagger in one hand. The caption said, *The vengeance of Hell boils in her heart.*

Molly read aloud, 'Dame Lily will be charged with the cost of replacing four sets of doors which were altered to facilitate her eviction from the premises. In the comfort of her country home, Dame Lily is thrilled to be able to finally write her autobiography.'

At the time of her premiere her outstanding Queen of the Night costume had made the front page of most newspapers, but this photo was a grand finale for Molly's career as well. Molly nursed this fact with learned resignation.

Horatio drank tea and ate biscuits and stayed for lunch –
vegetable patties and fresh eggs – and the talk was of war and
Leander and Mrs Sidebottom's posters:

YOUR KING AND COUNTRY WANT YOU.

Molly walked her friend to the tram stop, sad that he too was
leaving but happy he would avoid conscription, if it ever came
to that.

'I'll come to Dungatar one day, wherever that is.'

'I hope you do.'

'We'll write.'

'We will.'

They embraced and she waved Horatio off at the tram stop
and turned to head home. Instead, she was drawn to the square,
where her father was nailing a poster to the rotunda, directly
opposite Mrs Sidebottom's front window, right where Freddy had
perished.

6TH COMMANDMENT, THOU SHALT NOT KILL.

Evan Pettyman watched Molly Dunnage walk her policeman
friend to the tram stop, her arm through his, the sound of the
radio warbling up the stairwell – war, war, war, it was all about
war. He wrapped his mother's nightie around his neck, like a
scarf, and held the sleeve to his nose, breathing it in.

That night, every night, Molly climbed into her bed, pulled the
covers up and lay there, numb, unable to stop her thoughts. Why
did everyone leave? Gladys, Leander and now Horatio. Why had
she been given this impossible life?

Unable to sleep, she got up out of bed and paced, then swept
the back veranda and found it appeased her a little. Then she did

something she had not done in fifteen years or more. She climbed to the top of the chicken coop and over the side fence, negotiated the spikes of the bougainvillea, and lowered herself down into the Sidebottoms' yard. Near the back veranda, coals glowed under the copper and the ground around it was muddy. The house was dark; nothing moved. Molly removed the supporting branches that held Mrs Sidebottom's clotheslines aloft and the day's washing – nice white sheets, towels, aprons, dishcloths, tea towels and napkins, all sparkling clean – settled into the wet dirt and possum poo. Molly made a point of walking over it to get back to the fence.

Confident her neighbour's week had been ruined, she slept. The next morning, she scraped aside the mosquito netting, flung back her blankets and got up quickly, pulling up the covers to seal Leander's scent in her bedclothes.

In the mirror over the trough, she saw a sad girl with puffy eyes and a dry, red-tipped nose, but a girl who was content, sustained by one miraculous and tender night with Leander, her true and only love. Reaching for the cold cream, she smelled the stench of Mrs Sidebottom's copper fire and felt ashamed. Her small revenge in the middle of the night had achieved nothing.

She did her best with her face but had no joy organising her hair, so got on with her day, cooking breakfast, searching for a newspaper, gardening, shopping for bread and butcher's bones, taking Leander with her, walking as though he was beside her.

Chapter 39

As they prepared to leave for the campaign, April paused at the front door and looked at her brother, sitting up in his bed holding a cup of soup. 'Once more unto the breach,' said Aunt April.

And her brother replied, 'Dishonour not our mother.'

Molly kissed her father goodbye and tidied his scarf around his throat.

'Mare tails and mackerel sails,' said Aunt April, looking at the foreboding sky.

Molly concurred. 'We'll get wet.'

But there was a banner to hold, and not enough hands to carry a mackintosh or umbrella, and neither was inclined to go back inside, dismantle, find their galoshes and struggle to drag them over their boots.

They shared a look, *we'll risk it,* and proceeded.

Evan Pettyman, unshaven, disappointed and drunk, watched from his window, his mother's nighties under his pillow, empty beer bottles at his feet and dirty dinner plates from the Kent Hotel kitchen outside his door. 'Aha,' he said to no one, brightened at seeing something of interest, finally.

He watched the big old rocking woman come out and, hot on her heels, the treacherous girl, Molly. They paused on the street to wrangle a huge rolled-up banner between them, the old girl leading with one end and Molly following with the other, heading towards Nicholson Street, their sashes bright with propaganda – *I DO*

NOT APPROVE OF KILLING EACH OTHER'S CHILDREN AS A WAY TO PEACE and *OFFER YOUR SERVICE TO RELIEVE WANT AND SUFFERING.*

He raised a beer bottle to them and giggled, falling back on his bed. 'How fucking stupid, you don't approve . . .' He roared laughing.

The men sitting along the outside bench on the tram dummy saw the two women at the stop, armed for battle with a banner. They moved to the covered carriage and Molly and her aunt sat with the banner on their laps, holding on with one hand; they knew the grip man would speed around corners.

Protesters blocked the tram at the corner of Flinders Street. Molly and her aunt got off and joined the throng.

Eight WPA women stretched across Flinders Street, holding a single banner against their breasts: *THE WPA AND WOMEN, THE LIFE GIVERS OF ALL NATIONS, DEMAND THAT INTERNATIONAL DISPUTES BE ADJUSTED BY ARBITRATION.*

It was humid, but the air was sharp with friction. Molly and her aunt joined the members of the WPA, unfurling their banner that simply said, *PEACE.*

As fringe supporters of the WPA, Molly and April had no place among the upper hierarchy of the Women's Peace Army, an anti-war group newly founded by Vida Goldstein, who stood at the front holding a placard: *WE WAR AGAINST WAR.*

They found a position at the end, just in front of a handful of pacifists and anti-conscriptionists. Around them were National Anti-Sweating Leaguers, stragglers from various factions of the working class, a few Irish, some Catholics, liberal-minded people and unionists. Also taking the opportunity to protest were the Work Less Hours League and the Forty Hours a Week society – *WE WILL NOT WORK MORE HOURS TO MAKE AMMUNITION.*

Molly and her aunt nodded to the men and women around them, their comrades, proudly holding anti-violence posters and waiting to move with the throng. The aim of the protest was to disrupt the Elizabeth Street trams as well as automobiles and horse-drawn vehicles. They had joined a peaceful, orderly section of the march, roughly four-abreast, all looking to the WPA banner. Behind them was the entrance to Flinders Street Station. It was the perfect spot.

But before they could move, a melee broke out. It was instigated by the anti-Bolshevik, anti-suffragist and anti-socialists, the conventional Protestant, middle-class mass, appalled and outraged at the WPA. The melee was ignited when one of their number bellowed, 'Win for the homelands at any cost, kill the cowards.' Suddenly, rotten vegetables thudded on bodies all around and fell to slip up the protesters. A handful of horse manure missed Molly by inches and an enemy spat at them. The anti-pacifists chanted, 'Lazy cowards. Anti-patriotic German lovers, bludgers and weaklings.'

This gave permission for the pro-peace demonstrators to push back, shouting, 'Immoral butchers and murderers.' A group of men dressed in mock army uniform surrounded them and aimed guns at them, calling, 'Bang! Bang!' Molly called them gleeful bullies who manipulated their fellow man to kill and was shoved, but held upright by her comrades.

At this point, a member of the Australian Women's National League raised her megaphone towards her allies – the Temperance women and Christian anti-Socialists – and gestured towards the peace protesters. 'Everyone has a right to campaign.'

A traitor! How dare she endorse the pacifists, the anti-war and Suffrage campaigners! And so one of her fellow AWNL members – pro-war – hit the traitor with an umbrella. The battle took off as though someone had fired a starting gun. Women, men, children, all running, fighting, tearing, hitting, slapping, pushing and punching, falling and scrambling. The police arrived, but their horses were easily led in circles by protesters, the riders helpless in their shifting saddles. The scuffle continued and spectators witnessed many pantaloons and petticoats, stockings and garters.

Molly stuck with her aunt, back to back, swatting away the enemy, and then, as predicted, thunder rolled out of the distance and a dart of lightning cleaved the sky. Rain fell, loud fat drops that drenched their hats and shoulders in seconds. Molly took Aunt April's arm and dragged her away, shoving through the crowd. They headed up Flinders Street towards the gardens, their *PEACE* banner unfurling along the street, the sky dumping its watery ballast, which whipped sideways as the wind picked up. They would go home. It was not fair to have August out searching jail cells in this weather.

They arrived home much later, sodden. For the first time, Molly felt entirely defeated. She was morose and sick, and as she undressed she realised why and found herself disappointed. A tiny part of her had hoped she was carrying Leander's baby, but she was not.

Across the street in his fetid little room, Evan Pettyman was laughing again, rolling around on his bed and clutching a bottle. It was hilarious, those stupid women coming home soaked, utterly defeated and splattered with rotten vegetables.

Late in the afternoon, Molly took her father a cup of soup and sat with him while he drank it. He had trouble sustaining the weight of the cup so she held it for him. The storm had passed, it was a bright afternoon, the sun shining and the leaves on the trees in the park glittering. At the rotunda, the band struck up, making every bird on every branch squawk and flap away, a great swarm of them all at once.

They laughed, and August threw his head back a little, his smile so wide Molly saw all of his teeth, some of them still good. He sang along to the words, though breathlessly:

When I leave this town, I'll hurry,
To where they never frown or worry,
When I say goodbye no one will sigh when I am gone,
Give me back the brooks and clover,
With those shady nooks all over,
I could be content without a cent,
Where I was born . . .

'You know I always loved Yaambul,' he declared. 'Such fun we had there as kids, so much world to gaze at, all that living going on in the scrub.'

'We'll all live there, one day.' She kissed his forehead, and took his soup cup away, his bread and jam uneaten, though she'd assured him it was the fresh loaf.

'Nice little school there,' he said, when she had gone, thinking of Molly's children happy at their school desks.

In her room, Aunt April lifted her eye from the microscope. She could hear August talking to Myrtle, as he sometimes did.

Myrtle was at the window and he wondered why she was outside. Why didn't she come in? He felt her presence there beside him, the peace she always brought to him, and was relieved to place his hand in hers.

Something, a zephyr perhaps, hurried past Molly in the kitchen, and slipped out into the garden. She put down the tea towel, drawn towards the draught, and walked quietly up the passageway to kick the draught stopper back under the door. The front door was shut, the cylindrical stopper in place. She peeked in on her father. He was still sitting up, his hand on the bedclothes beside him, his head dropped forward and his eyes closed. She turned and looked at her aunt, saw that she was sitting on her bed, a blanket over her feet, and reading poems by Alfred Lord Tennyson.

Her aunt threw aside the book and came to stand beside her. They went to him. Molly put her ear on her father's chest and heard nothing.

Chapter 40

WHEN THE DOCTOR finally arrived, he was hatless, dressed in linen, his shoulder low with the weight of the leather bag in his hand. He looked far too young. Neither April nor Molly had ever seen him before.

From the doorway he took in the body on the bed and the women, grief-stricken and astounded, standing protectively at the bedside. The older one, rosy-cheeked and sturdy, stared numbly at the deceased, her hand on his, and the younger looked as if she'd fight this stranger in her house with her fists if he said the wrong thing. Indignantly, she said, 'Doctor Southy is our usual doctor.'

'I apologise, I happened to be the doctor on roster, they are training a lot of us up . . . The war . . .'

The deceased man on the bed was wasted and his lips stained. They had laid him flat, brushed his thin hair and put a pair of rolled up socks under his chin to keep his mouth shut. August's fingers were stained the same deep colour as his mouth.

The young doctor approached the bed. 'He was a painter?'

April whispered, 'Famous for his fine brushstrokes.' She pressed a hanky to her mouth.

The doctor nodded. 'I'm sorry for your loss.'

Molly managed to explain that he'd been ill. 'Bad blood.'

'Yes,' he said, and put August's hands on his chest and pulled the sheet up to cover the socks. The doctor said, very gently, 'It would have been the lead.'

They looked at him, uncomprehending.

'It's in the paint.'

The young one raised her clenched fists but thought better of it and bellowed instead, a sound like a trumpet. The older one fell, grabbing the sheet and pulling it from her brother. The doctor put down his bag and helped her up, feeling her body heaving with grief. The young one pounded her head with her palms. 'It is all too much, too much.'

After August had been taken away, Molly and April sat all night at the table. There was nothing to be done about it. It was true. August was dead and they would never see him again. But there was the pull to be together, so they stayed, looking at the table, one lone mosquito buzzing thinly and a barn owl screeching in the square.

Mr Luby arrived bearing flowers, geraniums from Curtain Square and daisies from Mrs Sidebottom's garden. Aunt April thought the rose was most likely one of Mrs Cross's. The pores in Mr Luby's skin were tiny and black, his collar worn and grimy around the rim, and his coat heavy with dust and soot.

'Is there anything I can do for you, Miss April?'

'Yes,' she said, and invited him in.

They emptied the wheelbarrow of old fired crockery, the dodo tea set, and Mr Luby set off with the barrow to search along the railway line for a discarded sleeper. He wheeled it home and when Mr Luby left her, Aunt April was hammering a chisel into the timber, carving out between the pencilled words.

Because the Melbourne General Cemetery had closed its books to paupers, Molly and April set off to push the headstone in the wheelbarrow all the way to Separation Street, a distance of three and a half miles, the Right of Burial letter in April's breast pocket.

No one offered to help them. It was a world of hardship and a war declared so there was no thought for downcast women wheeling a stolen railway sleeper in the warm rain on a sweaty spring day.

They dug a small trench and tipped the headstone into it, fortifying it upright with stones and sticks, and looked at August's mound of raw, damp clay. Aunt April bawled for the Dunnage family, once a neat square connected at all joints and then small, a triangle, and now a pair. One beside the other. Molly cried for her dear father, that he had been defeated by what he loved, and she wept for the life he should have had, the life *they* should have had, and for the bleak future that remained for her aunt and herself.

As rain bursts came and went, sunshine in between, they stood back, hems muddied and boot soles thick with clay. Molly's cloche was ruined. Aunt April had carved:

August Peregrine Dunnage
Jan 1850 – Oct 1914

Death has found a quiet pillow
For my dear brother's head.

Beloved husband of Myrtle, Dec 1895
Eternally loved by his daughter, Molly
This headstone worked by the devoted hand
of his sister, April Dunnage.

Their days were altered, sleeplessness and fatigue constant companions. They carried a sense that something was amiss then remembered, and the heavy dark thing descended and they had to remind themselves it was true. To cope, they roamed through the house and yard, almost reaching the studio then cowering, beating a hasty retreat to the kitchen. They stopped short of August's room, or hurried past. There was food preparation but no appetite, just sitting at the kitchen table looking at the wall, out the window, scraping away the split in the tabletop and blowing the minuscule boulders of excavated matter onto the floor. Molly chopped kindling and circled the small space in her sewing room and Aunt

April took comfort sitting before her microscope, around her the friendly fungus and multiplying bacteria and withered things in jars. The women picked up the basket to go to the grocer and put it down again and sat; they opened and closed curtains, and they wept when the heavy lurking thing slapped them.

They dusted August's failed ceramics – collapsed vases and wonky teapots and sculptures of distorted birds – and straightened his beautiful Yaambul landscapes – his beloved birds and his farm animals, which he depicted with great dignity – and his still lifes, things static but still living.

August was dead. And they cried again at how unfair it had all been.

Molly crossed the square to the Kent Hotel for more whisky and cried when she passed the rotunda steps, then cried when she saw a discarded newspaper, and again when she passed August's hat on its hook. They tried, but they couldn't put the dreadful fact to the rear and get on, though they knew they must. But get on to what? Time crept through the long day from sun-up to sunset.

Mr Luby left flowers, again, a bigger bunch. Although delivered by Mr Luby, they were taken from all their neighbours' gardens, by the looks of them.

A postcard arrived. It was postmarked Sydney, New South Wales, and it told Molly nothing, except that he loved her, hated the sea, the bunks were uncomfortable and the cabins both airless and hot with the smell of salt, men and tobacco. It said that Leander would write as often as he could, and that he would see her as soon as he possibly could, 'even if I have to swim, so keep your lamp burning for me'.

From all of my heart, Molly, my love.

It was nothing, but everything, and she understood this would be her life now: waiting for words that could tell her nothing, or, worse, waiting for letters that might one day cease.

She felt even more Leander's absence, but was reassured that he was alive and well, though seasick, and heading for a destination where there was no fighting, yet. If she could have found a tower to shelter in, she would have stayed there until Leander came for her, but he was sitting against a bulwark aft of a ship heading for German New Guinea.

It was a summer wind-gust that settled Aunt April's future, a falling branch from the gum which clattered onto the veranda roof and shattered her window, frightening the living daylights out of her in the middle of the night. Morning revealed the true extent of the damage. The entire front veranda was demolished, the giant limb resting across the front door.

Mr Luby stayed away; it was Aunt April and Molly who leaned the corrugated roof against the side fence and set about sawing and stacking branches for firewood. Aunt April was paused in the frame of the collapsed veranda, drawing breath, when a woman came to the gate. She wore a plain grey suit.

'Are you Miss Dunnage?'

'I am.' Aunt April put her saw down and scrambled through the branches to prise the front gate open. 'I do apologise, there was a storm. Are you here for a dress?'

The woman studied the path leading to the front door. 'I'm here to see Molly.'

Molly heard her name and waited.

Stepping efficiently over the branch and through the twigs and leaves, the woman said, 'It's fortunate no one was hurt.'

Molly heard the word *hurt*.

When she came into the kitchen, their eyes met and Molly knew exactly who she was. She removed her apron and attempted a smile. 'Would you like a cup of tea?'

'I would, thank you.'

Molly moved the kettle to the hot plate and stoked the fire, then fell into a chair and waited again, trying to settle her breathing, stop the rising dread.

Mrs Behan tugged at her collar. 'Leander is alive,' she said, evenly, and Molly breathed again.

Aunt April warmed the teapot and was conscious of the closeness in the warm room. 'Perhaps we'd be more comfortable in the backyard?'

'I am content in the kitchen,' said Mrs Behan. She was an upright and contained woman who took pride in her looks, her hair combed into a soft bun at her nape and her boater plain, a single white stripe through the navy-blue band. She smiled at Molly, but her eyes filled with tears and for a moment everyone in the kitchen struggled again.

Aunt April poured boiling water over the tea leaves and set out the cups. When the tea was poured, Mrs Behan inhaled and placed her hands flat on the table. 'He was with the Expeditionary Force, eventually he would have driven ambulances . . . His injuries are very serious.'

Molly looked to the ceiling. *How?* There was no fighting yet, no battles in New Guinea at all.

'It was a storm, the ship got into difficulty and sank.'

Molly was unable to fathom the cruelty of it.

Aunt April put her hand on Mrs Behan's shoulder, but she stiffened so April removed her hand. Mrs Behan stayed firm. 'He was rescued but he'd taken in a lot of sea water, so he will need care for the rest of his life.'

'He always said he was a strong swimmer. Can I –'

'No, you can't. *I* will look after my son. He'll come to Yaambul and stay with his family. There is nothing you can do. There's nothing anyone can do.'

Leander's brown eyes were softer than his mother's. 'Can I see him?' Molly asked.

She shook her head. 'He won't recognise you.'

He will, she thought.

'He does not recognise even me, Molly. It's best you remember him as he was. You can come and see him one day when you are older and settled, but not now. My tea is too strong, would you mind emptying half of it and topping it up with hot water? And may I have some sugar, thank you, Miss Dunnage?' Mrs Behan put a teaspoon of sugar in her cup and stirred her weak tea thoroughly. She drank and told them that Molly had made Leander the happiest she'd ever seen him, and she was grateful for that, but Aunt April detected a note of resentment in her unsteady voice. Mrs Behan declared she had no doubt Molly would have been a loving and devoted wife, and a fine mother. 'But you must get on with your life now, Molly, have a family of your own. As the Lord says, having a child is walking in truth.'

'We wanted to get married.'

'I know, and we would have accepted that, but your strong views . . . Well, it doesn't matter now.'

'I would do anything for Leander and I would never do anything to upset him or his family.' And as she said it, she knew it was true. She would have had to lead a life suppressing her impulses to campaign against the entrenched unfairness of the world. Molly Dunnage would have chosen Leander over her own convictions, whatever that might have meant for their union.

Mrs Behan stood quite suddenly. 'Thank you and good day to you,' she said, as if she'd just purchased some eggs.

Aunt April made a half-hearted attempt to see her out, but soon turned and sat with Molly again. On the table before them was Mrs Behan's teacup and saucer, a jug of milk, the sugar bowl and one fly dancing around a crumb from the breakfast toast.

At that moment Molly could have happily drowned herself.

It was finally too much for Aunt April. It was all too, too morbid. She came to Molly with a tot of whisky, flames from the stove flickering across her sad face and the postcard in her hand. She had been like this for days.

'This is no good, Molly. Neither Leander nor August would want us so sad. If you *do* something, weed the garden or tidy the shed, sew something, time will pass a little more easily, for both of us.'

Later, she tried again. A bit of music might brighten them? 'There's a tango exhibition at the rotunda – it's danced in lewd settings, Argentinian and Gypsy restaurants and the like, with workers and peasants, like us,' she joked.

'I don't want to go.'

'We'll steel ourselves with another tot,' said her aunt, looking at the darkening sky from the back door.

Molly shook her head.

'Mrs Bigbottom will be there with her Temperance cronies.'

Molly said nothing.

'Please, Molly, this is not good, it is not good for me.'

They'd already had whisky, both before their meagre dinner and after. Molly reached for the whisky glasses again, then they tidied themselves up and opened the front door. Over in the square, life was being celebrated and protested.

'Oh, Lord save us from them,' said Molly, seeing Mrs Sidebottom and her unlovely companions on the fringe of the crowd at the rotunda, a big, soft fence of them holding spiked posters, sashes crisscrossing their substantial presence, getting in the way of the eager crowd there to see the latest craze.

BE NOT DECEIVED: EVIL COMPANIONSHIPS CORRUPT
GOOD MORALS. FIRST CORINTHIANS 15:33.

SUCH CONDUCT EXCITES LUST.

THEY WHICH DO SUCH THINGS SHALL NOT INHERIT
THE KINGDOM OF GOD. GALATIANS 5:21.

DANCING IS A PRELUDE TO OTHER SINFUL ACTIVITIES, AND IT INVOLVES WICKED COMPANIONS.

'Off we go,' said April, and shoved Molly out the gate.

Evan Pettyman's money was running out, Christmas was mere weeks away and he had nowhere to go. No one to go to. He'd watched the women over the road, expecting his tenacity would be rewarded. It would be easier now the old man was gone. Somehow, Evan would have revenge. If he could just get close to them; all he needed was a chance.

And suddenly here it was, dancing in the square outside, and Molly Dunnage and the old girl opening their front gate. He watched them plunge through the line of Temperance ladies and into the crowd.

The program, listed on a blackboard displayed beside the rotunda, reflected that the Temperance Society had declared the two-step 'risqué' and drawn a line through it in red chalk. They had drawn a red line through the gallop – 'too invigorating' – and the foxtrot was banned for being more American than British. But they were unable to stop the tango demonstration. The band set up on the grass and practised loudly and the Latin Society simply barged through the human wall blocking the stairs to the dance floor. The dancers got on with warming up, their costumes tasselled and sparkling. The rotunda had never hosted such evocation.

Mrs Sidebottom whispered to her companions that the two mourners were out so soon after death and not at home praying. 'I am not surprised to see you, Molly Dunnage, at a tango dance!'

Molly concurred. 'Yes, but you and your friends have secured a very good view of the lewdness, Mrs *Bottom*.'

Molly

The Temperance ladies busily rearranged themselves so that they faced away from the dance floor.

The crowd was not like the usual Saturday rotunda crowd, always happy with their picnic and the oom-pah-pah band. These were modern girls, 'New Women' with their soft curls piled high and culottes, or very short slimline skirts – halfway up to the knee – dark stockings and plain blouses. The fast set, women who were eager for new sensations and experiences, sceptical that marriage and children would provide a fulfilling life.

'These are all Noras.' Thinking of Nora from *A Doll's House*, Molly wondered in her own pain if she was really cut out for marriage. But she quickly dismissed the thought, knowing that if Leander appeared before her, she would do anything he wanted, and she would have relinquished her own life to nurse and care for him for eternity.

She was drawn from her own thoughts by the tunes – profound, dramatic – and the musicians playing with gusto. A woman commanded the piano accordion, her fellow musicians on mouth accordion, a violin, drum and two guitars. The effect was jaunty, but deep and rich. Feet began to tap all around and, Molly noted, even some of the Temperance women's feet leapt about under their hems.

Several pairs of dancers took to the floor and held each other, frozen, looking into each other's eyes, and then they moved as one, legs beside each other, kicking, then entwined, scissoring and wrapping around each other, the male guiding his partner backwards and her yielding, then drawn forwards with her partner. It was a dance that required a corselet, a fitted bodice for what Aunt April would call 'gambolling breasts', but no one was wearing one. The ladies' costumes had roomy sleeves or none at all, and loose skirts, for there was a lot of entwining, especially of the legs. The men wore very tight-fitting, high-waisted suits. Each tempted the other, taking small steps away, then coming together to dance as one again, eyes locked, signalling what would happen next, receiving and giving, moving and responding. Most of the couples danced to the edge of the stage and stood watching the pair who remained.

They circled each other, their bodies close, glued. The female kneeled a little, swinging her hips from side to side, held by him, and he responded and danced around her, never letting go, their eyes only for each other, the music tense then joyful and then tense again, as in life. And then she stopped, and he moved backwards, holding her, and she let herself be lowered, balancing on her toes, her skirt skimming the floor, submissive, before he lifted her from her prone position and she fell back again, and he lowered her again, controlling her, suspending her above the floor with his forearm. He pulled her up, and they circled, entwined, embraced and ended, as one, close, their eyes still connected. It was a dance of minds and emotions, and Molly was breathless with the skill, the togetherness and the communication.

Aunt April was called home to the lavatory and was seized by her bed on her way back, the effects of whisky sending her sound asleep in her boots.

Evan Pettyman watched Molly Dunnage, betrayer and thief, sitting alone against the tree in the dark, no doubt thinking of the boy. She had no one to kiss now.

The Temperance women began rattling coins in tin cans, moving through the swelled, swaying crowd, who laughed at them and danced some of them to the music. People spilled from the pub. A war was coming, there was a need to be alive, but Molly was content in her spot away from the crowd and the dancers, remanded by her misery, the stolid mass that filled her, slowed her body and kept her mind a mire of angst. She hankered for Leander.

And then there was a hand in front of her, a man's hand, and Evan Pettyman said, 'Would you like to dance?'

She looked to the Temperance women. Someone took Mrs Sidebottom's tin can and threw it into the darkness. 'I don't know how to.'

'Nor me, we will make up our own.'

It seemed like a good idea to dance for Mrs Sidebottom. He levered her up, and led her to the floor, and held her. She kept her eyes on Mrs Sidebottom, who was struggling through the writhing throng, trying to get to her money rattle, but Evan guided Molly smoothly through the crowd, moved her, pulled her in to avoid collisions, spun her to the music, and said into her ear, 'I think you must have known, I think she paid you to keep quiet.'

Molly shook her head. 'I was used.'

'So was I.'

'She took your money?'

He wrenched her and everything around her spun and her legs were slow to follow, but he held her in the writhing crowd. He was strong, and she remembered Leander's firm arms, her hands holding his bare broad back and his chest on hers, her lips against his shoulders, and skin, Leander's skin.

'She took my money, and Alathea will make a fortune in a new style of ladies' underwear for women who work while the men are away fighting. She has the prototypes, your prototypes.'

The look on his face. She hadn't thought . . . She felt sick.

Molly untangled herself and turned to go home but was trapped, and Evan caught her again. He led her from the loud whorl of the dance floor. The music was fast and thumping, the Temperance ladies rattling and banging on the tin cans with spoons, and people had rushed onto the rotunda to sing and leap up and down. The floor bounced and she lost her footing and he saved her from falling under all the dancing feet, but it seemed to her that Evan Pettyman was weeping.

'She used us and it killed my mother, she is dead, and your father too . . .' In the dark, beside the Kent Hotel, he embraced her. 'Molly, I am so lonely and sad.'

Molly was angry, bleary with tears and tired. 'I trusted her, she's stolen my ideas, she betrayed me, intentionally, as if I was nothing. I need to go home.'

'We can help each other. Come with me, let's talk, somewhere quiet,' he begged.

She saw her home, Aunt April's lamp glowing and her father's room black. She wanted to lie down in her own bed where she had been with Leander, poor Leander. So sick.

Evan said again, 'Help me,' and guided her towards the hotel. 'I'll buy you a drink, a lemon squash, come with me, just for a little while.'

She allowed herself to be swept through the crowd to the hotel and through the empty bar, the customers all out on the footpath watching the spectacle of the tango. As he pulled her through the bar room, Evan grabbed a bottle of wine.

'I need to go home,' she said, but he put his big warm hand on the small of her back.

'I just want to talk to you, we'll have a drink, we must plan another future. I can help you set up a dressmaking and corset business. We can make something out of all this, help each other, does that sound like something you'd like to do?'

Of course it was; she had always wanted to do just that, and the thought of it made her yearn. Nothing in her life had gone to plan.

He shepherded her up some stairs and into a room, talking: '. . . my mother's money . . . advertise . . . magazines and news-papers, a shopfront in Flinders Lane, I know people there, all we need is fabric and pattern-making equipment . . . I have mother's money . . . one good thing out of her death . . . we can make something together . . .' and she was encased in a body, soft but firm, warm and enveloping and he lay her on the bed and held her. 'You'd know where to get cheap fabric . . .'

'Yes, I do.' He was embracing her, a familiar pleasant sensation but then he kissed her and, though it was comfortable at first, it wasn't Leander. She struggled, 'No,' but he was eager, and she was spent, weary and needed comfort, and then was shocked at how helpless she was to the fervour, the abandon. Something gave, finally, something she'd held in for so long, let go. What mattered? The world was all wrong for her, she would not get anything she wanted, nothing mattered anymore, and he was there.

When Molly woke, it was dark, and she was at first afraid, but nothing really mattered anymore. She crept from the room, injured – violated – and ashamed, but she was not the first nor the last girl to let herself be put in a vulnerable position, to have done what she had done.

As she walked through Curtain Square, littered and empty of people, someone's hat on the newel post of the rotunda stairs, the grief and regret came and she paused to gather herself, disgusted at what she had done, yet not. It wasn't a crime, she had not done anything others hadn't. But she felt bitter for what she had given, what she'd revealed about herself to him, and felt regret for her true love, her dear and ardent lover, Leander. But theirs was different. It was for love, and forever, though it was lost love.

What was left for Evan Pettyman was hatred.

What did people – Evan Pettyman, her neighbours, Alathea – see in her that Leander did not? What was it about her that made her a target? Alathea had seen it and used it. She had seen something in Evan Pettyman too, and duped him.

It was Evan Pettyman who had been truly taken in, and, though conned herself, Molly had helped Alathea outmanoeuvre him. But he was dangerous and Molly would always know that when others didn't. She was stronger – better – than snivelling, conniving, stupid Evan Pettyman. It was best that his ally, his mother, was dead.

Her self-respect was dented, certainly, but no one would mislead her again, she would not let it happen again. She was wiser now. Molly Dunnage was talented and strong and part of a clever, brave and loving family. It was the others, not her, that were flawed, nasty, small and petty. And she would not let them rouse her to anger, she would avoid them, outsmart them.

She spent a long time washing, standing in the cold in the middle of the night running the laundry tap, and as she pulled her blankets over her head she felt she was staining what was left of Leander, but he was safe in her mind and heart. As her father had said, ' . . . *here to reassure me while shepherding me gently.*'

Sleepless, she was soon up again and walking through the November dawn, searching for a newspaper, the birds waking, magpies warbling and lorikeets fussing in the foliage above.

She found a paper on the tram stop outside the Kent Hotel and pretended to read as she ate at home by the stove. An article distracted her; Vida Goldstein's attempt to gain election to the Federal House of Representatives as an 'Independent Woman Candidate' had failed. She had polled well, but she was outspoken, wanted to legislate to redistribute the country's wealth, and her position on pacifism lost her much support.

Chapter 41

HER AUNT WATCHED as Molly, plucky and vibrant a few weeks ago, now looked hard, a young woman at the end of her best years and defeated, possibly bitter. She slept late, had lost her appetite and spent a great deal of time in her cubby.

April tried. 'Life will go on, Molly, you might as well make the best of it, whatever it turns out to be.'

But Molly was secure in her shell, the carapace she'd worn to Pocknall's for years. She was coming to terms with the fact that she was defeated by everything she had fought to change.

Not entirely overcome, but others could do the fighting now.

As she watched her weary niece withdraw, Aunt April decided they would leave their home. They had always been happy there, but it was just a house where pain lived now.

Over egg sandwiches she said, 'I can't wander around in this house anymore. It's not a shrine. Let's move to Yaambul.'

Molly said, 'Leander is there.'

It was the raw meat in the butcher shop window that convinced her. Pressing a handkerchief to her nose didn't quell the nausea, nor did turning her eyes from the red and white carcasses hanging over plaited pink sausages and shiny purple livers, the bald sheep's heads with eyes and a brain, the flowery folds of tripe and the neat trotters and pigs' heads decorated with parsley fronds, their bellies cured and sliced and arranged in thin strips like a fan around them. It bothered her, like never before. And she'd been despondent and sluggish of late, bone tired.

As she walked, Molly did a quick count of the days of the month, and there, standing in the middle of Curtain Square, cradling a package of bones wrapped in paper, where Freddy Sidebottom had died and she had sat watching a dance, she felt hot, then a cold fear, revulsion, and finally wonder. She sat on the rotunda steps to absorb what she knew to be true.

The foetus wasn't Leander's – oh, how she longed for it to be! But there was nothing to do but just get on with things, and on her own terms. A child was to be born and that child deserved a home and a future. Her aunt would leave; the child would be all she'd have.

Her life now decided, some of her anguish quieted.

Across the road, Mrs Sidebottom came out of her front door, looked up and down the street and threw a bag of rubbish into the Dunnages' front yard.

Curtain Square was no place for a pregnant spinster, or an illegitimate child.

Her aunt was in August's studio, sitting on his stool as she sometimes did, and Molly said gently, 'You're right, Aunt. It will be easier in Yaambul with your allowance, and Eda.'

'We'll sell this place, the land is good, central to . . . things.' Tears spilled from her aunt's eyes then, and she took one of the paint rags from the table and blew her nose.

Molly put her arm around her. 'They'll probably tear it down, our lives will be rubble.'

Aunt April thought of Mrs Sidebottom, the Ravens and the Cross family pulling it down, brick by brick. 'I'd rather burn it all down first. Something good might rise from the ashes.'

And so over the days they set about preparing for their

future. Molly shoved many things into the kitchen fire, but it was small and burned slowly. She found her aunt emptying jars and throwing dishes and boxes and her treasures out through her window into her front garden, a heap growing.

'I'm giving my most interesting pathogens and dead insects to Mrs Sidebottom.' Aunt April's gestures were old now, her joints less pliable and the flesh not so convincingly attached to her bones. She stopped and looked carefully at her troubled niece. 'Out with it, Molly, I know you're about to tell me something.'

'I won't come to Yaambul, not under the circumstances.'

Molly's words hurt, but April understood. Dear Leander would be within sight of Eda's hotel, a light burning out on the plains, and forbidden to Molly: 'an arch through which gleams an untravelled world'.

'Horatio says there's work for me in Dungatar.'

Her aunt threw a frog skeleton pinned to cardboard out onto the pile. 'What sort of work?'

'Seamstressing.'

'No need for corsets in Dungatar?'

She shrugged. 'No upper class there.'

Her aunt came to her and held her, her soft old body shaking against Molly's and her nose and mouth wetting Molly's neck. They wept, wretched, exhausted and at wit's end. 'You were always the sun for us, Molly, you always will be.'

'You are my heart, my life and my soul and I will take you with me wherever I go.'

'And so, what of Horatio?'

Molly said, 'He's just my friend, Aunt. I won't compromise what authority he might have.'

'And all we need in this life is a single friend.'

'Indeed,' said Molly, mimicking her aunt.

*

Aunt April's pyre was large in the small front yard and she struck a match to it and put what was left of the veranda on top. Molly threw some old patterns into the flames, and then they added Mrs Sidebottom's posters:

STAND WITH THE AUSTRALIAN WOMEN'S NATIONAL
LEAGUE, MAINTAIN A WHITER AUSTRALIA.

NATIONAL SECURITY MEANS NO FOREIGNERS.

Then Aunt April threw the fat, tattered petition on top, her posters, sashes and badges along with the contents of her room, jar by jar, petri dish by petri dish, book by book, seashells, note-books, sketch pads, shoes, clothes, hats. And Molly came with her father's brushes and paints, notebooks and art books, sketch pads and paint palettes. Bit by bit, they emptied the rooms of anything that they could not take with them.

The furniture was next. They started smashing chairs and tables and throwing them on top of the coals, and the flames roared, singeing the trees.

Mrs Sidebottom didn't rush from her house to chastise them.

They added clothes that would never fit again, puzzles and toys, newspaper clippings and corsets that would never be finished. Together, aunt and niece went back and forth, back and forth, smoke billowing and the rancid air polluting the square until the rotunda disappeared in the smoke. The Crosses, the Ravens, Mr Luby and people from the Kent came out to see where the toxic smoke came from. All day they burned their life.

Lastly, they stood together to throw Molly's book of sketches, designs for all manner of underwear, into the flames, and then in went Dame Lily's *Favourite Arias* programs. They watched as the fire ate the shiny paper and sent the embers floating across the square.

*

And still Mrs Sidebottom didn't rush out to complain.

But Mr Luby loomed at April and Molly through the smoky air and, in an official tone, informed them that men in khaki had visited Mrs Sidebottom, staying for a very long time, and then the Sidebottom family loaded their suitcases onto a flatbed wagon and were driven away. The postman confirmed that Mrs Sidebottom's maiden name was Miss Schmied. German. The family was classified as 'enemy aliens', and were now resident internees at a camp in rural New South Wales.

Her sons, of course, could not enlist.

Without the furniture, the cracks and the floury concrete between the bricks were stark, and the walls patterned with mould where the pictures had hung. Fungus swelled along the rotted skirting boards, and a branch of ivy reached through the ceiling where the possums had caused the pressed tin to rust and fall away.

A freight wagon came and loaded Molly's trunk, clearly labelled for Dungatar, and took it away. As it turned the corner into Rathdowne Street, Evan Pettyman made a note of the name of the town.

Later, from the bar at the Kent, he watched the Dunnage women step out the front door, shutting it firmly behind them. Evan Pettyman went up to his room, collected his suitcase and slipped down the back stairs into the lane.

April Dunnage, rucksack in place, walked away from her childhood home and her entire life, her niece beside her. For a few steps a wisp of smoke was caught in their slipstream, then let go and dissolved. But as they turned the corner to Rathdowne Street, a leaf caught the edge of a smouldering branch and a few small blades of dry grass burst and the tiny yellow flames danced through the leaf litter.

Molly and her aunt travelled in silence, watching out at passing Melbourne. At Spencer Street Station they purchased one-way tickets and went to April's train, the steam engine hissing and sighing and the carriages waiting patiently, the smell of oil and steam and ash heady. They embraced, her aunt clinging to her like a joey to a koala, the sense of loss and the unfairness of it all choking any words.

April never imagined she'd lose Molly this way, would watch her, a small woman with messy hair wearing the lovely coat she'd worn to Dame Lily's concert and a ruined cloche, getting smaller as the train pulled away until finally she was engulfed by a steamy swirl.

She would take Molly into her future, what future was left for her. It was time to cease now, sit at Eda's stove and be as useful as she could. There was a lot to look back over – a vibrant and curious childhood in the paddocks and creek close by, and a wonderful urban life of art and books and science. A child she'd helped raise and a fine family she'd been vital to. And Hurtle, their great love, a short but profound love that lasted, providing her with a lifelong soul mate, many pages to wander through. She sighed and settled into her seat. Rìan would bring the ladder for her to climb up onto the cart, and Eda would serve preserved apples after dinner, and she would drink stout for breakfast. She would be warm, cared for by others she cared about.

Back at Curtain Square, the draught under the house drew the flames along the edge of the old timber veranda and sucked them under August's floorboards, where they found fumes and spilled paint. The fire grew strong, settled to eat its way along the skirting boards and adventure up into the space between the walls and the crumbling horsehair plaster.

As Molly boarded her train to Dungatar, the flames skipped along the rafters, sending the possums fleeing. No one took any notice of the smoke, not until it streamed from the holes in the roof, and then they came to watch the inferno explode out of the windows, shooting glass, then boil up and reach to the trees in Curtain Square.

Chapter 42

It took two days to get to Dungatar but Molly was content. Alone in the second-class carriage she found space for reckoning during the steady pace towards her future. Every so often, the train slowed, there was an exchange of mail bags, a whistle, and the train rolled on. In her corner, deep in her moiré coat, her cloche low, Molly confronted what lay ahead: she was a woman, therefore voiceless, also disgraced, fallen and almost penniless until the Curtain Square property sold. There was no support for single mothers, and she anticipated ostracisation. She would step off the train into Dungatar as someone who did not fit, as an exemplar of everything society thought wrong.

But she would not be alone, a child would be born. Things would be different for her daughter, surely?

Crossing the wheat-yellow plains around Dungatar, Molly first noticed a dark blot shimmering at the edge of the flatness. It was a hill and on top of it was a shabby brown weatherboard, a little house leaning a little on the grassy curve. Some would say the home she'd left behind was shabby, but it was snug in its trees behind the fence, a cosy tumbling place that nurtured love. She wondered what poor wretch lived in this lonely house on top of the hill.

Molly stepped down onto the Dungatar railway platform looking stylish in a waistless, ankle-length shift dress. The neck was square, unusually high and narrow, the sleeves capped over sheer net sleeves with beaded cuffs. The beads matched the oblong

bead insert that fell from her neckline to her waist. She held her
new cape draped over her arm, and a single suitcase. Horatio was
waiting to meet her, smart in his uniform and smiling. Her hat
had suffered rain damage; he would make a new one for her.

'Welcome, Molly.'

'Horatio!'

'Sergeant Farrat,' he corrected her, mindful of his professional
image in Dungatar.

'Of course!'

From the guard's van, left well beyond the end of the platform, someone chucked a mail bag out, and then Molly's trunk
thumped into the thick grass next to it.

'Edward McSwiney will deliver that for you,' Horatio said.
'I have found a house for you, it needs some love but it has a view,
you can look down onto the town and out over the plains.' He
took her arm. 'It will be wonderful to have a friend here, Molly,
but there's a lot you must know, I'll tell you over tea.'

He would not tell her that the ladies at the street stall had
asked, 'Why would a seamstress and corset maker move here?'

'Her husband has gone to war,' he'd replied.

'A likely story,' said Lois Pickett.

Beula Harridene said, 'They all say that.'

Molly would tell Sergeant Farrat over tea that his letters had
arrived, opened, creased along the wrong fold lines, read and
re-read, and ask if hers had come to him through the Dungatar
post office in the same fashion.

As Sergeant Farrat steered her towards his automobile, behind
them Evan Pettyman alighted the train from the first-class
carriage. He stood on the platform, the vast sky behind him,
watching Molly Dunnage and the policeman drive away. His
suitcase shot from the guard's van and landed in the grass next
to Molly Dunnage's. He eyed her trunk in the grass, big enough

to contain a sewing machine, or a dummy, fabrics and threads, paper for patterns. Evan would not starve ever again. From now on Molly would sew to support him. She owed him that much; if it wasn't for her, he'd have no debt and his precious, doting mother would still be alive. Mind you, should there be a rich spinster, or even a widow, Evan would have her instead of the dressmaker, or at least her money. In the meantime, there was Molly Dunnage, wounded and entirely alone in the world, and she'd been sweet in his arms.

He looked at the township, small and ugly with few trees and a giant tin silo – there'd be a creek. A town hall, quite new, stood majestically on the shabby main street, glowering at a few sad shops. Naturally there was a football oval and a pub.

Somewhere in there opportunity waited. He set off on foot, passing the post office, where a small, sharp, sun-burnished lass came out and stared, then ran back inside. Soon, another young woman came out of the chemist shop carrying a broom to watch him approach. An older woman who reminded him of a truck driver he'd once known peered at him as he passed the grocery shop, and at last he came to the pub, where a younger woman, disinterested, fair and pretty, booked him into room three, slapped a key on the bar without question and told him dinner was served at half-past six. 'It's sausages tonight.'

With anticipation, he came down for dinner and finally found some men, a bar full of them. They fell silent, stopped drinking and playing darts and turned to stare at him. He ordered his meal from a red-faced barman, and as he made his way to the dining room, someone remarked, 'He don't look like a footballer,' and the bar noise resumed.

Midway through his sausages and mashed potato, an older man sat down at his table and sized Evan up. Evan continued to eat, thinking he would definitely leave the town on the next train.

'Sausages,' said the man.

Evan kept eating.

'It'll be chops tomorrow night, then sausages again the next night, then chops again.' The man extended his hand. 'My name is Ralph Dankworth. I am the shire president.'

'It's an honour to meet you, sir,' said Evan, shaking his hand firmly.

'What brings you to Dungatar, son?' Ralph Dankworth thought he might be following the new girl up on The Hill. Everyone knew about her; if you wanted to keep secrets in Dungatar you had to drive to the next town to post letters or make phone calls, but chances were that whatever you wrote or said would be all over town the next day anyway.

Evan explained that he was 'in commerce' and travelling the rural areas, searching for locations that needed a Rural Bank of Australasia branch.

'Our post office does our banking,' Mr Dankworth said. 'And insurance.'

'Looks like I'll be on the train tomorrow then.'

'It's not until next week.'

Evan was about to ask about buses when Ralph Dankworth said, 'You must come for dinner. My daughter Marigold is quite a good cook.'

'As long as she doesn't cook sausages,' said Evan, and Mr Dankworth roared, laughing, and bought him a drink.

Not long after Evan met Marigold, a plain girl, shy, nervous and prone to worry, her widower father, Ralph, died, quite unexpectedly. But he died knowing his daughter had at last found someone. Evan had resigned his position at the bank to marry her and move into their very comfortable, well-appointed family home, as discussed. Evan's lawyer friend, Mr Hawker, would take care of her substantial inheritance, and Evan would take care of Marigold.

*

Molly

On a bright summer evening, the sky a silver-sequined fabric of stars, Mae McSwiney, pregnant with her third baby, heard a yelp and made her way up The Hill. Her husband trailed, carrying sheets and a big pot for boiling water, then went for Mr Almanac, the only medical person in the town.

Mr Almanac stood in the doorway and explained to the Dunnage girl lying on her bed that, because she had sinned, he could not deliver her baby. He cautioned her that eight out of a hundred babies died before their first birthday, and then left.

When Mae placed Molly's baby in her arms, Molly looked at her and said, 'Hello, Myrtle.' Any pain and tragedy seemed inconsequential in light of the joy she held.

On her illegitimate daughter's first birthday, Molly Dunnage stood on the veranda of her little house on top of The Hill, looking down on the town that had shunned her from the start. Despite the talk, the names Evan had called her and the lies he told, the women of Dungatar had walked or drove up The Hill for new, stylish dresses and corsets – all of them, even Marigold Pettyman – but when Evan took control as shire president, people stopped coming. But she would survive. The vacant block on Curtain Square had sold and Aunt April had set up a trust for her. Her small pension meant she could survive in the country, she would not need to work to live and so would be able to keep her daughter. And Molly had a feeling the future held better things. She looked to the horizon beyond the town, the plains leading towards a world full of mystery, a place of discovery and promise. She would raise little Myrtle to seek promise and one day, Myrtle would triumph.

On the top of The Hill Molly would live life her way and, each dusk, as her hill cast a shadow over the town, the people of Dungatar would feel the chill; each time they turned they would see her, they would see what they had done. And Evan Pettyman would know she was there, looking down on him.

Acknowledgements

Thanks to all at Pan Macmillan, especially Cate Blake, Belinda Huang and Emma Schwarcz for the guidance and editing, and to Clare Keighery and Charlotte Ree for the publicity and marketing. Thanks to Christa Moffit for the cover. Thanks also to Jenny Darling, and thanks to cousins Ben and Anne for the opera, and Sue Maslin for the impetus.

I'm grateful to my lawyer, and to my financial advisors, David and Jack, for their wise advice on swindle plots.

THE SAGA CONTINUES . . .

The Dressmaker

Tilly Dunnage has come home to care for her mad old mother. She left the small Victorian town of Dungatar years before, and became an accomplished couturier in Paris. Now she earns her living making exquisite frocks for the people who drove her away when she was ten. Through the long Dungatar nights, she sits at her sewing machine, planning revenge.

Set in the 1950s, *The Dressmaker* is a much loved Australian classic you'll never forget – a bittersweet comedy about love, revenge and haute couture.

Now a major motion picture starring Kate Winslet, Judy Davis, Liam Hemsworth and Hugo Weaving.

The Dressmaker's Secret

It is 1953 and Melbourne society is looking forward to coronation season, the grand balls and celebrations for the young queen-to-be. Tilly Dunnage is, however, working for a pittance in a second-rate Collins Street salon. Her talents go unappreciated, and the madame is a bully and a cheat, but Tilly has a past she is desperate to escape and good reason to prefer anonymity.

Meanwhile, Sergeant Farrat and the McSwiney clan have been searching for their resident dressmaker ever since she left Dungatar in flames. And they aren't the only ones. The inhabitants of the town are still out for revenge (or at least someone to foot the bill for the new high street). So when Tilly's name starts to feature in the fashion pages, the jig is up. Along with Tilly's hopes of keeping her secrets hidden . . .